Magnolia Bay
memories

BABETTE
DE JONGH

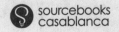
sourcebooks
casablanca

Published by Sourcebooks Casablanca, an imprint of Sourcebooks
P.O. Box 4410, Naperville, Illinois 60567-4410
(630) 961-3900
sourcebooks.com

Printed and bound in Canada.
MBP 10 9 8 7 6 5 4 3 2 1

*If you've ever worked or volunteered at an animal shelter…
driven a relay leg to take a rescue animal to their forever home…
coaxed a trembling stray to accept help…helped an animal find
their next right place…stopped to move a turtle off the road…
donated to an animal shelter or rescue organization…*

*If you've ever helped an animal in need, this book is dedicated
to you. By every kind act you extend toward another being,
you are raising the consciousness of the planet. And together,
we can save the world, one happy ending at a time.*

Chapter 1

ADRIAN CRAWFORD PARKED HIS LEXUS LC 500 CONVERTIBLE at the loneliest corner of the new animal shelter's gravel lot. Far from the handful of other vehicles and even farther from the centuries-old oaks that draped their scaly, fern-covered branches over the chain-link fence, the birthday bonus he'd given himself last month would be safe.

The construction/renovation of the shelter had progressed significantly since his last visit a week ago. The old Craftsman-style home's exterior face-lift was complete. Quinn, Adrian's old college buddy and the contractor in charge of the project, had already put up the new sign by the entrance. The sign, handmade with white lettering on a bluebird-blue background, matched the new paint and trim on the old house.

A bit bright for his taste, but as a business consultant working pro bono for the nonprofit shelter, it wasn't his place to argue with the three women in charge of this project. And Quinn was so crazy in love with the trio's leader, Abby, that he wasn't thinking straight.

"*Furever Love*," Adrian scoffed. "What kind of name is that for a business?" The unfortunately cutesy name the women had chosen for the shelter arched across the top of the sign in a curlicue font they had agonized over for hours. Beneath that, in more sedate lettering: MAGNOLIA BAY ANIMAL SHELTER.

Adrian pushed the button to close the car's top. He left the windows open a few inches to keep the car's interior from baking in the Louisiana summer sun. Halfway to the shelter's front porch, he pointed the key fob behind him and pressed the button to lock the car with a quiet but satisfying *blip-blip*.

"Gang's all here." Quinn's truck was parked by the outdoor dog runs, where the sound of heavy machinery droned. Reva—the organizing force behind the shelter even though her niece, Abby, was officially in charge—lived at the farm next door. Abby and Quinn were living on-site in the old estate's pool house until the shelter's grand opening, so unless Quinn was making a hardware store run, they were always here.

"Well, almost everyone's here." Heather's car, he noticed, was conspicuously absent.

Typical. Heather was just about always late. Adrian couldn't help but wonder why Abby and Reva thought they could trust her to be in charge of the day-to-day operations when she couldn't even make it to their weekly meetings on time.

Reva's dog, Georgia, trotted across the parking lot, coming toward him with a proprietary air. She was a funny-looking combo of dog breeds: a short, long dog with a thick speckled coat of many colors and a white-tipped tail that curved over her back. Her brown eyespots drew together in a concerned frown as she sniffed his jeans and then the treads of his new Lowa hiking boots. When she completed her inspection, she looked up at him with a "state your business and I'll decide if you can come in" attitude.

He knelt to pet Georgia's head. "I'm here to brainstorm with the team about another grant proposal for funding, if you must know."

Then he scoffed at himself. Quinn, Abby, Reva, and Heather all talked to animals like they were human. Now he was doing it too. "Assimilation is nearly complete," he told Georgia in his best imitation of the Borg.

Georgia stiffened and growled at something behind Adrian. He turned and looked, then bolted to his feet. The scruffy old black-and-white tomcat who'd been hanging around the area was walking tightrope-style along the top of the chain-link fence near Adrian's car. "Don't you do it…"

He could tell by the direction of the cat's gaze that he was about to jump from the fence to the hood of Adrian's brand-new, never-been-scratched car. "No!" He started running, but the cat was already gathering itself for the leap. "Bad cat!"

Too late.

Georgia took off like an avenging army of one, galvanized into action and ready to tell the cat what for, announcing her intention with a high-pitched, yodeling bark.

The cat was already mid-leap with front paws extended, body stretched out, and back toes spread when he spotted the dog barreling toward him. Eyes wide, mouth frozen in a grimace of terror, the cat twisted in midair to go back the way he'd come. Too late.

His spine hit the hood of Adrian's car with a loud *thwump*, then his body twirled like a corkscrew, all claws extended as he scrambled to get his balance.

"No…" Adrian ran, but Georgia ran faster. She leaped up, scrabbling at the side of the car in an impossible effort to reach the cat. Never gonna happen; Georgia wasn't even knee-high. But she didn't know it, the cat didn't know it, and none of that mattered to the previously shiny, immaculate finish of Adrian's new car.

"No, shoo, bad dog," Adrian yelled. Why hadn't he used the perfectly good, fitted canvas cover that he'd left in the trunk of the car? "Get down, right now." Why hadn't he bothered to toss it over the car the second he got out? "Hush, dog." He tried to push the dog away with his foot. "Get back. Go home."

The cat leaped up to the car's convertible top and hissed down at the dog, who barked even more ferociously, moving to scratch a different area on the side of Adrian's poor car. He snatched the little troublemaker up.

The little dog whined and squirmed but didn't bark. The cat, frozen in a bowed-up caricature of a Halloween cat, stopped growling long enough to catch his breath. In the sudden cessation of noise, Adrian heard a sound behind him.

Reva rushed up, all flowing hair and patchwork fabric—a prematurely gray hippie. She snatched Georgia out of his arms. "I'll put her up," she said. "You grab the cat and bring him inside. We've been trying to catch him for weeks."

As Reva hurried back across the parking lot with her Birkenstocks scuffing along the gravel surface, Adrian stood with his hands on his hips, surveying the damage. These scratches were not the sort that could just be buffed out with a good coat of Minwax. "Son of a bitch."

But there was nothing he could do about the damage now. He heaved a sigh and plowed his hands through his hair, then applied his business-consultant problem-solving skills to the situation. "Okay." First things first. "Come here, cat."

He held his hands out to the cat and made kissy noises. The cat backed away, growling low in his throat. "Naw, don't be that way." Adrian softened his tone even further. "Come on, little man." The cat *was* little but also a fully grown tomcat with a big jughead jaw. "Here, kitty, kitty."

The cat glared at him, so he used one of the tricks he'd heard Reva mention when she was talking to the shelter girls about taming wild cats. He half-closed his eyes, looking sleepily at the cat and blinking slowly. The cat settled onto his haunches, his glowing amber eyes not as wide-open as before.

Well, fuck me, he thought. It worked.

He started humming, not a tune, just random low tones.

The damn cat started purring, and damn if he didn't start doing that slow blinking thing too.

Which Adrian realized he had forgotten to keep doing, so he started it up again. His humming resembled a tune he'd heard his grandmother sing, so he added words to the tune: "What's up, stinky cat?" The cat did stink. He smelled like dirt, motor oil, and cat pee. "Whoa, whoa, whoa… Come here, stinky cat; whoa, whoa, whoa…"

The cat's body tensed, raising up a fraction off his haunches as if preparing to run.

Yeah, that shit wasn't working, so he went back to humming. The cat settled back down. He didn't seem inclined to move toward Adrian's outstretched hands, but at least he wasn't running or hissing or growling. Adrian eased forward and gently touched the cat, spreading his fingers lightly over the cat's bony ribs.

The cat's purring stopped. Adrian kept his fingertips on the cat's haunches, letting the skittish feline get used to him before he pushed the envelope any further. He did more of the blinking thing, still humming, and slowly began to stroke the cat's scruffy, greasy, black-and-white fur. It seemed peppered with tiny scabs.

No question, this dude was a fighter.

Adrian eased his fingers farther along the cat's back, then slowly dragged him forward. The cat resisted at first, but at some point in the process, he padded along the car's hood toward Adrian, assisted by the gentle pressure Adrian kept applying. They seemed to have reached some sort of unspoken agreement. Making soothing sounds, not even a hum anymore but a vibration in his throat that he could feel but barely hear, Adrian gathered the reluctant cat into his arms.

———————

Cat let the man hold him close, only because the hands that held him didn't grab too tightly or try to force anything. Cat knew, somehow, that if he changed his mind about accepting help, the man would let him go.

Cat had never been given any other name, though he had been called many different versions of it. As he rode along in the man's arms—carried toward the building into which he'd seen other cats come and go of their own free will—Cat thought of the many names he'd been called.

Damn Cat. Fucking Cat. Asshole Cat. Go Away Cat.

His personal favorite up until now: Go Away You Damn Fucking Asshole Cat.

That one had always seemed particularly impressive to him.

But this man called him by a new name, one that Cat much preferred because of the tone in which it had been uttered. Stinky Cat. He liked that one. He decided that would be the name by which he would refer to himself, whenever he wanted to think of himself as a cat with a name.

Despite the man's gentle reassurance, Stinky Cat felt himself becoming increasingly tense as they neared the door that would soon close behind him, cutting off the option of changing his mind.

He wanted to believe. He wanted to be like those other cats who seemed so confident, so unafraid. They even sat with the dogs—napped with them on the building's wide front porch!—and everyone seemed perfectly content. Even the bad little dog who'd come after him was nice to those other cats. She licked their ears the way mama cats licked their babies.

But Stinky Cat had a bad feeling that the dog he'd heard called Georgia wasn't going to lick his ears. She might not have used her teeth on him as she'd threatened to do, but she made it clear she didn't want him around. She had been ready to chase him right back over the fence he had climbed. He had wanted to see more of this strange place in which dogs and cats and people seemed to get along much better than the dogs and cats and people of his previous experience, who were more inclined to try to kill one another.

But now he wasn't so sure he was up for the challenge. He pushed his front paws against the man's supporting arm and leaned his head back against the man's chest.

"Shhh," the man said, "You're okay." Then he stopped walking and stood still, halfway between the metal hill Cat had been stranded on and the building where the dogs and cats came and went whenever they pleased. "Nobody's going to hurt you."

Stinky Cat didn't know what the words meant, and he was too worried about what might happen to understand the man's thoughts. But the tones of the man's voice soothed him, just as the man's fingers stroking his fur soothed him. He felt himself purring again, relaxing against the man's comforting bulk almost against his better judgment. He knew this human wouldn't harm him intentionally, as so many others had.

But he wasn't sure about the people inside that building.

Stinky Cat wanted to see if he could be one of those cats who seemed so confident and happy and unafraid. But he worried that something terrible may have happened to the ones who were caught in the traps. That's why he'd been so careful to avoid the wire tunnels that held enough fish-scented food to fill his belly for days. He'd been too afraid to risk it.

He'd been afraid all his life—or at least from the moment in early kittenhood when he'd woken with his siblings to find that their mother was gone. He even slept afraid—and lightly enough to wake completely between one breath and another, his ever-present fear fueling his ability to escape or fight for his life if a predator pounced.

Fear had kept him alive this long.

How could he give it up now?

———————

Adrian had the damn stinky cat within ten feet of the shelter's front porch when he heard Heather's car coming. He knew it was hers because of the loud rattling sound the old Honda's hinky motor made. She always brought her kids and her badly behaved dog. Knowing there was a high probability of mayhem about to ensue, he petted the cat and took another few, slow steps, hoping to make it inside the building before the car skidded into the parking lot. "What's up, stinky cat," he sang. "Whoa, whoa, whoaah."

Tamping down the sense of urgency that kept creeping into his head and infusing his tone, he took a few cautious steps closer to

the shelter. Balancing the need to move in sync with the cat's fluc-
tuating degree of compliance with the imperative of getting inside
before…

Heather's car careened into the parking lot, scattering gravel.
The dog's head hung out the window, barking as if he had something important to say.

The cat's claws came out like Wolverine's knives. Intent on
escaping, the frightened feline dug those claws into Adrian's flesh,
slicing effortlessly through his shirt. The back claws gained traction by digging deep into Adrian's abs, while the front claws latched
onto his chest. The determined cat used his claws like grappling
hooks to haul himself up to an unsteady perch on Adrian's shoulder, where with one last, mighty effort, he launched off Adrian's
back and hit the ground running.

Before Adrian could gather the presence of mind to say, "Ow,
shit," the cat had scaled the chain-link fence and leaped into the
thick underbrush on the other side.

Adrian watched Heather park her rattletrap car under the
shade of a live oak whose trailing, fern-covered branches were as
thick as a full-grown human body. She clearly had more trust in
the universe—or her car insurance—than he did.

Heather's dog—a honey-and-brown speckled Aussie with
flashy copper-and-white markings—rushed up to greet him.
Adrian reached down to pet the dog's head. "Hello, Jasper. You
don't even realize that you just ruined everything, do you?"

Jasper panted with enthusiasm, wagged his whole back end,
and grinned a doggy grin.

A second later, Heather's son, Josh, ran up to bombard Adrian
with the latest news. "I got in trouble at school today. See?" He
pointed to a small bruise on his cheekbone. His wheat-blond
hair stuck up in clumps, and his navy-blue polo shirt was gray
from what must have been a sweaty altercation on the school
playground.

"Wow, I bet that hurt." Adrian gave what he hoped was sufficient attention to the almost nonexistent but clearly exciting wound. "Did the teacher punch you?"

"No, silly." Josh grinned, revealing a gap where he'd recently lost a tooth. "Teachers don't get to punch kids."

"What happened, then?"

"I pushed Kevin for calling me a crybaby, and then he punched me. We both got in trouble, and Ms. Mullins—she's the principal now—said we'll have to apologize to each other in the morning, but after that, we're gonna forget all about it."

"Uh-huh."

"As long as it doesn't happen again," Heather added with a stern look at Josh. She and Josh's twin sister, Caroline, walked toward them hand in hand. Caroline seemed to be the complete opposite of her brother. Wearing a still-pressed-looking jumper, her white blouse and socks neat and clean, her long blond braids tied with crisp blue ribbons, Caroline was as reserved as Josh was outgoing.

Adrian couldn't help noticing how cute Heather looked, even dressed as she was in slightly baggy jeans and a simple white blouse with a modest neckline. What seemed like a deliberate effort to hide her femininity wasn't working. Had never worked, in fact, at least as far as he was concerned.

The needy kid who now clung to Adrian's leg in an effort to regain his attention kept him from reaching out to touch the bright blond curl that had escaped Heather's haphazard ponytail. It wasn't that the kid was physically in the way because if Adrian wanted to touch Heather, no one would be able to stop him. What stopped him was the fact that she had kids.

It wasn't because Josh's attention-seeking behavior could be exhausting.

It wasn't because Caroline was so unbearably shy that she often hid behind Heather with her thumb in her mouth.

It wasn't because Erin, the willowy girl who strolled toward the shelter with her nose in her phone, was prone to flare-ups of teenage angst.

There wasn't anything wrong with Heather's kids in particular. If not for all the hangers-on in her life, Adrian would have been up for a quick fling with her, as long as it came with a flexible expiration date. But her kids were a major part of her deal—as they should be—and he wasn't emotionally ready to be a stepdad.

So he kept his distance, and she kept hers.

She surprised him by reaching out and touching his chest. Her fingers spread across the fabric of his T-shirt, lightly stroking, barely even a touch at all. "You're bleeding."

Had she not seen what just happened? "That's the usual result of being climbed like a tree by a freaked-out cat."

"Oh?"

"Yeah, Mom," Josh supplied. "Adrian was holding that black-and-white cat y'all have been trying to catch."

Her eyebrows went up, two delicate blond arches of surprise over her wide, leaf-green eyes. "You caught him?"

"I *had* caught him, yes. I was almost at the shelter with him in my arms when y'all drove up."

"Jasper barked, and the cat went nuts." Josh hopped with excitement at the remembered event. "Huh, Adrian?"

He smiled down at the kid. "That sums it up."

Heather's pretty face was windowpane easy to read. Her cheeks washed with pink, and she brought a hand up to cover her mouth. "I'm so sorry!"

"Jasper tried to chase it when we got out of the car." Josh tugged on Adrian's shirt, encouraging him to look down. "But it ran too fast, didn't it, Adrian? It was already over the fence by then."

Adrian looked down and put his hand on the kid's shoulder. "Yep, it was."

"Lord help us," Heather said softly, her voice breathless, which had an unsettling effect on Adrian's peace of mind. "I am so sorry Jasper caused all this trouble."

As if to underscore her comment about Jasper, the dog took off after another of Reva's cats from next door who was stalking something in the shrubbery by the shelter's front porch.

"Jasper," Heather yelled. "Get back here."

The overexcited dog paid zero attention.

"Josh, Caroline, please go get that dog and put him in one of the kennels out back."

Josh ran after the dog and grabbed him by the collar. Caroline followed more slowly. "Caroline," Heather called out. "Open and close the gates for Josh, okay?"

Caroline changed course, heading for the walk-through gate that led to the kennels. "Yes, ma'am."

"Make sure they are securely latched once you go through, okay?" Even though there weren't yet any animals residing at the unfinished shelter, Adrian knew that Heather had been making a point of teaching her kids good safety habits.

"Yes, ma'am," Caroline said again. The child was a model of good manners.

Heather shook her head. "That damn dog." Then she reached out and took Adrian's hand. "Come on inside and let me doctor those scratches." She even tugged at his hand to tow him into the building as if he were one of her kids.

And he let her do it, without hesitation.

Chapter 2

HEATHER'S HEART FLUTTERED WHEN SHE WALKED INTO THE shelter's reception area with Adrian's long, strong fingers wrapped around hers. She had grabbed his hand without thinking, but the second their palms connected, an unexpected flash of adrenaline rushed through her. She let go to close the door behind them, then shoved her hands in her pockets.

Reva and Abby came into the room, each holding one end of an extra-large metal crate that they'd set up to house the feral cat. Abby was looking down, struggling to keep her wavy brown hair from falling into her face without letting go of the heavy crate. Short-stepping forward to accommodate Reva's backward steps, Abby looked up and stopped walking. "He doesn't have the cat." She set her end of the crate down.

Reva, who couldn't see them standing behind her, spoke to Abby. "But the cat said—"

"Nope." Abby shook her head. "You were wrong."

Reva eased her side of the crate down on the polished-wood floor, then turned to look. Her shoulders drooped. "Oh. What happened?"

"Jasper happened," Heather said with exasperation. "I'm sorry."

Reva shook her head. "Poor cat. How scared he must have been." The unspoken worry: They'd never be able to catch him after this. He would be much more wary from now on. "Jasper didn't hurt him, did he?"

"No. Jasper's a big goofball who wants cats to stand still so he can get to know them. He just doesn't know how to go about making new friends."

Reva nodded, but her mouth was tight, disappointment clear in her expressive hazel-green eyes. "We'll have to work on that.

Apparently, Georgia needs a refresher course in manners around cats as well."

The twins blasted through the front door. "We put Jasper up," Josh yelled, his voice loud in the empty room of hardwood floors and freshly painted taupe walls with white trim. The furniture that had been ordered for the reception area hadn't yet been delivered.

"Thank you," Heather said, lowering her voice in the hope that her son would also lower his. She didn't want to fuss at him any more than she'd already fussed today (pretty much the whole drive from the elementary school to here). "Would you and Caroline please go get a snack from the fridge?"

Josh's face fell. "But I wanna—"

Caroline took her brother's hand. "Yes, ma'am."

The kids went into the shelter's kitchen, and Heather heard the sounds of Caroline talking quietly to Josh and the refrigerator door being opened. Erin seemed to have disappeared. "Do y'all know where Erin went?"

Reva touched Heather's arm, a gesture of comfort. "She's next door, throwing the ball to Georgia, who has also been banned from the shelter for the rest of the day. Jasper wasn't the only dog who let his baser instincts take over today." Then she looked over at Adrian. "How's your car?"

"I don't know." Adrian made a sound of frustration. "Not good is my guess."

"I'm so sorry," Reva said. "Let me know what I owe you for repairs."

"My insurance will take care of it."

"Well." Reva patted his shoulder. "We'll discuss that later. You need to do something about those scratches so they don't get infected. And after that, we have a meeting to attend."

"I'll finish getting the conference room set up," Abby said. The shelter's conference room had been the dining room of the old house. Reva and Abby had furnished it just last week with an antique Persian rug and a lovely old dining table and matching chairs they'd found at an estate sale. "What should we do with this big ol' crate?"

"Let's leave it set up," Reva said. "Maybe we'll get lucky and catch the cat again soon."

Adrian picked up the crate and set it against the wall where it would be out of the way. Heather tried not to notice the way the muscles in his shoulders and back shifted under his ripped T-shirt. "Reva, would you mind taking the twins next door so Erin can watch them? I'll help Adrian take care of those scratches."

Adrian held up a hand. "No need—"

"Cat scratch fever is a real thing," Reva interrupted in her sternest tone. "And you don't want it. Let Heather help you."

"Yes, ma'am." Adrian's amiable smile made his deep-blue eyes sparkle. He really was too good-looking, if such a thing was possible.

In the kitchen, Reva herded the kids—who were sitting at the kitchen table eating yogurt pops—out the door with the promise of cookies. Heather pointed to the chair Josh had just vacated. "Sit." She made sure that her voice sounded strong, capable, nononsense. "Take off your shirt."

She turned on the faucet, and while the water warmed, she located the first aid bin. She took a washcloth from the drawer next to the sink, filled a big bowl with steaming water, then dropped the cloth in. Before she turned around with the bowl in one hand and the first aid supplies in the other, she steeled herself for what she already knew would be a compelling glimpse of gorgeous man.

Oooh, mama. Her imagination didn't do him justice.

Perched on the chair across from him, she poked through the contents of the first aid box, setting out a bottle of Betadine, a tube of Neosporin, a roll of gauze, and a dispenser of first aid adhesive tape. She wrung out the cloth, then dispensed some Betadine into its folds.

Finally, she met his eyes. Closer than she'd ever been to him before, she noticed that one of his dark-blue eyes had a chocolate-brown occlusion across the top third of the iris. Sitting this close, she could see the shadow of his beard beneath the clean-shaved skin of his square jaw and strong chin with a slight cleft in the center. He smiled at her, a gentle, soft smile that brought out the dimples in his lean, tanned cheeks. Then he closed his eyes and leaned forward. "Do your worst," he said. "I can take it."

As gently as she could, she cleaned the scratches then took the bowl to the sink and dumped it. When she turned back, he was watching her, his eyes heavy-lidded, his long dark lashes obscuring the brown spot in his left eye.

She smiled.

He didn't.

He just watched her with that smoldering, sexy gaze.

She felt like a gazelle being studied by a lion. Her cheeks heated.

Snatching the tube of Neosporin off the table, she moved to stand behind Adrian, where she could escape his steady gaze. Her fingers shook as she twisted the lid of the slippery tube.

"You okay back there?" he asked, a hint of laughter in his voice.

She dangled the tube over his shoulder. "I can't get it open."

Wordlessly, he reached back, took it, uncapped it, and plunked it into her outstretched hand. She applied a bead of the medicine to one of the scratches, dragging her fingertip lightly down his bare skin. He shivered.

Now there was nothing but the intimacy of her skin touching his. She smeared the antibiotic cream on the angry red welts, then covered the worst gouges with gauze and tape. Self-sticking bandages would have been easier, but the scratches were too long for those.

She came around to sit in front of him. Keeping her eyes focused on each scratch as she applied the cream, she managed to get through the process without blushing. She finished applying cream to the last remaining wound and reached back for the gauze.

He covered her hand with his, pinning it between his palm and his warm, hairy chest. "That's good enough."

Startled, she knocked the gauze onto the floor. "Huh?" She would've leaned down to grab the gauze—Weren't medical supplies subject to the three-second rule?—but he didn't release her hand.

He kept her hand pressed to his chest. She could feel his steady heartbeat, his slow breaths in and out, his warm skin heating her palm. Her heart started doing that fluttering thing again.

"That tape isn't gonna stick. It's fine to leave it uncovered."

"Oh." She drew her hand back and put it in her lap. "Okay." She realized with a shock that until now, with the exception of a few brief handshakes, she had never touched a man's bare skin—other than her husband's, of course.

No wonder she'd felt so unsettled.

She was still pondering when Adrian leaned in close…

Her fluttering heart flopped over in her chest. Anticipating the kiss, she sat frozen in place, unable to protest or flee when…

He reached past her to take his shirt off the table, then leaned back to slip it over his head. Her lungs started working again about the time his head emerged from the neck of the shirt.

A slow, sexy grin grew slowly out of the knowing smirk on his lips.

Heart hammering, cheeks flaming, her breathing more shredded than his shirt, Heather pushed her chair back and bolted for the bathroom.

———

Reva herded Heather's twins through the swing gate between the shelter and Bayside Barn. She left them in her kitchen with a plate of cookies, a pitcher of Kool-Aid, and strict instructions to mind their big sister and stay put. Then she closed the doggie door in the laundry room and told Georgia to stay put too. Georgia had always had a strong desire to play Miss Manners with the cats—and with other dogs—but that trait had gotten out of hand today when she chased the feral cat.

While Reva walked back to the shelter and across the parking lot, she had a telepathic conversation with Georgia, promising to let her out at the end of the workday when the two gates—one drive-through and one walk-through—between the shelter and Bayside Barn had been closed for the night. She also delivered the bad news that Georgia would be denied permission to go back to the shelter until the feral cat had been caught.

Georgia pouted, sending a mental image of herself turning her back and sticking her little nose in the air. Reva had no doubt that Georgia would also choose to sleep on the couch instead of the bed tonight. Fair enough. Bad behavior had consequences.

Reva stood by Adrian's car and assessed the damage. Not as bad as she'd feared; it looked like none of the scratches were deep enough to require a new paint job. She would insist on paying for Adrian to take the car to the dealership and have the scratches buffed out or whatever they did to restore the factory finish. If it was too much to pay out of pocket, her homeowner's insurance would pay, since it was her dog who'd done the deed.

With that settled in her mind, Reva scanned the heavily wooded area on the other side of the chain-link fence. The strip of vine-covered trees and shrubs was dense but not wide because it bordered the road that dead-ended at an old boat launch into the marshy bayous that edged Magnolia Bay. She didn't feel that the cat was hiding in that narrow strip of land. She didn't sense him in the marshland between here and the bay either. She felt that he was somewhere high and dry. Probably across the road in the vacant lot between here and the next block of estates. Or maybe he was hiding across the street from Bayside Barn in the Cat's Claw forest.

"Where are you?" she asked. Closing her eyes, she reached out with her intuitive abilities and imagined the cat's black-and-white face with its amber eyes, its wide, testosterone-muscled cheeks, and its tattered, battle-torn ears. Slowly, his image shifted, showing her mind an image of his entire body, though it was shrouded in darkness. Hiding under something.

No…in something. A dilapidated structure of some kind. There were plenty of those: the fallen-in house that had been consumed by the Cat's Claw vines across the street, the various sheds out back of the aging estates on this road and the next. "Oh, well." She sent a mind message to the cat. "You're safe enough for now. But you'll be safer if you'll let us take care of you."

She leaned against the front bumper of Heather's car (she knew better than to lean against Adrian's beloved hunk of metal) and spent a few more minutes conversing telepathically with the cat. She tried unsuccessfully to assure him that, contrary to his unfortunate experiences today, it would be better for him to come back to the shelter and allow himself to be brought inside than to remain untethered to humans.

She showed images of the inside of the shelter, in particular the upstairs area that would house the shelter cats. He would be the first resident, the first to climb the treelike cat towers, the first to use the cat doors that led into the two-story outdoor play enclosure full of interesting places to play and climb and hide.

No luck, though. In the image he sent of his reaction to all this, he turned his head away from her and licked his paws. He wasn't impressed.

"Well, then," she asked. "What would it take?"

He showed an image of Adrian cradling the cat loosely in his arms.

"Well, all righty then. I'll tell him."

Not wanting to disturb the planning meeting that had already started, Reva hung around outside the shelter, watering the potted ferns that hung above the white porch railing, then pulling a few weeds that had dared to spring up in the new flowerbeds around the old-growth gardenias.

After a while, she heard the planning committee folks go outside to look at the cats' outdoor play area. She joined the group and stood at the back, listening to Abby's fiancé, Quinn, who was the project's contractor, explain what he'd done so far and what he still had to do.

While Quinn pointed out the way he had attached the cats' two-story play enclosure to the outside of the old house and installed several cat doors in the exterior wall, Reva noticed Abby watching Quinn with a half smile on her face. Reva couldn't help smiling too. Her niece had found a keeper. Quinn was kind, hard-working, and good to Abby. He wasn't hard to look at either; tall and good-looking, with silky light-brown hair that somehow always managed to be a bit too long.

"Quinn," Heather said. "Where's my hose connection going to be?"

"I haven't run that line yet, so you get to choose."

While Quinn and Heather conferred about hose connections and site drainage, Abby told Adrian and Reva about her plans for the enclosure's landscaping and climbing structures. Despite Abby's animated hand gestures, Adrian's gaze kept drifting to Heather, who stood with her back to him, her hands on her curvaceous hips while she nodded at something Quinn was saying. It seemed that Adrian couldn't keep his eyes from lingering on Heather.

"Hmmm," Reva murmured. "Isn't that interesting?"

"Oh, definitely!" Abby agreed. "Not only will it give the cats plenty of enrichment and exercise, it doubles the amount of space they'll have."

"Um-hmm," Reva agreed. But she hadn't been commenting about the cats.

———————

After the meeting broke up, Adrian hung around and talked to Quinn while Reva and Abby went back inside to clean the conference room and lock up. Halfway listening to Quinn, Adrian watched Heather walk through the gate between the shelter and Reva's house to collect her kids.

He really hadn't meant to scare the bejesus out of her by leaning in so close. Yes, he admitted he was teasing her, just a little, by coming in close enough to kiss while reaching for his shirt. She was such an easy mark, though, that it was hard to resist. All he had to do was look at her and lower his eyelids a fraction to get her to blush. He realized too late that he shouldn't have pushed the envelope quite so far. He'd been half-hoping she'd lean in too and invite a kiss for real, but instead, she had jumped up like a scalded cat and rushed out of the room, leaving him to clean up the mess from her Florence Nightingale routine.

Only fair, he supposed.

Next time, he'd be more aware of her subtle cues. He had only wanted to flirt, not to embarrass her. She hadn't met his eyes since the almost-kiss; for the entire meeting and the site tour that followed, she'd managed not to look at him.

He figured that hiding back here with Quinn until Heather left would save her further embarrassment and that by next week's meeting, she'd be over it. He'd thought about apologizing, but (a) that might make things worse, and (b) he wasn't sorry he'd invited an opportunity for kissing. If anyone needed kissing in a bad way, it was Heather. That woman was wound tighter than Dick's hatband.

"See?" Quinn was saying. "We subdivided the existing three-car garage into kennels and added a doggie door on the exterior wall of each one. Every kennel will have a separate chain-link dog run and 24/7 access to the outdoors. Heather says that'll cut down on cleaning. And Reva says it'll provide natural house-training for the dogs because they'd rather do their business outside if they can."

"That's genius," Adrian said.

A second later, he was tackled from behind. He stumbled but managed to stay upright as Josh grabbed his hand and walked up his jeans. What had seemed, at first, to be a good attempt at a run-up-the-wall back flip ended with Adrian's shoulder possibly out of joint and Josh rolling in a giggling heap on the ground, leaving red-dirt footprints as high up as Adrian's hip.

"Josh!" Heather ran toward them, her eyes wide with alarm. "What are you doing?" She snatched her son up by the arm. Adrian tried not to look at her heaving bosom as she spoke to her son in a curiously firm tone for such a soft voice. "That was not okay."

Quinn put his hands up. "Uh-oh. Family drama. I think I hear Abby calling me."

Quinn quickly absconded, brushing past Erin and Caroline, who were standing behind Heather.

"Erin, please go get Jasper out of the kennel and put him in the car." The five-star-general aspect of Heather's personality emerged, apparently banishing her embarrassment more effectively than anything Adrian could have done to talk her out of it. "Caroline, please go with your sister and close all the gates securely behind you. Josh, please stand exactly where you are and tell Mr. Crawford how sorry you are that you ambushed him."

Erin and Caroline went off in the direction of the kennels, and Josh looked up at his mother, innocently blinking his wide blue eyes. "What's 'ambushed' mean?"

That didn't cut it with Heather. "I will show you how to look the word up in the dictionary when we get home. And to make sure you remember the meaning, I'll get you to write it down five or ten times. Now. You know what you did, and you know it was wrong. Please apologize." The unspoken threat behind her polite wording hovered in the air.

Josh looked down at his feet and drew a line in the clay-rich red dirt that had been hauled in to level the construction site outside the existing buildings. "I'm sorry," he mumbled.

Heather crossed her arms. "I'm not sure anyone heard you, and when you apologize, you are supposed to look the person in the eye and say what you're sorry for. Let's try that again."

Adrian knew how excruciating this kind of chastisement in front of others would feel to any kid, much less one who wasn't yet knee-high to a grasshopper. And he owed something to Heather after taking his natural tendency to flirt a little too far.

He knelt down in front of Josh. "It's okay. I know you didn't mean anything by it. But your mother is right. When you…" He struggled to find a small enough word for *accost, invade, violate.* "When you sneak up on someone without their permission, it's…" Shit fire; again, he struggled to come up with a ten-cent word to explain a five-dollar concept. "It's a… It's a *good thing* to apologize."

Josh looked down at his feet, continuing to scrub lines in the dirt with the toe of his shoe.

"Josh…" Heather said in a warning tone.

Adrian held out both hands, and Josh grabbed hold. Adrian squeezed the kid's fingers lightly, giving encouragement. "I'm right here, and I'm not mad. Just say what you need to say, and I promise, it'll be fine."

"Um…" Josh's voice shook, then faltered.

Adrian looked down at the boy's short little fingers clutching his much longer ones. Josh's hands were so small, still bearing the marks of babyhood in the dimples above each knuckle. Adrian looked up into Josh's ice-blue eyes that he must have gotten from his father. "It's okay, buddy," Adrian said, even though it seemed that the hint of understanding he showed made the kid's bottom lip tremble with emotion.

Josh clutched Adrian's hands and stared into his eyes. "I'm sorry, Mister…" He glanced up at Heather, obviously unable to remember Adrian's surname, since he'd probably only heard it this once.

"Hey." Adrian brought Josh's attention back to him. "You know what? You can call me Ade, like Quinn does, because he's my buddy from way back. We can dispense with the Mister."

Josh's blond brows drew together for a second while he looked off to the side (probably wondering about the word *dispense*); then he looked into Adrian's eyes again. "I'm sorry I sneaked up on you and climbed up your legs." The words tumbled out in a rush, and then he leaned close and whispered into Adrian's ear. "I hope I didn't hurt you. I didn't, did I?"

Adrian patted Josh's back. "No," he said quietly. "You didn't hurt me."

"I'm glad." Josh's small body relaxed in relief. "I wasn't thinking." He wrapped his arms around Adrian's neck and held on. "I was just so happy you were still here so I could say goodbye before we left."

Adrian's heart cracked open at the kid's raw honesty. A kid, he realized, who hadn't been able to say a last goodbye to his father because Dale had died so suddenly that goodbyes weren't possible. Nobody had ever mentioned to Adrian what, exactly, had happened to Dale, and Adrian hadn't felt comfortable asking for details that weren't given freely. He only knew from talking to Quinn and Abby and Reva that Dale's death was so unexpected and upsetting that the whole family was still struggling with PTSD along with their grief.

Heather reached down to touch Josh's shoulder. "That was a good apology, Joshua. I'm proud of you."

Josh nodded, then pulled away from Adrian just far enough to look at him. "I'm glad you're okay." His face brightened. "You want to come to dinner? My mom cooks great."

"Maybe one of these days." Adrian smiled at Josh, then chanced a look at Heather. Her pink lips were curved in a soft smile.

"You could come tonight," Josh insisted. "Friday is spaghetti night. Mama makes toasty cheese bread then. And salad, but you don't have to eat it if you don't want to. *I* have to at least try it, but she won't make you do that."

"Josh," Heather said softly. "I have a Zoom meeting with Sara tonight so we can prepare for Monday's PTA meeting. And we need to get going."

"Well, when *can* he come?" Josh asked, a mulish expression on his face.

Heather blushed. "I don't know, Josh. We'll have to figure that out later."

"Promise?" Josh whined. He sent an imploring look to Heather, then to Adrian. "Do y'all promise you'll figure it out?"

Heather sighed heavily. "I promise. Now let's go. I can't be late for the meeting, and I still have to cook your dinner."

Josh looked back at Adrian. "You promise too? You'll come to dinner? Soon?"

Adrian tried to give Josh a reassuring smile, but it felt pasted on. Family dinner night at Heather's was a fate he hoped to avoid. He was happy to flirt—and to follow that wherever it led—but he didn't want to put down roots. He had to say something though, and making idle promises didn't sit right. "I'll try."

It was the best he could do, and even that felt like too much commitment.

He stood and received Josh's fervent hug.

Heather blushed. "Sorry about all this." She took Josh's hand and urged him to take two steps in the direction of the car, even though he reached out for Adrian dramatically; a brilliant career in the theater definitely awaited. She dragged her son another few staggering steps. "See you next Friday, Adrian."

"I'll be here." He watched the struggle, almost halfway wishing he could help, but mostly glad he didn't have to.

Erin and Caroline led Jasper through the gate from the kennels to the parking lot, and Heather stooped down to get her son's attention. "We really do have to go now. Please say goodbye, Josh."

"Goodbye, Josh," the kid mimicked with a silly, clownish look on his face. Unlike his twin sister, Josh was not a wilting flower.

But it was clear that his manic appeal for attention covered deep insecurity and sadness.

Adrian waved, his face carefully expressionless. "See you next week." Because his presence seemed to ignite Josh's veering emotions, Adrian turned back toward the shelter, planning to hide out of sight by the kennels until Heather left, then hightail it to his car and get the hell out of Dodge.

That evening, when Heather and the kids got home from the meeting at the shelter, she couldn't help noticing Charlie, Dale's lonely and pitiful horse, standing alone in the field behind the house with his head low. With his head down like that, the retired racehorse—who had loved nothing more than to run like the wind with Dale on his back—was reduced to a sad brown blob of misery in the distance.

She wondered for the millionth time whether they should get Charlie a goat or a donkey for company, but it wasn't fair to ask Erin to take on even more responsibility. She already had to feed the poor thing, scoop his stall out every evening, and deep-clean his stall every weekend. Dale had done those jobs because Charlie had been his horse, but Charlie, like everyone else in the family, had lived a diminished existence ever since Dale died.

"Erin," she said as they sat in the car and waited for the garage door to creak open. "Please go out to the barn and take care of Charlie before you do anything else, okay?"

"Dammit, Mom," Erin groused. "I have a ton of homework to do."

"And the whole weekend to do it," Heather replied, ignoring the fact that Erin had just said *dammit*. There were some arguments she didn't have the strength for, and right this minute, Erin's little outburst was one of them.

Heather parked the car in the garage and got out before her temptation to be a better mother got the best of her. It was fine, she told herself, to let Erin's bad language slide, just this once. "Get all your stuff out of the car," she said over her shoulder. "I don't want any Monday-morning hysteria about not being able to find something you left in the car."

In the kitchen, Caroline and Josh fed the dog while Heather set a pot of salted water and a skillet on the stove. Erin hefted her backpack onto the granite-topped island then slammed out the door on her way to feed Charlie Horse.

Heather thought about the weeks she and Dale had spent picking out that countertop when they built this house. They'd gone to every granite store in the state of Louisiana (and a few in Mississippi) until they found a beautiful slab in the subdued browns and grays Dale could live with that also contained the interesting striations of silver and crystal formations she insisted upon.

Everything, everything—from the distressed-leather wall treatment she had chosen to the unimaginative white ceilings and trim she'd let him have—everything reminded her of him. And every time she noticed or remembered anything about the building of this house, she sent up a prayer of thanks that Dale had insisted on buying more life insurance than she'd thought they could afford.

Dale's life insurance had paid off the house and covered the bills for a year so she could continue being a stay-at-home mom. That gift had allowed her to keep their lives as consistent as possible. Taking a job would change a lot, but at least they could afford to keep living here.

Heather sighed and went back to smashing the browning ground beef and seasoned sausage in the skillet into ever more tiny chunks. The time of respite and recovery she had resolved to give herself and her kids was now over, and time continued to march onward.

Dale's birthday would have been next Wednesday. The first missed birthday after Dale died came when they were all still shell-shocked, so the kids hadn't remembered. This time, though, they might. Heather wondered if she should plan something to com-memorate the date—maybe a visit to the cemetery followed by a special dinner.

Jasper nosed her leg, looking for a handout, his little stub tail wagging. She handed him a chunk of cooked carrot, which she'd been chopping finely enough to hide in the spaghetti sauce. He took it from her fingers so gently that it warmed her heart.

Jasper nosed her leg again. "Ever hopeful," she said to his plead-ing brown-and-blue-marbled eyes. She gave him another carrot and stroked the whirlwind-shaped cowlick in the middle of the white blaze at the bridge of his nose.

Aside from the cowlick, Jasper was a perfectly marked red merle Australian Shepherd. The pure-white blaze that started at the tip of his nose went up his forehead to widen between his ears and join up with the ruff around his neck. His feet and legs had white socks edged in copper, and the rest of his thick wavy coat was speckled in shades from the lightest honey to the darkest brown.

"You're gonna like working at the shelter, aren't you, Jasper?"

The dog panted, smiling. Always happy, always spreading joy. Jasper was actually one of the reasons Heather had decided to take the job at the shelter. Where else could she work that would allow her to bring her kids *and* the dog?

The only fly in her ointment at the shelter was Adrian Crawford and her conflicted feelings toward him. Because sometimes, when she noticed him looking at her with those deep, dark midnight-blue eyes or when he brushed past her with his overtly masculine presence (because even in those leather loafers he wore some-times, there was no denying his masculinity), she would remem-ber that she wasn't just Dale's widow; she was a woman.

And every time it happened—those little wisps of connection that clung to her skin like strands of spiderweb for hours afterward—she felt as guilty as if she'd just woken from an erotic but disturbing dream in which she had cheated on Dale.

Her husband, the love of her life, was gone. She knew that it wasn't possible to cheat on a dead man. But her newly awakening womanhood felt as uncomfortable as the pins-and-needles feeling of a gone-to-sleep limb whose circulation was just beginning to flow again. In a way, it felt good. But it also hurt, maybe more than she could bear.

Chapter 3

ADRIAN SAT ACROSS FROM QUINN IN THE HOT TUB AT REVA'S house and gazed out over the green pastures that rolled out behind Bayside Barn and eventually led to the marsh-lined bay.

Quinn leaned back and sighed. "Glad you decided to stay a while."

"Your offer of a cold beer by the hot tub was hard to argue with."

Reva and Abby stepped onto the patio with their hands full. Reva set a couple of hors d'oeuvre plates on the edge of the hot tub, while Abby handed out Stella Artois to the guys and wine to the ladies. Abby sat beside Quinn, then Reva sat between the two men and held her wineglass out for a toast. "I'm so glad you agreed to stay a bit longer before heading home."

"Me too." Adrian joined in the toast and took a sip, then set his bottle aside. "Thanks for the invite."

"Mind that bottle," Reva warned. "Georgia will knock it over if it gets between her and the tennis ball."

Quinn hurled Georgia's ball into the gathering darkness beyond the patio lights. Georgia took off like a bullet after it. "Yeah, she will," he agreed. "She's obsessed."

"I'll be careful." Adrian could see how the combo of Georgia's game of fetch and glass bottles might be a problem. The hot tub and the pool were built-in level with the patio slab and within easy reach of the super-focused cattle dog mix who clearly cared about nothing but playing ball.

Wolf, the elusive wolf hybrid who'd chosen Quinn as his person, sat at the edge of the patio where the solar lights met the clipped-grass lawn. He seemed to care nothing about chasing the ball and everything about guarding everyone within his domain.

"Dinner's in the oven for those who are staying," Reva said. "And, Adrian, I won't insist, though the invitation remains open." She reached for one of the hors d'oeuvre plates and drew it closer. "But meanwhile, this should keep your stomach from thinking your throat's been cut."

"Disturbingly morbid," Quinn said.

Adrian wasn't sure whether his friend was talking about Reva's comment or the serving dish. He helped himself to one of the toothpicks that stuck out of a sculpted mummy in the center of the dish, then stabbed a tiny sausage.

"Grayson and I found these serving dishes at some hole-in-the-wall shop in the French Quarter. Can't remember where, though. It was years ago." Reva's voice didn't sound sad, but Adrian felt her sadness all the same. She and Heather were both widows—that was how they'd met, at a grief support group—and even though they were both cheerful and upbeat on the surface, there still seemed to be an invisible, protective cloak of sadness around them.

Big reason—the biggest—why Adrian kept reminding himself to stay away from Heather. Even though he regularly managed to forget the fact that flirting with Heather was flirting with fire. He wasn't averse to some level of commitment to the right woman, preferably someone as driven and success-minded as himself. But Heather was a whirlpool of unacknowledged needs that he could too easily get sucked into if he let himself get too close. And now that he'd witnessed firsthand how messed-up Josh was…

Georgia brought the ball back to Quinn and dropped it a hair too close to the snack tray. Abby grabbed the ball and dropped it into the hot tub. "Done playing, girl."

Clearly not convinced the game was over, the dog dropped to the ground and eyed the ball.

Adrian looked at Reva as she sipped her wine. Probably about the same age as Adrian's mother, Reva was young-looking and beautiful, her shiny hair silver-gray but lush and long and pulled back in a barrette.

Conversation circulated above the bubbles in the hot tub. But Adrian was thinking about the differences between Reva and his mother, who, while still attractive, looked older and more matronly than Reva. Adrian's parents' example of what not to do was another reason he needed to keep a distance from Heather.

Gordon and Eileen Crawford were still in love after however many years, but they had each given up many of their goals and dreams in order to stay together.

Even after Hurricane Katrina, when Adrian's parents and younger siblings had moved back into the rebuilt family home, Eileen had prevented Gordon from taking promotions that would've required them to move, just as he had prevented her from going back to school and getting a degree once their kids were grown.

Maybe Hurricane Katrina had been a blessing in disguise, at least for Adrian. Though the storm had torn through his relationships, washed away opportunities, and trashed his senior year in high school, the complete derailing of his life at such a pivotal time had changed him and shifted his priorities. Adrian's potentially glorious senior year of high school had been sucked up by the storm. He'd lost his girlfriend and the college scholarship that had been all but promised to him as the star quarterback of his high school football team.

He'd lost everything he thought he wanted and become a castaway in a big city where he knew no one—other than his college-age cousin, who'd been forced by his parents to give Adrian a place to sleep but was under no obligation to make him feel welcome.

It hadn't been easy, but Adrian had learned how to take care of himself and depend on no one.

Every disappointment had been followed by a lesson that made him better off in the long run. He'd become successful by learning not to want or expect anything from anyone other than himself.

Adrian didn't want to be in the kind of relationship that caused both partners to get beaten down by life. And the only way he knew to avoid that was to avoid falling in love.

Luckily, that wasn't difficult. He had perfected the art of enjoying close relationships while still keeping his distance.

"Adrian," Reva said, "can I get you another beer?"

"No thanks. I'm good." He'd be driving back home to New Orleans—just an hour from here—soon.

A low, moaning yowl in the distance escalated into a hair-raising scream. Adrian sat forward and looked out over the rolling hills behind Reva's house and the big red barn. But all he could see was a gorgeous violet-streaked sky over the bay that glittered just beyond the fenced pastures. Another, deeper yowl echoed from a different location nearby. "What in the hell was that?"

"Feral tomcats," Reva said.

"You think one of them is the black-and-white one I caught today?"

"Pretty certain of it," Reva answered. "That's why I was so disappointed when you didn't manage to hold on to him."

"We've been trying to trap both of them," Abby added. "But those old tomcats are wily. They know better than to be fooled by the smell of canned tuna."

Quinn chuckled. "I think the cats around here have told them they'll be relieved of their testicles if they fall for the old tuna-in-a-trap trick."

"We've caught a bunch of raccoons though," Reva said. "I think at least a few of them were disappointed when we let them go. They wouldn't have minded a small surgical procedure if it led to a lifetime of luxury."

The yowls and screams eventually clashed in the crescendo of a truly vicious-sounding cat fight. "How far away do you think they are?"

"Sounds carry a long way around here," Quinn said. "We can easily hear boats on the bay, and it's, what? A mile down the hill?"

"That depends on whether you count the marsh between here and the bay as land or water," Reva answered. "But yes, it's about a mile from here to the bay."

"The sound carries, though," Abby said, "because there's not much to absorb it. Just the marsh grass and that big oak tree in the pasture."

The catfight broke up, and the sound of crickets and bubbling water took over again. "That sounded seriously violent," Adrian said. "I wonder if they both walked away."

"Yeah," Reva said. "They probably left a significant amount of fur on the ground, though." Her phone chirped, and she stood. "That's my cue to check on dinner and make the salad, which gives everyone about a half hour before it's time to mosey back inside."

"Need any help?" Abby asked.

"No, thanks. Y'all finish your drinks and come on in when you're ready. Adrian, even if you decide not to stay for dinner, I hope you'll come inside and say goodbye before you leave. There's something I want to give you."

Nobody else jumped up, so Adrian relaxed and enjoyed his beer. The violet-and-lavender sky turned to pearl gray, and a few stars emerged in its cotton-soft depths. The little pond under the oak tree glowed dimly with reflected light. "It's peaceful here," Adrian decided out loud.

"Catfights notwithstanding," Quinn agreed. "Not quite so peaceful during school days, though. I'm not looking forward to the beginning of field trip season."

Abby put a hand on Quinn's shoulder and patted lightly—a there-there-honey pat. "Field trips will be few and far between until October."

Adrian knew that Bayside Barn was a field trip destination for schoolkids as far away as New Orleans. It was essentially a petting zoo, though Reva and Abby used a more highfalutin term: animal-assisted education center.

"Thank God we've nearly completed the Great Wall of China between the shelter and here." Quinn's description wasn't much of an exaggeration. What had once been a hedge-covered chain-link fence between the two properties was now a nine-foot-tall concrete-block wall. The imposing edifice was broken only by a sliding drive-through gate and a smaller walk-through gate.

"If you hadn't gone so far overboard on that wall, it'd be long since done by now," Abby said to her fiancé with a slight tone of I-told-you-so in her voice.

Quinn scoffed. "It'll be worth it. Kids screaming and yelling next door all day every day couldn't possibly be good for the shelter animals' mental and emotional health."

Now it was Abby's turn to scoff. "Yours, you mean. Funny, since we'll be living on the Bayside Barn side of the fence once the shelter opens."

"Only until after the wedding," Quinn said. "Then we'll start looking for our own place."

Abby gave Quinn another there-there pat. "Whatever you want. Meanwhile, we'll have fun playing house in the little cabin you're building behind Bayside Barn."

The lovebirds weren't kissing or even sitting up against each other, but without Reva's balancing presence, Adrian started feeling claustrophobic. "Welp…" He finished his beer in one gulp. "It's been fun, y'all." He stood and wrapped a towel around his waist. "But I really need to get home."

He changed into his clothes in the guest bathroom at Reva's house, leaving the towel and borrowed swim trunks hanging on the shower curtain bar. Then he found Reva in the kitchen, where she stood with her back to him, fiddling with something on the counter.

"I'm about to head out," he said.

She turned around with a covered dish in her hand. "For you to heat up later."

"Thanks." He took the warm container. "I'm glad I stayed to visit. I enjoyed it."

"I hope you'll hang out with us after these shelter meetings more often. You have a standing invitation." She linked her arm in his. "Let me walk you out."

"There's no need."

"I have to lock the gates anyway." She took a flashlight off a hook by the door and led the way from Bayside Barn to the shelter. "I also wanted to talk to you about that cat."

"What about him?"

"He seems to have bonded with you." She opened the gate between the dogs' play yards and the parking lot, then held it open for him. "I believe that he will come to you again if you work to regain his trust. Would you be willing to do that?"

Adrian walked beside Reva toward his car, its black surface appearing gunmetal gray in the glow of the flashlight's beam. "What exactly does *work to regain his trust* mean?"

"I know it's asking a lot."

"Just ask. I can always say no." Though he hadn't been very good at that lately.

"I know you've been donating your time for this shelter project once a week. But if you could see your way to come more often, maybe twice a week—just for an hour or two each time—he'd sense your presence, and he'd be more likely to come back to you. You could call out to him, leave treats by your car, let him know you want to make a connection with him."

"I don't see why I'm the one who needs to do this. What makes me so special?"

"You're special to all of us for helping us get this project off the ground." She patted his arm in a motherly fashion. "But there's something about you that makes this cat feel safe. I don't know what it is, but I think that together, we can figure it out. I think we need to try before he gets hurt more than he already has been."

Adrian had noticed the cat's many injuries.

And hell, it wasn't like Adrian couldn't spare the time. He worked from home 90 percent of the time. He could bring his laptop, pull up a chair, and sit by this fence a few hours a week without it touching his bottom line. Even the hour-long drive here and back wouldn't be wasted because he could use the time to make phone calls from the car.

"Okay, fine." He took the keys from his jeans pocket and clicked the unlock button. "I'll be here Wednesday afternoon."

Heather woke just before dawn on the morning of Dale's birthday and watched the sky outside her bedroom window lighten from gray to lavender to pearly pink to pale blue. Though she had made plans to commemorate the occasion in the afternoon, she resolved not to tell the kids that today was anything special until then. The twins definitely wouldn't remember the date, and Heather hoped Erin wouldn't either. Heather didn't want a sense of loss to sabotage their school day.

The plan, Heather decided, was to drop everyone off at school, then make a grocery store run to get a birthday cake— that wasn't weird, was it?—for the family to share after dinner as a way of remembrance. After school, they'd stop by the cemetery to put fresh flowers on Dale's grave. If everyone felt okay afterward, they might swing by the animal shelter on the way home, just to see how things were going. It would be fine. They'd get through the day together. And maybe next year, it wouldn't be so hard.

Luckily, the kids didn't notice anything different about the morning, and the school drop-off happened without a hitch.

Jasper's feelings were hurt when he didn't get to come along. But the summer heat didn't allow him to wait in the car while Heather shopped, so he had to be left behind. Erin exited the car with a breezy goodbye, and five minutes later, Heather waved goodbye to the twins.

She turned up the volume on her *Happy Music* Spotify playlist and sang along to "Don't Worry, Be Happy." The gaiety was forced, sure. But fake-it-till-you-make-it was a baked-in component of her personality. She had made the cheerleading squad that way. She had started out her adult life that way, masquerading as an adult until she became one. And when Dale died, she pretended to be able to cope until she figured out a way to cope for real.

That afternoon, when Heather parked outside the middle school, Erin was one of the first kids out the door. She breezed up to the car and hopped in, tossing her backpack on the floor. "Hey, Mom." Leaning across the seat, she kissed Heather's cheek, then buckled her seat belt. "How was your day?"

"Fine, thanks." Heather merged into the line of cars leaving the school. "You look happy today."

"I got invited to join the yearbook club. They're meeting at Sierra's house tonight; she said her mom would pick me up and bring me back home after."

"Oh." Heather hoped Erin's opportunity didn't interfere with her afternoon plans. "What time?"

"Five. They'll have pizza, so I won't have to eat first."

Cutting it close, but still doable. "That's wonderful, sweetie." They would still have time to go by the cemetery. She drove a few more miles debating how to break the news that they'd be going to visit Dale's grave today. She wasn't sure why she expected a blowup from Erin, but she did. Better to get it over with before the twins got out of school. "I have a surprise for you too."

Erin looked up from her phone with an excited smile. "Yeah?"

"After we pick up the twins, we're going to have a special little celebration, just the four of us."

"What are we celebrating?"

Heather took a breath. "Today's your daddy's birthday, so I thought—"

Erin drew back as if she'd been slapped. "We're...celebrating? Mom, that makes absolutely no sense."

"I thought—"

"I was having a great day, the first great day I've had in *ages*, and you just had to go and ruin it, didn't you?" Erin's cheeks stained red with anger. "You can't stand that I'm happy. I'm finally just a regular kid at school, not *that girl whose daddy just died*." She flung up her hands. "Daddy is *dead*, Mom. Get over it already."

"Well...but..." Heather sputtered. She had expected some grumbling from Erin, but not such a vitriolic attack. "I thought it would be nice to commemorate his birthday. It's not a big deal."

"It's not? Well, good." Erin flounced around in her seat, crossed her arms, and stared out the window. "Because I don't want any part of it. You and the twins can do whatever stupid thing you've cooked up, but you can take me straight home. I need to take a shower and change clothes and get ready for tonight."

Heather clutched the steering wheel. Dale would've probably pulled the car over and...well, she didn't know what he would've done because Erin had never stood up to either of them the way she'd done just now. But Dale would have known how to handle it. Heather didn't. Should she force Erin to go along? That would ruin the whole afternoon for everyone and defeat the purpose of remembering Dale in this small and meaningful way. But if she let Erin stay home, she would be rewarding a tantrum. "It won't take more than an hour..."

Erin cut a sideways look of fury toward Heather before responding. "I have homework to do too."

Heather felt a headache begin to throb behind her left eye, and she realized that her teeth were clenched, her shoulders tensed, her whole body geared up for a confrontation. She forced herself to relax.

She drove the rest of the way to the elementary school in silence. Erin fumed silently, her fingers flying on her phone's touch screen. Probably texting a friend to say how horribly she was being treated.

Outside Magnolia Bay Elementary School's red-brick building, the twins piled into the back seat. Caroline sat quietly and buckled her seat belt, while Josh filled the car with his loud chatter and the smell of little-boy sweat and playground dirt. Erin sighed, rolled her eyes, and took a pair of headphones from her backpack, pointedly plugging herself into her phone.

At that moment, Heather decided to take Erin home. Then she could talk to the twins without Erin's argumentative presence tainting the conversation. She reminded herself that her intention was to make a new family ritual that would help the kids remember Dale in ways that cemented good memories and made even more good memories going forward. Forcing any of them to participate would only accomplish the exact opposite. Erin was old enough to remember Dale; the twins were the ones who most needed those memories to be nurtured into the future.

When they got to the house, Erin slammed out of the car and stormed toward the house before any of the others had even shifted in their seats.

"Hang on, kids," Heather said. "I want to talk to y'all a second."

She explained her plan for the afternoon and the reason for it. Then, instead of telling them they had to come along—because making Erin babysit while Heather went by herself would be a nice bit of passive-aggressive poetic justice—she let them decide for themselves.

"Sure," Josh said. "I want to go. Can we get ice cream too?"

Caroline bounced in her seat. "Yes, please, but can I go inside and pee first?"

"Sure, honey." Heather cut the engine. "Let's all go in for a few minutes before we leave."

Heather knocked lightly before opening the door to Erin's room. It wasn't quite a pigsty but wasn't far from it either. Erin had flung herself onto the messy bed, clearly prepared to sulk whether she got her way or not. "You told me you cleaned your room this past weekend."

"I did." Erin's voice was muffled by the mattress. "It got dirty again."

"I see." Heather waited a few seconds, but Erin didn't say anything else. "Well, the twins and I are going to the cemetery, and you are welcome to change your mind and come along if you'd like."

Erin shook her head and mumbled something.

"Suit yourself." Heather closed Erin's door softly and walked away.

———————————

Charlie stood in the field and watched the family's car drive away again, though it had only been in the garage for a few minutes. Charlie's people spent a lot of time coming and going but very little time interacting with him. He understood; he didn't deserve their time or attention.

He stood with his nose to the ground, though he wasn't grazing. His belly hurt, so he hadn't eaten this morning, but Erin didn't know that because she always poured his daily scoop of sweetened oats into the bin without looking. He hadn't eaten the hay that she'd tossed into the hayrack in the corner of his stall either. He had torn at it in frustration, so most of it got scattered on top of his droppings or stuck to the peed-on mass of wood shavings that squished under his hooves.

Dale had always made sure that Charlie had a fluffy layer of shavings to stomp through and to lie on at night if he decided to relax fully instead of sleeping standing up. But Erin rarely took the time to scrape the stall down to the bare-dirt floor before adding fresh bedding. The substrate of Charlie's stall was often so soaked with urine that it irritated his skin if he decided to lie down to sleep. He had always tried to avoid messing in his own stall, but sometimes Erin put him up too early in the afternoons. And when that happened, he just couldn't help making a mess.

Life after Dale wasn't really worth living.

No more than Charlie deserved, he knew.

He hadn't meant to do it.

A hot breeze blew across the pasture, sending tufts of milkweed tumbling across the too-tall alfalfa grass.

Dale had kept the pasture mowed-down so the blades Charlie nibbled were always juicy and sweet. Ever since Charlie had killed the person he loved most in the world, the grasses and weeds had been left to grow tall and bitter.

Charlie hadn't meant to do it.

But that didn't matter.

Nothing did. If Charlie had known how to will himself to die, he would have done it already. Maybe now that his belly hurt so much that he couldn't bring himself to eat, the release he longed for would finally happen.

When Adrian got to the shelter that afternoon, he laughed out loud at the sight that greeted him. He pulled into his usual parking spot next to a folding chair and tiny worktable with an even tinier ice chest on top. He hadn't confirmed that he would actually show up to help tame the feral cat, but apparently, Reva had faith in him.

He put his phone and laptop on the table, then covered his car with the tarp. When he opened the ice chest, he laughed again.

"Thanks, Reva," he said out loud, popping the top on a cold beer. He took a swig and poked through the contents nestled into a bed of ice. A bottle of water, a baggie of sesame sticks in a paper bowl (for him, he assumed), and another baggie… He turned it over to read the label written with a Sharpie in flowing longhand: *Kitty Crack*. And, in another baggie, a small squirt bottle of citronella bug spray.

He set his beer on the table and settled in to begin the campaign to lure the feral tomcat to his eventual fate as a domesticated house cat. "Better you than me, dude," he said to the cat who was still nowhere to be seen. "Here, kitty, kitty."

After opening his laptop and connecting to the shelter's Wi-Fi, he clicked on an email, then tossed a cat treat through the fence and into the tangle of trees beyond. "Well, shit." That was stupid. He tossed the next one with a little less oomph. It bounced on the gravel and through the fence, landing a couple of inches from the wire. "Better."

He dealt with emails, calling, "Here, kitty, kitty," every now and again. Ten emails later, his relative inattention was rewarded; Stinky Cat sat hunched on the other side of the fence, crunching on the Kitty Crack. "Hey, buddy." Adrian threw another morsel. "What's up in the big, bad world?"

The cat declined to answer—or even to look up. He crept over to the new treat and started munching, so Adrian threw another few treats, this time making sure some of them landed on his side of the fence. Reva came across the parking lot carrying a small cat crate. "How's it going?"

Adrian leaned back in the folding chair. "As you see. That crate might be a little premature."

Reva set the crate down next to the fence, several yards down from Adrian's impromptu office space. "I'm setting this up for later to get him used to the crate." Reva propped the crate's open door against the fence and set a plastic container of food inside. "Also, I just got a text from Heather. She and the twins are on their way here." She stood slowly. The tomcat looked up but kept eating the treat he was working on. "I thought I'd let you know in case you were thinking of picking up the cat. I wouldn't want you to get flayed alive again."

"They're bringing that horrible dog, I take it."

"Not this time. They're... They've just left the cemetery. Today was Dale's birthday. Apparently, the visit to the gravesite didn't go as planned."

This was precisely the sort of shit Adrian didn't want to get involved in, but it seemed that a response was expected. "Oh?"

"Heather was hoping it would be a...celebration of sorts, but it didn't turn out that way."

He snorted. "No shit."

Reva narrowed her eyes at him. "Be nice."

Chastised, he retreated behind his charming half smile. "Yes, ma'am."

She drifted closer, her arms crossed. The cat looked up but didn't move. "I'm going to take the kids across to Bayside Barn and get them involved in feeding critters. Take their minds off missing their dad."

"Sounds like a plan." Adrian closed his laptop, since Reva was distracting him from finishing his emails anyway. Maybe he'd head home earlier than he'd planned. The cat wouldn't cross the fence until all the coming and going had stopped for the day, so he was officially wasting his time now. "I guess I'll—"

"I was hoping," Reva cut him off, "that you'd talk with Heather. Maybe go for a walk or something. Cheer her up a little."

"I've actually got a lot of work to..." His voice drifted off in the face of Reva's disapproving expression. With her crossed arms and her pursed lips, she reminded him a lot of his mother right this minute. "Um...I really do have a bit of work to do still." He wasn't lying; once he finished with emails, he had to edit a draft business plan for a new startup company he was advising.

But Reva's silent stare was scarier even than his mom's. "I guess I could…um…spare a few minutes before I head home."

Reva's pursed lips stayed pursed, and her squinting eyes stayed squinted. She tightened her crossed arms.

"Maybe I'll take her for a quick spin in the convertible."

Reva smiled and patted his shoulder. "That's a wonderful idea. I'm so glad you thought of it."

———————

Heather arrived at the shelter with two very subdued kids in the back seat. Maybe Erin had been right after all. Heather needed to stop living in the past and allow Dale's shadow to fade away.

She parked near the shelter's front porch, and Reva opened the back door for the twins. "Hey, you guys," Reva said with excitement to the kids who crawled out of the car. "You want to come see the baby bunnies?"

Caroline nodded soberly, her thumb still in her mouth.

"I guess so," Josh answered, sounding sullen and unhappy.

"Come on then." Reva held out her hands. "You can help me feed the barn critters too."

Heather got out of the car, feeling lost. She needed a hug, but Reva's attention was all on the twins. Reva tipped a chin toward the far end of the lot, where Adrian was folding the canvas tarp and putting it in the trunk of his car. "Go see that one. Ask him how the cat taming is going. No talking—or even thinking—about you-know-who allowed."

She looked over at Adrian. "I don't think he wants to be bothered with me and my problems."

"I'm sure he doesn't. So don't bother him. Just go somewhere and have fun. He'll be able to remind you how that's done, in case you've forgotten."

Heather shook her head but schlepped across the parking lot toward Adrian, who had climbed into his low-slung car and started the engine. The automatic convertible top started folding back all by itself. "Fancy," she said when she drew even with the passenger door.

"Of course," he replied with a wink and a grin. "Get in."

She hesitated a moment, glancing to where Reva had taken the kids, but then got in and slammed the door harder than she'd intended to—her old Honda's doors had to be hauled shut with some force to close completely. "Sorry. I didn't mean to do that. I see you got the scratches taken care of already."

"Friends in high places." He slid his sunglasses down to cover his eyes. "You ready to go for a joyride?"

She forced a smile. "I'd be a fool to say no to a little joy, wouldn't I?"

Adrian drove aimlessly, Sunday driving on a Wednesday afternoon. Whenever someone got behind them, he pulled over to let them pass. "Wonder what's down this road?" he'd say, turning down one potholed track after another.

"Ooh, look at that," she said, pointing out a modern farmhouse perched atop a gentle rise. "How pretty."

"I claim that tractor," he said, referring to the big John Deere some guy was driving across a quaint wooden bridge spanning a winding stream at the foot of the hill.

"What on earth would you do with a tractor?" Heather lifted her face to the breeze as the convertible zoomed around a curve, leaving the farmhouse and tractor behind. "Do you even know how to drive one?"

"I know how to do a lot of things." He gave her a comical leer. "You want me to show you a few of them?"

She smiled, feeling…well…maybe a tiny hint of joy. "Maybe one of these days."

———

Realizing that he couldn't drive aimlessly forever, Adrian turned back toward the main drag, a narrow backcountry blacktop that wound around the bay. Sometimes the bay was visible; other times they passed long stretches of woodland interspersed with fancy pillared gates that guarded some of the more expensive waterfront estates. He thought he knew where he was going, unless he'd turned the wrong way onto Bayview Drive.

But no, here it was. He slowed just in time to ease into the gravel parking lot of Big Daddy's Bar & Grill. He parked under a cypress tree festooned with Spanish moss and hoped for the best; there were no out-in-the-open spots available. He folded his sunglasses and put them in the console. "Fancy a drink?"

A dozen different excuses flitted across her face before she smiled and said, "Sure. Why not?"

She undid her seat belt and reached for the door handle, but he put a hand on her thigh, a silent cue for her to stay put so he could do the gentlemanly thing and open her door. She nodded and settled for wrapping the long strap around her tiny pink leather purse.

He suspected the tiny purse revealed something about her. She didn't carry around a bunch of cosmetics and beauty implements or a day-runner and iPad to keep abreast of her important and ever-evolving business concerns or a ton of other unnecessary minutia. He wasn't sure what that revelation meant about her personality, but he decided he was interested in finding out. Could it be that she was one of those rare people who had the ability to inhabit each moment as it came without obsessing over appearances, thinking ahead to the next thing, or planning for every eventuality?

He opened her door and held out a hand to assist her out of the car. She rose gracefully, looking down until the last second when he didn't immediately release her hand. Her eyes met his, a look of hesitant anticipation in those clear, leaf-green depths.

He thought about kissing her. This time, he hoped she wouldn't freeze in dismay. This time, she might even lean into him. He looked at her soft, prettily curved lips, then back up to meet her eyes. He lowered his eyelids in that way that always made her blush. And blush she did, but she also smiled, a tiny secret smile. "Are you going to buy me that drink or what?"

Chapter 4

FRIDAY EVENING, ERIN CAME INTO THE KITCHEN WITH HER backpack slung over one shoulder. She'd gone home with Sierra after school that day and had been dropped off in time for dinner as instructed. "I'm so glad it's the weekend."

"I know. TGIF, right?" Heather gave the pot of noodles she was tending another stir. She'd taken the twins to the shelter after school, and they'd only just gotten home a half hour ago. Spaghetti night had turned into shrimp Alfredo night because frozen shrimp thawed faster than ground beef. "How was the yearbook meeting?"

"Fine. We all got digital cameras on loan from the school, but honestly, I think I'll just use my cell phone." Erin took a clean glass down from the cupboard and filled it with water from the fridge. "I'm gonna head upstairs and do my homework now so I can rest and relax for the rest of the weekend."

"Good plan."

Erin headed toward the stairs.

"Wait up," Heather said. "You fed Charlie before you came in, right?"

"Jeez, Mom." Erin dropped her backpack on the floor and set her water glass on the counter with more force than necessary. "Why do you always jump on me the minute I walk in the door? Why are you punishing me?"

Heather swallowed a sudden surge of temper. "It's not punishment to take care of Charlie. He is your responsibility, and I shouldn't need to remind you that he's the reason you get such a generous allowance. The twins take care of Jasper, you take care of Charlie, and I take care of you kids."

Instead of replying, Erin sent a daggered glance that Heather didn't have to turn around to see because she could feel it boring into the back of her head.

"We all have to help each other," Heather reminded her daughter, as if that would help.

But of course, it only poured oil onto the fire. Erin made a hissing noise that was eerily similar to the one Dale used to make whenever things didn't go his way. "Why don't we just sell Charlie? We might as well, since you won't let me ride him without Daddy here to teach me. He just stands out there in the field, all alone, all day long. It makes me sad."

"I know." Heather blinked back tears. "It makes me sad too. But that horse—"

"The horse you're too scared to even go near," Erin spat.

"Yes. But the horse I'm too scared of…was Dale's horse. And I'm sorry, for Charlie and for you and for me, that I'm just not ready to let him go." She'd thought of it, even gone so far as to contact an equine rescue group. But in the end, she couldn't go through with putting Charlie up for adoption. "Seeing Charlie all alone in that field is sad, but not seeing him at all would be sadder still. So I'm trusting you to take care of him. Maybe we can find someone to teach you how to ride next summer."

"It doesn't make sense!" Erin yelled. "Why are you hanging on to a horse you're too afraid to even touch?"

"Because letting Charlie go would be like letting your dad go all over again, and I'm just not ready to do that."

Erin slumped with a sigh. "Fine. I'll go feed Charlie."

Heather drained and rinsed the noodles, then melted a big chunk of butter over low heat. She poured heavy whipping cream into a jar, dumped in a tablespoon of plain flour, closed the lid, and shook the jar vigorously. The thought of throwing the jar across the room crossed her mind, but she carefully opened the lid and poured the frothy mixture into the saucepan, then stirred in a container of shredded Parmesan cheese. While the sauce thickened, she sautéed the thawed shrimp in a small skillet.

Erin slammed into the kitchen in a huff. "Well, I tried to feed Charlie. I set up his stall, but he wouldn't come. He's just standing out in the field with his head down."

A feeling of dread crept over Heather. "Did you call him?"

Erin made a huff of irritation. "Of course I did. He just stood there."

Heather glanced at the clock. It would be getting dark soon. "Go out there right now, put a halter on him, and make him come in."

Erin groaned. "Why don't *you* do it?"

Heather held on to her temper by the barest tendril of a fraying thread. "I am cooking your dinner, that's why. Look, Erin, I know that you help out more than a lot of kids your age. But this is our life now, whether we like it or not. We all have to pitch in and help each other."

Erin's ice-blue eyes—Dale's eyes—grew sharp as glass, and her mouth drew into a lemon-sucking pucker. After a moment of tight-lipped silence and staring, she stomped her foot. "Fine." She flounced out the back door, slamming it behind her.

Heather went back to stirring the pasta. Her hands trembled, from the argument as much as a sweat-producing fear that something might be wrong with Charlie. The Alfredo sauce was done, so she turned off the heat. The shrimp had curled up and turned pink, so she moved them off the heat and turned that burner off too.

Closing her eyes, she coached herself to take a few deep breaths. Willed her hands to stop shaking. Released tension on a sigh and settled her shoulders, which had crept up to her ears while she'd been arguing with Erin.

They had been such a happy family before.

———

Cat watched Adrian—whose name he'd figured out by listening to the people who talked to him—from the safe distance of the bushes outside the fence. The other people had finally left, and Cat wondered if Adrian would leave now too. But he sat in the chair and set the flat thing with the hinged lid on the table, then opened it up and started tapping on it as usual.

Humans seemed to be interested in the strangest things.

The flat thing made noises every now and then, but other than that, it seemed to have no use whatsoever. And yet Adrian had an endless capability to stare at the thing and tap on it for great swathes of time.

Enough of that, Cat decided. He came closer and rubbed against the fence, enticing Adrian to come closer so they could study each other with the safety of the fence between them.

Adrian didn't notice.

Cat meowed, arched his back, and paced in the other direction, leaning against the fence.

Adrian threw another of those tasty but rich treats through the fence. Cat had eaten the first two but ignored the rest. He'd eaten too many of those a few days before, and though they tasted better than anything, they gave him the squirts. He'd learned his lesson about those things.

He didn't blame Adrian, though. He knew, without knowing how he knew, that Adrian was a good person who didn't wish him harm. He was also beginning to like that colorful lady who moved like a tree blowing in the wind. She'd been giving him a container of predigested meat every evening. He had to jump the fence and then venture into an open box to get it, but so far, no harm had come to him. Apparently, it wasn't a trap.

Adrian closed the flat thing and stood, stretching. Cat thought at first that the man would come closer, maybe pet Cat through the fence. Cat meowed, a sweet meow of invitation, but Adrian folded the chair, then the table, and leaned them against the fence.

Then Cat heard the low, menacing moan of the big gray tomcat. The one who'd beaten Cat before but didn't seem satisfied with his victory. His wavering yowls meant he was coming to chase Cat away from the predigested food that was his by rights. Cat put his ears back and screamed at the interloper. That was *his* predigested food.

Old Gray could have the treats. Adrian had thrown dozens of them through the fence, and they were incredibly delicious, guaranteed to keep Old Gray busy while Cat scarfed down the gooey meat the tree lady had left for him. Cat could eat his food and abscond before Old Gray found and ate all those scattered treats.

All he had to do was stay out of sight until Old Gray got the squirts. Then the old tomcat wouldn't feel like chasing Cat again for a good long time. But Cat realized that sooner or later, he would have to choose between freedom and safety.

———————

Heather called the twins down to dinner. She had just set their plates in front of them at the kitchen bar when Erin slammed through the back door.

"Mom." Erin's eyes were wide with panic; her breaths came in frantic huffs. "Charlie's lying down in the field. He won't get up."

A frisson of fear skittered up Heather's spine. "He… He won't get up?" She'd heard Erin but hoped she had misunderstood somehow. She didn't know a lot about horses. But she did understand enough to know that a lying-down horse who wouldn't get up was a serious problem.

Josh and Caroline had stopped eating, forks suspended in midair. They both spoke at once. "What's wrong with Charlie?"

Heather put a hand up to shush them and turned back to Erin. "You tried to put a halter on him?"

Erin nodded. "I got it on him, but he didn't even pick up his head."

Heather chewed on a fingernail. The vet's office was already closed. She could call the office and leave a message, but it would take as much as an hour for Mack to call her back.

"Mom," Erin said in a pleading tone, "I think Charlie is really sick. We need to do something."

"I know that," Heather snapped. Then she put a hand on Erin's shoulder. "I'm sorry. I'm thinking about what to do."

The kids were all staring at her, waiting for her to make a decision. "I'll handle this," she told them. "Y'all finish your dinner."

She took her cell phone into the den. Reva probably had Mack's cell number. Maybe she could get in touch with him right away. She sat on the couch and called her friend. Relief flowed through her when Reva picked up immediately. "Hey, you."

Heather didn't waste time on pleasantries. "Charlie is lying down in the field, and he won't get up. Do you have Mack's cell number?"

"I do. I'll call him for you and then head that way myself. If Charlie is already down, it may take us all working together to get him up again."

"Oh, thank you, thank you." Having Reva's support made this whole situation seem a little less dire. "What should I be doing for him while I wait?"

"First priority is to get him standing. What you don't want is for him to roll over because he could twist his intestines, and then you'd be talking about surgery."

"I'll try." But she couldn't imagine herself having any success at moving Charlie from five feet away. She knew her phobia of horses wasn't logical, but that didn't lessen her fear.

"Get Jasper to help. But if you can't get Charlie up, at least try to keep him from rolling. I'll call Mack and head your way. See you soon."

When Heather ended the call, she noticed Erin hovering in the archway between the kitchen and the den. "What now?"

Heather tucked the phone into the back pocket of her jeans. "Reva says that if we can't get Charlie up, we at least need to keep him lying still. If he rolls over, it could hurt his insides."

"I'll go out there and sit by him," Erin said. "If I hold his head still, he won't be able to roll."

A vision of the horse kicking out at Erin or rolling over her invaded Heather's mind.

"He won't hurt me." Erin had correctly read Heather's expression, a feat Heather knew wasn't difficult because every fleeting emotion showed on her face. "I'll be sitting next to his head," Erin added, "not by his feet."

"I understand that, honey. I just worry."

Erin gave Heather a quick hug. "I know; you're a mom. Worrying is your job."

Heather kissed Erin's cheek. "Let's do this."

Erin called Jasper and headed that way. Heather paused in the kitchen to give the twins instructions to stay inside and watch something on TV until Erin came back in to supervise bath time and tuck them into bed. Then, with her heart thumping against the lump in her throat, she hurried to catch up.

———————

Charlie felt the cool, damp earth beneath him, seeping into his body and cooling the pain in his belly. But the griping pains didn't stop. They built and then eased, built and then eased, never completely going away, always coming back stronger than before. He closed his eyes and ground his teeth against the pain.

Something he couldn't understand kept him tethered to the earth. Tethered to the pain. Tethered to the people who didn't understand him or care about him or have time for him. Why? Was it because he hadn't yet suffered enough to make up for his failures? Was it because he had to be punished for his sins?

He was willing to be punished. He knew he deserved it. So he closed his eyes and kept his focus on the twisting pain in his belly. He let the pain come. He didn't turn away from it, and he didn't want to. Because he deserved it. It belonged to him. It was all he had left.

Moments later, he felt Erin's gentle touch on his face. Then Charlie felt Heather's hands on him too. She smoothed back the mane along his neck, and Charlie shivered as the warm evening breeze reached his sweat-damp skin.

"Mom," Erin said. "I can't believe you're sitting this close to Charlie."

"Neither can I." Heather's voice sounded as soft as her touch felt. "But he's a little less scary when he isn't standing upright."

"I hope he's gonna be okay." Erin's voice wobbled. "I'm so scared for him."

"Me too, honey," Heather said. "Me too."

Jasper whined, nosing at Charlie's face. Charlie tried to lift his head to greet his old friend, but even that small movement seemed impossible.

"Reva said that maybe Jasper could help us get Charlie up," Heather said. "Let's try it."

Erin tugged at Charlie's halter, and Heather tried to lift his neck, while Jasper barked in Charlie's ears, a ringing, annoying repetition of "Get up, get up, get up."

Charlie pedaled his feet weakly, but it was no use. He couldn't get his feet under him now, even if he wanted to.

————————

Adrian had spent a good hour working through emails and tossing treats through the fence. But after eating only one or two morsels, the cat had ignored the treats. Meowing and rubbing at the fence, he seemed to be begging for some other kind of food, which Adrian didn't have. Reva had already set up the crate with the canned food, but she said the cat wouldn't approach it until everyone was gone, so Adrian figured he might as well leave so the cat could eat.

He gathered his stuff and folded the car cover. In the woods nearby, a tomcat yowled threats at Stinky Cat, apparently demanding satisfaction for whatever slights he may have endured in previous fights. "Stinky Cat, you really ought to consider coming over to this side of the fence before you get hurt."

But, of course, Stinky Cat didn't listen. He put his ears back, stared into the trees, and yowled a challenge to the interloper.

"If you won't listen, I can't help you." Adrian got into his car, shaking his head. He hoped the cat would allow himself to get caught soon. But sitting here wasting his time wasn't going to make that happen. Not today, anyway.

He started the motor and looked over his shoulder to back up, then noticed Reva running across the parking lot with her skirts flying out behind her, her hands waving to catch his attention. He rolled down the window. "Have I forgotten something?"

"No, but…" She clung to the car's doorframe and caught her breath. "We need your help. Heather's horse is sick. Abby and I are going to help, and Mack is on his way, but we might need a bit more muscle."

Adrian looked over at Quinn's work truck, which was parked in its usual spot. "What about Quinn?"

"He's got his son, Sean, this weekend. They've already taken my car to go…" She flapped a dismissive hand. "I don't know. Somewhere. Anyhow, I'll pack up the dinner I just made to bring along. We might have to take turns eating, but at least we won't starve before morning."

"What's wrong with the horse?"

"He is lying down in the field, and Heather and Erin can't get him up."

Adrian knew what that meant: The horse probably had colic, a severe abdominal pain that, depending on its cause, could lead to fatal consequences. An impaction or obstruction could result in tearing or twisting of the intestines, so getting the horse on his feet was a life-or-death proposition.

Adrian's family had owned a horse before Hurricane Katrina turned everyone's world upside down. He knew how to handle horses, so his help could be critical in this situation. "Okay. I'll follow y'all in my car."

"Thanks, Adrian," Reva said. "It'll take me a minute, though. Abby's packing up the food, and I'll have to change into jeans and get some lead ropes and a lunge line from the barn. I don't know what all Heather has at her place."

"Bring a whip too," he suggested.

"I'll do that." Reva turned to go.

Then Adrian thought of something else. "Hey, Reva. Do you know if Heather has a horse trailer? If we can get Charlie to go inside, it might help." Being trailered might generate enough adrenal activity to loosen the horse's impacted bowels. Horses who weren't used to being loaded onto a trailer were often just scared enough to shit the moment they were forced to load up.

Adrian knew this because horse, Bluebell, had done the same thing when they'd loaded him onto a rescue transport just before Katrina hit.

"We can take the barn's trailer," Reva said. "Can you hook it up to Quinn's truck while I finish getting everything else together? The keys are in the ignition."

"Yeah, sure." Adrian rolled up his window and turned off his car. Having learned his lesson the first time, he took the canvas cover out of the trunk and tossed it over the car before trekking across the parking lot toward Quinn's truck.

Adrian drove the truck around to Bayside Barn and hooked up the trailer, still thinking about everything his family had lost in Hurricane Katrina. His old horse, Bluebell, had been adopted out wherever he ended up after the evacuation. Their black-and-white cat—who had looked a lot like the feral tomcat—had refused to come out of hiding when it was time to pack up and leave before the storm hit. He was unlikely to have survived. Their neighborhood had been hit hard; the houses had flooded to the rooftops. It had taken over a year to accomplish the necessary renovations, including a very costly undertaking to lift the entire house up past the newly calculated flood level. Katrina had, literally, blown their lives off-kilter.

"Enough," he said out loud. "Stop thinking." It wasn't like him to dwell on the past, but every now and then—especially when faced with an emergency situation reminiscent of their flight out of New Orleans—those old memories rose up to bite him.

He parked the truck and trailer on the drive next to Reva's house and helped Reva and Abby load up all the stuff they'd gathered. "Y'all want me to drive?"

"I've got it," Reva said. "Take your car so we have more than one vehicle in case Mack decides to transport Charlie to the vet."

"Okay. See y'all at the road."

The sky had darkened while they'd been rushing around, so Adrian used his phone to light the way to his car. When he made it past the shelter and its outbuildings, he lifted the beam to pinpoint his parked car. The hair on the back of his neck prickled. For a half second, he'd thought that the jughead tomcat sitting on the canvas-covered hood was his family's old cat. Impossible, of course. It was just another old ghost, rising up. "Here, kitty," Adrian called softly.

At the sound of Adrian's voice, the cat sprang off the hood of the car and hit the ground running. In less than a minute, it had climbed the eight-foot-tall chain-link fence and leaped into the thick wall of trees, bushes, and vines that stood as a natural barrier between the shelter and the road.

Adrian shook off the spooky feeling of having seen a ghost.

———————————

Charlie's gut twisted. The pain pulsed with every heartbeat, consuming him, shutting out all but the pain that writhed inside him like a live animal trying to claw its way out.

Dimly, Charlie heard Jasper's frantic barking. The dog, his friend, circled and barked, circled and barked. He even nipped the air beside Charlie's face, trying to force Charlie to get up. To stand. To live.

Charlie was past that point. The pain was too great, the effort of moving too impossible.

A pair of blazing lights came toward Charlie across the field. Then another pair, from a slightly different direction. Charlie closed his eyes, but the bright lights pierced through his closed eyelids. Slamming sounds as loud as gunfire made him flinch.

Loud voices buzzed around Charlie's head like flies. Rough hands smacked his hide, stinging his skin, keeping him from sinking further into his belly pain. He heard the sounds of a whip cutting the air, then felt the whip's tassel flickering at his hooves like hissing snakes. Charlie pedaled his feet to escape the feeling of snakes slithering all around his feet. He twitched his ears to shut out the hissing sound of snakes rising up from the ground. Hands clapped loudly beside his head. Jasper barked, barked, barked. People yelled. "Get up, Charlie. Get up. Get up."

He couldn't get up.

Another set of lights came toward him across the field, surrounding him in a painful bright glow. More loud slamming sounds.

"This isn't working."

"We're losing him."

He heard Erin's wailing cries and Heather's soft voice saying, "We've got this. Go inside and take care of the twins. Make sure they get their baths and then tuck them in."

"Clip those lead ropes together," someone else said. "Let's try…"

Charlie felt many hands behind him, rocking him forward, urging him up onto his legs. But his legs trembled and crumpled beneath him.

Voices came at him from all sides. "Get up. Get up. Come on, you can do it."

No, he couldn't.

Something behind him, a rope under his rump, pulled him forward across the ground until he got his back legs under him. Shaky, he tried to stand, but only pitched forward onto his chest, plowing his nose in the dirt.

Hands pulled at his head and tugged at the straps of his halter. Charlie lifted his head, but that was all he could manage. "Come on, buddy. That's it."

Another rope came around him, this time from the front, lifting his chest. "Good boy!" Firm hands patted his shoulder. "Good boy, Charlie."

Dale? Was Dale here now? Charlie opened his eyes, turned his head to look at who was speaking to him so kindly, but his head weighed too much. He dropped his chin, but the hands holding his halter kept his head up, even though his legs wanted to collapse under him. "No, no. Don't lie down."

The slithering snakes came back, flickering at his feet. Forcing Charlie to move.

He took a staggering step, then another. The man with the kind voice walked beside him, urging, encouraging, patting him, and calling him Charlie Horse in a low voice. Someone pulled at the lead rope attached to Charlie's halter, forcing him to keep moving, even though the ground dragged at his hooves, causing him to stumble.

The man who reminded him of Dale took the rope and urged Charlie to a slow trot. "That's it." He made clicking sounds in time to the beat of Charlie's hooves against the hard ground. "Good boy, Charlie Horse."

The man trotted beside Charlie inside the ring of lights made by the cars parked in the field. People came and went, going to the house and coming back again. Different hands took the lead rope, keeping Charlie moving, making him go even faster when his legs tried to fold beneath him.

The man came back. Coiling the lead rope up under Charlie's

chin, he let Charlie walk instead of making him trot. Then, finally, the man stopped walking. "You want to try the trailer?" he asked one of the other people. They were all gathered around, a concerned knot of humanity.

"If he falls in the trailer, we'll have an even bigger problem."

Words swirled around Charlie, and he swayed on his feet. "Watch out, Adrian," someone yelled. "He's going down!"

Adrian must be the man holding him because he quickly tugged the lead rope and made a clicking sound.

Trotting again. Charlie's breath rasped out of his lungs in ragged gasps. Every step jarred his belly.

Adrian slowed to a walk, gasping for breath. "Come on, buddy." He led Charlie to a two-stall horse trailer that smelled of other horses, donkeys, and goats. "Let's load up." Someone came with the whip, flickering the tassels at Charlie's feet. Primal fear rose up in Charlie's chest, and escape was the only thing he could think of. With the snakes behind him, his only option was to leap forward into the trailer.

He stood, shivering, waiting to be tied to the crossbar, expecting to be hauled somewhere behind the truck.

Trailer rides were frightening, though, even when they were worth it in the end, and anyway, Charlie didn't feel like going anywhere.

"It's not working," somebody yelled. Someone whose voice Charlie recognized. "Bring him on out. We'll have to tube him."

Adrian pushed against Charlie's chest, forcing him to back out of the trailer, step by anxious step, never knowing when he'd take that last step back only to find there was nothing beneath him but air. But Charlie's new friend moved with him, one arm around his chest while he held the lead rope coiled at his chin and whispered encouraging words in his ear.

Then he was out. Adrian tugged at the lead rope and let it play out to the end, trotting beside him once again. Someone whistled, and Adrian slowed, turning back toward the sound.

Mack was there.

Charlie remembered Mack.

Mack came to see Charlie once a year to do very bad things to him. Mack was a nice man with a gentle touch, but his kind energy and gentle hands didn't make it any better when Mack poked Charlie with needles in his neck. Or when he shoved a tube down—

Oh, no. Not the tube...

Adrian wrapped the lead rope in his fist and walked Charlie toward a metal bucket that glinted in the car lights. Mack held a long, clear tube coiled up in his hand, looping over his shoulder. Charlie tried to back up.

"Adrian." Mack grabbed Charlie's halter. "Can you hold the twitch?"

Adrian took the twitch: a short stick with a narrow loop of chain on the end. Murmuring apologies, he put the chain around Charlie's soft nose and twisted it tight to keep him from moving. Then Mack proceeded to feed the end of the long tube down Charlie's throat.

Would they never stop torturing him?

It seemed like hours later—and maybe it was—that Mack coiled up his tube and stuck it into the metal bucket, along with the twitch that had hurt Charlie's nose. Charlie swallowed, tasting the residue of the thick oil that Mack had forced into his empty stomach.

Then the walking started up again. Different people took turns holding the lead rope, walking or trotting in the same unending circle made by all the cars' headlights. Whenever one person got tired, another took over.

Charlie didn't get to stop, and his beloved friend Jasper kept pace beside him.

Adrian held the lead rope and tugged to get Charlie moving, while Jasper trotted alongside. Round and round they went, beating down a circular path in the field grass. Mack got into his truck and drove away. The other truck drove away too, leaving the trailer behind.

Heather stayed.

Adrian stayed.

Jasper stayed, Charlie's constant companion no matter who held the lead rope.

Only one car remained, its motor purring softly, its lights cutting through the darkness of the lonely field. Heather took the lead rope from Adrian, who leaned on the hood of the car while she pulled Charlie around in more circles.

Charlie knew that Heather had always been afraid of him, but now, her concern outweighed her fear. To let her know that he wouldn't hurt her, Charlie chuffed softly as they plodded along. She patted his shoulder, her touch light and soft. "Good boy."

Slowly, the griping pain in Charlie's gut began to ease. He could hear it gurgling, feel his tense insides relaxing as the tight knot inside him began to loosen and release. "Adrian," Heather called. "I think I can hear his stomach growling."

"Yeah?" Adrian walked toward them. He leaned close and put his head against Charlie's belly, listening. "This could be it. Let's get him back in the trailer."

Charlie wanted to lean on Adrian, to let the man's gentle hands soothe his aching belly, but Adrian took the lead rope and pulled him forward, forcing him to step up into the metal box. When they got there, Adrian wrapped his arms around Charlie's chest and held on, even took some of Charlie's weight and let him rest his neck over the man's shoulder.

"Come on, buddy," Adrian said, his voice deep and soothing while his wide palms and long fingers stroked Charlie's belly on both sides. "Just relax. I've got you."

Heather came into the trailer too. She smoothed gentle fingers over Charlie's face, murmuring sounds of comfort and assurance. "Sweet boy, sweet boy, sweet boy."

Could he trust? Could he believe? Did he even want to?

Heather whispered into his ear, her breath warm and full of life. "Please, Charlie. I know that Dale isn't here, and he was your person. But I'm here now, and I want to be your person, if you'll let me."

Charlie twitched his ear away from Heather's warm breath and felt a shudder go through his body. He wanted to believe, but believing could be so much harder than holding onto despair.

"I'm here now," Heather whispered into his ear. "I'm here. And I want you to live."

Charlie hadn't quite decided yet whether he could trust Heather. But Adrian's energy felt so loving, and Charlie knew that he had to take a chance. He had to risk the pain that could come from loving someone new, even if it meant losing everything all over again.

Chapter 5

WHEN THE POOR HORSE'S BOWELS FINALLY RELEASED, ADRIAN gave a whoop of joy, then glanced at his watch. Just after 2:00 a.m. He patted the horse's sweat-coated hide. "About damn time, buddy."

He guided Charlie out of the trailer, handed the lead rope to Heather, and closed the trailer door. "I hope you don't mind cleaning that trailer out tomorrow," he said. "I'm too tired to do it right now."

"Thanks for everything you've done tonight." Heather held Charlie while Adrian went to his car, turned off the engine, and pocketed the keys. "We couldn't have gotten him up without your help."

"I don't know about all that." Actually, she was probably correct. Not because he did anything special, but because it took a team of people working together.

They walked together across the dark field toward the barn, Jasper leading the way and Charlie trailing behind. The weak light of a crescent moon tipped the tall grasses in silver. "Do you think it's safe to put him up in his stall now?"

Adrian glanced back at the horse. "I think so. He clearly feels a lot better. And since he pooped, we know that his intestines are moving again. But we'll stay in the barn and keep an eye on him for a while, just to be sure."

"I can't thank you enough for staying. Charlie seemed to respond to you better than to anyone else."

"I like him too."

Just outside the barn, Heather handed the lead rope back to Adrian and went in search of the light switch. After a minute of feeling along the wall—and one shriek of terror when she touched something—she found the switch and flooded the barn with light. The corners of the place were laced with dust-covered cobwebs, explaining Heather's shriek.

The barn held a total of four stalls, two on each side of the central aisle, which appeared to be made of packed red dirt. The stalls were well made if not well maintained. The dust-covered walls and sliding doors were made of sturdy two-by-six boards in metal frames to a height of about four feet. Above that, every wall contained rows of metal bars. Each stall had an exterior window opening covered with bars.

Open spaces for storage flanked the stalls on both sides, and all of them were filled with a hodgepodge of junk. A dusty lawn mower half-covered by a dirty canvas tarp. Dirt-caked buckets. Metal trash cans with dented lids, one of which had a brown-stained feed scoop turned upside down on top of it. Several bales of old-looking hay stacked in a corner.

Jasper hopped up onto the top bale and curled up, rested his nose on his paws, and watched Adrian with a worried expression.

Heather was looking around the barn too, her expression one of dismay.

"Which stall is his?"

"It's this one." Heather slid open one of the stall doors.

Adrian led Charlie Horse to the stall but stopped just outside it. The bedding that remained was scattered with piles of horse droppings and saturated with urine. "We can't put him in there."

"I didn't know it was this bad." Heather flushed, her cheeks turning crimson with embarrassment. "Erin takes care of Charlie."

"Or not," he said with a snort of disgust. He refrained from making a comment about the irony of Heather being hired to care for shelter animals when she clearly didn't take care of her own.

"I'm sorry," Heather said. "I thought Erin was taking care of Charlie. I feel bad that I didn't know she wasn't doing her chores."

"Isn't it your job to make sure your kid does her chores?" Maybe he was being unfair—he wasn't a parent, so who was he to judge her parenting? But this horse deserved to be more than a teenager's chore. A lot of people—including him—would love to have a horse but couldn't afford one because of money, time, or space constraints. It chapped his ass to see Charlie so neglected.

Adrian knew Heather was busy, but this was completely unacceptable. And why was she planning to take a full-time job at the shelter—taking care of animals, no less—when she couldn't cope as it was?

He took a breath and told himself to simmer down. He'd seen the results of extreme equine neglect before, so he had to admit, this situation triggered him just a little. He tied Charlie's lead rope to one of the stainless-steel bars and looked into the other stalls. They were piled high with junk. He tried to soften his tone. "See if you can find a bag of pine shavings somewhere. And bring a shovel."

He went into the barn's darkest crevices in search of a wheelbarrow.

———

Heather found a dozen bags of shavings stacked in a corner of the barn and covered by a musty, mold-spotted quilt. She pulled the quilt off the stack, and a dog-eared copy of a teen magazine fell to the ground.

Heather rolled up the magazine and tossed it into a cluttered corner of the barn. She had been buying a bag of shavings every week, intending for each bag to be used up before her next trip to the feed store. And instead of doing the work of cleaning Charlie's stall, Erin had been hiding out in the barn reading magazines.

Heather remembered when, at the beginning of the summer,

Erin had offered to start unloading the truck and driving it back to the pole barn each week. To Heather, that offer had signified that Erin was showing a renewed interest in life, in the future, after Dale's death. Dale had been allowing Erin to drive from the field to the barn—which wasn't illegal because even though Erin was only thirteen, she wouldn't be driving the truck off their property.

Heather had been proud of what she saw as Erin's effort to help out even more.

But now it was glaringly obvious that Erin had made the offer to cover her increasing laziness. Instead of cleaning up properly after Charlie, Erin had been spreading layer after layer of clean bedding on top of dirty shavings. Shameful.

Shameful that Erin, the seemingly helpful child Heather was so proud of, would treat Dale's horse this way. Even more shameful that Heather, the adult, had neglected to check behind her teenage daughter to ensure that everything was getting done. A responsible parent gave instructions and then followed up. Without Heather's inattention, Erin couldn't have neglected Charlie as she had. Erin had dropped the ball, but it was Heather's job as a parent to pick it up, and she had failed. Adrian was absolutely correct; it was Heather's job to make sure Erin did her chores.

If it wasn't the middle of the night and if Adrian wasn't here, Heather would march into Erin's bedroom and drag her out to the barn. They'd clean Charlie's stall together while Heather pelted her eldest daughter with a few choice words.

But it was the middle of the night, and Adrian was here.

So Heather would deal with the situation in front of her now. And tomorrow, she would handle the situation that was upstairs sleeping blissfully unaware of the wrath that awaited.

Adrian tossed two rubber buckets out of the stall. "These need a good scrubbing."

He didn't look out at her, but she heard the steady scrape,

thunk sound of the shovel as he dug out the sludge in the bottom of the stall and dumped it into the wheelbarrow.

How could Heather be trusted—how could she trust herself—to be in charge of caring for a shelter full of animals when she had allowed this to happen to her own horse? Because Charlie *was* hers now.

Ignoring the buckets for now, Heather eased closer to Charlie, the horse she had always feared too much to get close to.

Charlie didn't seem so scary now, as he stood with his head low, exhausted and dispirited, tied to the bars of his stall. Just as he hadn't seemed scary when Heather had taken her turn walking him in circles around the field. She hadn't been worried then that he would step on her or rear up or run her down. Her biggest fear then was that he would stop plodding along and try to lie down again.

Heather reached out to touch Charlie's nose. It was soft as velvet, with long whiskers that tickled her palm. He blew a warm gust of air into her hand. Startled, she drew back, then forced herself to try again. This time, she stepped a bit closer to touch his chest. He raised his head and then lowered it, leaning his face into her belly.

A powerful wave of remorse and contrition rose up inside her, making her heart feel heavy and full, pushing against the back of her throat.

She had allowed this horrible situation to happen.

Heather's kids couldn't be ignored.

Even Jasper, always underfoot and ever in the way, couldn't be ignored.

But Charlie could be ignored. Charlie could disappear into the distance, a brown blob of misery on the distant horizon. His grief had been so visible, so inescapable, that it had seemed to equal Heather's own inconsolable grief. Her fear of horses hadn't entered into it, she realized now.

Her fear of being consumed by Charlie's grief on top of her own had.

She stepped closer to Charlie until the two of them stood chest to chest, heart to heart. She wasn't overwhelmed by the massive bulk of the big animal. She was, instead, comforted by it. Wrapping her arms around Charlie's sturdy neck, she held on and let her grief pour into his heart. Then, with a shuddering sigh of release, she allowed his grief to pour into hers. And to her surprise, the sharing didn't make her grief more unbearable. Instead, her sorrow eased. And she thought that maybe she felt Charlie's sorrow ease just a little bit as well.

"I won't let you disappear again," she promised, a whisper against Charlie's warm neck. "I won't let you disappear." She would do better from now on. She would spend time with Charlie, at least a few minutes every day. She would make sure he was well taken care of.

Adrian wheeled the shit-filled wheelbarrow out of the stall backward, bumping the flat tire against the metal threshold. "Where can I dump this?"

She let Charlie's comforting bulk insulate her from Adrian's judgmental tone. "There's a mulch pile just outside the barn door."

He didn't say a word as he manhandled the flat-tired wheelbarrow down the aisle, but his entire being radiated disgust. He seemed to be trying to soften his demeanor and act less irked with her, but it wasn't really working.

Fine. Heather knew she'd done wrong, and she planned to do better. Adrian could judge her all day long, but he didn't know what she'd been through. He might not be so high-and-mighty if he knew what it was like to lose the love of his life. He could bang that wheelbarrow around and shoot narrow-eyed glances all he liked. It wouldn't bother her.

Heather patted Charlie and kissed him on his velvet-soft nose, then took the buckets around to the hose outside the barn—which was thankfully located opposite the door where Adrian was dumping the wheelbarrow's contents. She rinsed the buckets, then left them to soak while she located a scrub brush and a squirt bottle labeled in Sharpie: *50% Dawn / 50% Clorox*. She worked on the buckets till they felt clean, then rinsed them again and filled the water bucket to the brim.

As she tilted the feed bucket upside down on a shelf to drip-dry, she noticed an old metal currycomb on the shelf above the food bins. It was rusted and warped, the wooden handle peeling and cracked. She'd go by the feed store and get a new one tomorrow, but for now, this one would do just fine. She went up to Charlie and started brushing his salt-caked brown hide with slow, smooth strokes.

Charlie's eyes drifted closed, and he shifted his weight to rest one back leg, then blew out a soft chuffing sound. As Heather worked the currycomb over Charlie's coarse brown hair, she felt his unconditional love and acceptance pour into the jagged fissures of her wounded heart. "I'm so sorry I didn't take better care of you."

She imagined that if he could have replied, he'd have said, "I forgive you." And in that moment, she felt his forgiveness as clearly as she felt his love. She realized then that she had no reason to be afraid of Charlie.

His love had cured her fear, and his forgiveness was beginning to cure her sorrow.

———

Adrian finished cleaning Charlie's stall and added fresh bedding. While he'd been doing all that, Heather had cleaned and filled Charlie's water bucket and hung it on the hook inside his stall. Now, she was brushing him with a currycomb, dropping great gobs of horsehair onto the barn's dirt floor and leaving his coat slick and shiny. She cleared the comb's serrated metal edge by tapping it on the stall's thick wood wall. "Should we give him anything to eat?"

"Mack said to just give him water for now." He untied the lead rope and led Charlie into the stall. "You were walking Charlie when Mack left, so he gave me instructions to relay to you." Adrian removed the horse's halter with the lead rope still attached and handed them both to Heather.

"And?" She hung the halter and rope on a nail outside the stall. "What else did Mack say?"

Adrian closed the stall door and slid the latch home. "Wait until after he checks Charlie out to feed him. Mack will swing by around noon thirty tomorrow on his way home from the vet's office. You're supposed to call the office and report how Charlie is doing in the morning." He glanced at his watch. "In about four hours."

Heather sighed. "I am so sorry." She put a hand on his arm. "And I really appreciate your help."

He shrugged. "I did it for Charlie." Then he realized how cold that sounded, how dismissive of Heather's feelings. She shouldn't have let Charlie's stall get in such bad shape, but he knew she didn't harm the horse on purpose. And even perfectly well-cared-for horses could come down with colic for no discernible reason. It might not have happened because of anything Erin and Heather did or didn't do. He patted her hand. "I'm glad I was here to help." A wide yawn caught him by surprise, and he covered his mouth. "Sorry."

She yawned too, then smiled behind her hand. "It's contagious."

"It's no wonder we're yawning. I don't know about you, but it's way past my bedtime, and the clean sheets I put on my bed yesterday are calling me." He dug the car keys out of his pocket. At the sound, Jasper hopped down from the hay bale and sat next to Heather, wagging his stub tail. Clearly ready for a car ride, if one was imminent.

"My guest room has clean sheets too," Heather said. "Egyptian cotton. They might give your sheets a run for the money, especially since they're here instead of an hour away."

He looked at her sideways.

"Really. You should spend the rest of the night here instead of driving back to New Orleans."

He hadn't been looking forward to the long trip home. "You sure it won't be an imposition?"

"Positive." She smiled. "The guest bedroom is all made up and ready for you."

"In that case…" He yawned again. "I'll gratefully take you up on the offer."

"I'll even make your breakfast in the morning." She turned toward the house, and in a way that felt entirely natural—though he wasn't expecting it—she slipped her arm through his. Linked at the elbows, they leaned against each other on the short walk between the barn and the house. "What's your opinion of pancakes with whipped cream, strawberries, and organic maple syrup?"

His mouth watered, and his stomach growled. Suddenly, he realized he was even more hungry than he was sleepy. "That depends on whether I have to wait till morning to eat them."

"You don't have to wait." A security light outside the garage door illuminated the gravel path and the concrete driveway. They walked toward the house, a traditional red-brick structure that managed to be squatty and imposing at the same time. It was one of those 3,000-square-foot mushrooms that had popped up in dozens of new suburban subdivisions outside New Orleans since Hurricane Katrina. "We can eat first and then sleep."

In the two-car garage, she released his arm to open the door into the house. "Come on in." Jasper charged past, and Heather laughed. "It's past his bedtime too. He'll be under the covers with Josh in another minute."

The door from the garage opened into a wide hallway. Heather flipped a light switch, illuminating a long bench seat across from the door with a row of shoes underneath, while school backpacks hung on a row of hooks above. Cubbies on the wall above the hooks held fabric baskets with little brass-edged chalkboard charms dangling from the handles, each marked with someone's name in bright block letters. All very neat and organized.

To the left, he could see an open doorway with a metal sign above: DO YOUR OWN LAUNDRY HERE! Heather turned right and led the way into a large kitchen with a granite-topped island in the center. She took down two glasses from the neat rows he could see when she opened a cupboard door. "You want ice in your water?"

"Just water is fine, thanks."

She dispensed water from the fridge door. When he took the glass, their fingers touched, igniting a feeling of connection he hadn't felt with anyone for a very long time. He didn't know why such a simple touch felt so compelling, but time slowed in the moment their fingers touched. Her lips parted, and he thought he heard her draw in a soft breath.

Then she turned away to fill her own glass. "I'll start cooking before we faint and fall over. But maybe you'd like to take a shower first? I don't know about you, but I don't want to have to stand next to myself much longer."

Adrian couldn't help but laugh; he was drunk on exhaustion. "Is that your diplomatic way of telling me that I stink?"

"Not at all." She let out a surprised giggle, and her cheeks turned pink. "I would never."

"Just kidding. I would love a quick shower before breakfast."

She slid a sheepish glance his way. "You had me worried for a minute." Then she straightened and smiled. "Let me show you to the guest suite."

She led him through a large family room with a fireplace to a formal entryway with a carpeted staircase on one side. He followed her up the stairs, watching the hypnotic sway of her hips. He couldn't help thinking what it would be like to reach out, to put his hand on her waist and turn her toward him… He shook his head to dispel the thought of touching her and just about bumped into her when she stopped beside an open door.

"Why are you shaking your head?" She reached around the doorjamb to turn on the light.

He shook his head again, this time to clear the strange, almost floating sensation of being asleep on his feet. "I have no idea. I think my brain quit functioning a few hours ago."

She laughed. "I know what you mean. Mine too."

The bedroom she walked into looked like it belonged on the cover of a *Southern Living* magazine. The queen-sized bed was made up with fancy pillows and a homemade quilt, each scrap of fabric edged in embroidery thread with many different stitching patterns.

She opened the door to the guest bathroom. Simple, clean lines, white or off-white everything, including white, lace-edged towels on the bronze towel bar. "I feel like I'm too dirty to touch anything in here." And it just occurred to him that he had no clean clothes to change into. He was beginning to rethink his decision to stay here for the rest of the night. If he had headed home when they first put Charlie back in his stall, he'd have reached the interstate by now.

"These white towels don't mind bleach. There's soap and shampoo and everything you need, new toothbrushes in the top drawer…" Her voice got quiet. "Oh. You'll need clean clothes to change into."

"Don't worry about that." Being clean inside dirty clothes would at least be a slight improvement.

But she had already turned away. "I'll be right back," she said softly.

She came back holding a stack of folded clothes: a T-shirt and a pair of sweatpants. "Sorry, there's no underwear." Her cheeks, the visible barometer of her feelings, registered something between attraction and embarrassment. "I only kept the things I could wear myself."

Or, okay, maybe just embarrassment.

So did that mean that all the times he had entertained the idea that she might be attracted to him, he'd been wrong? Maybe the subtle flirting he'd managed to tease her into doing didn't mean anything. Maybe he wasn't as *all that* as he thought he was. He took the clothes from her, feeling an uncomfortable twinge in the region of his heart. Yes, they were just clothes, and they would wash up as clean as new after he returned them. But he knew it must feel like a sacrifice for her to lend them out. "Thank you."

She smiled—a sunny smile that made her pink cheeks go as round as apples under her clear green eyes. That smile made him wonder how often she smiled and acted like nothing was wrong to put others at ease when she was still hurting inside. "If you'll leave your clothes outside the bathroom door, I'll put them in the washer before I start cooking."

"If you're tired, you can wait on cooking breakfast until we've had some sleep."

"Nah, this works. The kids will be up soon, so I can feed them their breakfast too. Then you and I can take a nap before Mack gets here to check on Charlie—" Her eyes got wide and her cheeks flared crimson as a double meaning for her innocent words dawned. "I mean, we can each take naps separately. In different rooms."

He wanted nothing more than to take her sweet face in his hands and kiss those hot-pink cheeks until her blush subsided. But that would be the pinnacle of idiocy, wouldn't it? So he turned away and set the neatly folded stack of clothes on the bathroom counter. "I'll put my clothes outside the door. See you downstairs."

———

Heather backed out of the guest bathroom and closed the door behind her. She paused a second to put her hands against her cheeks. Their heat burned into her cool palms.

Why did Adrian affect her so much?

She heard a soft sound—Adrian's clothing hitting the floor in the bathroom, brushing the door on the way down. She scooted out of the guest bedroom, grateful that the carpeting muffled her footsteps. Easing the guest room door closed behind her, she hurried downstairs to the master bathroom to take the world's fastest shower.

Her hair dripped on her shoulders when she dressed in a fresh pair of denim shorts and a boat-neck tee with *Yo mama's a llama* in sparkly pink letters above an ironed-on image of two llamas kissing. She gave her hair a last squeeze from the towel she'd left hanging over the shower stall door, then went back upstairs to grab Adrian's dirty clothes.

She paused in the hallway outside the closed guest room door. Shouldn't have shut that door, she realized. What if she got caught traipsing toward the bathroom door when he just happened to come out?

That didn't bear thinking about. But… She put her hand on the doorknob. What if…

The knob turned under her hand, and in the next second, she stood face-to-face with Adrian. Fresh from the shower, wearing clothes that she had worn enough times to call them hers, Adrian took a step back. His dark-blue eyes widened, no more shocked than if she'd taken a flying leap at him, wrapped her legs around his waist, and plastered her lips to his.

"Oh, hey." He held the balled-up wad of his dirty clothes.

She took the clothes from him. "I was just coming to get these." She wondered, just for a second, whether he'd left his underwear in this mass of dirty clothing or put them back on. She resolved not to look. Not at the wad of clothing and not at him. At least, not at any part of him that was located south of his chin. "I'll put these in the wash. Do you want coffee? Tea? Juice?"

"The water you already gave me is fine for now."

"Okay. I'll drop these in the wash, then start cooking." Thank goodness, she didn't feel the prickle of a blush rushing to color her fair skin and give her discomfort away. She turned her back on him and headed down the stairs, not quite congratulating herself but at least feeling that maybe she was getting a grip on her runaway emotions around him. Maybe, if she were lucky, she was beginning to become immune to him.

———————

In the kitchen, Adrian watched from a seat at the kitchen island's raised bar while Heather rummaged in the large pantry. The sky outside the window above the sink had lightened to a pearl gray near the horizon, merging into a deeper gray above. Soon, it would be morning. "Can I do anything to help?"

She came out of the pantry with a mason jar of syrup and a box of pancake mix. "You could reach the big mixing bowl for me, if you don't mind." She opened a cabinet door and pointed. "It's up there, top shelf."

He came around the counter and reached past her to grab the bowl. Her hair, damp but drying, smelled like lemons. Her skin…

He stepped back before he could decide what her skin smelled like. "What else can I do?"

"Not a thing." She touched his arm. "Sit. Keep me company while I cook."

Yeah, he could do that, but staying busy would be easier. He leaned against the counter and watched her take a bunch of ingredients out of the refrigerator. She lined everything up in a row on the counter, setting the eggs on a folded dish towel so they wouldn't roll. She measured and poured batter mix into the bowl and cracked an egg one-handed over the bowl. Adrian came around behind her and snagged the container of strawberries. "I don't find relaxing relaxing. So maybe you'll allow me to wash the strawberries and slice them up?"

"Sure. Knife's in the—"

"Yep, I see it." Her kitchen was very organized, with a big set of chef's knives in a wood-block holder and a whole bunch of other kitchen implements right next to it in a big, homey-looking ceramic crock. He rinsed the strawberries, then took a paring knife from the block. The cutting board was easily accessible too, right next to the knives. Everything laid out in an ergonomic fashion, closest to the first point of use. "You must cook a lot."

She looked at him sideways, a teasing little smirk on her lips. "Three kids, yo."

He started slicing off the berries' green ends, and she handed him a couple of bowls. "One for the strawberries, one for the ends. I compost."

He popped a plump strawberry into his mouth. Then, without overthinking it, held one up to her lips. "You don't feed your kids prepackaged box food?"

She took the strawberry into her mouth, her lips barely touching the tips of his fingers. Closing her eyes, she savored the taste. When she opened her eyes and smiled at him, her lips glistened with a hint of berry juice. "Not often. Fresh strawberries beat strawberry Pop Tarts any day of the week. And I want my kids to have a healthy relationship with food. So I cook." She covered the strawberry bowl with some kind of waxy-looking cloth, molded it to the bowl's edge, then handed the bowl back. "What about you? You look pretty comfortable in the kitchen."

"I can cook." He'd be a lot more comfortable if he could just go ahead and kiss her. Get it over with. "But I do live minutes away from the best restaurants on the planet. And most of them deliver." He put the bowl of sliced strawberries in the fridge, then rubbed his palms together and glanced around the kitchen. "What else can I do?" Anything to get his mind off the thought of touching her.

She hefted an iron skillet onto the stove, drizzled a bit of oil, and turned on the gas burner. "If the cream cheese is soft enough, you can make the whipped cream."

"Um…okay. Just tell me how."

"One block of cream cheese, one container of whipping cream, and a half cup of confectioner's sugar. The blender is in the cabinet right in front of you."

They made breakfast together. She coached him on what to do and how to do it, the tension between them eased, and Adrian was able to stop thinking of their close proximity with such unfamiliar longing.

Difficult when everything about her was sexy—from her lush curves to her lemon-scented hair to her fresh-washed skin. But working with her this way was easy. They found a natural rhythm, reaching this, handing that, quietly moving together in an almost-dance of synchronicity. Standing at the stove, she pivoted and reached back to turn on the sink tap.

"What do you need?"

"Nothing. Just—" She held her fingers under the water, turned back to the stove, and flicked water on the skillet. The water droplets danced and sizzled, skipping across the pan until they evaporated. "Making sure the skillet's hot enough."

"Oh." He turned off the tap and came to stand behind her. "Neat trick."

"I'm full of neat tricks." Using a ladle, she dropped measured amounts of batter into the pan, making four neat pancakes that immediately started sizzling at the edges.

He took a metal spatula from the crockery jar and handed it to her. She held it over the pan and sprayed it with oil but made no move to flip the pancakes.

He leaned forward to get a better look, resting a hand lightly on her hip without even thinking about it. "You gonna flip them?"

"Not yet. Not until the little bubbles on top burst. Have you decided yet about coffee?"

"None for me, thanks. I'm still planning to get a little sleep after this, if that's okay. I'm looking forward to determining whether your sheets are softer than mine."

When the pancakes were all done, stacked on a plate and covered with a dish towel, Heather carried the plate to the kitchen table, which was nestled in an alcove with a bay window that looked out onto the horse field.

He helped her set the food on the table, and she set out plates, silverware, and napkins. She stuck a serving spoon in the bowl of berries and another in the whipped cream, then went back to the kitchen. "Have a seat. Fix your plate." She took the lid off the mason jar of syrup and poured some into a small ceramic pitcher, then zapped it in the microwave. "Don't be shy. Get as much as you want."

He loaded his plate, then drizzled hot syrup onto his masterpiece. "Aren't you gonna call the kids to breakfast?"

She sat next to him and started serving her own plate. "Don't worry. The pancakes are already calling them. They'll be down soon enough. If we're lucky, we might have a few quiet moments before the hordes descend."

Chapter 6

THE HORDES DESCENDED. FIRST, JASPER BARRELED DOWN THE stairs to skid into the kitchen, his body vibrating with excitement. He lapped some water from his bowl, then put his wet face in Heather's lap and gazed up at her adoringly with his blue-and-brown-marbled eyes.

She rubbed his silky ears. "Every new day's an exciting event, huh, Jasper?"

Josh trailed behind more slowly, wearing a pair of rumpled summer pj's Heather had sewn herself. Josh went straight for the food, catapulting into a chair and grabbing a pancake off the stack. "Yay! Pancakes!" He took a bite before putting the rest of it on his plate and dousing it with syrup.

Then he noticed Adrian. "Hey! You came!" He abandoned his pancake to leap into Adrian's lap and hug his neck.

"Josh, be polite. It's not good manners to choke our guest to death." Heather had been just the teeniest bit worried what the kids would think when they came downstairs and saw a man—even one they knew—sitting at the breakfast table.

Josh, apparently, couldn't be happier. He sat back, his face alight with joy. "What are you doing here?"

Adrian grinned. "I heard this place had great pancakes. Thought I'd check it out." Adrian's smile made his already-handsome face almost unbearably beautiful. Heather felt her cheeks grow warm, then even warmer when Adrian caught her eye.

His smile widened.

He had to know that she was blushing because he was so damn good-looking. It was like having a movie star sitting at her kitchen table. Josh was starstruck too, so starved for an adult male role model that any glimmer of attention from Adrian had about the same effect as plugging the kid into a light socket.

"Josh, would you please let Jasper outside?"

"Yeah, sure!" Jasper jumped out of Adrian's lap. "I'll be right back," he assured Adrian, "as soon as Jasper does his morning poops."

"Can't wait," Adrian replied, smiling at Heather's embarrassment. She knew that her windowpane face showed every thought that crossed her mind, so she 'fessed up. "It's hard having a kid with no social filter between his brain and his mouth."

Adrian laughed. "I bet it is."

Caroline came into the room quietly and hung back behind Heather's chair for a minute before easing forward and climbing into her lap. Heather knew that Caroline wouldn't show any outward response about Adrian's presence here, but the wheels were turning behind her solemn green eyes. They'd have to talk about it later, after Adrian left. Heather kissed her daughter's cheek. "Good morning, sweetie pie."

Heather didn't prompt Caroline to say hello to Adrian. Caroline's extreme shyness had worsened after Dale's death. She took a while to warm up to new people, and though she'd been introduced to Adrian at the shelter, she hadn't spent much time in his company. Forcing her to be sociable would only result in a quick and tearful exit. "Do you want me to fix a plate for you?"

Caroline stretched up to whisper in Heather's ear. "Can I eat in the den?"

"Yes, you can eat in the den. But just for today."

"Me too," Josh yelled as he came back inside with Jasper. He loaded another pancake onto his plate and soaked it in syrup. "I want to watch cartoons."

"Just be careful with all that syrup, okay?" Normally, Heather didn't allow the kids to eat in the den, except for special popcorn movie nights. But she knew Caroline wouldn't eat in front of Adrian. She'd just pick at her food and look down at her lap, and that would be awkward for everyone. Heather reached past Caroline to put a pancake on a plate but had trouble reaching the whipped cream.

Without speaking, Adrian spooned a dollop of whipped cream onto Caroline's pancake, then stuck a strawberry in the center. Heather shook her head no when he reached for the syrup. "That's perfect, thank you."

Adrian nodded but didn't speak. He seemed to understand that Caroline's anxiety around new people was less severe if there wasn't too much noise and activity going on.

Josh headed toward the den with his plate in one hand and juice glass in the other. "Come on, Caroline."

She slipped out of Heather's lap and carried her food carefully into the den. Jasper fell in line behind Josh, looking up at his syrup-laden plate.

"Do. Not. Feed. That. Dog." Heather stressed each word. "You remember what happened last time."

"What happened last time?" Adrian whispered when the kids left the room.

"Josh never would listen when we told him why it was wrong to sneak food to Jasper. Dale threatened that if it happened again, Josh would have to clean up the mess. So even though Josh was only four at the time, when he fed the dog syrup and pancakes, Dale made sure that Josh learned the hard way that people food can be hard on a dog's digestive system."

"You're telling me that *last time* was two years ago?"

Heather chuckled. "Yes. And it made a never-to-be-forgotten impression."

"Wow. So Dale was a tough disciplinarian, huh?"

She nodded. "Absolutely. I could never have followed through with that threat, but Dale never said anything he didn't mean. He was dependable that way."

The TV came on in the den, and after a brief argument, Caroline came to the doorway to complain about her brother hogging the remote (a usual thing), then saw Adrian and scuttled back into the den. Adrian waited a second, then spoke quietly, his expression compassionate. "I guess Caroline is a little bit shy."

Heather couldn't help letting her frustration show. "Thank you for putting it so kindly in that colossal understatement." She folded her napkin, then folded it again and again into ever-smaller squares. "Caroline used to be a little bit shy. But when Dale died, her shyness became off-the-charts paralyzing. She turned into a different child overnight."

"How is Josh doing?"

"Fine, except for the fact that he spends every other afternoon in the principal's office."

Adrian's eyebrows went up. "What for? He seems like a sweet kid."

"He is. But he doesn't take kindly to bullying, and when someone hurts his feelings, especially on purpose, he sometimes forgets to use his words instead of his fists."

"I'm sorry to hear that. It must be hard for you."

"It's been hard on everyone. Erin has been a big help, but..." Heather hesitated but reminded herself that Adrian already knew the truth of what she was about to say. "I realized last night that I've been depending on her too much. She's been so grown-up, I've..." She cleared her throat, but the lump she felt forming there didn't go down. "I thought that since she was so good at taking care of her siblings, I could trust her to take good care of Charlie too. I should have checked behind her."

Adrian opened his mouth to say something, then closed it again without speaking. Anyway, he didn't need to. He had already told Heather what he thought last night, and she really didn't need to hear it again.

"Don't worry." She unfolded her napkin and started rolling it against the table instead, forming the flimsy paper into a tube shape. "I'll take care of Charlie from here on out. Erin needs to get back to being a normal teenager, not just my mini-me."

Adrian put a hand over hers, stilling her nervous fingers. "Would you like to start working on my napkin?" He handed it over. "Yours is about shredded."

She chuckled, though his lame offer had the opposite effect of the comic relief he had intended. She felt her eyes fill with tears. Slipping her hand out from underneath his, she used the napkin to blot her eyes. At least she hadn't put on any makeup after her shower. She had deliberately left her too-blond eyelashes naked so he wouldn't think she was trying to seduce him.

Which, when she thought of it, was ridiculous. She looked sideways at Adrian—who made tons of money and made Henry Cavill look like a troll by comparison. Adrian Crawford was not about to fall for an overcommitted single mom with three troubled children. He probably dated a different Victoria's Secret model in every city he traveled to for his work. And Heather was no Elsa Hosk.

She didn't mind not being Elsa Hosk, though. She never had. Even in high school, she hadn't let her generous curves give her a body image complex. She hadn't let her buxom bosom and shapely hips stop her from trying out for cheerleader and making the squad or from becoming head cheerleader by her senior year. She liked to think it was because of her intrinsic emotional stability, but it was also because Dale had loved her, every inch of her, exactly as she was.

Adrian's lips quirked in a charming, slightly quizzical grin. "You gonna cry or what?"

She snorted. "No, I'm not gonna cry. It was touch-and-go there for a second, but I'm okay now."

Heather heard Erin come down the stairs, and she took a breath to steady herself. Against what, she wasn't quite sure. Erin could be mercurial. How she'd act when seeing Adrian sitting at the breakfast table was anyone's guess. Heather turned to look over her shoulder as Erin walked into the room, her slippers scuffing on the tile floor. "Erin, you remember Adrian from the shelter."

"Oh." Erin wouldn't have sounded any more shocked if she'd come into the kitchen to find a spaceship had landed inside their house. She tightened the sash of the thin cotton robe she wore over her pj's. "Yeah. Hey."

"I stayed to help with Charlie," Adrian explained, his deep voice casual.

"Is Charlie...?" Erin's shock forgotten, she rushed up to sit at the table. "Is he okay?" Her blue-eyed gaze pinged between Heather and Adrian. "Is he going to be okay?"

"The vet's coming to check him out in a couple hours," Heather said, "but, yes, we think he's going to be okay."

Erin wilted with relief, and even reached out to touch Adrian's shoulder. "Thank you so much for helping with him. Mom and I couldn't have gotten him up on our own. We tried."

"I know you did," Adrian said. "I'm glad I was close enough to come and help out."

Heather was grateful he didn't mention the state they'd found Charlie's stall in last night. She would have the conversation with Erin sometime today, but not until they were alone. She passed an empty plate to Erin. "Eat your pancakes before they get cold."

A light tap on the guest room door woke Adrian from a sound sleep. He wasn't sure whether Heather's sheets were better than his, but he'd slept like a rock from the moment his head touched the fluffy down pillow. He sat up and rubbed his face.

"Adrian, it's Heather."

"Yeah. Come on in."

She didn't. She spoke through the closed door. "Mack's on his way, but you don't have to get up."

"No, I'll come. I want to check on Charlie."

She opened the door a crack and peeked in, then opened it all the way. She held his clothes, clean and folded. "Here are your clothes." She stepped into the room and set the neat stack of clothing on the bedside table, then stepped back again to hover in the doorway. "I already checked on Charlie once before I went to sleep."

"And?"

"He's doing good."

Adrian sat up on the edge of the bed, blinking to clear the cobwebs.

"There's coffee downstairs." She was apparently the kind of person who knew what was needed before being asked.

"That sounds good." He'd be willing to bet that she made good coffee too.

"See you downstairs." She closed the door behind her.

He changed back into his clothes and made the bed, leaving the sweats and T-shirt she'd loaned him folded at the foot of the bed. When he got downstairs, he found her sitting at the table with a mug of coffee, gazing out the window with her chin propped on her hand. He couldn't decide whether she looked sad, pensive, or just relaxed. She straightened and turned toward him, then smiled. "Everything's on the kitchen counter. Help yourself."

Relaxed, he decided. He poured his coffee, added sugar but no cream, then joined her at the table. Jasper sat at her feet—actually, he was lying on her feet—but the kids weren't around, and the vibe of the house seemed to reflect their absence. No TV playing in the den, no video game sounds from a bedroom, no sounds of kids yelling outside. A sense of quiet calm reigned, sort of like at his loft but without the loneliness—which, he reminded himself, he was totally used to and didn't mind one bit. He enjoyed his own company. "Where are the kids?"

"Erin's at a friend's house."

Noting his incredulous expression, Heather lifted her chin. "I know she deserves to be punished for neglecting Charlie and lying to me, and she will be, but not until we have enough time and privacy for that discussion."

"Makes sense. And anyway, not my place to judge."

"And yet…" She gave him a quick, steely-eyed glance before looking away. "Josh and Caroline went to spend the night with Sara's son, Max. She picked them up about an hour ago. Sara's a good friend; we help each other out a lot. She took over the PTA meeting last night when I couldn't make it because of Charlie. You met her at one of the shelter's brainstorming sessions, I think."

He nodded. Willowy redhead who hovered over her son a lot.

"Sounds like you've been busy while I was sleeping. Did you get any sleep at all?"

She grimaced. "I tried, but my brain wouldn't stop churning." Then she shrugged and smiled. "Anyhow, when you've got kids, it's kind of hard to check out of life during the day. I'll catch up tonight."

Jasper sprung up as if someone had stuck him in the butt with a hatpin. Barking maniacally, he scrabbled across the kitchen's tile floor and hurled himself at the back door.

"Great alarm system," Adrian yelled over the earsplitting noise.

Heather stood. "That'll be Mack."

They met Mack in the barn. Mack fit the part of a country vet—broad-shouldered and muscular, his dark, no-nonsense hair clipped short. Mack had parked his dirt-caked pickup on the grass by the open door to the field. His assistant sat in the passenger seat looking down.

Beyond Mack's truck, Adrian's car sat in the center of the horse field, alone and unprotected from the elements. Adrian had forgotten all about it; he had shut it off intending to come back a few minutes later and head home to New Orleans. He hadn't even locked the doors, though the chances of someone traipsing through a horse field to hot-wire an unlocked car seemed a less-than-remote possibility.

Jasper leaped up on Mack's leg, and the man reached down to rub Jasper's ears. "Hey, good boy." Mack looked over at Charlie.

"Looks like y'all worked a miracle last night. I was mighty worried about that old horse."

"I was plenty worried myself." Adrian and his dad had been active in a horse-riding club, so he'd heard a few horror stories of colic cases gone wrong.

Heather went up on tiptoe to wrap her arms around Mack's burly neck, then held tight for a minute with her head on his shoulder. She didn't say anything, and neither did he, but he must have been used to this kind of display from his clients because he just stood there and patted her back until she was done hugging. He met Adrian's eyes over the top of Heather's head with a *you know how it is* look.

Mack McNeil was a fifty-ish country vet with a rugged yet tenderhearted appeal that Adrian thought probably made many female hearts go pitty-pat. Mack was also a man's man who looked capable of making a backwoods camp of weatherproof huts out of willow limbs and palm fronds using only a Swiss army knife and a wedge of flint. Adrian would bet cash money that Mack cut his short, dark hair with the same clippers they used to shave down dogs at the vet's office, and if he had ever owned a comb or a hairbrush, he had probably long since misplaced them.

When Heather quit hugging Mack, he ambled over to Charlie's stall and opened the door. He walked inside, leaving the door open but somehow knowing the horse wouldn't try to walk away from him. As Mack slid his hands over Charlie's hide, communing with the horse and intuiting his physical health, Mack's truck door slammed outside, and his assistant, a young slip of a girl, came into the barn. Dressed in green scrubs scattered with cartoon images of dogs and cats, she carried a dented metal tackle box, which she set down in the center aisle with a resounding clank. She knelt by the box and swung her ratty brownish-purple braid over her shoulder. "What you want, boss?"

"Stethoscope would be nice," Mack answered in a mild tone. "If you have time."

"Sorry, boss." She located the stethoscope. "I was on the phone for a minute."

Mack lowered his brows and made a growling sound low in his throat, but he took the stethoscope without further comment and focused on listening to Charlie's gut. It was clear that Mack's bark was worse than his bite, and his bark wasn't even all that scary.

After examining Charlie, Mack took the horse out into the field and ran him in circles on a lunge line, then brought him back in and fed him a flake of hay from a stack of bales in the back of his truck. As Charlie munched on the hay, Mack pronounced Charlie officially on the mend. But then he asked, in his quiet, understanding, nonthreatening way, for Heather to show him Charlie's grain and the hay they'd been feeding him.

When Heather pulled the old quilt off the pile of hay, he shook his head and made a quiet tsking sound. "The bale on top is good, but everything under it is old and moldy." She took the lid off the metal can that held the horse's feed. He leaned down and took a sniff. "This grain's okay, but it's a full bin, and I'm not sure what's on the bottom."

Mack gave Heather a sympathetic look. "I know that Erin's been helping out with Charlie. You need to be sure that she hasn't been pouring new grain on top of old." He stepped back and put his hands on his hips. "To be safe, I'd say you ought to toss all of this"—he waved his hands at the mess of hay and food bins in the barn—"on the burn pile, then run to the feed store today and start over with all new."

He kindly didn't mention the abhorrently dirty conditions of the rest of the barn. He was clearly used to dealing diplomatically with people who loved their animals but had no idea how to take care of them. "You still have the truck, right?"

Heather nodded. "It's in the pole barn on the other side of the house."

"It runs?"

She nodded again. "I crank it every week."

"Okay, well." Mack brushed his hands off on his jeans. "We'll get out of your hair so y'all can make a feed store run." He patted Heather on the shoulder and wished her luck, then took Adrian's hand in a goodbye handshake. Adrian didn't consider himself a lightweight, but Mack's grip ground his knuckles together.

"It's good that you're here to help Heather get everything back on track," Mack said in a quiet tone. "Her heart's in the right place, but she can't handle all this by herself. It'd be great if you could come a couple times a week and work with Charlie. It's pretty clear that he's depressed; he needs more interaction than he's getting."

Adrian's heart fell like a stone to settle into the soles of his Lowa hiking boots. "I'll do what I can to help."

It wasn't his place.

It was none of his business.

He didn't even live near here.

He had a life of his own—a life he was quite happy with, thank you very much.

But he couldn't turn his back on Charlie, and as it turned out, he couldn't turn his back on Heather either.

His mind flashed back to a time when, as a teenager living on the Gulf Coast, he had been out partying with friends who had decided to drive onto a beautiful moonlit beach, only to find out too late that the car's tires had spun down into deep sand. They struggled to get the car out, dragging up driftwood to put beneath the tires in a useless effort to gain traction. But none of it worked. They watched helplessly while the tide came in, and by the time the sun came up over the horizon, the car bobbed like a cork in the Gulf.

Like that car, he was stuck. And he had a sinking feeling that he'd soon be drifting out to sea.

Charlie watched all the commotion going on outside his stall. He'd been mostly ignored and forgotten for the last year, but now, he seemed to be the center of interest and activity. Heather and Adrian drove through the field in Dale's truck, then backed it up to the barn's field-facing entrance.

Then another truck arrived, and all the same people who'd been there the night before swarmed out of the vehicle, bringing rakes and push brooms and wheelbarrows and all manner of implements designed to stir up dust. After much coming and going, the dust began to settle on a cleaner barn. Still not satisfied, the women wiped down shelves and bins with wet cloths while Adrian brought in fresh bales of hay and new bags of feed to stack into pallets in the corners of the barn.

A fire blazed up in the center of the horse field, sending billowing streams of light-gray smoke into the air. Charlie wasn't worried. It wasn't close to the barn. But he kept an eye on it, just in case. Being locked into an enclosed space could be comforting (predators couldn't get to him) but also horrifying (he wouldn't be able to get out if he needed to).

Heather rinsed Charlie's water bucket and refilled it with fresh water. Adrian—or was it Ade? Charlie had become confused because he'd been called by both names—dropped a fresh flake of hay into the hayrack, and a woman put a scoop of sweet feed in his food bin. Charlie half-closed his eyes and focused on enjoying the crisp, molasses-coated grains that always tasted best when they'd just been poured from a newly opened bag.

He nibbled up the last remaining grain in the food bin, then moved to the hayrack and started teasing out bits of fresh hay to munch. As with the grain, hay always tasted best when it had just been unloaded from the back of Dale's truck. This hay was a clean, bright golden-green. The last stuff had been brittle and brown.

While Charlie enjoyed this undeserved feast, he wondered why he had suddenly become such an item of interest to all these people.

Was something about to happen that he didn't know about? Something good? Or maybe something terrible?

Was this his last good day?

He remembered when one of his dog friends was given a last good day before Mack came to the house and gave him the injection that relieved him of his body. The family had given Benji all the treats he loved best but wasn't usually allowed to have, even ice cream.

While Charlie was wondering whether this was his last good day, one of the women came up to the stall's closed door and started wiping down the metal rungs with a damp rag.

He wished with all his heart that Dale could still be here. Dale and Charlie had shared a deep bond, so deep that Charlie only had to think of a thing for Dale to show that he heard the thought and understood. Charlie wished that he could find someone to hear his thoughts. Someone to love him and be loved by him the way he and Dale had loved each other.

"Hello, Charlie," the woman said. "I can hear your thoughts, if you want to share them with me." He stopped chewing and swung his head toward her to see why he heard her voice in his head but not his ears.

"Hello, Charlie," she said again. Strangely, she was able to send words into his mind without moving her mouth or making a sound at all. "I'm Reva. I don't mean to invade your privacy, but I couldn't help but notice that you're wondering about a lot of things right now. I will be happy to answer your questions if I can."

The strangest thing about all this wasn't that Reva could talk into his head without speaking out loud. It was that he could understand every word in a way he usually couldn't when people spoke to him with their mouths moving and sounds coming out.

Then he could understand only some of what was said. This

way, he knew exactly what she meant. He took another bite of hay and thought about this strange phenomenon. It was a bit like the way he and Jasper communicated.

"Yes, it is," Reva replied in his head. "In fact, it's exactly the same, except that people and dogs and horses sometimes have different ways of thinking and communicating. People use more words, while many animals prefer to communicate by sharing images. Everyone is different, though. Which way do you prefer to communicate?"

Charlie thought this over but couldn't decide. He and Jasper spoke in images and emotions, sending pictures and feelings to each other about what they wanted and what they missed.

"We can communicate any way you like," Reva's silent voice said. "Whatever is easiest."

He looked at her, then back at the delicious fresh hay. Mack had apparently been satisfied with Charlie's appetite, and he drifted into the house along with everyone else. Everyone except Reva. She slowly wiped each of the metal bars along the top half of Charlie's stall.

"You can keep eating, and I'll keep cleaning while we chat."

Charlie turned back to the hayrack but kept part of his attention on his conversation with Reva. He found that it didn't diminish his enjoyment of the hay.

"It seemed to me earlier that you were wondering about what is happening?"

"Yes." Charlie chewed a mouthful of hay. "Is this my last good day?" He shared with her the memory of talking to Benji about *his* last good day. Benji and Charlie had communicated before Benji left his body and then again afterward.

Benji had explained to Charlie what had happened inside the house and how it felt when Mack gave him the shot that made it easy for Benji's spirit to rise above his body and leave it behind. He showed Charlie that all of Benji's aches and limitations had stayed in the lifeless husk that had once belonged to him but was no longer necessary once it had outlived its usefulness to the spirit within.

"No, it's not your last good day," Reva responded. "But you got very sick, and Heather asked us to come and help you get better."

"What next?" Charlie asked. That was the only part of his thoughts that felt like words; the rest was emotion: his grief and remorse and his fears of an uncertain future. But then out of those emotions, the questions that had been niggling at his consciousness rose up like ghosts to haunt him. Had he been punished enough for his role in Dale's death, or would he go back to being shunned by his family?

"Oh, Charlie," Reva said out loud, her voice full of concern. Then she went back to sending silent thoughts. "You didn't kill Dale."

He stopped eating and looked around at Reva. She had stopped polishing the bars of his stall and now just stood there, her hands gripping the bars, looking at him with an expression of love and understanding.

He didn't believe her, even though he wanted to. "Then why was I being punished? Why did my family stop loving me?"

"They didn't stop loving you." Reva turned away to take something off the shelf, then opened Charlie's stall door and went inside. She laid one hand on his shoulder, sending such love through her palm that he closed his eyes and let his head droop. Then she started brushing his coat with the soft brush that felt so good.

The currycomb felt good too, because its metal teeth gobbled up masses of shedding hair that kept Charlie from feeling the breeze on his skin. But this brush, with its stiffly soft bristles, stimulated his skin and scratched all the itchy fly bites he couldn't reach with his teeth.

"You remember how much you grieved when Dale died?" Reva asked by sending the words from her mind to his. "Well, Heather and the kids were feeling that way too. They didn't know what to do with those feelings, so they all had to…disappear…inside their own pain for a while."

"Jasper didn't disappear."

"No, he didn't. But he's different, you know? He remembers what it was like to be here before, in his other body. He knows that the body is just a thing and that Dale's spirit can still be here whenever it wants to."

Reva continued to brush Charlie's coat with long, soothing strokes while he thought about what she'd said. Benji had told Charlie that he would come back one day and inhabit another body. Charlie only just now realized that the body Benji had come back to inhabit was Jasper's. The two dogs were the same in a lot of ways. But they were different in others. How could Benji come back to live in a different body and be the same dog but not the same dog?

"I don't know," Reva said. "It's a mystery that maybe we're not supposed to solve entirely."

"Can Dale come back?"

"Yes, but I don't know if he will. And I don't know if he would come back in a body that you could recognize. Even his personality wouldn't be exactly the same. After all, there's no point in coming back to do exactly the same thing, be exactly the same person all over again, is there? Dale might want to try something different, slip into a new persona along with the new body. Like Benji did when he became Jasper."

"The same but different." Charlie understood. Next time, he might decide to come back as a blond horse, maybe one with white spots. He would definitely want to come back as a horse who wasn't quite so afraid of snakes.

"Yes. And you don't have to be a horse all the time either. You could be a dog or a person even."

Charlie and Reva communicated for a while longer, then Reva left to join the other humans who were outside in the field, tending the burn pile. Charlie went back to eating his hay and thought about the idea that he could leave his body and come back as a different kind of animal. He couldn't think of anything he'd want to be other than a horse. But he would rather be the kind of horse whose family loved him. He had been that kind of horse once. But he wasn't sure he was that kind of horse anymore.

Chapter 7

HEATHER MADE SANDWICHES AND FILLED A COOLER WITH ICE and canned drinks for her friends who were beginning to gather on the river dock behind her house. After the marathon cleaning session in Charlie's barn, they deserved an afternoon picnic, and Heather intended to empty the cupboards to satisfy everyone's appetite. While Abby and Reva carried food and drinks to the picnic table on the dock, the guys dragged the floats and inner tubes from the shed and gave them a few blasts of air from the air compressor in the garage.

Instead of going out there to join her friends, Heather strolled to the barn to visit with Charlie. She could hear the men whooping and yelling as they dove off the end of the dock and splashed around like kids. The women were probably popping the tops off wine coolers and floating in inner tubes with their feet up.

Heather would catch up in a minute, but for now, it felt important for her to stand outside Charlie's stall and stroke his velvet-soft nose. She had been afraid of him for so long—afraid he would bite or step on her or knock her down or rear up and kick out at her.

She wished Dale could see her now, petting Charlie's nose without fear. Or last night, when she had taken her turns holding his lead rope and walking him in circles.

"I'm sorry," she whispered to Charlie for the hundredth time. "I didn't know Erin wasn't taking care of you. I should've checked. I should've made sure she was doing the work."

Heather probably wouldn't have been able to tell whether the horse food and hay were fresh enough. But the disreputable state of the barn—and especially of Charlie's slimy feed buckets and uncleaned stall—was impossible not to notice.

Undeniable and unforgivable.

Charlie had forgiven her. But she would never forgive herself.

Mack had told her that the colic could have been caused by bad hay or bad food or from eating some weed in the field that disagreed with his digestive system. And some horses, he said, were just prone to colic for no discernible reason.

But she knew that Charlie had almost died because of her negligence. She had to do better. She couldn't *just get over* Dale's death and get rid of Charlie, as Erin had insisted. But she could put on her big-girl panties and figure out a way to do what had to be done.

And part of that equation meant bowing out of some responsibilities that didn't work so well any more. She needed to redefine her priorities and refocus her attention where it needed to be. She had been trying so hard to keep everything the same as it had been before Dale's death that she had been unable to adapt and change in order to cope with her family's current reality.

Tomorrow, she would ask Sara to take over as the president of the PTA.

She would talk with Erin, and together, they would come up with a plan to make sure that Charlie's needs were taken care of. Heather knew that she had been depending on Erin too much, but giving the teenager less responsibility wasn't an option either. They would have to have a long talk about working together, reallocating tasks, and ensuring that everything got done.

Because Mack had said that Charlie's colic could have been caused by eating some weed or other in the field, mowing the field was another thing to add to Heather's to-do list. But Quinn had tried to start the mower earlier, and it wouldn't work. He and Adrian tinkered with it for a while, then used ramps to load it onto the back of Quinn's truck to take it to the repair place down the road.

Heather knew it took hours to mow the yard and the horse field.

Heather couldn't see herself sitting on that mower wearing a straw hat and getting a farmer's tan on the back of her pale-skinned, sun-sensitive neck. But once she started working full-time, she would be able to afford to hire someone to do that work.

"We'll figure it out," she said to Charlie, stroking his face through the stall's bars. "Somehow, we'll make it work. I promise."

———

Reva found Heather in the barn, standing in front of Charlie's stall and communing with the big horse. Fifteen or more hands tall by Reva's reckoning, Charlie was on the high side of horse height, unless you were talking about heavy horses like Clydesdales, Percherons, or Shires. She touched Heather's back. "How y'all doing?"

Heather sniffed and turned a teary-eyed look Reva's way. "Fine, I guess, unless you consider the fact that I'm a bad, bad person. Charlie almost died because of me, and yet he seems to have forgiven me completely."

"He has." She didn't say the old platitude about there being nothing to forgive. Because it was true that Heather could have done better. But she'd been consumed with her own guilt and pain along with the seemingly insurmountable task of taking care of her three children alone.

Reva reached through the bars of the stall's closed door and petted Charlie's neck. "But unless you can forgive yourself, you won't be able to make his life better." She kept her tone soft while counseling her friend. She wasn't trying to lay blame. But she did want Heather to realize that until she could move past self-blame into a more open-hearted way of relating to Charlie, she wouldn't be able to give him the care and connection he needed to become whole again. "Do you understand that?"

"I think so." Heather took a shuddering breath. "But…" A sob escaped before she swallowed it back down. "I don't know how to forgive myself. Not just for this"—she waved a hand at the now-clean barn—"but for so many things."

Maybe because both women were touching Charlie at the same time, a window opened from Reva's consciousness to Heather's, showing Reva a glimpse of a memory that Charlie and Heather both shared, of Dale lying on the ground, unconscious. In the vision, Charlie stood near Dale's prone form, still saddled and with reins trailing, feeling confused and contrite, trying to come close enough to find out what was wrong with Dale. Heather knelt beside Dale, consumed with panic, crying hysterically and swishing a riding crop at Charlie's legs to make him back away.

Reva had never told Heather about the extent of her ability to communicate telepathically with animals, even though the two women had become good friends ever since their meeting at the grief support group.

But it was time to come clean. "Heather, I'm going to tell you something about myself that I don't tell many people, and I hope you'll keep an open mind and hear me out until I'm done explaining."

Heather looked at Reva, her leaf-green eyes wide. "Okay."

Reva took a breath for courage and let it out slowly. "When I was little girl, I had the ability to hear an animal's thoughts, if they were inclined to share them with me. My parents convinced me that it was just my imagination, and they punished me for what they saw as telling lies to get attention. So I began to hide my abilities, even from myself, in order to fit in. But throughout my life, my abilities kept breaking through the wall I'd built around them, so when I became an adult, I started working on tearing down the wall by deliberately practicing my telepathic abilities.

"I was lucky enough to find a good teacher who helped me learn how to control and expand them. One of the rules she taught me was to only go where I'm invited, so I would normally not communicate with your animal companion without your permission.

But sometimes, an animal reaches out to me, or their thoughts about needing help are so strong that I can't help but overhear. When that happens, I believe that they are giving me the permission I need. So when Charlie had questions about what has been happening to him, I offered to answer them. May I share with you some of what he communicated to me?"

Heather nodded, an expression of shock on her face.

"Charlie feels responsible for Dale's death. He believes that you blame him and that you're punishing him."

Heather drew in a breath. "No, I don't. Of course I don't blame him. It wasn't his fault."

"Well, he believes that it is."

"But… but…" Heather shook her head. "Why would he think that?"

Reva closed her eyes, and with her hand on Charlie's neck, she reached out with her mind and heart to connect to his. As the images started flowing into her mind, she narrated them to Heather. "He's showing me images of Dale riding him along a wooded trail. Jasper is running alongside. Then something frightens them all—I'm not getting a clear image of what it is, but it seems to be all around them. Jasper yelps and runs back toward home. Dale is yelling and waving his arms above Charlie's head…"

"It was a hornet's nest," Heather whispered. "I never told you that."

Reva nodded but didn't reply; she was still watching the images Charlie was sending. "Charlie is startled by the yelling and commotion, and he wheels around and bolts toward home. Dale falls off, and Charlie doesn't realize it right away, but when he does, he stops. Dale climbs back on, and Charlie takes him home.

"When they get there, Dale falls off again. You run up to him. The kids run up too. There is a lot of loud noise—everyone yelling, screaming, crying. Charlie comes close to find out if Dale is okay. Then you… I'm sorry… You hit at him with Dale's riding crop. You chase him away from Dale. You tell Erin to catch him and put him up in the barn, and he never sees Dale again after that." Reva opened her eyes. "He thinks that you blame him for what happened. You need to let him know that's not the case."

Tears streamed down Heather's face, and she wiped them away with her hands. "I was afraid he would step on Dale. I should have known better." She reached through the bars of the stall and caressed Charlie's face. "I'm so sorry." She looked at Reva, her expression pleading. "Can you tell him I'm sorry? Can you tell him that I didn't mean it? I was just so scared."

Reva began to communicate what Heather had said to Charlie, but Heather interrupted. "I told Erin to put Charlie up and then run to the house and call 911, and I told the twins to run inside and get the EpiPen. It was my fault; I should have had Erin call 911 first, and I should have run for the EpiPen myself. It just never occurred to me that I could safely leave Charlie in the field with Dale lying there."

Reva nodded. "I'll tell him all that."

"I was just so scared; I couldn't think straight."

"He knows. He was scared too. He didn't mean to get in the way, and he wouldn't have stepped on either of you."

"I feel so terrible for what I did and then for everything I didn't do. Please tell him I'll make it up to him. I promise."

Reva knew Heather was sincere in her intention, but having good intentions and having the wherewithal to follow through were two different things. "Heather, I know you mean well. But I can't relay a promise to Charlie if I'm not sure you can keep it."

"But I—"

"You would never have allowed Charlie—and his stall—to get in such a state if you'd known what was happening. I know that. But—"

"I won't trust Erin to take care of Charlie by herself anymore," Heather interrupted. "We'll work together from now on—or take turns—and I'll check behind her. From now on, I'll make sure everything gets done."

"I know you will. But that's not enough. Charlie needs more interaction than that. He needs to be ridden. He needs to be worked with."

Heather slumped. "And I don't know how to do that."

"So before I can relay your promise to Charlie, you and I need to come up with a plan that will work. Adrian has already agreed to come to the shelter twice a week to help tame that feral tomcat. I'm sure he'd be willing to stay a little longer to ride Charlie."

Heather sent her a sideways smirk. "You think he would?"

"If not, I can twist his arm." She winked. No need to let Heather know that she had already approached Adrian about it last night because even before chatting telepathically with Charlie, she'd had a sense that the horse was depressed and would need more attention than he was currently getting. And she knew that Mack had also spoken with Adrian earlier today. "He could come around here to ride Charlie while you're working at the shelter. Would that be okay?"

"I'd hate to impose on Adrian, but...yes. Whatever Charlie needs, I'll make sure he gets it."

"Good." Reva completed the conversation with Charlie, ending the way she always did, by asking the animal if there was anything else they wanted to say. When he replied, she smiled and patted his neck before relaying the message to Heather. "He says that he will never harm you or the kids or any human, for that matter. You can trust that you are all safe around him."

Heather blinked back tears. "Erin wanted to ride him, but I wouldn't let her. Please tell Charlie that it wasn't for fear of him... Well, actually, it was, a little. Please tell him that I trust him now, but I still don't trust that Erin would know how to ride him safely. So I'm not ready to allow that yet, but it's not because of him."

Reva relayed the message, again ending with her query of

whether Charlie had anything else to add. When he answered, she laughed. "He says he doesn't trust that any of y'all are ready to ride him either. But he would be willing to let Adrian have a go, as soon as possible. Charlie is tired of being a brown blob of misery in the middle of the field."

"Oh, my God," Heather said softly, putting her fingers to her lips.

"What?"

"I've thought of him that way before—a brown blob of misery. Are you telling me that he's been reading my mind?"

"Maybe sometimes, yes. It's not like our animals stand around listening in on our every thought. But when our thoughts have a lot of emotion behind them, we can be pretty good at projecting them unintentionally."

Heather gave a wide-eyed look at Charlie, then slowly turned that same incredulous stare to Reva. "So you...?"

Reva shook her head. Once people heard a communication from an animal that turned them into believers, their next question was almost always whether Reva could hear the thoughts of humans too. (In other words, *their* thoughts.) Reva chuckled. Though she was always honest in her responses, she didn't feel obliged to give away all her secrets. "You can relax. Even if I wanted to know what the people around me were thinking, I ain't got time for that shit."

Heather poured a glass of wine and sat by herself at the kitchen table in her quiet house, soaking up the silence. The twins would be spending the night with Max at Sara's. Erin would be home any minute to face the reckoning Heather dreaded but knew she had to deliver.

Heather's friends, who'd been so incredibly wonderful, had

all gone home, as had Adrian. They'd worked like field hands all afternoon, cleaning not only Charlie's stall but the rest of the barn as well. When Quinn and Abby drove off with a flatbed trailer full of junk to take to the heavy trash facility on their way home, Reva had joked about bringing a few friends for Charlie over from Bayside Barn, now that his barn had three empty stalls.

"No, thanks," Heather had said. She knew Charlie needed company, but she also knew better than to take on even more mouths to feed and stalls to clean. The company Charlie needed—and, she resolved, the company he would have—already lived right here in this house.

When headlights sent twin spears of light down the long driveway, Heather took her wineglass with her and walked outside through the open garage door. Erin hopped out of the back seat, all smiles. "Hey, Mama."

Heather smiled too and waved at the parent who'd been kind enough to bring Erin home so Heather wouldn't have to come and get her. "Thanks so much," she yelled to the man who waved back but didn't roll down the window.

"Don't go in yet," Heather said to Erin, who had started to head inside. "I want you to see something."

"Okay," Erin said, sounding perplexed but not arguing. They both stood and watched the car do a three-point turn and head back down the driveway. "What is it?"

"Follow me." Heather led the way to the barn, walking quickly down the path illuminated by the security light on the side of the house. She still didn't know how she was going to handle this; a lot of it depended on Erin's attitude.

Would Erin be combative? If so, they'd probably be engaged in a screaming match before long, and Heather would have to watch her own temper. She had a long, slow-burning fuse, but once it was lit, an explosion was sure to follow.

Would Erin be contrite and remorseful? If so, Heather would

have to guard against being too soft in return. She couldn't afford to be as lax as she had been.

"What's wrong?" Erin asked. "Is Charlie not okay?"

"He's fine." Heather flicked a switch, flooding the barn with light. Charlie nickered softly from his stall, confirming Heather's words.

"Oh!" Erin glanced around the barn, her face lit with delight. "It looks great in here!" She went up to Charlie's stall and petted him on the nose. "How'd this happen?"

Heather took a sip of wine; it tasted sour, and the small amount of alcohol wouldn't help her through this. She set the glass on a nearby shelf. "Charlie's stall was so filthy that we couldn't put him back in it when we finally stopped walking him this morning at about 2:00 a.m. That's why Adrian was still here when you woke up. He stayed to clean the stall before we could put the poor horse up for the night."

"Oh." Erin took a step back but still seemed confused. "I'm sorry. I put fresh shavings in there on…I don't know…Thursday, I think?"

"And when was the last time you scooped the stall?"

"Um…" Erin's cheeks flushed. "I don't know."

"And when was the last time you completely scraped out the shavings and started over with fresh bedding?"

"Last weekend."

"Oh, yeah?" Heather walked through the barn to the huge pile of used shavings Adrian had dumped out there. "So where did all this come from?"

"Um…"

"And why were there more than a dozen unused bags of shavings stacked in the corner…with a magazine on top of them?" Heather paused to let her words sink in. "How many afternoons have you spent sitting in here reading a magazine instead of doing the work I've been paying you to do?"

"Um…"

"Pouring new food on top of old in the bins?"

Erin hung her head. "Those bags are heavy," she mumbled.

"Sure they are," Heather agreed. "And I was the one doing the work of refilling the bins each week until you offered to take on more responsibility. You offered!"

"I'm sorry, Mom," Erin said, a hint of tears in her voice.

Heather stiffened her spine and held on to her righteous anger. "I was so proud of you for wanting to help out more. I was happy to increase your allowance, even though I had to watch every other penny to afford it."

"Is it my fault Charlie got sick?" Erin's tears spilled over, and she reached through the stall's bars to rub Charlie's neck. "Because I wasn't taking good enough care of him?"

"I don't know, but we threw away the food just in case. We also tossed out some stale hay because you weren't using it fast enough."

"I'm sorry, Mom. I didn't know it could make him sick."

"It might not have been your fault," Heather admitted. "Charlie could have eaten a weed out in the field that made him sick. If so, that would be my fault for not having the field mowed often enough."

Erin sniffed and wiped her face. "I could mow the field," she offered. "You wouldn't have to pay me either."

Heather allowed a small smile but didn't reach out to comfort her daughter. She needed to keep up the stern parent act a little longer. "I will take you up on that offer. As soon as the mower gets back from the repair shop. Quinn mowed the field with his tractor today, but the next time, it will be your turn. The job will probably take you all weekend, but since you're going to be grounded for the next two months, you won't be missing anything important while you're out there sweating in the hot sun."

Erin nodded. "Okay. I know I deserve to be punished."

"Your punishment is for lying to me and for taking advantage of my generosity by accepting an allowance for work you weren't doing."

"I know. I'm sorry."

"As to Charlie's care, you absolutely should have done better." This time, she let herself reach out and touch Erin's shoulder. "But you and I both let Charlie down, and we are going to work together to make sure that never happens again."

"I'll take better care of him from now on," Erin promised, turning to hug Heather. "You don't have to worry about that. I've learned my lesson."

Heather accepted the hug and even returned it, but she didn't allow her voice to soften. "Unfortunately, my darling girl, you have lost my trust when it comes to taking care of Charlie." She patted Erin's back, then pulled away to make eye contact. "And trust, once lost, has to be earned all over again."

"I understand. I'll do the work, and you can check behind me."

Heather shook her head. "You and I are going to care for Charlie together. We'll come up with a schedule and a plan so we'll each be coming out to the barn to care for Charlie on a daily basis."

Erin looked down, her expression contrite. "Okay."

"And in addition to mowing the field twice a month, you will also take over doing the laundry so I'll have more time to come out here and spend time with Charlie."

Erin's eyes got big, her first look of dismay.

"And I'll be withholding your allowance until you make up for what you got paid but didn't earn all summer long. After that, you'll go back to earning what you earned before I increased your allowance, even though you will continue to mow the field and do the laundry."

To be honest, Heather wasn't going to make Erin mow the field once she started getting a paycheck from her job at the shelter. She had looked into hiring someone to mow it with a tractor—a hefty amount of money, but one she'd be able to afford. Still, she wanted to impress Erin with the enormous potential punishment Heather had at her disposal should Erin decide to shirk her responsibilities again.

Erin's eyes got even bigger, and her mouth dropped open, but then she blinked and closed her mouth. "I guess I deserve all that."

Heather crossed her arms and gave her daughter a hard look. "You guess?"

Erin looked down again. "No, you're right. I do deserve it."

"And Charlie deserves better than he's been getting from both of us. So going forward, you and I are going to work together to make sure he gets the care and attention he has a right to expect. Right?"

"Right." Erin's lips turned up in a tiny smile. "Am I done getting fussed at?"

"I'm not sure; maybe not." Heather pursed her lips, determined not to smile back. She knew she was a sucker when it came to her kids, and she had been especially easy on them lately. But it was time to lay down the law. "I'll think about it while you're drawing up a new chore list on the poster board I left on the kitchen table."

A few days later, just after lunchtime, Heather was cleaning the house when Jasper went nuts barking at the sound of a vehicle coming down the drive. He scrabbled at the back door, his usual song-and-dance when a delivery truck arrived. Overcast skies threatened rain, one of those early-afternoon summer monsoons that blew up out of nowhere, and Heather didn't want the package to get soaked. She grabbed the garage door remote, then rushed out into the garage with Jasper bounding ahead of her. After snagging him by the collar, she opened the door.

It creaked up by slow degrees, showing...

Not the big tires of a FedEx van but the shiny bumper of Adrian's fancy convertible. Not the...whatever kind of footwear FedEx employees wore, but a barely worn-in pair of tooled leather cowboy boots, tight-fitting jeans, and, well, Adrian. Damn but he was fine.

With his hands on his hips and a slight smirk on his gorgeous face, he waited until the door had stopped squealing and squeaking to speak. "I'm here to ride Charlie."

She released Jasper, who bounded up to Adrian and—thank God—barely restrained himself from jumping up. Adrian rewarded the dog's good manners by kneeling to pet him. "You wanna come with, Jasper?"

Jasper wiggled all over and barked agreement.

Heather looked up at the dark clouds that scudded overhead. "Are you sure it's such a good idea to go riding today? The weather doesn't look so cooperative just now."

"It's all bluster." Adrian continued to rub Jasper's ears, eliciting whimpers of joy. "I'll keep an eye on it. Not supposed to actually start raining till about 3:00."

"Okay, well... Are you sure you want to fool with Jasper too? I mean, I wouldn't want him to get in your way and get stepped on or anything."

Adrian shrugged. "Your call."

She gave another glance at the dark clouds overhead. "Maybe he can come with you next time, and this time you can just concentrate on working with Charlie."

Adrian stood, the easy smile still on his face. "No problem."

For a second, they just looked at each other, then both spoke at once.

"Listen—"

"You're not—"

He grinned and motioned for her to continue.

"You're not gonna ride Charlie off the property just yet, are you? I mean, I think maybe you should work with him around here a few times before going out on the trails." She swallowed. "Just in case."

Adrian's grin faded. "I won't ride Charlie off the property without your permission. Promise."

She nodded. For some reason, that promise didn't make her feel much better. "Okay, well…" She looked back at the house. "I guess…"

Adrian stepped forward and ran a gentle hand down her arm. "I'll be careful. I won't even ride him until I've done enough groundwork to know how he responds. I know it might be hard at first, but try to forget I'm here."

"Okay." She called the dog to heel. "I'll do my best."

For the next couple of hours, Heather continued to do her housework but couldn't stop herself from looking out the kitchen window every fifteen minutes. Adrian spent an hour doing groundwork, making Charlie walk and trot and canter in circles on a long line before saddling up. Then he rode Charlie along the edges of the field, first walking, then trotting, then cantering.

Now, they were full-out galloping. Adrian bent low over Charlie's neck, and Charlie's hooves flung clods of dirt out behind them. Heather backed away from the kitchen window. Just watching those two fly along like that made her nervous. What if something happened? What if they had a…a wreck? Charlie had promised not to hurt anyone—a "conversation" Heather still had trouble wrapping her mind around—but he might not be able to help himself if something startled him.

What if lightning struck, scaring the horse and making him rear up?

Adrian seemed to have no worries for the weather, no concern for the heat lightning that skittered along the undersides of the menacing dark clouds. Should she go out there and get him?

No. He probably wanted to finish Charlie's workout, and surely he was old enough by now to know when to come in out of the rain. He was, as her granny used to say, *growed up and haired over*. And he'd gotten that way without her advice or interference on matters of weather safety. But what if…?

"Shut up," she said to her disasterizing thoughts. To distract herself, she opened the refrigerator door and got busy organizing the condiments. One of the kids had opened a new bottle of ketchup even though the previous bottle still had plenty in it. She checked the expiration dates and hid the new bottle behind the old one.

Heather rearranged the tall bottles and boxes on the top shelf, then noticed that the orange juice container had been leaking. With her head in the fridge, she wiped at the thick, slimy sludge. A loud boom shook the house—she shrieked and bumped her head when she straightened up too fast. The hum of the refrigerator went silent for a second. The lights flickered, followed closely by another boom.

"That's it." She slammed the refrigerator door, then dropped the rag into the sink with a splat. She was bringing that fool inside the house whether he liked it or not. Having made the decision brought her anxiety down a notch.

She peeked out the kitchen window on her way to the garage. Adrian and Charlie weren't visible in the field anymore, so at least he'd had the good sense to go into the barn.

Maybe she didn't need to drag him inside after all.

She stood at the open garage door and looked toward the barn. Its door was open too, but the angle was such that she couldn't see inside. He was most likely unsaddling Charlie, wiping down the tack, and putting everything back where it belonged. Then, he would probably brush Charlie with a curry comb to remove the sweat marks left by the saddle.

Peaceful moments spent doing those quiet, homely tasks were some of the best things about having a horse. Heather twisted her hands in indecision but decided not to intrude.

She reminded herself that although Adrian was helping her by helping Charlie, she wasn't obliged to turn it into a social call. Reva had said that Adrian wanted to work with Charlie because he missed having a horse of his own. This thing was between him and Charlie. Adrian could get his horse-riding fix, then get in his car and leave. Heather didn't need to take him to raise just because he would be coming around here a lot.

"Pretend I'm not here," he'd said when he first showed up here this afternoon.

But Adrian Crawford wasn't an easy man to ignore.

———————

After tying Charlie's lead rope to one of the stall's bars, Adrian put up the saddle and tack, scooped the stall, and dumped and refilled the water bucket. With both barn doors open, a hot breeze pushed through ahead of the coming storm. Adrian took his time brushing Charlie, patting him and murmuring praise. "Such a good horse."

Adrian wouldn't mind getting wet if it started pouring rain and he had to make a run for it to his car. He had parked on the driveway next to Heather's house, and figuring he would be dusty and sweaty after the ride, he had draped a big beach towel over the leather seat. He wasn't worried about his car, but if this horse-riding thing worked out, he might buy a truck. He patted Charlie's shoulder. "We're gonna do this a lot more. I promise."

For a first time working together, they'd done great. Charlie had been responsive and eager to please, and the headlong gallop under the lowering clouds had been exhilarating. "Thanks for the ride, old boy." Maybe, after another few practice runs in the field, they would try out the riverside trails.

He led Charlie into the stall, unbuckled his harness, and hung it on the hook beside the door. "See you in a few days."

Adrian walked out of the barn, congratulating himself that he'd made it out before the rains hit. But halfway to the car, the bottom fell out.

Without even one drop of warning, the rain descended in a deafening roar.

He put his head down and ran, barely hearing a high-pitched sound rising above the noise. He had left his car unlocked and the keys on the passenger seat, so his only thought was to get inside the car as quickly as possible.

Then the high-pitched sound his mind hadn't registered as anything other than noise resolved itself into the organized tones of Heather's voice calling his name.

He looked up to see her running toward him, holding a big black umbrella over her head. Her Keds slapped on the wet pavement, scattering raindrops. Then he was under the umbrella with her arm wrapped around his waist. "Hurry. Come inside."

He shivered, suddenly cold, suddenly realizing that he was already soaked to the skin. He wrapped his hand over hers on the umbrella's handle, and together, they rushed into the shelter of the garage. He shook out the umbrella and set it upside down on the concrete floor. Heather wiped his face with her hands, then shook her fingers, splattering droplets on the floor where puddles formed under the umbrella and their feet. "You're soaked!"

"So are you." Her jeans were soaked to the thigh and damp up to... Well, he wasn't going to look up high enough to figure that out. "You really didn't have to come out there and rescue me. In another ten feet or so, I'd have made it to my car."

She gave him a mischievous grin. "And mess up your precious leather seats? I don't think I could allow that to happen. Not on my watch."

Leaving the umbrella lying where it was, she hooked his arm with hers and led him into the house. Instead of turning right into the kitchen, she led him into the neat-as-a-pin laundry room and brought a towel down off the shelf. She started to wipe him down with it, then paused, blushing. "Here." She handed over the towel and pointed to a closed door he hadn't noticed—but if he had, he'd have thought it was a closet. "There's a mudroom with a shower through there. Get cleaned up, and I'll leave out some dry clothes for you."

Great, he thought. I'll be going commando again. Not that he minded hanging loose in theory, but going commando around Heather was maybe not the best idea.

"I promise I won't peek," she said. "In fact, I'm gonna have to rush to change into dry clothes and get the kids from school, so if you don't have to leave right away and you know how to work a washing machine…"

He nodded. "I think I can manage that."

"Great. I'll put some sweats and a T-shirt on the dryer. Meanwhile, make yourself at home until I get back. Wash and dry your clothes, make a cup of hot tea, pilfer the fridge for a snack, whatever. If you have to leave before I get back, just leave the back door unlocked and the garage door open."

"Okay." As if. He would never leave here with everything unlocked. Anything could happen. "Will do."

"Barring any complications, I'll be back soon."

"Okay, thanks." He took a step toward her, hoping to dissolve her tendency to hover over him like a mother hen. "Please don't make yourself late because of me."

"Oh!" Her cheeks turned bright pink. "Of course. I need to hurry." Then she whirled around and ran in the opposite direction. "I'll be back in a minute with dry clothes," she said from the kitchen.

"I'll wait here until you get back." Because somehow he could imagine her tiptoeing into the laundry room, terrified that she might inadvertently see him naked.

She hustled back in two minutes later, carrying the same clean folded sweats and shirt she'd given him before. "Here you go. I'll see you when I get back from picking up the kids…I guess?"

"Yep. I'll be here."

"You're welcome to stay for dinner." Her cheeks turned rosy when she met his eyes.

Her shy blush made it impossible to say no. "Thanks. I'll take you up on that offer."

She smiled, her cheeks going apple-round in her sweet face. "Josh will be so happy to see you here when he gets home from school. There's shampoo and soap and stuff in the shower." She turned to go, all but closing the laundry room door behind her before she turned back at the last minute. "But there's dog shampoo in there too, so be warned."

"No worries." He couldn't help but grin at her concerned expression. "Either way, I guess I won't have to worry about fleas."

Chapter 8

HEATHER DROVE TO THE MIDDLE SCHOOL IN THE POURING rain, the windshield wipers going only slightly faster than her hammering heart.

At this very moment, Adrian Crawford was naked...*naked*... in the mudroom shower at her house. And unfortunately, she'd seen enough of him uncovered to imagine exactly what (or mostly exactly what) that would look like.

She didn't know what to do with that thought, so she called Reva.

Reva's breathless "Hello, hey, Heather. What's up?" couldn't compare to Heather's inability to catch enough oxygen to answer.

"H-h-hey, Reva." She might have been close to hyperventilating. "I'm on my way to get the kids."

"What's wrong? Do you need help?"

"Not help," she clarified. "Just advice. I need to know what to do next."

"Okay, shoot."

"Adrian is naked...probably, I think...in my shower...at this moment."

Reva made a laughing/choking sound. "And yet you're on your way to pick up your kids? Are you sure you wouldn't rather have me pick them up instead and bring them to my house? I'll be happy to do that, just saying. You could turn the car around and go back right now."

"No, no." Heather felt herself blushing, all alone in her car with her fingers clutching the steering wheel and her foot on the gas pedal. "I just need to talk it through with you about what to do once the kids and I get back home."

Reva laughed. "I don't know, honey. Unless you want to bring the kids here to spend the night, I'm not sure what to tell you."

"I'm not bringing my kids to spend the night with you. I invited Adrian to have dinner with us. But…I haven't done that since…" She felt an unwelcome surge of self-pitying tears crowd behind her eyeballs like a mob of protesters pushing against a chain-link barrier. "I don't know how to act around a man anymore. What am I supposed to do?"

Reva sighed. "Baby girl, all I can tell you is to be yourself. Either he'll love and accept you the way you are, or he's not worthy of you. Either way, being yourself, without restraint or apology, will give you the only answer you need."

―――――――

Adrian showered with the kids' shampoo and soap-on-a-rope in the mudroom shower, then dried himself with the dark-brown towel Heather had given him.

The colors in the mudroom were designed to hide dirt. Brown, forest green, black iron. Hooks on the walls crafted from bent railroad nails welded together. A leather belt with a rodeo buckle hung from one; an old sweat-stained cowboy hat hung from another. The wall art was an assortment of framed collages made from chopped-up license plates.

Adrian dressed in the sweats and T-shirt Heather had left on top of the dryer, then started the washer. In the kitchen, he met up with Jasper, whose little stub tail wagged.

Adrian reached down to pet the dog's silky head. "Where's the tea, do you know?" Even as steamy hot as a Louisiana summer could be, on rainy afternoons, a warm mug of Earl Grey hit the spot.

In the search for tea, he didn't have to hunt much. As organized as Heather kept her kitchen, everything was easy to spot and located closest to the first point of use. Mugs above the coffee maker and the electric teapot, spoons and a steeping ball for loose tea in the drawer below, boxes of assorted teas and coffee beans in the pullout pantry drawer below that. He was beginning to see why Abby and Reva had hired Heather to be in charge of the shelter's daily operations.

Standing barefoot on the cool kitchen tile floor, he waited for the tea to steep and noticed how clean the floor felt under his feet. He couldn't help but contrast the difference between the immaculate house and the dusty, cobweb-filled barn. He had given Heather a hard time—maybe somewhat unfairly, he realized now—about the state of the barn.

Adrian had been critical of the state of Charlie's stall and his feed-and-water bins, and yes, the whole setup could've been better. Charlie's stall should have had fresh bedding. (It wasn't as if a bunch of bagged pine shavings hadn't been gathering dust in the corner.)

But he had to admit that barns everywhere were dusty because hay created dust. Horse bedding made from pine shavings created dust. Dirt tracked in on horse's hooves created dust, and wind blowing through open windows and doors created dust.

He would take the first opportunity he could find to apologize to Heather. And, if she would listen, explain why he had overreacted. Maybe not tonight, when they were surrounded by her kids, but some other time soon. Even if he had to steal her away from the shelter one day and take her out for coffee or something.

Sipping the tea he'd made, Adrian looked out the kitchen window toward the barn. Rain still pelted down in sheets, but it poured off the roof in a torrent, which made it clear that the gutters were clogged.

Another task—like horse care—that if Heather was aware of it, she didn't know how to do it or was so overwhelmed with everything else that it had slipped far down the to-do list. Next time he came, he would take care of that. Preferably when Heather wasn't here to know about it because even though he wanted to help, he didn't want to get involved.

The washing machine made churning noises from the laundry room. Adrian took his tea and wandered into the beige-carpeted family room next to the kitchen.

Jasper followed him, step for step. Quiet and unassuming but definitely on it should Adrian want to give him some affection or send him on a mission, Jasper stayed glued to his side. Thunder boomed, and Jasper whined, sending a worried glance toward the shaded windows where flickers of light bloomed along the shades' edges.

A wall of dark-stained bookshelves held a multitude of books but even more pictures. Framed photographs of family vacations and memorable moments marched in rows, standing guard in front of forgotten books that had been pushed back to the wall.

Ski vacations.

Beach vacations.

School events.

Rodeo competitions.

Ballet recitals.

Birthdays.

Babies' first steps.

All over again, Adrian felt like a bully for criticizing Heather for the way she handled the mess her life had become in one hot minute of misfortune. Charlie had suffered, yes. But he had suffered right along with the rest of the family, even though he'd been a step removed, all by himself in the barn.

Adrian's mind flashed back to the chaos leading up to Hurricane Katrina.

After sending the horse on a transport and leaving the AWOL cat behind to fend for himself, the family had piled into the car and crept out of town at a snail's pace along with thousands of evacuees, the windows rolled down and the AC turned off to conserve fuel. Adrian and his parents had taken turns driving north on packed roads in stop-and-go traffic in search of a motel with two vacant rooms. Finally, after nearly two days of nonstop driving, they found a place where the family could hunker down in anticipation of heading back home as soon as possible.

That was bad enough, but the aftermath was even worse, with his family fractured and staying with different relatives for the better part of a year. He knew how Charlie felt, being stuck some distance away from the rest of the family, navigating a deep sense of loss without their support. Adrian hadn't blamed his parents; they'd done the best they could. The situation was what it was, with everyone struggling. A lot of people—and animals— had fared a lot worse. Adrian was lucky that his parents had an extended family network to reach out to for help.

Heather hadn't, yet she had managed to preserve a sense of continuity for her kids.

Adrian walked through the downstairs living area of the immaculate house, looking at all the photos and mementos. This house was filled with reminders—if reminders were necessary—of why Adrian had no business getting involved with Heather.

Not that he was considering it because he wasn't. A ready-made family wouldn't fit in with Adrian's lifestyle, which he had crafted specifically to avoid all but the most superficial emotional entanglements. The right woman might come along one day to change his mind, sure. When he was old enough to see his own mortality staring him in the face, he'd probably want someone to share his eventual decline into senility.

Did he want to exchange his freedom to pick up and go anywhere, anytime, for life with Heather and her kids? *No.*

Did he want to exchange his ability to spend the money he earned in whatever way he chose for the kitchen-table talks he'd seen his parents have over which bills to pay and which to defer? *No.*

Did he want to exchange ski weeks in Switzerland or beach

weeks in Portugal for family vacations to Yellowstone Park in a camper van? *No.* (Although he did have to admit that Yellowstone was beautiful, and it seemed from the photos on the bookshelves that Heather and the kids hadn't yet been there.)

The big question, the one he refused to ask himself, let alone try to answer, was whether he dared to act on his attraction to Heather, given the risk of turning his life—and Heather's life and her kids' lives—upside down.

"No," he said out loud. Definitely, positively "no."

Jasper whined, and Adrian reached down to pet the dog's head. "I wasn't talking to you," he said, giving the dog another reassuring pat. "You're a good dog."

With Jasper at his side, Adrian padded barefoot through the quiet kitchen to the laundry room, where he moved his clothes from the washer to the dryer. At the sound of the garage door squeaking open, Jasper barked and ran for the back door.

"Ade!" Josh's excited voice echoed through the short hallway between the garage and the mudroom. "Where are you?"

He slammed the dryer door and got it running. "In here, Josh."

Tennis shoes squeaked on the tile floor, and Adrian turned in time to intercept the tackle as Josh leaped into his arms for an exuberant hug. "You came!" Josh's thin arms squeezed Adrian's neck with choking force while one narrow shoulder dug into his Adam's apple.

"Ack," he croaked, unwinding Josh's arms. "Hey, buddy." He peeled the kid off him and set him on the floor. The dog, who'd been calmly following Adrian through the house for almost an hour, was now leaping and slobbering with excitement. With Josh's arrival, the energy of the house changed drastically. Before, it had been a quiet shrine; now it was bursting with hectic energy. "How was school?"

"Great!" Josh bounced around for a few seconds, then grabbed Adrian's hand and dragged him into the kitchen. "I didn't get in trouble at all today."

"That's awesome. Congratulations."

As agile as a little monkey, Josh climbed onto the kitchen counter and took down a huge ceramic bowl from the cabinet above.

"Can I help?"

"Nope. I've got it." Josh scrambled down from the counter. "Mom said I could make popcorn and we can watch a movie while she cooks dinner." He zipped into the pantry and yelled from its depths. "She's making cheesy bread, even though it isn't Friday. I told her you'd want that, since we talked about it."

The kid came out of the pantry closet with his arms full (popcorn popping machine, olive oil, and a jumbo-sized jar of popcorn kernels), but Adrian had figured out by now that the best thing to do was just stand back and watch while Josh fulfilled his mission. Adrian put his empty tea mug in the sink and leaned his butt against the kitchen counter. "Let me know if you need any help."

"No, thank you." Josh set the popcorn machine on the island and hopped up to belly-surf on the counter long enough to plug in the cord. "I do this all the time."

"Where's your mom?"

"All the girls went out to the barn to see Charlie. It isn't raining anymore, so Mom said she's gonna let him out into the field for a while."

"That's good." It sounded like Heather was getting more comfortable around Charlie. The long night of the horse's bout with colic had broken down some barriers. "Maybe I should go help."

"No!" Josh paused in pouring seeds into the popper, his pale brows drawn together in a frown. "The *girls* are doing that. Us *guys* are gonna make popcorn and decide which movie to watch."

"Okay, fine." Adrian felt duly chastised for even thinking of deviating from Josh's master plan. "But I'm not good at lounging, so what do you need me to do?"

"Ummm…" Josh bit his lip, thinking. Then his face brightened. "Drinks! Glasses are up there…" He pointed at one of the cupboard doors. "Sodas are in the pantry. We are allowed to have one each. That's the rule."

The back door slammed, and a second later, Erin breezed past the kitchen on her way upstairs. Backpack slung over one shoulder, her face in her phone, she didn't look up or sideways.

"Hello," Adrian said, testing the kid's emotional temperature. Was she pissed off that he was here or just focused on what she was doing?

She stopped, glanced around. "Oh, hey. I have a ton of homework to do. See you at dinner."

"Okay." Adrian relaxed. He hadn't realized he'd been tense until that moment. But now, he had to admit that he'd been halfway worried he might be subjected to some teenage angst. "Two down, one to go," he muttered under his breath while he filled two glasses with ice. Another thing he hadn't realized till just now: Kids scared him.

———

Caroline sat on the kitchen counter, swinging her feet while Heather cooked dinner. "Please stop bashing the cabinet with your heels," Heather said for the third time. "Are you sure you don't want to go in the den and watch TV with Josh and Adrian?" Heather could hear Josh talking nonstop, but she couldn't make out the words over the sound of the *Iron Man* movie playing on TV. She could tell that the only time Josh stopped talking was to draw enough breath to fuel the next torrent of words.

Poor Adrian. She'd have to make it up to him somehow.

"I wanted to watch *Dr. Dolittle*," Caroline whined. "But Josh said they'd already picked *Iron Man*." She kicked the counter again, light little bumps with her bare heels.

Caroline wasn't hurting anything, really, but the intermittent tapping sound was getting on Heather's last nerve. She lowered the heat on the rice, then turned around and plucked Caroline off the counter. "I'll watch *Dr. Dolittle* with you after dinner. I need you to butter the bread before I put it in the oven."

Heather helped Caroline wash her hands, then set her up with a footstool in front of the counter. Heather sliced the baguette lengthwise and laid it open on a parchment-lined cookie sheet. Then she gave Caroline a butter knife and the bowl of garlic-and-herb-infused butter she'd made earlier. "Make sure you get the butter into all the little holes."

That should keep Caroline busy and out of Heather's hair—for about five minutes. If Heather had to keep herself sane five minutes at a time, that's what she'd do. She opened a fresh bag of shredded cheese, poured some into a bowl, and set it on the counter beside Caroline. "When you're done buttering, sprinkle this cheese on top." It wasn't spaghetti-and-cheesy-bread night, but since Josh was convinced it was important to Adrian, Heather agreed to make it to go with the baked salmon, jasmine rice, and steamed veggies. Not a perfect fit for the menu, maybe, but at least his stomach wouldn't growl. "Spread it out thin, all the way to the edges."

So maybe she'd have seven minutes of peace instead of just five.

She knew better than to try to encourage Caroline to go into the den with Adrian and Josh. Painfully shy at the best of times, Caroline just wasn't capable of it. While Josh... She tuned her mom-radar to pick up the sounds coming from the den.

Yep. Still talking.

Poor Adrian. Maybe alcohol would help. She'd seen him drink beer with Quinn; maybe he would enjoy a glass of wine with dinner. She searched the pantry and didn't have white wine to go with the fish, but she found an inexpensive bottle of red wine that she kept on hand in case of guests. "Better than nothing," she said to herself. "Maybe." Heather's girlfriends weren't too picky; most of them said that anything red would do. This wasn't the kind they sold at the corner store, but not the kind you had to go to a specialty shop for either.

Heather could tell by the way Adrian dressed and the car he drove that he probably drank the kind of wine you had to ask the wine department at Rousses to special-order. A certain extra-special something to go with the exact menu—which probably didn't mix Italian cheesy bread with baked salmon.

"If he complains about the wine," she muttered to herself, "I'll just hit him over the head with it."

She took the bottle to the den.

Adrian looked up, and unexpectedly, Heather's heart melted like candle wax to puddle at her feet. Adrian was darkly handsome with his thick, mahogany brown hair, dark-blue eyes, and forever-tanned skin. But what tugged at Heather's heart was the way Adrian was sitting, slouched against the couch cushions with his hands crossed behind his head and his feet propped up on the ottoman.

Josh sat cross-legged next to him, cradling a big bowl of popcorn in his lap. "Hey, Mom," Josh yelled as if she were across the world instead of across the room. "We're watching *Iron Man*." He crammed a fistful of popcorn into his mouth and chewed, grinning so wide she could see every kernel.

"I see that," she answered with a smile. "And I know it might be too late for me to give you this advice, but please don't scarf down so much of that popcorn that you can't eat your dinner."

"I won't," he answered with his mouth so full that his cheeks puffed out like a chipmunk's. "Ade ate a bunch of it already, didn't you?"

Ade. How cute. "*Ade*," she said to Adrian with a smirk she couldn't keep off her face. "Dinner's almost ready." She held up the bottle of red wine. "Shall I open this to go with?"

"Yes, ma'am. Is there anything I can do to help?"

"You're doing it." Josh hadn't looked this happy in ages. "I'm about to set the table. Five-minute warning."

"Aw, Mooommmm," Josh whined, sending her a dramatic, mortally wounded look of woe. "Pleeeease? The movie is almost over. Can't we watch till the end?"

Adrian pointed the receiver at the TV, showing that the time remaining wasn't but about seven minutes anyway. "Aw, Mooommmm," Adrian mimicked (but not unkindly). "Pleeeease?"

She laughed. "Okay, fine. You boys watch the rest of the movie, then wash your hands and come to the table." She got a little kick out of calling Adrian a boy and lumping him in the same category as Josh. But he'd started it, so she figured he could take it. She knew it for sure when he high-fived Josh over their victory, grabbed a handful of popcorn, and turned back to finish watching the movie.

———

When the credits started rolling, Josh grabbed the remote and turned off the TV. "Come on, Ade." Josh tossed the remote and pulled at Adrian's arm. "Dinner's ready, and you can sit next to me."

"That sounds great, Josh, but let's see what your mom says about that first." He followed Josh into the kitchen, where the mingled aromas of baked fish, garlic, and cheese filled the room.

He looked over at Heather, who stood near the sink spooning cooked rice into a serving bowl. "Can I help with anything?"

"Yeah, sure. Please pour the wine." Heather plunked a spoon into the steaming bowl and carried it to the table. Jasper followed her, then collapsed under the table with a groan. "Y'all go ahead and sit. Josh, if you don't mind, please let Adrian sit in your chair so he can sit between you and me."

"Okay, Mom." Josh hopped into a chair next to the window and patted the seat next to him. "You still get to sit by me," he said in a hushed tone, as if they were getting away with something.

Adrian winked. "I'm glad." And he was. Josh could be a bit

exhausting, but other than that, he was easy to be around. Just about everything made him over-the-moon happy.

Adrian poured a measure of wine into each of the two stemmed wineglasses. He swirled his wine in the crystal glass—good legs. Took a whiff: a nice-enough aroma for a wine that had probably come from the local grocery store. He took a sip: oaky, not too fruity, nice bite.

Strange combo for the platter of baked salmon fillets surrounded by steamed veggies that Heather was bringing in from the kitchen, but he wasn't a wine snob.

When it came down to it, wine was wine, unless it was terrible.

Caroline came into the room, carrying two glasses of ice water as if they held nitroglycerin. Without a word, she walked around the table to set a glass next to Josh, then eased around Josh's chair to slide the other glass close to Adrian.

"Thank you, Caroline." He kept his voice quiet, the way he'd done with the feral cat.

She blushed and tucked her chin. "Welcome," she whispered, then scuttled back into the kitchen.

Heather brought the sauce and bread, while Caroline carefully carried two more water glasses to the table. As she went back for the final glass, Heather went to the foot of the stairs. "Erin," she yelled. "Please don't make me come up there and get you."

"I *said*, I'm *coming*," he heard Erin yell back in a voice full of teenage rebellion. "I'm on the phone. Please start without me."

Heather came back, a look of apology on her face. "Let's go ahead." She sat at the end of the table between Adrian and Caroline, who sat across from him. "Erin will be down later." She held her wineglass up and looked at Adrian with gratitude. "Thanks for helping with Charlie. It means so much to me, and I know it means even more to him."

He clinked his glass to hers. "It means a lot to me too. I didn't know how much I missed riding until I got the chance to do it again."

They each took a sip of wine, looked into each other's eyes and shared a moment of…well, he didn't know, but before he could figure out what kind of moment it was, it was interrupted when Josh bounced in his chair, waving a fork. "Let's eat! I'm starving."

Heather served Caroline, and Adrian took her cue to fill Josh's plate. A cloth-lined wicker basket filled with chunks of cheesy bread got passed around. The sight and scent of the perfectly buttery and crusty bread made his mouth water. "This is amazing." He set a piece of bread on the edge of his plate. "Y'all eat like this all the time?"

"Nope," Josh said around a mouthful of salmon. "Only on Wednesdays."

Heather grimaced. "Are you saying that I starve y'all the rest of the week?"

Josh giggled. "Mmmm-hmmm."

Adrian looked across the table at Caroline, who was quietly and politely eating while staring down at her plate. "What else does your mom cook for y'all, Caroline?" he asked in an effort to draw her out of her shy little shell.

She looked up, briefly, then back down again. "Mexican on Mondays." Her voice was barely audible. He had to lean close to hear.

"What else?"

Caroline shrugged. "I don't—"

Josh interrupted by yelling, "On Tuesday—"

"Josh." Heather quelled his outburst with a sharp glance. "Give your sister a chance to think."

Erin walked into the room. "Vegetarian on Tuesday, seafood on Wednesday—"

"We already know what's on Wednesday, duh," Josh said. "Because today is Wednesday."

"Okay, smarty-pants." Erin stuck her tongue out at her brother, a teasing gesture with no malice behind it. Then she started filling her plate and redirected her attention to Caroline. "Thursday is…?"

Caroline smiled at Erin, who sat in the empty chair next to her sister. "Chicken on Thursday."

"What's on Friday?" Erin prompted Caroline.

Caroline looked up at Adrian. "Spaghetti on Friday, soup on Saturday."

"Y'all make it sound like our culinary life is very boring," Heather complained. "But there are a million different ways to prepare chicken or fish or even soup."

Of course she was right, but it did sound kind of boring. "What's on Sunday?"

"Lost on a desert island!" the twins said at once.

He raised an eyebrow at Heather. "Did y'all mean lost on a dessert island? That sounds a like a lot more fun."

"Lost on a desert island," Heather said in a prim tone, "means that we eat whatever we have on hand in the fridge and the cupboards before I shop for next week's groceries."

He put up his hands. "I'm not judging."

She sniffed. "It's a sin to waste food."

"Absolutely." He wondered how they'd gone from his complimenting her cooking to her thinking he was judging her. Quick change of subject required. "So, Erin," he said, "did you get your homework done?"

She scowled. "All but math. I hate math."

"I'm pretty good at math. I could take a look at it after dinner." The offer burst from his mouth before his head had a chance to think it over.

"Thanks, but…" Erin shook her head and let him off the hook. "It's not due till Friday. I'll do it over Skype with a friend tomorrow." Then she started telling Heather something about her need to shop for more school supplies, and the conversation began to flow about family stuff, giving Adrian the chance to observe rather than participate.

All these family traditions that revolved around food, around days of the week, around daily events, reminded him of the comforting routines of his own childhood. His mom hadn't cooked certain meals on certain days, but dinner had always been served at six on the dot, and anyone who wasn't sitting at the table on time had to pitch in for kitchen duty afterward, whether it was their turn to clean the kitchen or not.

Maybe these comforting routines were necessary for staying sane when so many different people—along with their unique personality types, emotional needs, and age levels—lived under one roof.

Adrian had almost forgotten those dynamics from his childhood. He hadn't considered back then all the practical and logistical considerations his mom must have contended with, getting four kids from point A to point B (and also points C, D, and E) and back again every day.

He hadn't thought much, he realized, about his mother's struggle to raise four kids. But he did remember, vividly, one evening when his father came home from his work at the cement plant, covered in cement dust as usual so he looked thirty years older than he really was. Gordon had looked so tired and used up that Adrian had gasped. "Dad," he'd said, "are you okay?"

His father had dropped into a chair by the kitchen table and lit a cigarette. "Son," he'd said, taking a long draw and blowing smoke at the ceiling, "you might ought to consider making this lifetime be all about you."

And in that moment, Adrian had decided that he wasn't going to live an all-work-no-reward life like his father did. Because even though his parents were always loving and affectionate toward each other, he couldn't help but see what the relationship took out of each of them. Who knows what they might have been able to accomplish if they hadn't been shackled with each other and the passel of kids they ended up having?

Adrian wasn't going to let a family and kids drain him dry and make him old before his time. He made all his choices—his education, his career, even his hobbies—around that paradigm.

It was nice, though, spending an evening surrounded by this family's sense of comfort and connection. It would be even nicer to get back home tonight to relax in the solitude of his quiet loft in NOLA, where the traffic sounds faded into background noise occasionally punctuated by the distant wails of ambulance and police sirens. He enjoyed living on his own in the big little city of New Orleans, where the restaurants were many and varied, the people unique and interesting, the nightlife so wild and unrestrained that the streets had to be swept and hosed down at dawn each morning.

This was nice. But when Adrian thought of all the effort and angst it took for Heather to keep this peaceful illusion of family togetherness afloat, it only proved that family life was the exact opposite of what Adrian wanted for himself. He didn't have what it took to help this family knit itself back together.

Adrian knew how to leave.

He had never learned how to stay.

Chapter 9

FRIDAY AFTERNOON, HEATHER WALKED INTO THE SHELTER'S conference room carrying a pitcher of lemonade. Sliced lemon wedges and sweet mint leaves from Reva's garden floated on top.

"Oh, Lord," Abby fretted, wringing her hands. "I hope everything is going okay out there." Abby's honey-brown hair straggled down her back in a mass of semi-wild waves, but her white pedal pushers and tucked-in cotton shirt were sedate enough to make up for the unruly hair that seemed to defy her efforts to tame it.

Heather could tell that Abby had done her best to look businesslike today. They all had. Heather had even left Jasper at home this morning, poor dog. She set the pitcher on the ecru linen table runner in the center of the antique mahogany table. "I'm sure it'll be fine," Heather promised, though she could promise no such thing. "All we can do is wait and see."

Either the shelter would pass the inspection or it wouldn't. The county building inspector and the mayor were both outside walking the shelter grounds with Quinn right now. Adrian was supposed to be here soon, but he hadn't yet arrived.

Heather arranged alternating swirls of turtleback cookies and snickerdoodles on the platter, then nestled a sprig of fresh sweet mint from Reva's garden in the center. Lucky for Abby, one lone turtleback cookie remained, and fitting it in would have ruined the artistic appeal. "Here." Heather held the cookie out to her boss. "Have a cookie."

Abby broke the cookie in half instead of taking the whole thing. "Only if you eat half."

Heather took her half and tapped it to Abby's in a cookie toast. "I'll make the sacrifice."

Abby took a bite and groaned. "So good," she said with her mouth full. "Makes me want to slap my mama."

Heather laughed. "Is that different than usual?" She took a bite of her half of the cookie, her teeth cracking the fine layer of hardened icing on the top as her taste buds exploded. She ate the rest of it, so sweet and tasty it flooded her mouth with joy and filled her mind with a false sense of well-being.

Maybe everything would be okay after all.

Abby finished her cookie and rubbed her palms together to brush off the crumbs. "I think we both needed a bit of sugary self-medication today."

"Yep, I agree." They had worked hard to get everything ready for the inspection. After all the work they'd done to get ready for this day, Heather didn't feel one bit bad about indulging. And they still had a planning committee meeting to get through. Hopefully, Quinn would have good news to relate about the inspection.

Reva walked in with an antique blue-glass mason jar of daisies and zinnias from her garden nestled in lacy sprays of fiddlehead ferns and green cockleburs from the nearby swamp. She looked pretty in a tie-dyed peasant dress and red Birkenstock sandals with rhinestone buckles. A fresh daisy was tucked into her silver-gray hair. "Hey, Heather. Hey, Abby."

She moved the cookie platter over and set the arrangement in the middle of the table. Any gathering in the Deep South—even a business meeting—was worthy of attention to detail. But this one was especially important. Reva put her hands on her hips. "Is Adrian here yet?"

"I haven't seen him." Heather felt a blush coming on, so she turned to fold a stack of paper napkins into neat triangles. It was annoying and embarrassing that her fair skin had an opinion of its own about Adrian Crawford.

A widowed mother of three had no business dreaming about

a dreamboat business consultant who had no room in his life for romance, kids, or even pets. She knew better than to respond to his shameless flirting. She'd spent too much time with him lately; that was the problem.

She needed to remember that Adrian was part of this team only because his college buddy Quinn had invited him. The second the shelter was open and running smoothly, he would go back to doing whatever he'd been doing before.

Abby looked out the window. "Adrian's car is here." She snorted a laugh. "Wearing its pajamas."

"Don't make fun," Reva said. "He just got all those scratches fixed. I don't blame him for being extra careful."

Heather stood beside Abby to look out the window at Adrian's fancy sports car that he'd covered with its tailor-made fabric tarp to protect it from falling leaves, jumping cats, and drifting dirt. "He does love that shiny hunk of metal," Heather commented, "doesn't he?" She didn't blame him though. If she could afford a car like that, she'd take extra-good care of it too.

Abby snorted. "His life will be complete if he ever finds a woman to love as much as he loves that car."

"That ain't gonna happen," Adrian's deep, masculine voice said from the arched entrance of the room. "But don't worry about me. I'm happy enough as I am."

Abby choked on a hastily stifled laugh and squeezed Heather's arm. Heather felt her skin go up in flames. But she had no choice except to turn from the window and face Adrian's self-satisfied smirk. In fact, he did look extremely happy with himself and life in general. From the aviator sunglasses perched on top of his perfect hair to the treaded soles of his fancy expensive hiking boots, he looked perfectly...well, perfect.

Adrian noticed Heather's flaming cheeks; it was impossible not to. Her fine porcelain skin mirrored her every emotion. He'd seen it all—from the delicate pink tint of attraction to the ferocious blush she had going on now to the mottled dull-red flush of anger. He'd seen it all because those had all been her reactions to him.

And those wide green just-got-caught-gossiping-about-him eyes, also impossible not to notice. But what *his* eyes really wanted was to devour the rest of her. His gaze stayed stuck on her face, though, because he was disciplined enough to avoid looking farther down than her obstinate little chin.

He didn't have to look down to know that her voluptuous body curved in all the right places, even though she often seemed to dress to minimize her sex appeal. From her minimal makeup to her blond ponytail to her plain pink tee and modest denim skirt, everything about her screamed *don't look at me.*

So he didn't look—unless of course she couldn't see him looking. Then he looked plenty. He knew that she had a little crush on him because her skin told on her, every single time.

What she didn't know was that he had a pretty hefty crush on her too. He was lucky that his tanned skin didn't tell on him and luckier still that he knew better than to act on his impulses. Because no matter how compelling Heather was all by herself, she came with a bunch of baggage that he was incapable of lifting.

"Hey, Adrian," Heather said, her voice Marilyn Monroe breathless. That was another thing about her that just about did him in: her voice. It made him feel like they were the only two people in the room. Hell, when he was near her, it often felt like they were the only two people on the planet.

"Hey, Heather," he replied, doing a pretty good imitation of her tone.

And just like that, the fading pink of her blush turned that mottled red color, setting the tone for their last big meeting about the shelter's upcoming grand opening and fund-raiser. She didn't say a word, but her lips tightened, and her eyes narrowed.

"Aw, don't be that way," he said. "I was just teasing." He didn't even know why he'd done it, unless maybe some part of him was trying to put the brakes on feelings he wasn't quite ready to handle. Heather's anger was better for his peace of mind than any other emotion she might feel toward him.

"I'm not being any sort of way," she announced. Then she brushed past him with her chin in the air.

Heather scooted her chair just so to put Reva's beautiful flower arrangement exactly between herself and Adrian. She'd prefer to look at daisies and zinnias instead of his disturbingly attractive features. She wasn't mad at him for pointing out the obvious. She couldn't help sounding breathless around him; he had that effect on her.

She wasn't mad at all. She was used to his teasing manner that seemed to veer between mocking and flirtatious.

In fact, she ought to be thankful that he sent her that little reminder of some of the less-attractive aspects of his character. After last week's riding session with Charlie, and the week before when he'd literally helped save Charlie's life, she had allowed herself to become a little too chummy with the idea of letting Adrian get close to her and her kids.

He could get close to Charlie. That was fine and necessary. But Heather needed to keep herself and her kids out of the equation. She needed to remember that once the shelter opened on Labor Day—which was, yikes, just a little over a week away—Adrian wouldn't be coming around so much, and eventually, once the shelter was running smoothly, he wouldn't be coming around at all.

What that would mean for Charlie, Heather hadn't yet considered, except to promise herself that by then, she would be making enough money to pay someone else to ride Charlie twice a week.

"Okay, y'all, let's get started." Abby stood. "We've got a lot to cover before Quinn is done showing the inspector around." She clasped her hands in front of her and smiled, a look of pride and relief on her face. "First of all, I want to thank y'all for your hard work in turning a crumbling old estate into an animal shelter we can be proud of.

"Heather, thanks for all the donations you got from local businesses. The donation of fencing and work crews from the fence company made all the difference. Adrian, thanks for expediting all the paperwork and forms. Reva, thanks for helping Quinn supervise the work crews and make sure everything got done right the first time. Y'all are miraculous."

"Yay, us," Reva hooted.

Everybody clapped.

Abby picked up her notebook and started reading from it. "On the agenda today, the biggest octopus we have to wrangle into a jar is the Labor Day picnic and shelter fund-raiser at Bayside Barn. As y'all know, we were hoping to do the shelter's grand opening at the same time, but whether we can do that hinges on today's inspection."

"It'll be fine," Reva said. "It'll be fine."

"Lord, I hope so." Abby held up crossed fingers. "At the end of today's meeting, Quinn is going to give a tour to some of the folks who helped us get the shelter approved by city hall. I'd like y'all to follow along to answer any questions but also to get a fresh look at what's been done recently and what we still have to do before we can open our doors to the public. And…Adrian's going to give us an update on the grants we've applied for."

She sat back down. "Adrian, you're up."

"Yes, ma'am." Adrian stood and passed a stack of papers to

Abby. "We've been approved to receive a grant that will reimburse us for the replacement of the leaking pool steps with a beach-style ramp. That will make it easier for the shelter dogs to safely enter and exit the pool. It's been done already thanks to the donations Heather managed to get from the local merchants..." He nodded at Heather without meeting her eyes. "But once we receive that payment, we can allocate that money for other projects."

A quiet ripple of whoops, cheers, and claps erupted. Adrian made a mock bow, then straightened and pinned them all with a serious gaze. "Don't get too excited. What this grant means, aside from the money, is that y'all will have to chronicle the rehabilitative benefits of swimming for a minimum of ten canine amputees, each of whom will be fostered here for twelve months. So that means over the next two years, the shelter will have to actively acquire dogs who have recently undergone amputations, keep them here for a year each, follow a specific pool-exercise protocol, survey their recovery rates, and document everything. Mack has agreed to provide veterinary care and fill in the reports for these dogs free of charge."

"That's awesome, Adrian," Abby said. "Thanks for taking the initiative on getting that funding."

"Happy to do it," he said. "We have a few more outstanding grant proposals I haven't heard back on, but I'll keep y'all posted."

"Great, thanks." Abby gave an appreciative little clap for Adrian, then looked at Heather and Reva in turn. "Everybody grab another cookie. We've gotta finalize the details of the grand opening and fund-raiser."

Adrian turned to leave the room. "Well, I'll leave you girls to that. Event planning is not my—"

"Sit," Reva commanded, softening the harsh word by handing him a cookie. "Event planning is not just for girls."

"But I'm really just here to give business advice, so—"

"Well," Reva said in her comforting, motherly voice, "we might have to fill in a form or get a permit or something, so I think you should stay. Abby? Heather? What do y'all think?"

Heather would be just as happy if Adrian left now. But Abby put a hand on Adrian's forearm and coaxed him back down. "Stay, please. Quinn wants you to be here in case anything comes up in the inspection that y'all need to talk about. And I'm sure he'll want to have a cold beer with you by the pool after that."

Adrian sighed a long-suffering man-sigh. "Fine."

When he sat back down, he moved his chair a fraction of an inch, and Heather could now see the side of his face, almost enough to catch the impossibly dark-blue iris of his right eye. She scooted her chair over and focused on the daisies again. "I have kids to pick up after school, just so y'all know. Let's talk fast." (An oxymoron to most Southerners—including the ones sitting around this table—but still. Her time constraints were worth mentioning.)

"We'll hurry," Reva assured everyone. As promised, the meeting was short—if not sweet—and everyone was happy enough to take on responsibilities they'd rather not have in order to have the thing over and done with.

Reva was nothing if not persistent. If anyone on earth had ever won an argument with Reva, Heather hadn't heard about it, and she was sure that such an event would've made the evening news.

Quinn came around the corner. Dressed in jeans and a dark T-shirt, he only looked slightly wilted from trekking around the shelter's grounds with the inspector. He held a folded sheaf of papers in one hand. "Welp, which do y'all want first, the good news or the bad news?"

―――――――――――

"Good news first," Abby demanded.

Quinn sat in one of the vacant chairs at the long table. "Good news: We *mostly* passed the inspection."

Adrian leaned back in his chair and crossed his arms. He was past ready to go home. "What didn't we pass?"

"The existing generator is old, it's not up to code, and even if it was, it doesn't have enough power to keep all the buildings and outbuildings cool in case of an extended outage. We will have to buy and install a new generator for each of the different zones: the house, the garage, and the pool house—a.k.a. the shelter, the kennels, and the infirmary."

"Okay," Adrian said. "So how long will that take?"

Quinn gave his friend a sheepish look. "That sort of depends on you."

"Me?" Adrian pointed to himself, as if there might be another person Quinn was talking about while staring straight at him. "Why me?"

"The inspector told me about a place in New Orleans where we can get the generators we need at a good price. But Abby can't go—she has a bunch of wedding-planning appointments—and Reva can't go because she has something scheduled at Bayside Barn. That leaves Heather—"

"I can't go," Heather piped up. "I have kids."

"So," Quinn said with a shrug, "that leaves you, Ade. You can take my truck and the flatbed trailer. They're expecting you to pick up the generators anytime after 10:00 Wednesday morning."

"Great. Fine." Not great, not fine, but Adrian reminded himself that this whole gig had a fast-approaching end date. He may as well pitch in as much as they needed until then.

"Yoo-hoo," a high-pitched female voice yodeled from the front room. "Where is everybody?"

"In here, Edna," Reva answered with a smile in her voice. "Come on in."

Edna, a short, rotund, grandmotherly woman with tight gray curls and a commanding presence, came into the room followed by a tall woman dressed in CEO style. "Y'all know Tammy Goodson, the city council's president?"

Everybody but Adrian nodded, and a couple of the women said, "Hey, Tammy."

Adrian stood and introduced himself.

"And Mayor Wright?" Edna introduced the slightly stooped, silver-haired man who'd come in last.

Adrian shook hands with the mayor.

"Well," Reva said, "since we're all standing, shall we let Quinn take us on the grand tour? I just got a text from Mack that he can't get away from the vet's office. Let's all grab a few cookies and some lemonade or tea and let Quinn show us around."

Everyone helped themselves to refreshments, then followed Quinn through the main level of the renovated Craftsman-style home.

"Quinn built the laundry room of my dreams," Heather said to the group when Quinn opened that door. "Two washers, two dryers, a long table for folding, and an entire wall of storage cupboards and shelving."

"I aim to please," Quinn said. In the main building's hallway, he opened doors one by one, then stood back for the visitors to look inside. "These used to be bedrooms, but now we have playrooms where we can do behavior training or where visitors can get to know a shelter animal one-on-one."

Then they all followed Quinn upstairs. "The second floor will house the shelter cats and small animals," he explained. "The first room on your right has been outfitted with floor-to-ceiling stainless-steel enclosures with wire doors and pullout trays for easy cleaning. These enclosures will be for any of the smaller incoming residents, including cats, kittens, ferrets, rabbits, whatever."

Everybody on the planning committee took turns peeking into the room, while Edna and Tammy and Mayor Wright walked in for a closer look.

"The first room on your left has adjustable shelving to accommodate any cages and hutches that might be surrendered along with the animals they belong to."

Quinn opened the new, glass-windowed door to the communal cat colony residence. "This used to be the master suite. The master bathroom has been renovated to provide a mop sink, extra storage, and a laundry chute to the downstairs laundry room."

Quinn stood with his hands in his pockets until everyone filed into the room. Built-in cat towers went from floor to ceiling in all four corners, and built-in shelves and ramps and steps and hiding spaces filled each wall. Quinn stopped next to a set of wider-than-usual shelves on the exterior wall, where several cutouts had been framed in and installed with cat doors that led out to the two-story outdoor play area.

Heather sidled up to Adrian. Quinn started talking about the Formica laminate he'd used for the climbing installations, chosen for their ability to endure spray-downs with antibacterial cleansers. She bumped Adrian on the arm with her elbow. "I'm sorry about before," she whispered.

What was she talking about? He tried to find the answer in those green eyes of hers, but all he ended up doing was noticing the gold starburst around the iris. "I didn't mean to hurt your feelings," she whispered. "Talking about your car, I mean."

Quinn had moved on to explain how he had cut into the exterior wall to install several cat doors at different levels so that cats could access the outdoor play area attached to the exterior of the renovated house. "Having multiple doors accessed at multiple levels was Reva's idea," Quinn was saying. "Otherwise, one or two cats could decide to guard the door and keep the others from going outside or coming back in."

Adrian hadn't thought twice about her little comment. He'd known at the time that she was working just as hard to shut him out as he was working to stop thinking about her. And that little joyride that Reva had sent them on hadn't helped. "Forgiven," he whispered back.

Of course, she blushed. Her rosy cheeks got a shade rosier,

which made the tightrope he was treading all the more dangerous. The thing was, no matter how much he wanted to lure her into a light flirtation that could lead to something more, he knew that nothing lasting would come from it, and Heather wasn't the kind of woman to accept anything less. She was all wrong for him, and he was even more wrong for her.

"Ade, Heather, y'all coming?" Quinn said from the doorway. Apparently, everyone had begun trooping downstairs to view the cats' outdoor playground.

"Sure," he said, keeping his tone as even and smooth as always.

"Lord," she muttered, blushing all over again.

He refrained from putting his hand at her waist as they both turned to head downstairs.

━━━━━━━━━

On Wednesday morning, Heather drove straight to the shelter after cleaning Charlie's stall and dropping the kids off at school, but as she turned into the gravel lot, Adrian's car was already in its usual space in the far corner. Covered with its fitted tarp, the car's hood sported a new ornament: a black-and-white cat. At first, she thought it was Reva's cat, Glenn, but as she got closer, she noticed the feral tomcat's big-jawed jughead.

Jasper whined from the back seat, pressing his nose against the glass.

"Oh, no you don't," she warned. "You're not gonna mess things up this time."

She took her foot off the gas and let the car coast through the lot, then eased to a stop as far from Adrian's car as she could manage.

Jasper whined again, making a gearing-up-to-bark sound in the back of his throat. "No speak," she commanded.

He knew what she meant. He sat, sending her a worried glance before gazing out the window again.

She turned off the car and sent a group text to the shelter team. The tomcat is sitting on Adrian's car. I am stuck in my car with Jasper. Please advise.

Reva texted back. On our way. Sit tight.

A minute or two later, Adrian and Reva walked casually toward Adrian's car from the shelter's main building. Abby followed some distance behind with a small cat carrier. Quinn walked toward Heather's car from the direction of the kennels, while his wolf dog shadowed him from a safe distance. The whole event was beautifully choreographed, and all Heather had to do was watch.

Quinn tapped on the back-seat window with one of Georgia's tennis balls, distracting Jasper to keep him from barking.

Adrian and Reva eased up to the cat, and Adrian gathered the sleepy-looking feline into his arms. Abby held the crate and opened the wire door. With no apparent hesitation, the cat allowed Adrian to shift him into the crate, and Reva gently closed the door. It all happened in less than five minutes.

Quinn stood by Heather's car, waiting until Reva had carried the crate up the front porch and into the shelter before giving Heather the go-ahead to open her door. Then he let Jasper out of the back seat. The dog, who apparently had the attention span of a goldfish, danced around Quinn's legs, ready for him to throw the ball.

"Wow, that was amazing." Heather got out of her car and clipped the keys to her purse strap. "I can't believe they managed to catch that cat so quickly."

"Reva and Adrian have been working on him," Quinn replied. "Thanks for letting us know he was out here." Quinn tossed the ball, and Jasper eagerly scuttled across the parking lot after it. Wolf, apparently uninterested in the ball and unconcerned about Jasper, sat near the play yard gate, watching.

Jasper trotted back with the ball, eager for another toss. He dropped the ball at Quinn's feet and wagged his whole self, quietly idling side to side like an off-kilter ceiling fan.

"Do you think it's okay to let Jasper come into the shelter? Or should I put him up in a kennel?"

"He can come in." Quinn hurled the ball again. "Reva will take the cat straight to the vet to get neutered and vaccinated. I'm sure she's got him in her car by now."

"That's good." They walked toward the shelter together. "Do you know what's on tap for today?"

Quinn took the ball from Jasper and threw it again. "You'd have to ask Abby. I know Adrian is getting ready to go to NOLA to pick up those generators. Reva has a group of folks from the Magnolia Bay retirement community coming to Bayside Barn in"—he glanced at his watch—"under an hour. So maybe Abby's the one taking the cat to the vet." He shrugged. "You know how it is. We go with the flow, and around here, the flow keeps changing course."

At the shelter's front porch steps, Quinn held the ball up and made eye contact with Jasper. "Last one, buddy. Are you ready?"

Jasper barked with excitement, and Quinn launched the ball. The dog took off, and Quinn wiped his hands on his jeans. "He's all yours now. I'm heading back to get some more stuff done before something else happens."

"Okay." Heather and Jasper went into the shelter, where Jasper flopped down on the wood floor in the reception area. Heather went to her desk. Abby had left a note on the computer keyboard. Normally, there would be a long list of things for Heather to do to prepare for the shelter's opening, stuff like *Please wash/dry/fold the donated towels* or *Talk to Quinn about storage options*.

Today, the note only contained one impossible marching order: *We need you to go to NOLA with Adrian today. Please see me or Reva as soon as you get in.*

The dog beds in the office were all empty, and Georgia wasn't patrolling the area and inspecting everyone's work, so Reva must be next door at Bayside Barn. Abby must be halfway to the vet's office by now.

"Come on, Jasper," she called. Always on it, Jasper was at her side in half a heartbeat. Together they went through the shelter's back door into the kennels, then through the kennel's door to the pool area. Jasper bounded toward the pool's sparkling water, eager to try out the beach-style entry.

"No," Heather said sharply. "No swimming today." If she was going to go to New Orleans, she'd have to take Jasper back home first. And the trip would have to be a quick turnaround because she had to get her kids after school. It could be done, but honestly, it all seemed like a bit of a stretch, and Heather couldn't imagine why *she'd* been nominated.

When Heather and Jasper walked through the swing gate to Bayside Barn, Jasper bolted toward Georgia, who was standing next to Reva, Edna, and two other volunteers Heather didn't know outside the big red barn. Ready to welcome the crowd of retirees who would soon be arriving for a tour, the women were all dressed in jeans, barn boots, and assorted colors of Bayside Barn T-shirts. Jasper dropped Georgia's ball. Georgia took it and ran, instigating a happy game of chase-whoever-has-the-ball.

Reva waved and came toward Heather. "Hey. Did you see Abby's note?"

"Yes, but you know I have to be back by 3:00 this afternoon, right?"

"Sure, sure. No problem. But you do need to go with Adrian. Abby has back-to-back appointments, Quinn's up against his deadlines, and I'm expecting a tour group to arrive any minute. I've already spoken with Adrian, and he says that getting back in time shouldn't be a problem."

"Well yeah, but what if it is?" Heather's friend Sara was her only fallback plan, and Sara had taken her son, Max, to a specialist in New Orleans to find out what was causing his seizures. They were spending several days there while Max underwent tests. "Sara's my only option if I can't make it back in time, and she's out of town."

"If anything happens to hold y'all up, I'll get your kids and bring them here. The tour group will be leaving by two. That gives me more than enough time."

"But you're not on the list."

Reva's arched brows came together. "Huh?"

"You know, the list of people who are approved to take my kids from school. The middle school doesn't monitor that, but the elementary school does."

"Oh, of course." Reva smacked her forehead with her palm. "Why didn't I think about that? Why don't you get Adrian to swing past the school on your way out of town and put me on the list? Even if you don't need it today, I'm happy to be on call in case you can't get there for some reason or another."

"Thanks." It would be great to have more than one person she could trust to help out if she needed it. "I'd appreciate that."

The deep, rumbling whine of a large vehicle turning onto the street made Reva look up. "What info do you need from me to get me officially on the list?"

"Copy of your driver's license, front and back."

"Well, shit. All that's in the house." Reva winced at the squeal of the tour bus putting on brakes in preparation for turning down the drive. "Let's hurry."

Reva called Georgia, Heather called Jasper, and the four of them ran across the gravel drive toward the blue farmhouse. Once inside, Reva quickly made the necessary copies, while Georgia and Jasper flopped down on the polished-wood floor with their tongues hanging out.

"You never said why I need to go with Adrian to New Orleans today."

"Oh, yeah. Sorry. You remember that Abby had reached out to the nearest shelters about taking any canine amputees they might have when we won that grant?"

Heather took the printer copies Reva gave her. "Yes, I remember."

"Well, we got a call this morning from a rescue organization in

New Orleans that recently picked up a dog who'd been hit by a car. His right back leg was completely mangled and had to be amputated. He's ready to be released from the vet, and they wanted to know if we were equipped to take on any dogs yet. Abby said yes. They're expecting us to pick him up today."

Heather thought for a second about offering to take her own car instead of riding with Adrian in the truck but then thought better of it. She didn't want to be by herself with a dog she didn't know in case something went wrong. Better to have backup. "Okay, so I'm guessing I need paperwork?"

"Adrian has all that. He's already waiting for you, parked by the road with the truck and trailer. Jasper can stay here with Georgia. I'll make Georgia stay inside and keep him company instead of helping out with the tour this time."

"Okay, I guess." Heather felt too rushed to think straight, but Reva was hurrying them both out the door. "Is there anything else I need to know before—"

"Nope, nope," Reva interrupted. "Time to fly! Folks are waiting for me to start the tour."

She ran toward the barn. "Thanks, Heather," she yelled, giving a backward wave. "Have fun in New Orleans."

Chapter 10

ADRIAN HAD JUST HIT SEND ON A WHAT'S THE HOLDUP? TEXT to Reva when he saw Heather running through the gate, her shoulder-length blond hair flying. He couldn't help but notice that her breasts were bouncing quite nicely under the modestly cut white cotton blouse she wore over denim jeans. He tried not to think about that.

He turned down the volume on the stereo, then leaned across the truck's seat to open the passenger door. He would've gotten out and gone around to open the door for her properly. But by the time he did that, she'd have clambered in by herself, looked at him like he was crazy, and asked why he was standing outside the truck when they were already in a hurry.

She hopped in, all rosy cheeks and smiling green eyes. "Hey." Out of breath from running, her voice sounded even sexier than usual. If he got through this day without kissing her, it would be a miracle. She slammed the door and buckled her seat belt. "I got nominated to pick up that dog. I hope you don't mind I'll be tagging along."

"Not at all." It did mean he'd be doing more than loading up, turning around, and going straight back to the shelter. Reva had given him her credit card (which of course he wouldn't use) with instructions to take Heather somewhere nice for lunch. "I'll be glad for the company."

He had already called the manufacturing company to explain that he'd been tasked with several errands besides picking up the generators. The lady on the phone was kind enough to say that he could unhook the trailer and leave it in their lot, then take the truck into the city. Driving in downtown New Orleans—let alone the French Quarter, where he planned to take Heather for lunch—wasn't something you could do pulling a flatbed trailer. Driving this big-ass pickup through those narrow streets would be bad enough.

While he eased the truck and trailer onto the blacktop, Heather brushed a hand across the flip-up console between the two front seats. "Quinn's new truck is fancy."

Quinn's old truck had given up the ghost about the time he donated his estate to the City of Magnolia Bay for use as a badly needed animal shelter. The girls were still campaigning to paint the old truck bright red and park it out front. They had some hare-brained plan to fill the truck bed with dirt and plant flowers in it. The old truck was now sitting on flat tires at the back of the property while Quinn and Abby duked it out.

Heather breathed in deeply, then released the breath on a sigh and relaxed into her seat. "It still smells like new leather too."

Adrian snorted. "That smell was probably sprayed on."

She looked at him sideways, and he could hear her thoughts as surely as if she'd said them out loud. Why did he have to be such a killjoy?

When even the sound of her breathing turned him on, he had to do something to combat the impulse to pull this truck over right now, flip that console up out of the way, unbuckle her seat belt, and…

Heather's phone dinged with an incoming text. She glanced at it and sat up straighter. "Can't believe I almost forgot. We need to stop by the elementary school." She glanced around at the landscape beyond the truck's windows. "I'm sorry." She chewed on her pinkie fingernail and sent him an apologetic look. "You should have turned left back there."

He took his foot off the gas. "And turning this rig around right here is impossible, so…?"

She nodded to herself. "Keep going straight. We'll have to double back around in a bit."

"Okay, fine." Not fine. They hadn't traveled three minutes, and already the complications were piling up. His list of errands had been expanded even before Heather's mission to pick up a three-legged dog had been tacked on to the agenda. They also had to pick up a load of hurricane-proof roll-down shutters, and now this. He'd told Reva that they could make it back by 3:00, but that was before she began adding to their tasks.

Adrian felt a bit like Indiana Jones embarking on an impossible adventure, but Reva had assured him that everything would work out perfectly if he just had faith. That sort of shit seemed to work for her—and, in fact, it also seemed to work for everyone around her—so he bit his tongue. He clutched the steering wheel and gave Heather an easygoing smile he didn't quite feel. "Just tell me where to turn."

By the time they'd stopped by the elementary school so she could *just run inside quickly and be back in a minute*, it was almost ten.

They hit the open highway a half hour later, and Adrian had high hopes that they'd still make it to The Palace on Canal Street in time for a late lunch. He hadn't had more than cereal and coffee for breakfast, and his mouth was already watering for the restaurant's famous crab cheesecake appetizer.

Then they hit stop-and-go traffic on I-10.

And the *stop-and-go* traffic turned into *straight-up-stopped* traffic. Adrian gave up and put the truck into Park because the whole interstate had ground to a complete halt. Cars and trucks lined up behind them, and folks started getting out of their cars and talking on their cell phones. Heather chewed on her pinkie fingernail and looked over at him, her green eyes wide with worry. "I have to be back at three."

"No, you don't." He reached across the console and squeezed her hand. "That's why we went to all the trouble of stopping by the elementary school. Reva will handle everything if we don't make it back in time."

With her left hand clasped in his, she continued to chew on the pinkie fingernail of her right hand. "I wonder what happened up ahead." Her posture conveyed an anxiety all out of proportion for the situation as she sat forward to look out the windshield, craning her neck in an effort to see any clues that might be visible along the line of standstill traffic ahead of them.

"I don't know, but it's pretty clear there's nothing we can do about it, so why worry?" He squeezed her hand again. "We'll get there as soon as we can."

An ambulance blasted past, driving along the breakdown lane with lights flashing. Another ambulance followed close behind.

She looked at the line of traffic forming behind them. "Maybe we should just go back."

"Honey..." The endearment slipped out, but she didn't notice. "We can't go back. Even if I wanted to, I couldn't back this rig down the highway to the last exit any more than I could successfully turn it around. Besides, either of those moves would be against the law. All we can do is wait."

She nodded, her forehead furrowed. "I'm sorry. I know that. I'm just...worried."

"What are you worried about?" Since the truck was in Park and the interstate had become a long, narrow parking lot, Adrian felt fine about undoing his seat belt and turning fully toward Heather, who blushed and looked away.

She shrugged. "I know it doesn't make any sense. It's just, I wouldn't want my kids to worry that something might have happened—or might happen—to me. I've been very careful to always be on time to get them after school."

"Okay."

She was chewing on her fingernail again, so he grabbed that hand and held it too. "Let's talk this out. What could we do that would make you feel better about the possibility that you might be late to get your kids?"

She shook her head and looked down, almost as if she was fighting tears. This seemed to be about so much more than simply running late and having her kids go home with a trusted friend.

"Would it help if you talked to Reva?" He knew they were good friends and that Reva, being a widow too, would understand what Heather was going through.

"I can't bother her right now. She's hosting a tour group."

"What about calling your kids? Maybe if you talked to them, you might find that they're happy to go home with Reva." He forced a light chuckle. "Bayside Barn *is* pretty much a kids' paradise."

"It's not so much that they won't like going there. What bothers me is the thought that they'll be upset if I'm not there as expected."

"So why not call the school and ask the twins' teachers to let you talk to them about it? If they know ahead of time that they may be going to Reva's, they won't be upset."

"But they would be worried if they got called to the school office."

He gave her a *come on now* look. "Even Erin?"

She looked up at him, a glimmer of relief lighting her green eyes. "Erin does have a cell phone, even though she has to keep it in her backpack during class."

"Great." He grinned, eliciting a small smile from her. Releasing her hands, he took her phone off the charge port in the console and handed it to her. "Text Erin and ask her to call you when she gets a break. That way, she'll have advance warning, and you'll know that she's prepared for whatever happens."

As Heather sent the text, the traffic ahead of them started inching forward. He put the truck in gear and eased forward as well. "And now we're moving. All is not lost."

When she hit Send, he glanced over at her. Her body language and facial expressions were so easy to read. She had relaxed a bit, but not enough. "Maybe now you should call the elementary school and tell them—"

Her phone chirped, and her face brightened when she looked at the screen. "It's Erin." With the phone held to her ear, she sent Adrian a smile and a quick thumbs-up. "Hey, Erin. Thanks for calling me."

Adrian turned the music up, just a little. Not enough to distract Heather from her call, but enough to give her at least the feeling that she had a measure of privacy. When she ended the call, he turned it down a bit. "And?"

"She's fine with the idea. In fact, she's excited. Told me I should get you to keep me in New Orleans all day."

He wouldn't mind doing that. He'd take her to a hole-in-the-wall wine bar he knew about that had live jazz every evening. "Oh, really?"

"Apparently, Quinn's son, Sean, is working at Bayside Barn after school today and staying for dinner afterward."

"So…?"

She gave him a sideways glance that said she was deciding whether she could trust him. "Well, you can't tell anyone, but Erin has a tiny secret crush on Sean."

"Oh, yeah?" News to him, but then again… "Sean is a good-looking kid."

"Yes, and he has always been kind to Erin and the twins. Erin has been a little starstruck ever since the first time she saw him at the shelter."

"Even though he's…what? Two years older than her?"

"Are you kidding?" Heather laughed. "Especially because he's two years older than her." She laughed again, her eyes sparkling. "If he were her age—I don't care how cute he is—she wouldn't give him the time of day. And she's not hard to look at either."

"Almost as pretty as her mother," Adrian couldn't help saying. He shot a quick glance her way, but no more than that. Traffic had loosened up a bit, and cars were beginning to change lanes and pick up speed. Even though it meant he had to go slower than just about everyone else on the road, Adrian kept to the right. The truck and trailer together were too long to allow much jockeying for position, and he had to be wary of cars cutting in front of him. "I guess they've cleared the accident."

"Looks like it." She sighed and sat back, her good humor restored. "I guess I don't have to worry about being late after all."

"What?" He raised his eyebrows at her. "And disappoint Erin after getting her hopes up? This could be her big chance to snag a boyfriend who's already in high school. You're gonna deny her that opportunity?"

Heather snorted at his teasing. "Erin isn't looking to snag anybody. She just wants to bask in the glow of his dazzling smile and sweet personality. She would die if she thought he knew she even looks at him." Heather pointed a finger. "And don't you dare let on that I told you anything."

"I don't know about that..." He knew it was wrong, but the opportunity to tease her got the better of him. He trailed a finger down her forearm where it rested on the console. "I might have to hold it over you. See what kinds of concessions I can blackmail out of you."

She slapped his hand away and crossed her arms. "You don't want to see me in mama-bear mode." But her tone was teasing, her expression a fake scowl that she couldn't hold on to for more than a second.

"I'll remember that." He put his hand back on the steering wheel, his eyes back on the road. "But I still think you should consider *planning* to be late instead of worrying that it might happen. You could call the school, let the twins know what to expect, and tell Reva we'll be back to pick them up before their bedtime. I'll take you out to lunch in the French Quarter, and then we'll go to a wine bar I know of on Frenchmen Street that has live music every night."

He kept his attention—most of it, at least—on his driving and let that thought settle in.

"But I'm not dressed for all that."

He glanced over at her. "You look a damn sight better than all those tourists who've been bumming around the Quarter all day, sweating in the Louisiana heat."

"We'll have a dog with us." She flung that excuse out like she thought it had some merit.

"Also not a deal breaker. It's N'awlins, baby. Everybody and their brother has a dog, and they're welcome just about everywhere. We can go somewhere that has a patio, and they'll even bring the dog a bowl of ice water. Or a beer, if he'd prefer."

She shook her head. "We don't even know this dog. He might be scared. He might be—"

"Fine, fine. I give up." She did have a point about not knowing the dog. But he wasn't *really* going to give up. The idea of showing Heather something about his world had taken hold, and he wasn't ready to let it go. He would, however, give the subject a rest for now and come at it from another angle later. "Let's talk about something else."

———

Heather readjusted the AC vents. The sun was straight overhead now instead of beaming through the back window, so the interior of the truck was cooler than she liked. "What do you want to talk about?"

"You cold?" Adrian looked over at her, and she could have sworn he glanced down at her breasts to determine exactly how cold she might be. But if it happened at all, it was only for a second. He met her eyes, his expression entirely innocent. "You want me to make it warmer in here?"

She crossed her arms. "Yes, please."

He bumped the digital temperature up a notch or two. "So, I did want to talk to you about something."

"Yeah?"

He sounded a little nervous—a word she would never have

attributed to Adrian, the most confident, smooth-talking man she'd ever met. "What?"

"I want to apologize for giving you such a hard time about Charlie's stall and the barn in general."

"Oh, you don't have to apologize." The place had been terrible beyond her worst nightmares. She twisted her fingers in her lap. "It was horrible, and I'm so ashamed that I didn't check behind Erin to make sure she was doing the work. I mean..." She made a huff of chagrin. "The irony hasn't escaped me that I'm about to take a full-time job with a good-paying salary and my primary responsibility will be to make sure the shelter animals are properly cared for. And yet I didn't take care of my own horse."

"It wasn't like you were starving him."

"Animal neglect doesn't have to be terrible to be bad." She shook her head. "You only said what I needed to hear."

Adrian looked over at her. "I could have kept my mouth shut instead of piling on criticism. I could have shown a little compassion."

She shrugged. "Like I said, you were only telling the truth. His stall was dirty, his buckets and bins were dirty..." She looked down at her fingernails.

"Here's the thing, though." He reached over and touched her hand, an invitation. She turned her palm up, and he took her hand in his. "Yeah, you could've done better. I bet you could've done better if you'd paid a dozen farm hands to do the work every day, right? Why didn't you do that, huh?"

She chuckled and looked sideways at his teasing smile. "Because I'm not rich?"

He smirked. "Oh, you mean, you don't keep Charlie in a fancy, high-dollar racehorse barn with a rubber-coated concrete floor and central air-conditioning because you can't afford to? And here I thought you were just being mean."

"I could have at least made sure Charlie got the same level of care as the animals at Bayside Barn." The big red barn at Reva's place was kept clean but not immaculate; the stalls were picked clean daily, the shavings replaced weekly. The shelves got wiped down and the barn got swept every week.

Heather knew all this because she'd had to document the information for the shelter's animal care plan, since any farm animals that were brought into the shelter would be housed at Bayside Barn until the shelter had its own barn. "Erin and I have been doing that, by the way. Erin feeds Charlie first thing every morning and lets him out into the field, and I scoop the poop in his stall before I get ready for work and take the kids to school."

Heather's come-to-Jesus meeting with Erin had resulted in a reallocation of duties; Erin had taken over laundry duty to allow Heather the time to do part of the daily work in the barn. As part of Erin's punishment, her allowance had been docked while her total amount of chores had been increased. Weekends with friends were gone too: Instead, Erin and Heather spent Saturday afternoons working together to clean Charlie's stall completely and sweep the barn.

But they had learned that dust in Charlie's barn was just a fact. The packed-dirt floor meant that red dirt drifted everywhere to coat everything, maybe even more when it was swept than when it wasn't. "Charlie's barn will never be as clean as Bayside Barn because of the dirt floors, but I'm trying. Erin and I both are."

"I can tell." Adrian squeezed her hand, which he was still holding. Their clasped hands rested on the center console between the two seats. "And I do realize that there are only two of you, while Reva has…what? Five volunteer interns to help with the field trips and Sean working part-time to help with the animal care and cleaning?"

"Something like that." Reva had more help than Heather, but she also had more animals. "I just wish I had more time to do everything that needs doing. All the junk Dale piled up in the pole barn is starting to sneak into my nightmares."

"Maybe we'll schedule another cleanup day to deal with that sometime. Meanwhile, you and Erin are doing a great job of taking care of Charlie with the resources you've got. And when you and Abby hire the people who'll be doing animal care for the shelter, you'll do a great job supervising them too."

"Abby and I are interviewing someone next week. Whoever we hire will start working the day after the grand opening."

"And soon after that, you'll be working together to save animals and make people's lives better. That's actually kind of incredible, isn't it?"

"You know, it kind of is." She felt a flood of gratitude for Adrian. He held up a believing mirror of the kind of person she meant to be and hoped she could be. "Thank you for the pep talk. I didn't realize how much I needed one."

"It's nothing. And for real, I'm truly sorry I overreacted that night. I've been thinking about it a lot, and I realize that it was partly because I was tired as hell and partly because I lost my own horse..." He seemed about to say more but didn't. She watched flickers of emotion cross his face, quickly suppressed and just as quickly gone. He glanced over at her, then back at the road. "And partly it was because I've seen truly horrible conditions in a horse barn, and I guess it affected me more than I thought."

"Do you want to talk about it?"

Muscles in his jaw moved as he briefly clenched his teeth. "When I was a kid...I dunno, maybe about nine or ten years old, I went to a little mom-and-pop feed store with my dad. It wasn't the place we usually went to, but our regular feed store was out of the brand my dad liked to feed Bluebell." He looked at her and flashed a smile. "My little sisters got to name the horse. I was campaigning for Flash, but I got outvoted."

"Awww, you poor thing." She thought of the way Adrian might have looked as a nine- or ten-year-old. Tall for his age, maybe, skinny, probably. "What did you look like back then?"

He scoffed. "Nobody knew. I was always covered in dirt."

"Hmmm. I bet you were a very cute little boy with those big blue eyes of yours." He gave her a surprised look, as if a compliment or a thought about his looks was the last thing he'd expect to hear coming from her. No wonder; they'd always kept things businesslike up until now, even though she was pretty sure she wasn't the only one who felt an undercurrent of attraction running through every encounter between them. "I'm sorry for interrupting. Tell me more about what happened."

"So, we were at this little backwoods feed store that was just a shack in front of somebody's house, and I was bored with the whole process, so while my dad was inside buying feed, I wandered to the barn out back."

He probably didn't realize it, but he was squeezing her fingers tight enough to cut off the circulation. She watched his face as he stared out the windshield, his attention on driving while the faraway memory seemed to move behind his eyes. "I still remember how shocked I was. There was this…this little brown pony with a shaggy coat and a fat belly, standing fetlock-deep in a slurry of urine-saturated shit. His front legs were swollen…" He swallowed. "So swollen that the skin had cracked open in long vertical fissures that oozed blood and pus."

"Oh, Adrian…"

"The water bucket—maybe a fifty-gallon rubber container—was half-full of thick greenish-black liquid that looked more like used motor oil than water."

"What did y'all do?"

"I went running to get my dad. He had always fixed everything in my life up until then, and I fully expected him to fix this too. I wanted him to get that pony out of there and bring him home with us, even if he had to pay a gazillion dollars to do it."

He was telling the story the way people do when they're unloading their grief for the first time. She'd seen it happen enough times at the grief support group to know what that kind of outpouring looked like. She eased her hand out of his, unbuckled her seat belt, and flipped up the center console.

"What are you doing?"

"Scooting closer." She sat beside him, fastened the lap belt, and wrapped her hands around his arm. "You looked like you needed a hug." She hugged his arm, then took his right hand and wove her fingers through his, settling their clasped hands in his lap. "Carry on. Tell me what your daddy did."

Adrian swallowed. "He didn't do anything. He said he didn't want to start any trouble; we were so far out in the boonies that if the guy decided to shoot us, no one would find us."

"Did he buy the horse feed?"

"Yep." Adrian's tone was bitter. "To be fair, he had already bought it and loaded it up in the back of the truck. I tried to get him to go look at the pony, but he told me to mind my own business and get in the truck. Then he just drove away."

She put her head on his shoulder and hugged him tight. All the times she had avoided touching him—or even looking at him—seemed silly and juvenile to her now. "I am so sorry that happened to you."

"I've never told anyone else—except ranting to my mom about it when we got home."

"I'm glad you told me." She reached across his chest and put her hand on his shoulder, giving him the best semblance of a full-on hug she could manage while he was driving. "I'm sure it was a traumatic experience, seeing that pony's suffering and not being able to do anything about it."

"I've never been able to forget that poor pony. I'm sure he's long since dead, but even the thought that he died alone and in pain is embedded in my mind." He shrugged, and the hard muscles of his biceps and shoulder moved smoothly under Heather's hands. "I guess it's one of the reasons I'm donating so much of my time to help y'all get the animal shelter off the ground."

"You're making sure that little pony's life meant something."

"I never thought of it that way. But maybe you're right. I hope so."

———————

Heather fell asleep with her head on his shoulder long before they reached the exit to the industrial complex just outside New Orleans. Traffic had clogged up again when they passed the wreck site and everyone had to funnel into one lane to avoid the cleanup. When he got to the exit, he tried to make the turn slowly, but she sat up a little straighter and rubbed her face. "Where are we?"

"Almost there. We have two stops to make: Quinn wants us to pick up some hurricane shutters he ordered, and then we'll go pay for the generators. They're going to let us drop the trailer in the parking lot. They'll load up the generators so we can pick them up whenever we're ready."

"What time is it?"

He glanced at the truck's clock. "Noon thirty."

She dropped her hands into her lap. "Oh no. Can we get everything done in time?"

"Nope, not unless we skip lunch, and I am *not* skipping lunch."

She gave a sigh of resignation. "Well, that's that then."

"Yup." He didn't say anything more, just gave her time to come to terms with the fact that for the first time in over a year, she wouldn't be picking her kids up after school.

Adrian figured the kids wouldn't care; they'd be happy to get their very own personal and private field trip to Bayside Barn. But Heather had the after-school pickup all balled up with her own feelings of loss and guilt and a need to make sure her kids felt safe. Telling her things would be okay wasn't going to help anything, so he turned up the volume on the stereo and kept driving.

He drove about ten miles past the compressor company to the

shutter place—which also made custom garage doors—and followed the signs to the drive-through warehouse. The load-up took less than ten minutes.

The whole time, Heather chewed on that fingernail and looked worried. With one knee crossed over the other, her supporting foot was arched up like a ballerina on tiptoe. She had removed her shoes awhile back, and her toenails, he noticed, were painted a shiny bright red. Her ankle jiggled nervously, rattling the cupholders. He decided to ignore all that and let her stew for a bit, since she didn't seem to be in a mood to accept comfort or listen to reason.

At the generator place, he left the truck running and went inside briefly to find out where they wanted him to drop the trailer. The place was busy—who knew generators were in such high demand? It took a while, but he got instructions on where to park, along with an assurance that they'd load the generators when they had a minute. The lot would be closed by 7:00 p.m., but the night security guard would let him in to get the trailer if they got back later than that. He gave his name and driver's license number for the guard to check in case that happened.

When he got back to the truck, Heather had moved over to the passenger seat, and she was talking on her phone. It sounded like she was speaking with someone at her kids' school. She didn't say anything to him but sent him a quiet smile.

The jiggle was gone, and she seemed more relaxed. He moved the truck, unhitched the trailer, and got back in. Heather was still on the phone; this time it sounded like she was talking with one of her kids. "I'm sure Reva can take y'all past the house to pick up your swimsuits." She looked over at him and rolled her eyes. "Yes, I'll tell her to do that… Yes, I promise… No, you will not be spending the night."

Even though Heather didn't have her phone on speaker mode, he could hear Josh's whining voice loud and clear. "But, Mom…I *want* to spend the night at Aunt Reva's. She has baby rabbits."

"I know she does. And I also know that she's not going to let you touch them."

Adrian motioned for her to buckle her seat belt, which she did. Then he drove out of the parking lot and hit the road toward New Orleans. After a few more minutes of back and forth with Josh, Heather ended the call. Adrian gave her a questioning look. "Feel better?"

She released a breath. "I texted with Erin and talked to both of the twins." She chuckled and slid a rueful glance his way. "Every dang one of them wants to spend the night at Reva's."

He laughed. "*Aunt* Reva is what I heard."

"Yes. She has recently become my kids' honorary aunt. Josh heard Abby call her that and decided she could be his aunt too."

"So you were worried for nothing."

"Seems that way, but don't rub it in. I'm entirely willing to adjust my perspective."

"Good to know. And what are you going to do with your new perspective?"

She stacked her hands in her lap and looked out the windshield with renewed interest. "I'm going to stop worrying about things I can't control and enjoy our time in New Orleans." Her stomach growled, loudly enough for both of them to hear. She clutched her belly and blushed, then laughed. "Are you ever going to take me out to lunch? I'm starving."

"I'm driving as fast as I legally can."

She looked at the speedometer and made a prim-and-proper face. "I'd say you're going a little faster than the legal limit."

He scoffed. "Are you hungry or not?"

She made the prim face again. "Hungry enough that I don't want to waste time sitting by the side of the road while you get a speeding ticket."

"Fair enough." He took his foot off the gas and set the cruise control. They were almost at the exit to his loft in Bywater anyway.

He planned to park the truck there and take her on a quick ten-minute walk along the river to one of the nearby restaurants in the French Quarter. "Let's talk about food."

Her stomach growled again, and when his roared back, they both laughed. "What are you hungry for?"

"Anything. Everything. I don't care," she said. "I'll happily eat your arm if you don't get me to a restaurant soon."

"Yes, ma'am. I'd like to keep my arm, so I'll do my best." Enjoying the banter, he thought about taking her hand but then thought better of it. Best to go slow and easy, he decided. He wasn't even sure what he hoped to accomplish by luring Heather into enjoying the afternoon bumming around with him in the Quarter. Maybe it was pride in showing off his hometown.

New Orleans, especially his corner of New Orleans, was a place unlike any other on earth. Or maybe it was his recognition that Heather needed and deserved a break, and he knew the day could be a fun diversion for them both. Whatever. He had to admit that his motives weren't entirely clear, even to himself.

He parked in the lot outside his condo building, a converted brick warehouse by the river. "Here we are. Home sweet home."

———

Heather unbuckled her seat belt and looked around. "Wow." She gazed out the windshield at the renovated mellowed-red-brick warehouse. "What a beautiful view." The side of the building overlooked the river, while the front faced the French Market and the New Orleans skyline.

"Do you want to come inside for a pit stop before we walk to the restaurant?"

She hadn't thought about it until now, but her bladder was beginning to fuss at her just a little. "Yes, please." Besides, she was curious to see where Adrian lived. A cautious corner of her brain raised the question of *why* she was curious. She decided she didn't want to think too much about that.

Adrian walked around the hood of the truck to open her door while she slipped her tennis shoes back onto her feet and unplugged her phone from the charger. She tucked her phone into the side pocket of her mini-purse, then followed Adrian through a pressed-concrete patio where several beautiful people hung out beside a huge lap pool.

"Hey, Adrian," one of the beautiful people yelled, waving to catch his attention. The scantily clad, stunning young woman rose gracefully from her lounge chair and glided toward them. Her tanned skin glistened with suntan oil. Her short hair was white-blond at the roots with blue tips that stood up in heavily gelled spikes. "Didn't think you were coming home today."

Heather had always been comfortable in her own skin. But as the model-thin bikini-wearing woman's electric blue eyes looked her up and down, she couldn't help feeling dumpy, frumpy, and old-fashioned.

Adrian made introductions. "Heather Gabriel, Jamie Echols, my neighbor from across the hall."

Jamie gave Heather a warm smile and a slightly limp, slightly greasy handshake. "It's nice to meet you, Heather. Adrian has told me a lot about y'all's animal shelter project." She turned to Adrian. "Isn't it about done? We sure miss seeing you around here."

"I'll be helping out there for a few more weeks yet," he said with an easy smile. "And it's not like I'm *never* home."

Jamie laughed, a gentle trill. "Well, you've been gone enough to miss a package delivery. It's on my kitchen table." She reached out to take Adrian's hand and give it a gentle squeeze. "Feel free to use your key to my place and pick it up when you go upstairs."

"Okay, thanks." Adrian eased his hand from Jamie's and

surreptitiously wiped his palm on his jeans. "We've got a lot to do today, so…" He looked toward the entrance to the four-story brick building. "We'd better get going."

"Sure, of course," Jamie said smoothly, giving Adrian a wink. "I'll see you later."

As Heather followed Adrian through the glass doors into the building, she decided that Jamie's long lashes and compelling blue eyes had to be fake. But fake or not, they sure were arresting.

On the elevator ride up to the fourth floor, Heather looked at her distorted reflection in the elevator's brushed-steel walls. She remembered rubbing her face after waking up from her truck-nap on Adrian's shoulder and wondered whether the mascara she had applied that morning was still on her lashes or had migrated down below her eyes. The patterned silver surface she stared into held no answers. Maybe, if she was lucky, she had stashed a not-quite-dry tube of mascara in her too-small purse.

Adrian reached out and tucked a strand of hair behind her ear. (Did she look that disheveled? She hoped not—she might have mascara in her purse, but she knew she didn't have a hairbrush.) "Is everything okay? You're being pretty quiet."

"Just a little worried, I guess." No way would she let him know she was feeling insecure after meeting the beautiful Jamie, who had given Adrian a key to her condo. "Wondering when I should call Reva about getting the kids this afternoon."

He smiled, a quizzical quirk of his beautiful mouth. "I thought you were gonna call her a little after two, when she's done hosting the tour group."

"Oh, yeah." Great. In her effort to not seem jealous, she had instead made herself sound stupid. "Of course. You're right."

The elevator doors opened onto a long hallway with hanging pendant lamps that cast puddles of light onto a polished-concrete floor. She followed Adrian to the end of the hall and waited while he unlocked the door to unit 404. The doors across the hall weren't exactly opposite each other, but rather, each door on one side was located halfway between two doors on the other side.

Heather wondered whether the gorgeous Jamie lived in 403 or 405.

Adrian pushed open the door to his condo, allowing Heather to walk in first. The entry offered a short hallway to the right and another, wider hallway going straight ahead. When the wide hallway opened out to reveal the main living space, Heather's initial impression was one of spartan elegance. Concrete floors scattered with expensive-looking oriental carpets anchored modern furniture groupings: a velvet couch and two love seats in tones of gray and blue, a long dining table and sleek chairs of dark polished wood.

A baby grand piano sat in the corner of the room between two huge windows set into the old-brick wall. One window faced the river, a wide brown ribbon flowing silently past the pushed-aside curtains that puddled on the floor. The other window looked out onto the open market at the edge of the French Quarter.

"You play the piano?" she asked.

"A little." Adrian tossed the truck keys into an artfully crafted glazed clay bowl on a marble-topped cabinet by the door. "My mom made us all take lessons, whether we liked it or not."

"Play something?"

He sat at the piano and picked out a soft melody, nothing she recognized but soothing and beautifully rendered. "Feel free to look around," he said, still playing. "There are two bathrooms; the closest one is just past the door we came in."

"Thanks." She took him up on his offer to look around, taking her time getting the lay of the land while he seemed to lose himself in the music he made so effortlessly.

She knew he was giving her time to relax and get to know him better by checking out his living space—and maybe also to use his bathroom without worrying that he might be paying some sort of attention to how long she was taking in there. She appreciated his sensitivity.

The times when she could think of him as just a pretty face or even just a college buddy of Quinn's were long gone. His complicated personality was built on multiple layers she'd only begun to recognize. Had all his teasing and flirtation been a convenient mask to keep her from seeing the generous heart beneath? When he'd told her about the neglected pony who'd snagged his attention and captured his compassion, she had the sense that he'd revealed a part of himself no one else had ever seen.

"Your home is incredible." Even though the white kitchen at one end of the wide-open space seemed not to be integrated with the rest of the space. The white-marble countertops were glossy clean—and empty. No coffee maker, no chopping board or knife block, no nothing, really. The kitchen lacked the vibe of life that filled the rest of the place.

"It's home, I guess," he said without missing a note.

Heather wandered into the hall bathroom—all casual-like so he wouldn't realize she was a human being who might have to pee—then closed the door and leaned over the sink to stare into the mirror. Her mascara hadn't exactly held up, but at least it hadn't migrated down her face. She dug through her tiny purse but struck out. Not only no mascara, but no lipstick either. A lightly tinted Burt's Bees lip balm was all that stood between her and total disappearance. "Oh, well." Maybe that would cure her of the insanity of thinking she had any sort of chance with Adrian.

Wait. She watched her eyes widen in surprise at the direction her thoughts had taken. *Had* she been thinking that? Was she actually considering indulging in a fling with Adrian? Because if she did, it couldn't be anything more than a fling.

As she used the bathroom facilities, washed her hands in the fancy sink with the fancy spout that gushed water down a chute that resembled a Japanese-garden fountain, she tried to imagine a way in which she and Adrian might actually explore a real relationship together.

She scoffed at herself in the mirror. "No way."

The thought of her and Adrian getting together made about as much sense as a sparrow falling in love with a Japanese koi fish. Adrian fit in here, in this elegant, spartan place in this cosmopolitan party town.

She didn't fit in here.

And the thought of her children living here? Ridiculous. Heather and her kids belonged in the small-town culture of Magnolia Bay, where everyone knew everyone else and the only thing to do for fun was to go fishing or hang out on the river or the bay with friends.

He wouldn't fit in there.

But as she smeared a dab of Burt's Bees over her lips, she had to admit to herself that an undeniable sexual chemistry flowed deep beneath the surface of every encounter she'd ever had with Adrian. And now that she was getting to know him, the chemistry between them felt even stronger, even more impossible to deny.

Chapter 11

WHEN HEATHER WENT INTO THE FRONT HALL BATHROOM, Adrian hurried to the master bathroom, where he brushed his teeth, rinsed the sink, wiped down the counters, and changed the towels. He waded up the old towels, and on his way to the laundry room, he paused in his bedroom to take stock. His bed was made; his mother had drilled that habit into his brain.

When had he last changed the sheets? He couldn't remember.

Then he laughed at himself. He didn't have to worry about Heather seeing his bedroom or the master bathroom.

Why would she? Was he going to invite her in here for a little afternoon nookie? Of course not.

She had let down her guard when they were in the truck—he should have kissed her then, he thought, but then again, no. By the time she'd begun to thaw the boundaries between them, the traffic was moving again.

So, yeah, he'd missed the chance to kiss her earlier. That was probably a good thing.

Silly of him to even let the thought of Heather coming in here cross his mind.

He eased the bedroom door closed, dumped the wad of towels into the washing machine to deal with later, and went back to the piano. He played a made-up tune that wasn't much of a tune at all, but it took his mind off the push-pull of his attraction to Heather.

His desire for her kept overwhelming his rational mind: the devil on his right shoulder arguing with the angel on his left. His biggest problem was that between one minute and the next, he couldn't decide which side *he* was on.

Playing soothed him. It always had, even though he had

complained bitterly to his mother about having to practice. But she had never had to remind or force him to do it. Partially because he really did enjoy playing. Mainly because he'd been deathly afraid of his piano teacher's wrath. The man had an acute extrasensory perception of the times when Adrian had skimped on practice, and he gave the same lessons over and over again until they were mastered.

Heather came into the room, her green eyes shining in the afternoon light through the windows, her lips dewy pink and soft-looking.

Maybe he should worry about the sheets after all.

"You don't have to stop playing."

He realized that his fingers had come to rest on the piano keys. He stood. "I thought you were starving. I know I am."

"If you're waiting on me, you're backing up." She gave him a smirky smile. "I'm ready when you are." He thought how pretty her face looked when her cheeks plumped up the way they did when she smiled. Not stunning or gorgeous or compelling, but so pretty that he wanted to take her face in his hands and kiss her soft pink mouth. He wondered if her eyelids would flutter closed so he could kiss them too.

And maybe sometime today, he would find out.

He squinted at her. "Do you have sunglasses?"

"Nope." She looked down at herself. "I'm not sure where you think I might be hiding sunglasses—or anything else." She held up the tiny little purse with its tiny little strap slung crosswise over her white blouse. "Not in this excuse for a handbag, that's for sure."

"Okay. Hang on." He ducked into his bedroom, grabbed a couple of baseball caps from the closet, then got a tube of sunscreen from the bathroom drawer. In the living room, he dropped the baseball caps on the piano bench, then stood by the window and beckoned her close. "Come here." He uncapped the roll-up stick of sunscreen. "I'm not gonna let that lily-white skin of yours get sunburned today."

She came close but looked dubious. "It's not going to turn my skin white, is it?"

He shrugged. "Better white than lobster red, huh?"

"Yes, you're right." She tilted her face up to him and closed her eyes. "Go ahead. Make me look worse than I do already. I'm sure the lovely Jamie won't judge me too harshly."

The lovely Jamie? Hmmm. He grinned—couldn't help it—but she wasn't looking. Gently, he swiped the sunscreen stick across her forehead, then rubbed in the sunscreen with his pinkie. "Do I detect a slight note of jealousy?"

She snorted. "Of course not." Then, in the next breath... "Absolutely."

He applied the sunscreen across the porcelain-fine skin of her blushing cheeks, over the bridge of her actually very perfect nose—he hadn't noticed that before—and along her almost-but-not-quite-dimpled chin. "Now why in the world would you be jealous of Jamie?"

"Um...because she's beautiful?"

He smeared sunscreen on her neck—which was longer and more slender than he'd realized—and over her collarbones and into the very slight V of soft skin visible above the collar of her white sleeveless blouse. "She's one kind of beautiful, I guess," he conceded. "But then again, so are you."

She opened her eyes. "And maybe I'm jealous because..." She shook her head and closed her mouth against whatever she'd been about to say. "Isn't it enough to be jealous because she's beautiful?"

"Jamie is also very nice." He rolled the sunscreen stick over each of Heather's shoulders, giving the task his full attention. In a minute—or less than a minute—he was going to kiss her. "She receives packages for me whenever I'm not home and leaves them on her dining table so I can get them anytime that's convenient for me."

"And it's easy for you to do that," Heather said, watching his hands as they worked the sunscreen down her arm, "because you have a key to her condo."

He nodded. "Yes, all that's true." He applied sunscreen to her other arm, then recapped the tube and slipped it into his pocket in case they stayed out a while. "But you know what else is true?"

He made eye contact, noticing how her pupils dilated, making her leaf-green eyes look darker and more moss-green as the gold starburst around the pupil blended more fully with the green iris.

Her breathing quickened. "What else is true?"

"I don't want to kiss Jamie." He touched Heather's plump lower lip with the tip of his index finger. He realized with a sense of joy and relief that the devil had won, and he decided to be thankful for that victory and to never look back. "And I do want to kiss you."

———————

When Adrian put his arm around Heather's waist and drew her close, every nerve ending in her body *woke up*. A shiver of anticipation coursed through her, drawing her nipples into tingling buds and igniting a flood of sensation lower down that made her suddenly aware of the way her panties skimmed against her skin when she leaned toward him.

His expression was serious, intense, intent on what he was about to do.

He was about to kiss her.

He held her loosely; she could break away if she wanted. His lips hovered over hers for a heartbeat before allowing them to touch hers, ever so slightly. She could have stopped him at any time.

She still could.

If that was what she wanted.

He moved slowly, giving her every opportunity to change her mind. She could step back, make some quip about being hungry enough to eat his arm, and he would smile that easygoing smile he had perfected so well and usher her out the door with casual grace. It wouldn't even be awkward; he would make sure of that.

She opened her mouth to his, and given that small sign of assent, he claimed her. His tongue slipped into her mouth, skillfully sliding across her teeth, making the underside of her top lip tingle in response. He stroked the roof of her mouth, making that tingle too. He didn't just kiss her; he explored her mouth as if he wanted to get to know each separate part of it.

Dale hadn't kissed like this.

The thought crossed her mind without warning, and Adrian was so aware of her subtle shift that he ended the kiss and pulled back to look at her. She hadn't meant to compare the two men. But wasn't comparison inevitable? She had never kissed another man besides her husband.

Adrian smiled, a gentle, questioning smile. "You okay?"

She felt a blush spread across her face. "I've never kissed anyone but my husband."

Adrian's smile grew, morphed into one of delight—maybe with an added hint of confidence. "Until now," he added.

"Until now," she agreed. "It was...different."

His confidence was on full display now. "Yeah? How was it different?"

"It was..." Incredible. That's what it was. She tried to tone down her smile, to keep her lips primly closed. She failed, and finally allowed her twitching lips to show her true feelings, even though she wasn't about to go so far as to admit to him that he'd just blown her away. "I don't know yet." She managed to regain the prim expression she couldn't hold on to before. "I haven't quite made up my mind. I don't think I have enough data to go on."

"Good." He grinned because of course he could see the effect he had on her. "I'm glad to hear that. I'm a big fan of data analysis." He released her waist and took her hand, interlacing their fingers.

"We'll make a point of adding to your data set soon. But you'll have to choose which comes first: food or data analysis?"

Data analysis tempted her, but her stomach growled, threatening to derail any attempt to overrule the body's basic need for fuel. "Food, please. I'm afraid I'll die if you don't feed me right away."

He brought their clasped hands up to his lips and kissed her knuckles. "Let's go then."

He tried to set one of the ball caps on her head, but she refused to allow it. She put the cap back on the piano bench. "Sorry. I'm not gonna let you give me hat hair."

He made a tsking sound but didn't argue. He just tucked the other ball cap into the back pocket of his jeans and grabbed his keys on the way out the door. As they rode down in the elevator, he gave her some sultry looks that promised more kisses to come. But the most he did to ramp up expectation was to tuck her hair behind her ear and make a low growl in his throat.

She felt like a bandit when he took her through the building's exit on the opposite side of the building as the pool. Co-conspirators, they walked together, hand in hand, along a paved riverside walkway that led through Crescent Park to the French Quarter. A balmy breeze blew up from the water, softening the sweltering heat of the sun overhead.

Having grown up in nearby Magnolia Bay, Heather knew New Orleans very well. Adrian's loft on the outside edge of Bywater was almost within sight of the famous French Market. They were walking less than five minutes from some of the best restaurants in the world, and her stomach was growling. "Where are we going?"

"I had wanted to take you to The Palace on Canal Street, but considering how late it is, I thought we'd go to the Original French Market Restaurant instead. It's close enough to walk to, and the food is reliably decent. We've missed the lunchtime rush, so we can get a seat on the balcony, if that suits you."

"As long as you don't judge me for getting the fried seafood platter."

"Are you kidding? If they only had one platter left, I'd fight you for it."

She leaned over and bit his shoulder through his T-shirt. "If you deny me my seafood platter, I'll gnaw off your arm."

He stopped walking and twirled her toward him until they were chest to chest, hip to hip.

"Urp," she wheezed, then caught her breath.

He wrapped an arm around her waist and squeezed. "We might have a slight problem here. I think we'll have to agree to a compromise before we go any farther."

"What sort of compromise are you proposing?"

He kissed her lightly, not enough to convince, only enough to tease. "We'll share a dozen oysters on the half shell for an appetizer, a seafood platter for lunch, and a creole cream cheesecake for dessert."

That sounded better than good—she'd happily eat a McDonald's cheeseburger and fries by now—but she was determined to argue because this was fun. "Baked oysters—"

"Nope, nope." He kissed her again, deeply, before pulling away. "Fresh or char-grilled. That's all you get." Some guy on a bicycle went around them, the bike's gears clicking.

"Fresh oysters on the half shell, or…?" He pulled her close, his lips a breath away from hers.

She had a hard time standing upright but answered with conviction. "Char-grilled."

His hand drifted down the seam of her jeans. "Creole or garlic and herb?"

A biker zoomed past, yelling, "On your left!"

Adrian eased them off the concrete path and onto the short-clipped grass. "Come on, girl, focus on the conversation. You have a decision to make." He kissed her jawline, then her neck. "Creole or garlic and herb?"

How could she think of food now? She slipped her fingers into his back pockets and leaned into him. He kissed her, quick, then threaded his fingers through hers and pulled her back onto the path. "Too late. You get garlic and herb."

Hand in hand, they walked the short distance to the restaurant. Adrian brought their clasped hands up and kissed her knuckles.

"Adrian, I know this may be a stupid question, but...what are we doing?"

"I don't know." He swung their hands in a carefree gesture. "Enjoying a little time off? Does it matter?"

She sighed. "I'm afraid it does. I'm sorry." She gave his fingers a brief squeeze. "You've been flirting with me a lot lately—not just today—and I've been playing along because I was starting to find it fun. I didn't think there was anything more to it than that. But now..."

In the distance ahead of them, a couple of lovebirds were cuddling on one of the benches beside the walkway.

"What are we doing?" she asked again. "Is all this flirting about to lead to something more...physical?"

"I'm game if you are," he quipped. "Is that what you want?"

She chewed on that one poor fingernail she couldn't seem to leave alone. "I don't know."

"Tell you what." Adrian nodded at the lovers they were walking past. "Why don't we pretend that we're just another pair of lovers enjoying the city? That way, we can flirt and tease without worrying where it might or might not lead. It's not like we have time to follow through anyway, is it?"

"And then we go back to Magnolia Bay and forget this ever happened?"

He shrugged. "If you like."

Subject dropped for now, they crossed the street and entered the restaurant's dim interior. In minutes, they were seated on the balcony overlooking Decatur Street and St. Philip Street. She put her chin on her hand and looked over the wrought-iron rail. As always, the French Quarter bustled with tourists, cameras slung around their necks. A mule-drawn carriage clopped down Decatur and turned the corner while the driver gave his usual spiel to the folks inside the carriage, who craned their sunburned necks to see the sights.

Adrian ordered the shared entrée and appetizer they had agreed upon as well as crab cakes, crawfish bisque, and—though Heather tried to argue—both cheesecake *and* white chocolate praline bread pudding.

When the appetizers arrived, Adrian reached across the table, offering Heather a bite of crab cake on his fork. "You have to try this first." She hesitated, her own crab-filled fork halfway to her mouth. "Pretend, remember? For the next two hours, you can be whoever you want to be. Then we go back to Magnolia Bay, no harm, no foul."

The food was divine—of course it was; she was starving—but it would have been excellent regardless. What made it even better was the fact that she was sitting across from Adrian, and he had given her permission to try on the illusion of being the kind of woman who could sit on a balcony across from a good-looking man while they fed each other the way lovers do. And what made it even better than *that* was the fact that he made her feel like the most desirable woman in the world.

It reminded her—*sorry! Sorry! Stop comparing!*—of her and Dale's honeymoon, when they were young and in love and so poor that the only honeymoon they could afford was a weekend in New Orleans.

Heather expected the fleeting memory to ruin her enjoyment of the moment, but it didn't. For the first time since Dale's death, she was able to remember something they had shared without being swamped by sadness.

The entire meal became an exercise in decadence, a prelude to seduction. Good thing they wouldn't have time to do anything more than walk back to his place, get in the truck, and head to the vet's office to pick up that dog. "Thank you for taking me to lunch. All this decadence—the food and the company—is hitting the spot."

"Oh my god," Adrian said with his mouth full. "You have to taste this." He held out a forkful of bread pudding.

She took it into her mouth and rolled her eyes in bliss. "Oh, wow."

"So good, huh?" He swiped a finger across her lips, capturing a drop of the warm, gooey white chocolate sauce and then licking it off his finger. "So good."

He fed her another bite of dessert, this time the cheesecake. "I'm thinking you might be feeling even more satisfied by now if we had decided to skip lunch."

The thought that they could have made a different decision—and might have been together in Adrian's bed by now—made Heather's heart take a nervous leap into her stomach. A spur-of-the-moment fling wasn't like her at all. But her time with him today had reminded her in a big way that she wasn't just a widow; she was a woman. She wasn't just a mother; she was a sexual being. "Except for the fact that my stomach would be growling, I'm sure you're right."

"Damn straight, I'm right." He finished off the bread pudding, except one last bite that he gave to her. "How about we head back and gather some more data to prove how right I am?"

She'd gone way too long without sex. But he wasn't talking about sex…was he?

Anyway, they were on the clock. "Unfortunately for us, we don't have time."

Their server laid the bill on the table, and Adrian counted out several bills, then closed the folder over them. "If we hurry back to my place right now, we can squeeze in enough time for me to rock your world."

He *was* talking about sex! "Oh, God. I don't know… Doesn't this feel…a little sudden?"

"Not to me." He leaned forward and gave her that look that always made her blush. "I have to admit," he said quietly, "I've been thinking about luring you into my bed since the first time I met you."

And she hadn't been immune to him either. Would having sex with Adrian today be so spur-of-the-moment after all? No matter how much she had resisted feeling anything for him, their attraction had been simmering, just beneath the surface, ever since the first time they met.

Something about Adrian convinced her that she would be safe with him. Not just physically, but emotionally. She knew that if she said yes, he would take care of her, in every sense of the word. She knew that she could let him lead her all the way up to the actual act, and if she backed out at the last minute, he would exhibit nothing but kindness and compassion. "Well, if you're sure we'd have enough time, maybe we could at least…make out a little?"

He grinned like a kid who'd just been given a guitar—or maybe a pony *and* a guitar—for Christmas. "Aside from the fact that more is always better than less…" He glanced at his watch. "I think we might be able to fit a little time for…data collection…into our schedule." He stood and held out his hand. "Shall we?"

Just as they stepped onto the sidewalk outside the restaurant, a pretty young woman with blue hair and blue-painted skin skipped up Decatur Street, stopping to greet any tourists unwary enough to meet her eye. She wore a blue ballerina dress, tights, and shoes and a large pair of iridescent blue fairy wings. She carried an armful of pink roses with blue-tinted edges. She made a graceful curtsy, then plucked a rose from her bouquet and held it out. "A beautiful rose for a beautiful lady."

Heather shook her head no, but Adrian paid for the rose anyway. She might be used to denying herself small pleasures, but he wouldn't let her get away with it when she was with him.

Heather smiled at the woman and accepted the rose, then turned to him, her green eyes soft. "Thank you."

"You are very welcome." He turned his wristwatch toward her. "It's just after two. Do you want to call Reva?"

"Would you mind?" She sounded worried about hurting his feelings but was already digging her phone out of the side pocket of her purse. "I want to give her plenty of notice that she'll have to get the kids after all."

"Not at all." They ambled past the French Quarter shops toward his loft, and Heather had a conversation with Reva about the after-school arrangements. Partway through the call, she gave Adrian a concerned look. "Well," she said to Reva, "what do you think we should do?"

"What?" he mouthed.

"Reva," Heather said into the phone, "I'm gonna put you on speaker. Can you tell Adrian what you just told me?"

Adrian stepped closer to Heather and slipped his arm around her waist.

"I am so sorry, y'all," Reva said, "but I messed up on the timing about picking up that dog."

"Messed up how?" Adrian asked.

"I guess I got my wires crossed because we were extra-busy this morning. Because we caught that cat, you know, and because I was about to host a tour at Bayside Barn, and…well… I'm sorry, but apparently, I misheard the lady I was talking to at the New Orleans vet's office when all that was going on."

Heather started chewing on her fingernail. "Okay, so…"

"I got my days wrong. I heard her say 'today' and was thinking you'd have to get the dog today. But they're actually neutering him today, and you're not supposed to pick him up until tomorrow."

"That's okay, Reva," Heather said. "We'll just bring the shutters and the generators back today, and I'll make another trip to get the dog tomorrow."

"Or we will," Adrian offered. "I don't think you should go by yourself."

She gave Adrian a questioning look. "That's not a problem for you?"

He shook his head. "Of course not." But his mind was already churning on a different scenario. If Reva could keep Heather's kids overnight, Heather and he could spend the night—an entire, long, decadent night—together in New Orleans.

The trailer would be safe where it was; they could leave it until they were heading back to Magnolia Bay with the dog first thing tomorrow—or maybe after a leisurely breakfast of café au lait and beignets at the Café Du Monde.

"I can't let y'all do that," Reva insisted. "It was my mistake, and I'm not going to let you waste your time making a separate trip."

"Sooo…?" Heather said, drawing the word out. "Are you saying that you or Abby would get the dog?"

"No. I'm saying that Adrian has my credit card, and I'm authorizing y'all to use it to spend the night and then get the dog in the morning."

Heather gasped, then clapped a hand over her mouth. She looked at Adrian with wide eyes. "But…but…" she sputtered. "Reva, what about my kids?"

"What about them?" Reva asked with a touch of exasperation in her voice. "We've already decided that I'll bring them to my house after school. And we've already established that I'll stop by your house and let them get their swimsuits for the pool. Why not just tell them to grab whatever they need to spend the night and get ready for school in the morning? I'll take them to school, and you'll be home before they get out at the end of the day tomorrow."

Heather stopped walking and looked at Adrian as if she'd been stunned by a smack upside the head. Her green eyes widened and her mouth dropped open. She covered the phone's speaker and whispered "Should we?"

A few tourists were coming up behind them, so he guided her into the nearest alcove, a brick archway marking the iron-gated entrance to a traditional French Quarter courtyard apartment. He wanted to say yes, but this had to be her decision. "Up to you."

"Reva." Heather's voice wobbled uncertainly. "Can I think about it and call you back?"

"Absolutely. But before we say bye, I want to give you something to think about."

"Okay." Heather leaned against the moss-covered brick.

"When was the last time you spent a night apart from your kids?"

"Well, Erin spends the night at her friends' houses—"

"I didn't ask about Erin. I'm asking about you. How long has it been—"

"Point taken," Heather interrupted. "I'll think about it."

"I also want you to think about the twins. Maybe it's time you gave them a little space too, hmmm? A safe place where they can get out from under your coattails for a while?"

"I'll think about it."

"One more thing, and then I'll let you go: If you and Adrian come straight back today, what's the earliest you could get back?"

"Um…" Heather chewed on her fingernail.

"Dinnertime, maybe," Adrian answered. He leaned a shoulder against the bricks, his arms crossed over his chest. "If we don't run into any snags picking up the trailer or any bad traffic driving back. There aren't many alternate routes along I-10, so if we hit any snarls—"

"You could have the potential joy of sitting on I-10 for hours, or you could instead decide to spend your evening drinking wine at Bacchanal and listening to jazz music."

"That's what I'm saying," Adrian agreed. "Or we could have smooth sailing all the way home tonight, only to sit on the highway for hours tomorrow like we did this morning."

"Stop ganging up." Heather scowled at Adrian. "I said I'll think about it."

"Okay, hon," Reva answered. "That's all I'm asking. Even if y'all do decide to come back to Magnolia Bay tonight, I'll go ahead and make sure your kids pack everything they need for tonight and the morning, just in case. So don't worry about a thing. Just have fun and let me know what you decide. And I know you'll want to talk to the kids no matter what, so I'll keep my phone close."

"Thanks, Reva. Love you, bye." Heather ended the call, tucked her phone away, and gave him a *look*. Her expression was in equal measures agonized and hopeful. "I know we were already toying with the idea, but this makes it feel extra-real. I don't know what to do."

"I can't tell you what to do," he said, "but I guess I can do what Reva did and give you a few things to think about before you make your decision."

She crossed her arms. "Okay, shoot."

He leaned against the opposite wall, giving her plenty of space. "First, I don't want you to feel like deciding to spend the night in New Orleans means that I expect you to do anything you're not ready for. We can flirt the evening away and have a good time, and then you can sleep all by yourself in my guest room. As far as I'm concerned, it's all about giving you a fun and memorable experience…whatever that turns out to be."

She nodded. "Thank you for saying that."

"I'm not just saying it." And he wasn't. Sure, now that they'd come this far, he wanted her in his bed. But it wasn't about just that anymore. He realized that he cared about Heather—as a friend— and as a friend, he only wanted to give her whatever she needed. "If all you want is a friend, I can be that. I don't want you to feel pressured to do anything you're not ready for, and I'm here for you no matter what you decide."

"That means so much to me." She smiled her gratitude. "No matter what happens, I do want us to be friends. That's more important to me than anything right now."

"You've got it." For all the flirting they'd done today, she sounded far from making any sort of decision about the way the rest of the night would go, and that was fine. He stepped away from the wall and held out his right hand with his pinkie finger crooked. "Pinkie swear; no matter what happens, I'm committed to being your friend."

"Me too." She hooked her pinkie finger around his. "I still don't know what to do."

He put his hands on her hips and drew her close, hip to hip, chest to chest, her feet between his widespread legs. "I'm not done telling you all the things you should consider."

She looked up at him through her lashes. "What else should I consider?"

He thought about telling her the menu at Bacchanal or the musicians who'd be playing tonight or the fact that he couldn't decide whether to take her to the Café Du Monde or Riccobono's Panola Street Cafe for breakfast. Instead, he tipped her chin up, leaned in, and kissed her.

———————————

When Adrian kissed her, she could tell that he gave her his complete, focused attention, as if nothing else mattered to him in that moment.

Slowly, he pulled back from the deeper kiss to drop smaller kisses, like tiny blessings, onto each corner of her mouth. "Or maybe I should have told you about the menu and the musicians who'll be playing tonight at Bacchanal?"

An unexpected joy bubbled up inside her. Was she going to go through with this? Maybe… "I'm pretty sure that nothing Bacchanal has to offer could rival the way you kiss."

"I don't know…" He grinned, his confidence on full display. "Their charcuterie board is to die for."

"We can talk about food later." Completely forgetting—okay, maybe just happy to ignore—the fact that tourists were walking past on the sidewalk, she leaned into him, pressing her breasts to his chest. "For now, I think I need you to remind me... What was that last thing you were telling me to consider?"

Adrian kissed her again, and it wasn't just about the way he kissed, Heather realized. It was about the way he slid his hands down her back and spread his fingers across her backside to pull her even closer. It was about the way he smiled while they kissed, so she could feel his happiness at their connection. It was about the way he stayed fully present, responding to her shifting moods and, it seemed, even to the random thoughts that flitted through her consciousness like small, multicolored birds.

Could she say no to this?

No, as it turned out. She couldn't say no.

And before she even gave voice to her decision, it seemed that he felt it. "Let's go then." They walked hand in hand to his loft without talking. The walk took forever but also not quite long enough. Outside the gate, he stopped and looked down at her. His deep-ocean-blue eyes were kind and a bit more serious than his almost-smiling mouth. "You ready?"

"Absolutely." She nodded, then shook her head. "And definitely not."

He laughed. "I think I can help you and your adventurous alter ego reach a consensus of opinion."

He threaded his fingers through hers, and they walked past the poolside lounge chairs where a few people seemed to be zonked out, either sleeping or just soaking up the sun.

They didn't talk—or even kiss—in the elevator, but the silence felt comfortable. It seemed that Adrian was giving her the mind-space she needed to come to terms with what they were about to do together.

Inside his loft, Adrian dropped his keys into the bowl on the hall cabinet, then opened the doors and plugged his phone into a charger port hidden in its depths. A second later, soothing music filled the loft. Heather followed Adrian to his kitchen and leaned against the island bar's white-marble counter while he filled two glasses with water. She set her purse and the rose on the counter. "I was thinking I might need something a little stronger."

"I'm thinking the opposite." He gave her one of the glasses. "I selfishly don't want you to dull your senses."

She gulped her water while he sipped his. He seemed so confident, so relaxed.

"I'm not on birth control," she blurted out.

"I've got that covered." He left her standing at the counter and walked over to the piano, where he sat and played a melody that complemented the music coming through speakers that were set into the ceiling at the corners of the large room. "Just relax. Drink your water. We have plenty of time."

While he played, she wandered over to the couch, but she hesitated to sit for fear that the combination of sunscreen and sweat from walking the French Quarter in the hot sun would leave a mark on the velvet. "I don't know what to do with myself," she confessed.

"What do you want to do?" he asked.

"Lord, I don't know."

"It's almost 4:00. Why don't you call Reva and see how the pickup went? Maybe talk to your kids. You can sit out on the balcony if you want. Watch the river go by."

"Okay, you're right." Knowing her kids were okay would help her feel more settled.

Heather took her phone onto the balcony and sat in one of the chairs. With her feet up on the railing, she called Reva.

"Hey, girl," Reva answered. "How's it going?"

"You first," Heather said. "How it's going here sort of depends on how it's going there."

"All is well. We're on the way to my house. Your kids just collected their things, and they're planning to swim while I cook dinner. I just got a report from Sean that Jasper and Georgia are zonked out in my living room after playing ball for an hour."

Heather felt her anxiety level drop a notch. "That sounds good."

"And not to hurt your feelings, but just so you know, all of your kids are in favor of spending the night at my house. Have you decided which way you're gonna jump?"

Heather took a deep breath and let it out. "I'm going to stay." She felt a dropping sensation in her belly the moment she voiced her decision out loud. It felt like going down in an express elevator. "The phone isn't on speaker, is it?"

"Nope," Reva confirmed. "You are free to speak freely."

"I'm going to spend the night. At Adrian's loft. In his bed. With him. Probably."

"Probably?" Reva laughed. "Who are you trying to kid, me or yourself?"

Heather fiddled with the woven vinyl straps of the metal chair. "Just me, I guess. You'd tell me if I was about to do something really stupid, wouldn't you?"

"Yes, I would." Silence stretched out like taffy before Reva spoke again. "But I can't make your decisions for you. Only you know how you feel."

"I feel like…" Heather gulped. "I feel like it's time. And I feel like I can trust Adrian."

"Well, then…?"

"Please don't tell anyone. Not even Abby."

"I won't even tell Georgia."

"Can I talk to the kids?" Stalling, she knew, but hearing their voices, knowing they truly did want to spend the night away from her, would help her put them out of her mind for the rest of the evening.

"Sure. Here's Caroline."

Heather talked to each of the kids and reassured herself that they were as excited about the night to come as she was nervous. Before Heather ended the call, Erin said the exact perfect thing: "Forget about us, Mom. Concentrate on having fun. That's what we're gonna do, and that's what you should do too."

Heather sat for a few more minutes and watched the Mississippi River flow past. Something about the rushing water helped her let go of all the fear and anxiety she'd been holding on to. It felt right to reach out for a little happiness, a little normalcy.

It was past time she stopped being a widow and started being a woman again. Heather knew that she could trust Adrian to take her gently over that threshold. He would treat her with kindness and sensitivity. She could trust him. But even more important, she realized that she could trust herself.

"It's time," she said out loud. Then she left the river behind and went inside.

Adrian wasn't in the room. "Adrian?" she called.

He came in from the master bedroom she'd seen a glimpse of through its open door when they were in the kitchen. His hair was wet, and all he wore was a cocky grin and a dark-blue towel wrapped around his hips. "Kids okay?"

"Yes. Kids are fine. Everything is fine." Not nearly as fine as he was, though. Holy moly. "They are officially spending the night at Reva's."

"And does that mean you're…?"

"I'm officially spending the night here." Again, her stomach took the express elevator down. "With you. In your bed."

His cocky grin transformed into one of pure delight. "Well, let's get busy."

———

Adrian led Heather to the guest bathroom, the first stop in his planned seduction. He had filled the bathtub with steaming-hot water, then scattered the petals from the rose he'd given her on the surface. He wished he'd had a bunch of candles to really set the mood, but he'd only been able to scare up the one candle he kept in the kitchen cupboard in case of power outages. The flicker of its flame reflected in the mirror, lighting the dim room with a soft orange glow.

He had set out fresh towels and a newly unwrapped bar of fancy-smelling soap that one of his sisters had given him for Christmas last year. He hadn't opened it until now because it smelled too girly.

"Oh," Heather said when she walked into the room. He knew she hadn't expected him to leap on her the second she said she'd stay, but apparently, she hadn't expected to be wooed, either. He decided that he liked surprising her.

He backed her up to the sink, then slowly started unbuttoning her blouse. She closed her eyes and tilted her head back. A fast pulse thrummed visibly under the pale, delicate skin of her neck. He undressed her slowly, taking his time. She tried to help once, lifting her arms to unhook her bra, but he stilled her hands with his. "Let me."

He took charge, hoping to help her win the obvious struggle of turning off her overactive brain so she could concentrate on her body instead. He assisted her into the bath, then knelt beside the tub to scoop handfuls of warm water over her breasts and back.

Sitting cross-legged, she dropped her chin to her chest with a sigh of release.

With tender attention, he slid the soap over her wet skin, dipping his hand below the water's surface to follow the curve of her spine, the flare of her hips. He set the soap aside, then massaged her shoulders until her tense muscles relaxed. "Lean back."

Uncrossing her legs, she stretched out in the tub until her head rested against the porcelain rim and her feet bobbed up, exposing her brightly painted toenails. "Ahhh. This is so nice." She closed her eyes. "I feel so pampered. Thank you."

"You are very welcome," he murmured. Though as he caressed her luscious breasts and watched her nipples contract in response, he knew the gratitude went both ways. "Thank you for letting me pamper you."

He slipped a hand below the waterline, over her ribs and stomach, then even lower. When he slid a finger into the slippery folds between her legs, she sucked in a breath, tensing for a second before she sighed and relaxed, submitting to his touch.

As he moved his hands over her body, he watched her face, aware of the need to go slowly, to be sensitive to her shifting emotions. The lift of her brows, the flutter of her lashes, the softening of her lips were all clues to her boundaries and also to the spaces where he would be welcomed to explore her body. He was willing to back off at any time, should she change her mind.

So as he touched her body, he watched her face, attuned to the subtle expressions that told him when to press forward and when to retreat or redirect her attention to another aspect of the experience. When she tensed, he backed off and softened his touch. When she lifted her hips, he responded by pushing his palm more firmly against her and slipping in not just one finger but two.

When she clutched the sides of the tub and her breath came fast and shallow, he leaned over the bathtub and kissed her. He sucked her tongue into his mouth and swallowed her whimpers as he applied more pressure and mimicked with his hand the things he planned to do with her later, with his body.

When she squirmed against him, he stilled his fingers inside her and fondled her breasts, allowing her to rest a moment and catch her breath.

Then she reached up and captured his face between her palms. He kissed her again, this time swallowing her cries as he brought her to orgasm. She wrapped her arms around his neck, and he held her with one hand supporting her back, the other hand still holding her below the water, where he could feel her orgasm release its hold on her body by slow degrees. When her hands dropped to the sides of the bathtub, he stood and readjusted the towel around his waist. "Feel free to soak as long as you like." He had eased her past the first wall of resistance; a few minutes to acclimate might be welcome. "Come find me in the bedroom when you're ready."

Chapter 12

HEATHER WOULD'VE ENJOYED SOAKING A LITTLE LONGER IN the warm, rose-scented water, but that, of course, became impossible the moment Adrian said, "Come find me in the bedroom."

She hurried to finish, though she took the time to wash her hair and then do a little innocent sleuthing in the sink cabinet, where she found a tube of toothpaste. No brush, but she used a wet washcloth to clean her teeth.

Wrapping a towel around herself, she walked through the loft to the master bedroom, with her heart practically vibrating as far up as her throat and as far down as...

"Don't overthink it," she whispered to herself. "Just enjoy."

And oh, as Heather reached the open door of the master bedroom, the sight she saw could have graced the cover of a romance novel. Well, maybe not because he wasn't stretched out with his arms behind his head and a towel draped strategically across his lap.

He was, in fact, making the bed, smoothing out the sheets and turning back the dark-gray matelassé coverlet. He straightened, saw her, and readjusted the towel he had tucked around his waist. "Hey."

In the dim natural light that came through a long, narrow window near the ceiling, Adrian's every muscle seemed to be highlighted in gold against the shadowed dips and curves and hollows. She tucked in the edge of her towel too, a small gesture of self-protection. She felt safe with Adrian, but it had been a long time since even Dale had seen her naked, and he had always seen her through the eyes of love. "Hey."

Adrian folded the sheet and coverlet back again, then sat on the edge of the bed and patted the mattress beside him. "Come here."

She hesitated, not because she didn't want to sit next to Adrian but because she straight up couldn't get her feet to move. Then the logjam of self-consciousness that held her captive broke apart, and she walked across the carpeted floor and sat beside him.

Feeling awkward, she reached for Adrian's hand. They sat there for a minute, just holding hands, getting used to each other again after less than ten minutes apart. She listened to his easy breathing, felt the comforting strength of his hand holding hers, absorbed the warmth of his hard, muscular thigh against her leg. "Do you think we need to talk first?" she asked.

He huffed out a laugh and squeezed her hand. "Not too much, I hope." She looked up at him, reconnecting a little more firmly with that glance. "But yes," he said. His deep voice sounded as soft as a caress. "If you think we need to talk, we need to talk. Tell you what… Close your eyes."

He let go of her hand, and with her eyes closed, she could hear him moving: standing, then slipping under the covers and read-justing the pillows. "Okay," he said. "Now, I'll close mine so you can lose the towel and get under the sheets with me. I promise I won't peek."

She turned to look. He was reclining against the headboard with a pillow behind him, his hands stacked on top of the sheet and coverlet folded down over his washboard abs. True to his word, his eyes were closed.

"What should I do with the towel?"

"I tossed mine on top of the sheets I just changed," he said without opening his eyes.

In the corner of the room closest to the door, she saw the neatly rolled-up sheets he had just exchanged for fresh ones. She took a second to appreciate the courteous sensitivity Adrian displayed in changing the bed linens for her.

"You haven't gotten lost, have you?" Adrian quipped, still without opening his eyes. Did she detect a tiny note of worry in his voice?

Yes, she did.

His smooth self-confidence might not be as impermeable as he let on. "Should I whistle a tune," he asked, "to help you find your way?"

"No. Sorry. Just…" She sighed and tossed her towel on top of his. "Woolgathering."

She slid in beside him, propped a pillow against the smooth wood of the headboard behind her, and adjusted the sheets so they covered her breasts. "You can open your eyes now."

He gave her a tender look and reached for her hand. "Hey, again."

"Hey, again." She let out a huff of embarrassed laughter. "Am I being a real pain?"

"Absolutely." His lips quirked up at the corners; his gaze was soft and sexy. "And you're totally worth it. Come here." He slid an arm behind her and gathered her into his arms, fitting her body snugly against his. "Now." He kissed the top of her head. "How's this?"

"Better." With her head on his shoulder and her body curved around his, she felt more at ease. They seemed to fit perfectly together. "Thank you for indulging me."

"Oh, darlin'." He drew the word out in the Southern way, then chuckled, a dark, slightly sinister sound. "I haven't even started indulging you." He caressed her shoulder and upper arm with his fingertips. "But we have all the time in the world." He rolled her toward him until she was halfway on top of him.

Then he kissed her, a long and lingering exploration that derailed her churning thoughts. He tunneled his fingers through her damp hair and held her still while he kissed her eyelids, then the corners of her mouth, then her jaw, and then the side of her neck just below her ear. It tickled, so she brought up her shoulder and tilted her head, a silent plea for him to stop.

He made a low growling sound and rolled them again until she was lying prone, trapped beneath him. "Ticklish much?" He took her hands in his, and a second later, he held her with both wrists manacled in his right hand while he straddled her, his knees on either side of her hips. He made the low, slightly sinister chuckle she'd heard before. "I wonder what I should do with this new information?"

"Nothing," she said in a warning tone. "You'd better not tickle me; not if you want to get out of here alive."

"Oh, yeah?" The bedding between them had slipped—or maybe Adrian had managed the magic trick of making the sheets and bed-spread disappear. Her breasts and belly were exposed to him, and his gorgeous masculine form—even the part that was clearly very glad to see her—was bared for her to see...but not to touch.

"What ya gonna do about it if I want to do this?" Still holding her wrists in one hand, he bent to kiss that ticklish spot again, this time giving it a light nibble or two that did entirely different things to her nerve endings. He kissed—and bit, ever so gently—a path down her neck and then lingered on her collarbones. "What ya gonna do if I want to..."

He released her wrists and trailed his fingers down her belly. He knelt between her legs and sucked her nipples, first one, then the other, until she arched toward his mouth, begging for more even while she craved his attention a bit farther down.

His mouth followed his fingers, and then she felt the pressure of both his hands holding her hips and lifting them higher, baring her even further for him to explore.

She squirmed at first, but he held her firm until she subsided with a sigh of submission and then another of delight. All she could do was let her hands fall to her sides, let her trembling thighs fall open against the cool sheets, and let him have his way.

———

Adrian took his time learning the tastes and textures of Heather's body, from the soft skin of her inner thighs to the sweeping curve of her hips to the long arch of her neck. He took his time learning her signals, from the soft sigh when she relaxed into his hands to the shuddering indrawn breath when he touched her in just the right way to the quiet moans when he brought her closer to the edge.

He used every trick in his arsenal to bring Heather from thinking to feeling, from sighing to whimpering, from "yes, yes," to "oh, yes."

But he denied her the ultimate release of a full-on, crying-out, shuddering orgasm. Every time he felt her getting close, he gentled his touch, toning down her blazing response for a slower but ultimately hotter burn.

He wanted to prolong the experience for each of them, to be mindful…

But her gorgeous body spoke to his through its erotic movements and the scent of her arousal, and all his careful mindfulness dissolved. His determination to curate her experience had no more strength than a sandcastle scattered in the waves of an incoming tide. He'd been intent on crafting an amazing sexual experience for her, but instead, pleasing her had given him the most incredible sexual experience *he'd* ever had.

And he hadn't even been inside her yet.

At the thought of his body inside hers, the ability to hold off on his own pleasure began to shred like a paper kite in the wind. This time, when he used his mouth and his hands to bring her to the edge of orgasm, he didn't try to tamp down the fire. This time, he let her quiet moans intensify. And when "yes" turned to "don't stop," he obliged.

It wasn't until she lay there, gasping for breath, that his brain came back online and he had another thought for himself. He crawled up to the bedside table, keeping a physical connection between them by resting a hand on her thigh. He ripped open the condom's foil wrapper with his teeth, rolled the condom on one-handed, and then eased up close to lie beside her.

Past ready for it to be his turn, he still wasn't taking it for granted. He propped his head on one hand and looked down at her satisfied expression while he trailed an idle finger down the center of her body, from neck to navel, then down to touch the soft skin he could still feel twitching from the gradual slowdown of a massive orgasm. "You okay?"

She huffed out a laugh, and her eyelids fluttered open. "Okay?" She laughed again, a weak wheeze, and closed her eyes again. "I'm so much better than okay."

"Up for round two?"

"Round…" She looked down and noticed his predicament. "Oh. Round two." A sweet smile spread across her face, and she opened her arms to him. "You'd better believe I'm ready for round two."

When she took him inside her, her body was a revelation of softness and warmth.

He'd been expecting that.

But when she took his face in her hands, looked him in the eyes, and whispered, "Thank you" before kissing him with disarming sincerity, he found that the polished seduction he had attempted couldn't compare with the brutal power of her innocent honesty. Some latent emotion that had been hiding out in the unused corners of his heart twisted and snapped, and he knew he was done for. He'd known from the beginning this wasn't the casual sex he was used to, but it wasn't the carefully crafted experience he'd been determined to provide either.

This was something else entirely. Something he'd never experienced before.

Then she grabbed his shoulders, digging in with her fingernails. She wrapped her legs around his butt, hooked her ankles together, and squeezed to draw him in even farther. She bit the side of his neck and sucked so hard he knew he'd have a hickey in the morning. Then she bucked her hips, and after that, all he could do was hold on and hope he survived.

Thankfully, his body knew what to do. Because his mind had

been blown by the emotional explosion that broke open his heart when she held him close and tucked her face into his shoulder. Her muffled cries signaled her orgasms, one tumbling over another as he answered his need to bury his body inside hers, faster, harder, deeper.

He heard his own harsh gasps for breath, felt the cry of completion wrung from his lungs when the pulsing of her inner muscles forced his release. His arms trembled and then collapsed. Her soft breasts cushioned his heaving chest. Her cool skin absorbed his heat. Her heart pounded in time with his.

"Wow," he wheezed, his voice as ragged as an old man's. He dropped his face into the pillow beside her and tried to breathe normally.

She kissed the side of his ear, and he felt her lips curve in a satisfied smile. "You okay?" she whispered.

"Not..." he barely managed to mumble, "sure yet."

Powerless to move a muscle, he all but passed out. He might have been somewhat conscious of Heather shoving his dead weight off to the side and smoothing the sweat off his brow, but maybe that was just a dream.

He woke hours later with Heather draped over him, sleeping hard. His arms and legs were chilled, though the parts where he and Heather touched were toasty warm.

Maybe a little too warm.

He eased out from under her, found the sheets and coverlet on the floor, and then drew them gently over her, up to the shoulders.

If he were an artist, he wouldn't have covered her. If he were an artist, he would have found his sketchpad and charcoal, and he'd have drawn her naked body, sleeping and sated and so beautiful that the sight of her made his heart ache and urged his exhausted body to come alive again.

He padded out of the bedroom and closed the door silently behind him. He stood naked in the dark loft and gazed through the windows that overlooked the river. The sky hovered close, a dark, impenetrable blue. Through the windows that faced the French Quarter, lights twinkled, expanding the view. The faint sounds of music and revelry drifted in past the double-paned glass.

As he'd encouraged Heather to do earlier, he let himself pretend, just for a second, that he could be a different person if he chose. If he were the sort of man who actually wanted to settle down, could Heather fit into his life in this place?

Yes, of course. But her kids…?

No. The French Quarter loft lifestyle was not exactly a kid-friendly environment.

So the next logical question was, could he fit into her life?

He hadn't thought that far ahead—hell, he hadn't thought much past getting her in his bed. And he definitely hadn't thought that Heather might have the power to crack his heart open and burrow inside. He had planned to gift her with a stepping-stone that would lead her to a new beginning in her life. He hadn't realized that he might feel the need to go with her past that point.

Just pretending… What if he had the guts to abandon everything he'd thought he wanted and buy into a completely different plan, one he'd never considered before?

Adrian's imagination didn't stretch far enough to see himself stepping into a ready-made family. He wouldn't have any problem providing for Heather and her kids financially. (Honestly, he made a ridiculous amount of money doing work he enjoyed whenever he felt like doing it.) He could, if he wanted to, set Heather and her kids up in fine style and continue to live the life he lived, only popping over to Magnolia Bay whenever life on the road and partying in New Orleans got dull.

He had a sneaking suspicion that Heather wouldn't be satisfied with that.

But he wasn't capable of anything more.

Best to go back to plan A, giving Heather a respite from real life that she'd never forget, then going back to being friends. Or maybe friends with benefits.

His stomach growled, thankfully interrupting his circling thoughts. "Food," he said to himself out loud. He had thought that he would take Heather out for dinner and live music at Bacchanal, but by now, the place would be too crowded. To snag a table, they'd have to circle like sharks, looking for diners who might be making motions to pay their bills.

Not exactly romantic.

Frenchmen Street bustled with places that offered Cajun food and live music, and it was only a quick walk from the loft. If Heather were any other woman, he would make haste to get dressed and hustle them both out the door in search of a new adventure, a change of pace, a different vibe.

But he wanted to keep Heather to himself, at least until they had to leave here in the morning. Tonight might be all they had, so he decided to make the most of it. He ordered dinner to be delivered from the bistro in the building. He made the call and got way too much food in an effort to give Heather another long-overdue experience of being pampered.

No matter how this turned out or whether it lasted past tomorrow, Adrian wanted to remind Heather what it was like to be cherished.

―――――――――

Heather woke slowly in a pitch-dark room that smelled of sex… along with the drifting aroma of *food*. The cool, soft sheets that covered her moved aimlessly when she did. They weren't anchored to the bed, so she sat up and wrapped the bedclothes around her. The room wasn't entirely dark, she realized. A sliver of light barred the bottom of the closed bathroom door, behind which she could hear the hiss of water hitting a glass shower door. *Adrian*.

Adrian, with whom she had just luxuriated in several blissed-out hours of mind-blowing sex.

"Slow down," she said to her galloping imagination. She wasn't planning to allow Adrian into her life just yet, if ever. But she was damn sure gonna allow him to take charge of her life for at least the next fourteen or so hours because the last ten had been pretty damn incredible.

She left the sheets and coverlet piled on the bed and opened the door of the master bathroom, where Adrian stood in the shower, his arms lifted to comb his fingers through his hair while water pelted down his perfectly sculpted body.

Feeling her eyes on him, he wiped his face and opened the shower door. "Hey, honey. Come on in."

She joined him beneath the shower spray, and he closed the door behind her, then turned a tap that suddenly had water pelting them both from all angles. Surprised, she grabbed onto him and huddled close while she got used to the stinging spray. He rubbed his hands up and down her back, then cupped her backside and turned her so the water hit her with an oblique spray instead of head-on.

She turned her face up to his. "Did you just call me honey?"

He grinned, then dipped down to steal a quick kiss. His wet lips slid against hers, silky-sweet. "Yep, I guess I did."

"Okay. I'll take that." She took the initiative and kissed him back. "I'm okay with being called honey…but only by you…and maybe only in private."

He kissed her again, smiling against her mouth. "You do taste pretty sweet, so it's only fair, right?"

"Only fair," she replied, her voice already sounding breathy because he had backed her up against the shower's white-tile walls. He rubbed her down with a slippery bar of something that smelled suspiciously like cheap antibacterial soap, then set the soap aside and ran his hands over her skin while the water pelted down on them both.

He kissed her, and his mouth tasted clean and minty, like toothpaste.

She pulled away. "No fair. You brushed your teeth. I don't have a toothbrush."

"Aw, jeez. I'm sorry. I didn't think about that. I'll give you a new toothbrush. I have a drawer full of them."

"You do?" The only reason she could imagine was that Adrian liked to be prepared for the parade of women who ended up spending the night with him.

"Get your mind out of the gutter." He gave her a little pop on the butt, a playful spanking. "It's not what you're thinking."

"Yeah, well what is it?"

"I used to date a dental hygienist. She gave me a whole case of toothbrushes that some company gave her."

"Okay, you're off the hook." Not that he was ever on the hook in the first place. He most definitely wasn't on *her* hook. "As long as you deliver on the toothbrush before you kiss me again."

He narrowed his eyes at her, giving a sultry look. "I'm not sure I can do that. In fact, let's conduct a test…" He lowered his head and kissed her again. "All I can taste is my own mint."

"I don't care." She bit his bottom lip, gently sucking it into her mouth before letting go. "I still want my toothbrush."

He reached past her and turned off the water, then stepped out of the shower, giving her an excellent view of him in the altogether—as in altogether naked—this time unobscured by water or steam or even a clear pane of glass between his body and her ability to see it.

She resolved to look her fill, since this might be the last time she got to see such a magnificent sight.

With his back to her, he rattled around in a cabinet drawer, but she could see his front in the mirror. A near-panoramic view. He met her eyes in the mirror. "What?"

She grinned. "Just enjoying the view, in case it's the last time I get to see it."

He held out a new, pink, cellophane-wrapped toothbrush. "I'm not sure I want to sacrifice a brand-new toothbrush for you if you're not coming back again."

She tried to take the toothbrush, but he wouldn't let go of it.

She gave it a little tug. "I don't want to take anything for granted, that's all."

He held his end of the toothbrush in a firm grip. "Let's pretend for a minute that we both want to do this again. Are you willing to come back?"

"Well, yeah, if I can manage it. I do have three kids though. Getting away isn't as easy as you might think." This was ridiculous, standing here naked, drip-drying on the fluffy bathroom rug, arguing over whether he was going to give her a toothbrush. She gave the toothbrush another tug.

He tightened his grip. "But you're not discounting the possibility?"

"Not at all." She tried again to take the toothbrush, but he held on. She made a huff of frustration. "Are you gonna give me the damn toothbrush or not?"

He still scowled at her, and she searched his expression for some hint of a teasing grin, but he looked pretty grim. "I'm just beginning to wonder," he said, "if you were planning all along to take advantage of me and then cut me loose."

Her mouth dropped open. "I wasn't *planning* anything. For the first time in my fucking life, I was going with the flow. Enjoying myself. Pretending we could be…I don't know…whatever *this* is." She gestured to the two of them standing naked in his bathroom. "I thought that was what you wanted me to do. Was I wrong?"

He let go of the toothbrush. "No. Not wrong." He whipped a towel off the bar and wrapped it around himself, then handed her a folded one from the shelf above the toilet. "I ordered dinner. It's on the table. Let's eat it before it gets cold."

―――――――――

In the kitchen, Adrian took the lids off the food that had been delivered right before he got in the shower. He had already set the table with two place settings, with the unlit candle from the guest bathroom between them.

The candle seemed stupid now.

He stuck a serving spoon into every container but the soup, which he poured into two bowls. As he spooned a swirl of sorbet into each soup bowl and sprinkled croutons on top, he scoffed at himself for being such a dumbass.

What on earth had compelled him to act that way? For some reason even he couldn't fathom, he had gone from seduction mode to whatever mode he'd slipped into for no reason. He wasn't used to examining his emotions—he'd never been much into navel-gazing. But something had gone seriously off-course here, and he knew that the problem was all his.

Heather came into the room, wrapped in a bath towel and looking rightfully hesitant, since he had just tried to start an argument over a damn toothbrush. "I'm sorry," he said, straightaway. "I'm an ass."

"No, you're not an ass." She took in the table he had set with plain-white china and heavy flatware. "This looks beautiful." He had left a lighter next to the candle; she lit the candle and laid the lighter aside. "What can I do to help?"

He pulled out a chair for her. "Sit. I'll open the wine."

"Wow, look at all this food."

He pushed her chair in, taking the opportunity to kiss the side of her neck. "I wasn't sure what you'd like, so I got a bunch of different stuff for you to try."

"It all looks and smells delicious. But we'd have to stay here for a week to eat all this."

He poured wine into both their glasses, then sat across from her and gave a rueful grin. "I wish." And he realized that he did truly wish they had more time together. Maybe that was part of the reason he'd acted so childishly just now.

"Maybe..." He shook his head. "Never mind." He'd been about to try to explain his actions, but how could he when he could hardly figure them out himself? Better to just start over and try to recapture the romantic scene he'd been so careful to set before he messed it up.

She let his unfinished comment pass and held her glass up. "To our new friendship."

He clinked his glass to hers. "To our new friendship." He wanted to add more, to tack on an *and*... but couldn't decide what it would be. And *that*, he realized, was exactly his problem. He leaned back in his chair and crossed his arms, watching Heather eat her soup. "What do you think?"

She looked up, her green eyes smiling. "It's amazing." A tiny frown line appeared between her pale brows. "Aren't you going to eat yours?"

"I'm having too much fun watching you." She gave him a quirky look, and he picked up his spoon. "But yeah. I'm gonna eat."

By the time they finished dinner, he had managed to regain his sense of perspective. Mainly because Heather had so easily forgiven his momentary lapse of both manners and judgment.

Heather started putting the lids back on the containers.

"Nope, none of that. I'll do it."

"Okay." She sat back with a cheeky grin and put her hands in her lap. "I'm guessing you have a better idea?"

"I think so." He picked up the wine bottle and held it to the light; it was about half-full. "You want to split the rest of this wine and take our glasses out on the balcony?"

"Yes, please." She held out her glass. "I would love that."

He poured the wine, clinked his glass to hers, and took a sip. "You go ahead. I'll put all this away and meet you out there."

She grabbed her phone off the counter. "I'm gonna check in with the kids real quick."

"Take your time." After she went outside, he put away the leftover food, stacked the dishwasher, then went into the laundry room to put their clean clothes in the dryer. When he joined her on the balcony, she was leaning back in one of the patio chairs with her feet propped on the railing.

He had always appreciated her generous curves, her breasts and hips so lush and ripe with a softly inward-curving waistline that gave her a subtle hourglass shape. But he hadn't truly appreciated her legs until just this minute because she usually kept them hidden under slightly baggy jeans. Even the denim skirt she sometimes wore hid more than it accentuated. Perfect attire for her job, of course, but he would love to see her wearing a soft, curve-hugging dress with a short hemline.

Although he had no complaints about the towel she was wearing. "How are things back home?"

"Wonderful." She sighed. "My kids love Reva more than they love me, and they love Bayside Barn more than they love their own home."

"That's good." He sat beside her, then leaned over to steal a kiss. "Our clothes are in the dryer, so if you want to take a walk later, we can do that."

She sipped her wine. "We can if you want to, but I'm quite happy to sit here and watch the river go by."

"Works for me." He propped his feet on the rail right beside hers, close enough to play footsie. He stroked her pinkie toe with his. "We could go to bed early, if you want."

"Good idea," she said. "Then we could get up early and—"

He reached out to take her hand. "I wasn't thinking about *sleeping*."

"Ohhh." She drew the word out, slow and sexy. "I could be okay with that too."

"But first, I want to apologize again for being a butthead earlier."

"Not necessary; it wasn't even a thing, really."

"But it *was* a thing, and I think I've figured out why I temporarily lost my mind."

She laughed. "Okay, I'll bite."

"I was so busy trying to get you in my bed that—"

"Oh yeah? You were?"

"Yes. I was so intent on seducing you that I didn't think through what would happen afterward."

"Does it bother you that I want to keep this just between us?"

"No, that's not it. I understand that you want to protect your kids, and I admire that."

"So…"

"I thought, going into this, that I would be completely happy to seduce you and show you a good time and be your initiation into…into"—he swirled his hand—"all this, and then be just as happy for us to go our separate ways afterward."

"And now?" Her tone was gentle.

"Now, I'd like to… I mean, I'd like to if you'd like to…"

She squeezed his hand but didn't speak. With her green eyes glowing in the moonlight, she waited for him to gather his thoughts.

"I'd like to keep seeing each other, even if we have to do it in secret for a while." He took a breath in and let it out, surprised at how shaky it sounded, even to him. "I think I'd like to see where this goes."

She smiled, looking as serene and calm as he was nervous. "I'd like that too," she said.

Chapter 13

HEATHER HAD THOUGHT NOTHING COULD TOP ADRIAN'S expert skills in bed.

Until they finally wore each other out and he snuggled her close, spooning her from behind, with his arm draped over her waist, holding her breast lightly in his hand.

This, she decided sleepily, this blissed-out-in-the-afterglow cuddling, might be better than sex.

Adrian kissed the back of her neck. "If you wake up before me, check to be sure I'm still breathing, then make yourself at home."

"Unlikely that I'll wake up before you do." She sighed. "I may sleep till noon."

A second later, she heard his breathing slow and deepen. She smiled to herself and fell asleep, feeling protected and cared for and maybe even just a little bit loved.

She woke the next morning to the scents of coffee and clean laundry. "Coffee on the bedside table." He dropped her clean folded clothes on the bed beside her.

He was already fully dressed in khaki-green cargo shorts and a black T-shirt with a fleur-de-lis logo from the Three-Legged Dog Bar & Grill. His hair was still damp from a shower. "We can hit Riccobono's for breakfast on our way to pick up that dog, unless you'd prefer beignets at the Café Du Monde."

All this food talk was making her hungry. "What if I want it all?"

He grinned. "Darlin', if you want it all, I'll make sure you get it all."

"And yet," she said with a pout, "you are standing there with all your clothes on." She rocked forward onto her hands and knees and looked down. "Shoes too."

He smacked her backside. "Get dressed. I will be waiting for you on the balcony."

She showered and dressed in under ten minutes, then found Adrian leaning on the balcony, looking out over the river. She came up behind him and wrapped her arms around his waist.

He turned and gave her a coffee-flavored kiss. "Hey, you." With his back against the railing, he spread his legs wide and brought her hips up to his, linking his hands at the small of her back. "Reva called while you were in the shower. All is well; the kids had a good night, and she just got back from dropping them off at school."

"That's good to hear. Thank you."

"She also said that we can't get that dog until noon."

"Why?" It almost seemed like Reva was somehow colluding with that vet's office to manufacture reasons for Heather and Adrian to spend more time together.

"They want to give him a bath first."

"Does it feel to you like Reva might be…I don't know…instigating something between us on purpose?"

A slow, sexy smile grew on his face. "I don't know, but if she is, I'll be the first to thank her for it." He kissed her, and this kiss held a hint of goodbye, or maybe it was just sadness that their time together—at least *this* time together—was ending.

Though Adrian had committed to coming to ride Charlie a couple of times a week, Heather was about to start working full-time, so even then, he'd be at her house when she'd be at the shelter. She wouldn't see him unless they made specific plans.

He pulled away slowly and stared down at her, his deep-blue eyes somber. "Let's go make the most of our time in the Big Easy."

Adrian locked up, and the two of them strolled hand in hand through Crescent Park on the way to Decatur Street, where they paused often to window-shop. Heather appreciated Adrian's patience with her. She stopped to look in the window of an antique jewelry store and pointed to a poison ring in the display. "I've always wanted one of those."

"Then you should have one." He put a hand at her waist and leaned in for a closer look. "You never know when you might need to poison someone."

"I like the fact that it has a hidden compartment for hiding secret potions."

"Appeals to the witch within, huh?" He kissed the side of her neck.

"Something like that." She enjoyed the idea of intrigue, the sense of history. "Can you imagine the potential schemes and conspiracies and machinations that might have caused someone to need a ring they could fill with poison?"

"I dread to think."

She smirked at him. "I'm a little worried about your lack of imagination." Clearly, he had never read a Gothic romance novel.

She turned to go, but he held her back. "Let's go inside."

"I wasn't serious about wanting one of those rings." She'd never had the time or the money for anything so frivolous and unnecessary, no matter how intriguing it might be. "I don't need anything in there."

"I think you do." With both hands on her hips, he steered her through the store's open doorway and waved to the store's proprietors, a couple of gray-haired men sitting at the far end of the shop behind a counter. "She'd like to try on a ring we saw in the window."

"I really don't need a ring," she protested.

One of the men came out from behind the counter. "Which one do y'all want to see?"

"The gold poison ring with the blue stone."

The man unlocked the door to the window case and placed the ring in Heather's palm. "This blue sapphire ring is from the early Victorian era, eighteen-karat gold."

She slipped the ring on her finger. It fit perfectly. And she had to admit, it was pretty. But... She took it off and held it out to the shopkeeper. "Thank you for letting me try it on, but I don't need a ring."

The man took the ring back, his lips pursed with displeasure over being made to indulge a tourist who had nothing better to do than try on a ring she never intended to buy.

Adrian handed out a credit card. "We'll take it."

While the man toddled off to ring up the sale, Adrian wrapped his arms around Heather from behind and whispered in her ear. "It fits. Reva would say that's a sign from God."

"Somehow," she whispered back, "I don't think God interferes in jewelry purchases." But when Adrian slipped the ring onto her finger right before they left the store, she had to admit she was glad he'd insisted on buying it for her. Now, no matter what happened between them going forward, she would have a lasting memento of their time together.

———

After café au lait and beignets at the Café Du Monde, Adrian and Heather walked around Jackson Square toward St. Louis Cathedral. He noticed her glance into a couple of shop windows, but she didn't pause for a closer inspection. "Why aren't you stopping to look? We have plenty of time."

"I'd like to window-shop," she said, "but now I'm afraid you might decide to buy something else for me."

He put a hand over his heart. "I swear, I won't buy anything else for you today."

"Thank you." She dragged him toward a toy shop on the square. "Because I really want to go in here." The two window displays that flanked the old-fashioned wood-and-glass door were filled with the kind of dolls whose staring glass eyes had the power to keep people up at night.

"Those dolls are kind of creepy."

"You can wait outside if you're scared."

Actually, he kind of was. "I'll wait here." He pointed to a bench outside the store.

She smirked at him. "Scaredy-cat."

"I am pretty sure that at least half of those dolls come to life at night, and the other half probably bite without warning. But you go ahead and have fun."

He released her hand and backed away, waving as if it might be the last time he saw her. "If you don't come out in half an hour, I'll come in after you. But I've gotta say, I won't be holding out much hope of your survival."

She stuck her tongue out at him. "I'll see you in fifteen minutes."

He sat on the bench between the shops and the pop-up art displays outside the Cathedral Park's fence. He checked his texts and sent replies, then waded through emails.

He'd been very bad at checking in on clients, especially considering it was the middle of the week. He hadn't even looked at his phone or his laptop since yesterday morning, and now he was getting a few emails with subject lines that started with S.O.S.

He replied first to the one with the subject line of S.O.Fucking-S.

He was just hitting Send when Heather sat next to him. "I thought you said you'd come save me if I stayed longer than thirty minutes."

"Damn." He glanced at his watch. "I'm sorry. I got distracted." He made a big show of checking her arms for bite marks. "Are you okay?"

She slung a fancy drawstring bag from the shop onto the bench between them. "My checking account has suffered."

"Yeah?" He tugged at the drawstring. "If I look in there, will a zombie doll bite me?"

"I hope not because you're my ride home. But anyway, you can't see it. They gift-wrapped it already. It's a ballerina fairy doll for Caroline. That means I have to find something special for Josh and Erin too."

He stood and took her hand. "I know exactly where we need to go."

He knew how—and where—to shop because he had two younger sisters who had moved away from New Orleans but loved to come back and stay at his loft whenever they could get away from their jobs, husbands, and kids. Hand in hand, Adrian and Heather noodled back toward his loft, zigzagging from one interesting shop to the next. She bought a stack of artisan-made bangle bracelets for Erin and an assortment of cool fossilized shells for Josh.

Just after noon, they made it to the vet's office to pick up the three-legged dog, who had been named Bones by the vet staff. Heather paid the bill while Adrian took the dog outside for a pit stop. Bones—a handsome, mostly white Catahoula-and-American-bulldog mix with one blue eye and one brown eye—still hadn't quite figured out the logistics of hiking to pee with only one back leg.

"Nawww," Adrian said with a grimace. "Don't do it that way."

The poor dog had sidled up to a shrub to hike but was facing the wrong way, so he ended up aiming the wrong way and peeing on his front legs instead of out to the side.

You'd have thunk that peeing out past the missing back leg would have been a natural choice, but the dog—two years old by the vet's reckoning—must have been used to hiking the leg he now had no choice but to stand on. "Dude. That ain't right."

Adrian led the dog over to the truck and rummaged through the thoughtfully prepared bag Reva had packed for the trip. Under the dog toys, the paper towels, the poop bags, and a baggie of dog treats, he found a packet of wet wipes. "Come here, dude. Let's get you cleaned up." He knelt and cleaned the dog's front legs, then he walked over to the cleanup station outside the office and discarded the used wipe.

The dog moved awkwardly to keep up, taking a step with each

front leg, then hopping up with the back leg. The unnatural gait seemed to put a lot of strain on that back leg and hip but also on the dog's spine because it had to arch out long to accommodate the front legs' forward steps, then hunch over with every hop of the back leg to catch up. "You're gonna love the pool, buddy." Swimming would enable the dog to gain some fluidity of motion and build muscle without putting so much strain on his joints.

Heather came outside, carrying a bag of dog food and another, smaller bag with medicine and paperwork. She bent to pet the dog's head. "Ready to go home, Bones?"

The dog smiled up at Heather, his eyes half-closed with joy over being touched. But he didn't show any recognition of his name. Adrian took the bags from her and gave her the dog's leash. "I want to try something. Y'all stay right there. Keep petting him."

He walked toward the truck, then turned around and called the dog's name. The dog didn't take a blind bit of notice. "Now, stop petting him for a second."

Heather took her hand off the dog's head. "Bones," he called. Then again, a little louder. The dog glanced over when Adrian raised his voice, but again, didn't show any of the signs of name recognition he would have expected. "Did you see that? His ears didn't go forward. He didn't acknowledge that I was calling him."

Heather nodded, then went back to petting. "Well, he was a stray. He hasn't been named Bones for very long."

"I don't think Bones is the best name for him. I mean, he's not skinny, and he's not an orthopedic surgeon or a forensic pathologist, so the name doesn't make sense. We ought to change it."

"He was very skinny when someone brought him in after he'd been hit by a car."

"Well, he's not skinny now." Adrian put the bags on the back floorboard, then picked up the dog and put him in the large crate on the back seat.

"I don't mind changing his name. Reva says animals often want a different name to mark a new passage of life, and this qualifies." Heather tossed in a stuffed toy and a chew antler from the bag Reva had provided, then latched the crate door. "We can discuss it on the drive home."

But the dog wasn't up for any sort of discussion. He was in output mode only. They'd hardly gotten out of the parking lot before he started scratching at the crate. He whined, then he howled, then he whined some more.

Heather gave treats to the dog, hummed to the dog, sang to the dog.

Adrian turned up the music, turned down the music, changed the music. He tried cool jazz, soft rock, mellow instrumental. Nothing helped.

"Maybe we should pull over and get him out of the crate," Heather suggested. "He wants to sit up here with us."

"I'm not gonna stop on the side of the highway and take the dog out of the car to get him into the front seat. It's too risky. We're almost at the generator place; we'll handle it then."

Meanwhile, the dog kept singing the songs of his people. He might be one leg shy of a full complement, but there was nothing wrong with his lungs. "Maybe we should name him Pavarotti," Adrian suggested.

"I see your lips moving," Heather yelled above the dog's howls. "But all I can hear is this dog hollering."

When they reached their next destination, Adrian and Heather worked together to leash the dog, then Adrian lifted him out of the back seat and set his three legs on the ground. "Did Reva pack a doggie seat belt so he can sit up front?"

Heather leaned into the back seat to riffle through the bag, and Adrian took the opportunity to admire her backside. Even though her jeans were baggy, there was no hiding her curves.

"Found it." She came out holding a short strap with a leash-style clip on one end and a seat belt buckle on the other. Then she

MAGNOLIA BAY MEMORIES 221

noticed that he'd been ogling her and gave his backside a playful swat with the strap. "You are bad."

He grinned, unrepentant. "Is that a bad thing?"

She took the dog's leash and nodded toward a grassy patch by the fence. "I'll see if he needs a potty break while you check in with the office and hitch up the trailer."

The rest of the drive to Magnolia Bay was much more peaceful. The dog slept with his head on Heather's lap and his one back leg sprawled out across Adrian's thigh. While the dog snored, the two humans discussed likely dog names but didn't come up with any winners. They talked about shelter business, with Heather telling Adrian about all the vendors she'd secured for the grand opening fund-raiser on Labor Day.

"Was I supposed to have done something?" He had a sneaking memory that they'd tried to rope him into something during that last meeting, but he'd been surreptitiously texting with clients on his phone and only halfway paying attention.

"You were," she said with a pretend scowl. "But I took care of it. You will, however, be in charge of doing all the accounting afterward."

"I thought I told y'all to hire an accountant." In fact, he was sure that he *did* remember that part of the meeting. "Once y'all are up and running in not-so-many days, I won't be—"

He cut himself off too late. Though he and Heather had agreed to continue seeing each other, what he'd just said must have sounded to her like he was already backing out.

Heather sat a little more stiffly than before. "I am aware of that." Her shift in posture disturbed the dog, who woke and gave a concerned look around, then raised his head to lick Heather's chin. She petted his head, giving her entire attention to the dog and avoiding looking at Adrian altogether.

Why was she being so touchy? Not so long ago, he'd been the one asking her to consider taking their relationship further—or at least being open to the possibility. Now she seemed pissed that he wasn't planning to live in her back pocket. "You know that after Monday, y'all won't need me so much at the shelter."

She nodded, still without looking at him.

"But that doesn't mean I won't be coming to see *you*, Heather. And Charlie. I'll still ride him a couple times a week, like I promised."

"I'm sure you will." She crossed her legs and started swinging her foot. "And I'll be working full-time as of Monday morning, so I probably won't be there."

"I'll still come around to the shelter and check on y'all."

"Yep." She spit the word out. "Once a week for a month was the deal, I believe?"

He reached over the dog and took Heather's hand. The dog licked his arm, spreading love and saliva with liberal abandon. "And we'll still spend time together, yeah? Maybe you'll invite me to stay for dinner sometimes when I come over to ride Charlie? And maybe you can arrange for babysitting every now and then so we can spend time together, just the two of us?"

She smiled, but it wasn't the kind of smile that made her cheeks go plump. "Of course we can," she said. But it didn't sound like she really believed it. It didn't sound like she thought either one of them would follow through.

———

"They're here," Reva sang out to Georgia and Jasper when she heard the rumble of the truck's diesel engine in the shelter's parking lot next door. "Let's go see the new dog."

Ready to play, they rushed up to the closed gate between Bayside Barn and the shelter. Reva knelt to get their attention. "Listen."

Jasper sat; Georgia didn't. Reva knew Georgia didn't need

to be told about the new dog, but Jasper did. She sent a mental image of the way she wanted Jasper to act around the new dog: calm, respectful, friendly. She knew he'd get the last two behaviors because that was the kind of dog he was. She wasn't so sure about the first. "Can you do that, Jasper?"

Jasper leaned forward and licked her face. That was a yes.

"Okay then." She opened the gate. "Let's go meet the new dog."

Georgia and Jasper both ran to meet their new friend. Heather held his leash, and he wagged his black-tipped tail, lunging toward the other dogs. Heather gave Reva a nervous look and pulled back on the leash.

"They'll be fine," Reva called out. "Let them sniff each other." Even though she had only talked to two of the dogs about what to expect and how to act, she could tell by their demeanor that everyone would get along fine. She had also given Jasper a good talking-to about cat-chasing. Otherwise, he would be on a leash right now too.

"Where's Adrian?" Reva asked Heather.

"Gone to find Quinn so they can unload those generators and shutters."

"Quinn should be here any minute with the tractor. He put the front-end loader attachment on yesterday." The words were no sooner out of her mouth than the tractor's rumble could be heard from the direction of the drive-through gate. "Let's go inside. The new dog doesn't much like the sound of motors."

Inside the shelter, Heather unhooked the leash, and all three dogs began ripping and snorting. "Chill out, y'all," Reva said. She also sent a mental image of what "chill out" might look like.

Of course, they did no such thing. A dog's ability to hear and understand human words and thoughts didn't necessarily create a willingness to obey. In this moment, their need to play and let off steam dominated.

"You and Adrian had fun in New Orleans?"

Heather rolled up the leash and smiled, a pretty blush staining her cheeks. "We did."

"Good. I'm glad." Reva let a beat or two go by. "I'm not gonna ask what y'all did, but your kids might."

"We ate a lot of good food and did some shopping." Heather's blush intensified. "The usual things people do in New Orleans."

Reva patted her friend's shoulder. "Might want to rethink your plan not to tell anyone about you and Adrian. Your blush gives you away."

Heather fanned her cheeks. "I'll have it under control by the time the kids get off school."

Reva noticed the flash of new bling on Heather's finger. "Hmmm… Nice ring you've got there." She took Heather's hand for a closer inspection. "So y'all aren't keeping it a secret after all?"

"Um…" Heather's wide green eyes met hers. "I hadn't thought anyone would wonder about that."

Adrian walked in the door, filling the room with his aura of charming self-assurance. "Wonder about what?"

"Where Heather got this ring," Reva supplied.

Adrian and Heather exchanged shocked glances. "Um…" they both said at once, each looking at the other to come up with a plausible story.

Reva grinned, wondering if this whole keeping-secrets thing would shake Adrian's unshakable confidence. She made a big show of examining the ring, a beautiful antique gold-filigree design with a blue sapphire surrounded by tiny diamonds…with a small, almost invisible hinge and latch on either side of the gemstone-covered cap. "A poison ring?"

"You never know when you might need to poison someone," Heather said with a pained expression on her face.

"How romantic," Reva said with a puzzled glance at Adrian.

He shrugged, an easy grin lighting his almost-too-handsome face. "A fun memento of the day," he said. "That's all."

"Um-hmmm." Reva decided to drop the subject. A little light teasing was fun, but she didn't want to make either of them feel defensive.

"Where are the dogs?" Adrian asked, about the same time the trio came skidding into the room, their nails scrabbling on the hardwood floors. He knelt down to the new dog, who came up to him and licked his face. He scratched the dog's ears. "Hey, bud, how you liking it here so far?"

In answer, the dog pulled away and initiated another round of chase-the-leader through the shelter's main building.

"I see you can't bring yourself to call him Bones either," Reva commented to Adrian.

"Nope," he agreed, putting a casual arm around Heather before remembering their secrecy agreement and dropping it—just not quite as casually.

Reva took pity on them both. "I know y'all probably have a gazillion things to do before our meeting this afternoon…" She noted a semi-panicked look on Heather's face and a slight dimming of Adrian's congenial expression. "You hadn't forgotten, had you? We've got a lot to do to get ready for Monday's grand opening. I won't keep y'all long; just want to go over our next few days' calendar and to-do lists."

Heather grabbed Adrian's wrist and looked at his watch. "I've gotta go get the kids. I'm gonna drop them off at the house, but can I leave Jasper here? He's having so much fun, I hate to make him leave."

"Sure," Reva said. "I'll toss the ball to these three in the pool. Might as well get started with this dog's rehab program right away."

Heather and Adrian made an unconscious move toward each other, then stopped themselves. Their obvious desire to touch, to kiss goodbye before Heather left, fairly sizzled between them. It was going to be fun to see how long those two lovebirds managed to keep their relationship a secret.

During the entire shelter meeting—in which the new dog lay under the table with his head on Adrian's foot—Adrian could feel his phone silently pinging in his pocket. He knew it was a slew of neglected clients blowing up his phone. He hadn't realized how much time he spent interacting with clients until he'd stopped doing it for a couple of days.

No wonder they paid him so much. He was always on call.

At least, he had been until now, and many of his clients were low-key freaking out at his unaccustomed unavailability. He was sitting too close to Reva to take his phone out and text under the table, but he promised himself that he would catch up on texts and emails once he got home tonight, no matter how late that turned out to be.

"Adrian?" Abby leaned across the conference table and waved a hand in his face. "Hello?"

He sat up straighter. "Sorry. What?"

"How many people are you inviting to come on Sunday?"

"Sunday?" The grand opening was on Monday. "What's happening on Sunday?"

Reva let out a hoot of laughter. "I told y'all he was daydreaming."

Quinn shook his head and sent Adrian a look of commiseration. "I wonder why."

Abby, reading from her notebook, kindly filled him in. "As a way of apologizing for being mostly absent from all of the planning activities *due to his obligations as the only veterinarian in town…*"

Abby emphasized the last part of her statement by rubbing her index finger and thumb together in a gesture the gang all recognized as *This is the world's tiniest violin playing "My Heart Bleeds for You."*

"Mack is hosting a pre-grand-opening celebration for the team and any hangers-on we might like to invite, including kids and dogs. He has organized a party on the bay for us this Sunday. He is also renting motel rooms for anyone coming from out of town. He just needs a head count."

Adrian relaxed. "I wasn't planning to invite my folks to the grand opening, so—"

"Hold up," Quinn interrupted. "Abby already invited them." He made an *I told you so* face at her and grimaced at Adrian. "Sorry."

"Yeah, but my parents are homebodies most of the time, though, so—"

"They said they'd come," Abby piped up. "And since Quinn's folks—and even mine, God help us—are coming, yours have to come too. The only real question is whether your sisters and your brother are also coming."

"No," Adrian was quick to say. "They are not."

"So just your parents, then?" Abby asked with saccharine sweetness.

Adrian thought about putting his head in his hands but managed to sit still and adopt a genial and unconcerned poker face. "It'll just be my parents. Thank you for asking."

"Okay," Abby chirped. "Well, that's it then. See most of y'all tomorrow. Adrian, see you and your parents on Sunday. Mack has made reservations for y'all at the Bayside Motel from Sunday at 10:00 a.m. through Monday at…" She shuffled through her papers and then gave up with a shrug. "Monday whenever. We'll meet y'all at the dock next to the motel Sunday morning at eleven."

Adrian pushed his chair back, startling the dog who'd been snoozing at his feet.

"No, wait," Reva said. "We have to come up with a name for this new dog. We can't keep calling him New Dog forever."

Adrian sat back down and glanced at his watch. It wasn't but half past four, but jeez, he still had to ride Charlie before he headed home.

"He wants a real name, like a human name," Reva said. "So not Bones or Buddy or Tripod, but a real name like James or Duke or Jake. He wants a name that embodies his personality, so first we need to think about that."

They brainstormed traits like sweet, happy, resilient, friendly.

Meanwhile, Adrian's phone kept buzzing in his pocket. "Let's talk about names. How about Pavarotti?"

Reva closed her eyes, then opened them and shook her head. "He says no."

"Alan, Abel, Averil?" He paused and looked up at the ceiling. "Ben, Benny, Bevis?"

Reva crossed her arms and shot him a mean look. "Thank you for your input, Adrian. I know you're ready to get out of here, but going through the alphabet is counterproductive."

Abby ignored them both. "I think he does want a name that shows his resilience, so let's choose something that gives a nod to his past but then puts a stamp on the dog he means to become: friendly, smart, uncomplicated, and..." She paused to look at the dog, then smiled. "Debonair."

"Jack Reacher," Quinn said. "Jack is a good guy's name, short, uncomplicated, friendly-sounding. Reacher because he's reaching toward his future."

Adrian looked down at the dog, whose head had popped up at the name Jack but plopped down again. "Jack..."

The dog looked up, even sat up.

"Reacher?"

The dog looked away.

"Jack..."

The dog cocked his head, his ears perked forward.

"Skellington!" Heather yelled. The dog started jumping around, doing the Snoopy dance on his one back leg.

"The Pumpkin King," Heather explained, when Reva looked confused. "The skeleton character from *The Nightmare Before Christmas*."

The dog seemed to approve; he started hop-running around the room, while Georgia and Jasper looked on sleepily from their spots under the table.

"It's perfect," Heather said. "The vet tech said the dog was almost a skeleton when he got hit by that car and someone brought him to the vet. And now, for the rest of his life, he's going to be a king. We'll find him the perfect home, where he can be a friendly, kind, benevolent king."

The dog stopped running and put his head in Adrian's lap. Adrian rubbed the dog's ears. "Jack Skellington. What do you think of that name?"

The dog barked, a happy "Yip!" of approval.

"Okay, y'all," Abby said. "Meeting adjourned. Let's all head home." She and Quinn scooted out of there so fast it looked like they'd hyper-spaced.

"Hang on, Adrian." Reva stood and gathered her notebook and pen. "I need to talk to you before you leave."

Adrian sighed.

"Yes, I know," Reva said, doing the tiny violin gesture. "It won't take but a minute or two."

Heather made kissy noises to Jasper and patted her leg. "We're heading out. Will…um… Will you be riding Charlie today, Adrian? I know it's later than you planned."

"I'll be there. Tell Erin not to feed him; I'll do it after I've ridden."

Heather nodded, and she and Jasper left.

Reva patted Adrian's shoulder. "Come on." She led the way down the hall. "I want you to see something."

On the way, he remembered the semi-feral cat he'd caught. "How's that cat doing, by the way?"

"I picked him up from the vet this morning. The neuter surgery went well, but he is not a happy camper." She opened the door to one of the playrooms. "Here he is."

The cat was crouched in a shoebox at the back of a medium-sized plastic crate. "He's being pitiful. Sitting in the litter box."

"Awww. Why haven't you let him out into the cat room so he can go outside?"

"He's too wild for us to set him loose in the cat room. Also, he has a scratched cornea that will require medicine and ointment twice a day for two weeks. We would have to catch him to give him the medicine, and that would make taming him harder."

Reva approached the crate. The cat put his ears back and narrowed his eyes—one of which was already squinted shut, the fur around it smeared with a greasy-looking ointment. "He needs to be fostered by someone he trusts so that he can be allowed out of the crate and begin to be habituated to life with humans. With his current attitude, he isn't adoptable. And if someone doesn't work with him, he never will be."

Adrian dropped his chin to his chest. "Someone like me, I'm guessing."

"Yes." Reva picked up the cat's crate and put it in his arms. "Someone exactly like you."

———————

Cat crouched in the tiny pebble-filled box at the very back of his prison, watching. Adrian had set the carrier on a high shelf, where Cat could see everything in the large, dusty building but also be safe from *that dog* who had chased him before. The funny-looking strange-eyed dog couldn't get to Cat now. Adrian had made sure of that. But Cat growled a warning, just in case.

"Jasper won't hurt you," Adrian soothed.

Jasper. That bad dog had a name; why didn't Cat have one? Adrian had called him Stinky Cat at first, but not anymore. Reva had told Adrian that he would have to come up with a better name for Cat. Something with dignity, she said. Whatever that meant.

Cat didn't care what his name turned out to be. He only cared that someone thought enough of him to name him something, anything.

Other people came to see Cat. They were making a lot of words and calling each other by their names. Josh, Caroline, Erin, and Mom. Mom was also called Awww Mommmm and Mama.

Other words were said, words like *barn*, *stall*, *clean*, and *water*. But those were just words, not names. Cat could tell the difference because names were always said differently than those other words. The way names were said made Cat feel happy and safe. The way those other words were said didn't make Cat feel anything at all.

Adrian led a big animal into the building by a leash. Adrian talked softly to the big animal, whose name was Charlie. Adrian said Charlie's name with a great deal of affection. He took something off the shelf near Cat's crate and whisked it all over Charlie's brown coat. Charlie closed his eyes and made sounds that indicated pleasure.

The Josh human made whooping noises and ran around as if ants were biting him. Cat had been bitten by ants before too. He understood how that sort of itching, stinging pain would make anyone run and make noises like that. He wondered, though, why all the other humans seemed unconcerned. Maybe there was nothing they could do to help Josh.

Finally, Mom said something to Josh, and he ran out of the barn. Cat had figured out that the word *barn* meant the place they were all in right now.

Caroline climbed up on a big stack of hay and looked into Cat's crate. She stuck her fingers through the wire and said words in a high-pitched voice that sounded sweet and soothing. Cat didn't know what any of the words meant, but he kept listening and trying to learn. Maybe learning the words people said was the way animals earned their names.

"Don't fall off that stack of hay," Mom said. "Be careful."

"I won't fall, Mama," Caroline answered.

"I stacked that hay myself, Heather." Adrian stopped brushing Charlie and started strapping various objects onto the horse's body.

"Are you questioning my hay-stacking skills?" No one but Adrian called Mom that name: Heather. Her other names were said with love, but not with as much affection. Cat couldn't decide which of the woman's many names he liked best, but he thought that if he could talk the way humans did, he would call her Heather, the way Adrian did.

Cat watched with amazement as Adrian *climbed on top* of Charlie and *sat there*!

Adrian and Charlie seemed to understand each other so well that Charlie walked over to Caroline so Adrian could pluck her off the haystack and set her in front of him on top of Charlie.

Humans, Cat decided as he watched those two ride out of the barn on Charlie's back, were very odd creatures. And he was beginning to think that animals who hung around humans were maybe even odder than that.

Heather and Erin talked while they used long sticks to move Charlie's poop from one place to another. It hadn't taken Cat very long to learn that particularly odd fact about humans: They were very interested in collecting poop.

Humans were an unfathomable bunch. The more Cat saw of them, the more he worried that he might have made a mistake in choosing to throw in his lot with them.

Adrian and Caroline and Charlie came back into the barn, and it seemed to Cat that they all looked very pleased with themselves and each other. Caroline was saying words so fast that it sounded like birds chattering in the trees.

Adrian said something to Heather in his deep voice, then she replied back in her light, soft tone. Then Adrian lifted Caroline up and over the horse, and Heather reached up to take the small human and set her on her feet. "Go find Josh and Erin," Heather said to the little one. "Then y'all three go inside and wash up. I'll be in to serve dinner in a few minutes."

Adrian got down off Charlie, and Caroline wrapped her arms

around his legs. He picked her up and squeezed her, and she giggled. They made words, then he put her down and she ran off. Josh came whooping into the barn—still being eaten by ants, Cat figured—and leaped about until Adrian picked him up.

"Your sister is looking for you," Heather said, her voice not as soft as before. "Go wash up for dinner."

Adrian undressed Charlie and brushed him again, then led him into a big wood-and-metal box, similar to the one Cat was in now, but horse-sized.

"Are you sure you can't stay?" Heather asked Adrian.

"I wish I could." Adrian wrapped his arms around Heather. "But I am so far behind on my work, and with this all-day Sunday thing thrown into my schedule…" He looked over at Cat. "Plus this cat to deal with. I'd better get home."

Adrian and Heather started gently swaying together, similar to the way Adrian had rocked Cat to soothe him while walking to the shelter building. Then the two humans started doing things that looked a lot like cats fighting. While alarming, Cat had to admit that it didn't seem nearly as violent. Cat didn't feel that either of the humans was in any real danger. In fact, it seemed as if they both liked what they were doing, even when they started to eat each other's mouths, which to Cat looked very painful.

Erin stomped into the barn, and she must have also thought the mouth-eating thing was painful because she made a surprised sound, similar to the way a rat or a rabbit sounds when it is about to become someone's dinner.

"*Mother*," Erin yelled in a loud, angry voice. This was an entirely new name for Heather, one that Cat didn't like because of the way it was said, similar to when Cat had been called Stupid Damn Fucking Cat.

Cat had changed his mind about the name Stupid Damn Fucking Cat sounding important. As he spent more time near humans, Cat realized that names sounded better when said in a tone of love and acceptance. But Erin didn't sound very loving or accepting when she let out a stream of words that ended with "What are you *doing*?"

Chapter 14

AFTER ADRIAN LEFT, HEATHER WENT INSIDE TO FACE ERIN. She halfway expected Erin to be standing at the door, ready for a fight. She wasn't. Instead, she had set the kitchen table for dinner, turned off the oven, and set the foil-covered dish of chicken noodle casserole on top of the stove. "Erin?"

Heather followed the sound of the television to the den, where the twins were sprawled on the couch. Caroline looked up. "Is dinner ready yet? I'm starving-up hungry."

"Not quite yet," Heather said. "You can keep watching TV for a bit. I'll come get y'all when it's time."

At least it seemed that Erin hadn't blabbed to the twins.

Heather found Erin in her usual spot: flopped belly down on her messy bed, scrolling through her phone. The bedroom door was all but closed—a good sign, since it meant Erin hadn't run upstairs and slammed the door. Heather tapped on the door before pushing it the rest of the way open.

Erin looked up, but only briefly.

Heather sat on the edge of the bed. "Do you want to talk about what you just saw?"

Erin sat up cross-legged and set her phone aside on the rumpled bedspread. "Is there anything to say? I caught you making out with a hot guy. I guess you're entitled; Daddy's...dead. I just wish you hadn't been quite so brazen about it." Erin made a mock shudder. "I mean, ew, Mom."

"I'm sorry you saw that. I thought all of y'all kids were inside."

"I hope you'll be more careful in the future," Erin said, her tone stern.

"Yes, we will." The reversal of roles wasn't lost on Heather, but she wasn't quite sure how to turn it around. "But I think it is time for you and me to talk about the fact that I may start dating in the future. How would you feel about that?"

Erin rolled her eyes. "If you want to date, date. Just don't make out with your boyfriends in the barn."

"Adrian is not my boyfriend," Heather said. "We're just…good friends."

"Yeah? You're also good friends with Quinn and Mack. Do you kiss them in the barn too?"

Heather had to laugh at that one. Thankfully, her surprised chuckle made Erin's lips turn up at the corners. "No, I don't kiss Quinn or Mack. Just Adrian."

"Yeah. The guy you just spent a whole night with."

"Yes. We—" Heather didn't want to lie, but there were some things her kids didn't need to know. "We had to stay over to pick up the dog because Reva got the dates wrong. You know that."

Erin snorted. "Yeah, right. Whatever."

Best not to poke at that subject too deeply. "So, how would you feel if I decided to start dating Adrian?"

"Fine, I guess." Erin looked up at Heather under her lashes. "At least he's not a troll."

Heather grinned. "No, he's not a troll."

"So, okay." Erin picked her phone up and scooted to the edge of the bed. "Is it time to eat yet?"

Heather leaned over and gave Erin a hug. "Yes. Thanks for setting the table and taking the casserole out of the oven."

"There's buttered bread warming in the oven too. I turned the oven off, but it was still hot."

"Thanks. And thanks for understanding about Adrian."

"You could do worse." Erin bumped against Heather's shoulder in a teasing way. "Janelle's mom is dating an old, bald guy with a beer belly."

"And I'm sure he's a perfectly nice man," Heather answered. "Looks aren't as important as what kind of person someone is on the inside."

"And I guess you think Adrian's a nice person on the inside?"

"Yes, I do." Heather smiled. "I really do. But…until I know for sure that things are going to work out between us, I think it would be best if we don't tell the twins." Keeping secrets in the family was something Heather had always preached against, but she knew it was best not to let the twins know about her and Adrian just yet. "I don't want to get Josh's hopes up or upset Caroline over a relationship that might not happen. Adrian and I haven't yet decided what our relationship is going to turn out to be, but when we figure that out, we will let everyone know. Does that make sense?"

"God, yes," Erin agreed fervently. "Josh would be begging Adrian to marry you and be his new daddy. It would be way too embarrassing." She pretended to shudder. "And Caroline would be so shy of him that she'd forget how to talk. Better not say anything to either of them until you have a ring on your finger."

Heather laughed, then remembered that she *did* have a ring on her finger. She quietly stacked her hands on top of each other to hide it from view. "Adrian would probably run screaming, wouldn't he?"

"If he had any sense, he would." Erin's eyes widened, and her cheeks flushed. "I didn't mean that the way it sounded. A lot of guys date women who have kids. He probably won't *really* run screaming."

Heather smiled forgiveness. "If he does, that'll be his loss, right?"

"Definitely his loss," Erin agreed with a relieved smile. She hugged Heather. "But I hope things turn out however you want them to. You deserve to be happy."

"We all deserve to be happy. And I promise that no matter what happens between me and Adrian, you kids will always be more important to me than anything."

Heather stood, then she and Erin walked arm in arm to the bedroom door. Heather decided that she would show her new ring to the kids during dinner when she gave them the gifts she'd bought for them in New Orleans. And she figured that it wouldn't be too horrible for her to tell a little white lie about who paid for the ring.

This whole dating thing was getting a little too complicated.

———

Adrian had to make two trips from the car to his loft: one to carry the cat and another to carry all the cat's stuff. Reva had filled his trunk with bags of cat litter and food, plus bowls, toys, catnip, and a big-ass litter box—with a pooper-scooper that Adrian figured Reva expected him to use.

Reva had told him to put the cat in a small, closed-off area at first, so Adrian put the cat and all his junk in the guest bathroom. He set everything up, then opened the door of the crate and waited for the cat to come out on his own. Meanwhile, Adrian sat on the closed toilet lid with his phone in his hand and his laptop on the sink cabinet and took care of texts, emails, and phone calls.

He called Heather first but got a text back: I'm talking to Erin. Call you later.

He sent a thumbs-up emoji and started working. After a while, the cat came creeping out of the crate. Back hunched, neck stretched out, moving slowly, he acted more like a turtle than a cat.

"What's up, Stinky Cat," he started singing softly, but then he realized that the cat wasn't stinky anymore. Those vet techs must have taken their lives into their own hands and given the cat a bath. His black-and-white-spotted coat was now smooth and sleek, shiny and non-stinky. He changed the words slightly. "What's up, Winky Cat?"

The cat's cornea-scratched eye was half-closed and clearly irritated, causing him to blink a lot. It did sort of look like he was winking, so the new name fit—at least for now. "You like the name Winky?" Adrian asked the cat out loud.

The cat didn't seem to care much one way or the other. He sniffed around the edges of the room, then stuck his paws through the small gap between the bathroom door and the T-mold where the bathroom tile met the hallway's wood floor.

After a few minutes of that, Winky explored the litter box, scratching around a bit before coming out looking dubious. He sniffed at his food and water, then sat in the far corner by the door and stared at Adrian with a *you did this to me* expression.

"Well," Adrian said in his defense, "it wasn't my idea." In fact, he wasn't sure how long he was going to be able to handle this cat-fostering thing. Hopefully, the cat would soon be tame enough to go back to the shelter and get adopted out.

Winky huddled in the corner, and eventually, his eyes drifted shut. He seemed to be napping, but only lightly. Adrian worked a while longer, but the toilet lid wasn't the most comfortable seat, and the sink countertop didn't make the most ergonomic desk.

Maybe Winky would do better, sleep more deeply, if Adrian moved his stuff to a more comfortable location, like, for example, his office desk in the guest bedroom. "But first, medicine." Then he could leave the cat alone for the rest of the night, and they could start again on the taming program tomorrow.

Adrian followed Reva's instructions for medicine dosing. Moving slowly so he didn't alarm the cat, he prepared a dropperful of the oral antibiotic, then sat cross-legged on the floor with a towel spread over his lap. Then, by slow degrees, he eased closer to Winky, close enough to reach out and touch. Winky drew back, but he didn't hiss. With the tube of ointment and the dropper of oral medication on the floor beside him, Adrian reached for Winky with both hands, then brought the reluctant cat up into his lap. Adrian was supposed to quickly wrap the cat as tightly as possible in the towel so he couldn't scratch, then dose him.

But the damn cat started purring! So Adrian took a few

minutes to stroke Winky's fur and hum a tuneless tune before sneaking a bead of ointment onto his finger and stroking it over the infected eye.

Winky stopped purring and stiffened but didn't run or hiss. Adrian hummed a little and petted the cat some more until he started purring again.

So far, so good.

Feeling confident, Adrian stroked Winky's head and neck with one hand while he brought the dropper up close, then held the cat's head still and stuck the dropper in the corner of his mouth. Winky struggled to break free, and Adrian squeezed the bulb to dispense the medicine.

The cat's claws all came out at once, and he knocked the dropper out of Adrian's hand, sending a stream of pink medicine across the floor and onto the wall. Backpedaling over Adrian's thighs, he leaped onto the sink cabinet and tried to jump through the mirror. He tried once more, jumping at the mirror with such force that he bloodied his nose.

Adrian stood, trying not to panic. "Winky, don't do that." He reached out to restrain the cat, who was sitting in the sink, gathering himself to jump again. But when he touched Winky's back, the cat rolled, slashing out with his claws. "Stop. You'll hurt yourself."

Winky hissed and scrambled to jump off the slick marble countertop, knocking Adrian's phone and laptop onto the hard tile floor in the process. Upset even further by the clatter, he ran behind the toilet and hid, trembling.

Adrian was trembling too when he retrieved his phone and laptop and examined them. Both were fine; they were well protected by the best covers money could buy. But Adrian didn't think he was up for trying again with the pink medicine.

It wouldn't hurt Winky to miss out on one dose, and Adrian didn't want to do any more damage to their relationship than he'd done already. Tomorrow, he would try again. And tomorrow, he would follow Reva's instructions about wrapping the cat tightly in a towel before dosing him.

"Okay," he said to Winky. "You win this round. I'm gonna leave you alone for the rest of the night. Try to get some sleep." He turned out the light. "See you in the morning."

Adrian settled into his desk chair in the next room and handled a bunch of texts, emails, and calls, though in many cases, *handle* meant scheduling back-to-back Zoom meetings and conference calls that would eat up the entire day tomorrow.

In one of those meetings, he would explore the possibility of working with a new client he'd been courting for nearly a month.

If he landed this account, it would entail quite a bit of travel at first—and he would be raking in a serious amount of money—but once the work of merging the two companies was done, he would have forged an ongoing relationship that could produce a steady stream of small consulting jobs that stretched far into the future. Bread-and-butter jobs.

Heather called the second he'd shut down his laptop and plugged it into the charger. "Perfect timing," he answered. He leaned back in his chair and put his feet up on the desk. "How did your conversation with Erin go?"

Heather leaned against the headboard, put the phone on speaker, and closed her eyes. Hearing Adrian's voice, even over the phone, dropped her stress level. "Talking to Erin seems like walking a minefield some days, but I guess I could claim that the conversation went okay. She promised not to blab to the twins."

"Yeah?" His voice was deliciously deep and calming. "Did you promise her a car or something?"

"No, I just explained that I didn't want to get anybody's hopes up or, conversely, upset anybody prematurely. I told her that you and I haven't yet decided what our relationship is or if there even *is* a relationship and that when we figure that out, we will let everyone know."

"Sounds reasonable. How did she take all that reasonableness?"

"Very well, in fact. I think she understood. At the end, she hugged me and said she wanted me to be happy."

"That's good, Heather. I'm glad."

She took a breath for courage, then said, "I do think, though, that we'll need to be more careful in the future. No more kissing when the kids are anywhere near."

Maybe easier said than done, but yes. "I agree. We'll be more careful."

"Probably means no more touching or hand-holding, either, because both of those things lead to kissing."

"Understood. When we're not absolutely alone, we'll be good friends, nothing more."

"Thank you for understanding. I'm sorry this is so difficult."

"It's not difficult..." He chuckled softly, a wry sound. "Well, it is. But it's a difficulty worth navigating, right?"

"Right. I'm glad you think so. Because I was thinking..."

"Uh-oh."

"I was thinking that it would be a good thing if you and my kids could get to know each other a little better without me in the middle."

"Hmmm." He sounded dubious. "I thought you didn't want them to know anything about us."

"Well, yes. But I was thinking that maybe whenever you come to ride Charlie, you could plan to stay long enough to hang out with the kids when they get home from school."

"Hmmm." His tone was noncommittal, revealing nothing.

"I'm not asking you to babysit. I'm just suggesting that y'all can...I don't know...spend a little time getting to know one another."

"Well..." He drew the word out. "I may be working quite a bit these next few weeks."

"I don't mean to pressure you," she hurried to say. "If it's not convenient, then of course—"

"I'm not saying that." She listened for an inflection in his voice that would reveal his attitude toward her idea, but there wasn't one. "I'm just saying it might not happen right away."

"That's okay. I understand." She wasn't sure she did; was he backpedaling? Or did he really have a lot of work to catch up on? "Whenever you can do it will be fine." She let a small silence stretch out, then changed the subject. "How's the cat doing?"

Adrian laughed. "He won the first battle of the medicine-dosing wars. I'm regrouping and changing my strategy for the next battle in the morning."

"Awww, poor you. Did you get scratched?"

"Not too bad, but I wish you were here to doctor my wounds."

"Me too…" She yawned—silently, she hoped—then turned off the bedside lamp and scooted down to put her head on the pillow. "Did you catch up on work?"

"I successfully moved most of it onto tomorrow's calendar, so that's progress at least. I had just closed my laptop when you called."

"That's good." She ended the word on a yawn, and this time, she knew he heard it.

"Should I let you go? I know you have to get up early, and I didn't schedule my first call till ten in the morning."

"Rub it in, why don't you?" She yawned again, but sleepiness notwithstanding, she wasn't ready to let him go. "Let's talk a few more minutes."

"Shall I talk dirty to you?"

"I don't think I'm the talking-dirty type," she confessed. "I never understood the point of phone sex. Sorry."

He laughed. "So you're not gonna tell me what you're wearing?"

"I'm wearing a sleeveless cotton nightshirt from Target. It comes to about mid-thigh and has a panda on the front. It is very old, so the fabric is soft and comfy. But I might have to throw it away in a couple of years because it is developing a bunch of tiny pinholes... I hope that doesn't mean there are moths in my closet."

"So sexy..."

"Yes, I know," she said. "And just so you know, I'm not sure you're quite in my league when it comes to sexy bedroom attire. But I'm willing to be persuaded. What are you wearing?"

He started spinning a yarn that started with Spider-Man underwear and got more outrageous from there, and the next thing Heather knew, the neighbor's rooster was crowing, early morning sunlight had begun to brighten the windows, and her phone had gone dead on the pillow beside her.

———

Winky waited until long after the bathroom door had closed before slinking out from behind the toilet. The room was very dark, but not completely so. A sliver of light filtered through the bottom of the door, and Winky's eyes—the good one, at least—adjusted quickly.

The hurting eye, the one he'd allowed Adrian to smear grease into, was always blurry. It felt like it had sand in it all the time. It hurt whenever he blinked. It hurt when it was open, and it hurt when it was closed. The ointment seemed to help temporarily, but only after it stung like fire ants biting when it first went in.

He didn't understand why Adrian would squirt that horrible medicine into his mouth, though. There was nothing wrong with his mouth. But humans were an odd lot and often did things that made little sense.

After eating all the dry, meaty-tasting kibble he could hold, Winky hopped up onto the shiny white table with the strange depression in the middle. He crouched at the table's edge, then looked down at a papery-smelling white cylinder affixed to its side. He batted at the soft cylinder, and his claws sank into it easily.

It tore with a very satisfying sound. Then it started rolling, spewing out more of the white papery stuff. The faster Winky batted at it, the faster it spooled off and drifted down to the floor in a flowing heap.

This was fun!

He hopped down to the floor and skittered through the heap of soft white stuff until it covered the floor. Eventually, the only thing left on the side of the shiny white table was a hard brown cylinder that spun and spun but did nothing more, so Winky lost interest. He sat, tail twitching, wondering what to do next.

He wished Adrian would open the door and let him out of this room so he could explore the rest of the place. He knew there was more because he'd seen some of it through the bars of the crate when Adrian had carried it inside.

Winky sniffed at the crack where the light came in. He heard Adrian talking, so he slipped his paws under the door and yelled for Adrian to let him out.

Adrian didn't listen.

He sat up and scratched at the door, digging his claws in as high as he could reach, then raking his claws down the door, over and over again, until the smooth door began to develop a nice, satisfying texture, much like that of tree bark. He sharpened his claws, then sat for a nice grooming session. He ate the rest of his food, just for something to do, then paced around the room, meowing for Adrian to come.

Adrian didn't come.

Winky tried to climb the long curtain that hung across one end of the room, but it was harder than he thought. He realized that he had probably eaten too much, but he needed to remember to keep himself fit, just in case this thing with humans didn't work out and he had to go back to being a wild cat.

So he kept trying until he succeeded, but the jingly rings that held the curtain up popped loose, one by one, dumping Winky on the floor, where the curtain drifted down to cover him.

Exhausted, Winky tunneled under the curtain until he found his crate, where he curled up and slept for a long time. But he woke with a terrible griping pain in his distended stomach, a roiling, rumbling upset that proved his theory that he had, indeed, eaten too much of the food Adrian had given him.

Winky tunneled under the curtain again, this time in search of the litter box, but he couldn't find it in time. He did find a soft scrap of rug, though, which seemed as good a place as any to relieve himself, given the circumstances.

He curled up in the smooth bowl and hoped that Adrian would come soon and let him out of this tiny room, since it was quickly becoming very smelly, and Winky was a very fastidious cat. It was a long time later when Adrian opened the door, but Winky didn't hold a grudge. He meowed in gratitude, but Adrian didn't seem to understand his sentiment.

"Dammit, Cat!" Adrian bellowed.

Confused, Dammit Cat sat up. He'd thought his name was Winky. He meowed sweetly to let Adrian know that he really liked the name Winky much better than Dammit Cat.

But for some reason, Adrian didn't seem to be listening.

━━━━━━━━━━

Sunday morning, with his parents following behind him in their car, Adrian drove to Magnolia Bay with a yowling, unhappy cat in a crate on the front seat. He felt bad about it because Winky was doing much better. He hoped a two-day stint in the shelter wouldn't cause him to backslide. But since Adrian would be in Magnolia Bay for two days and Winky needed meds twice a day, there was no other option.

"You'll be okay, I promise. And we'll go back home on Tuesday."

Though Adrian still had to drop Winky off at the shelter, he first led his parents to the Bayside Motel so they could check in and get settled. The name of the place made it sound seedy, but it really was an okay place. The simple U-shaped concrete-block structure housed eleven units with a central courtyard facing the bay.

Adrian parked in front of the tiny office facing the road and rolled down his window. His parents' car pulled in beside his. "Thank you for leading us here," his mom said through her open window. "I know we'd have gotten lost on all these back roads."

"No worries. Y'all check in for us and hang on to my key. I'll be right back after I drop off this cat at the shelter."

"Yes, yes," his mom said. "I'll text you with the room numbers."

He drove to the shelter, where Heather's car was the only one in the lot. He had passed Quinn's truck heading toward the boat launch. It bristled with water toys: inner tubes and water skis strapped to the hood, kayaks and paddleboards in the bed. People and dogs were packed into the crew cab. He thought he saw Josh bouncing in the back seat, but they had blasted past so quickly, he couldn't be sure.

He parked next to Heather's car and took Winky's carrier inside.

Heather came into the room dressed in a gauzy light-green sundress over a darker-green two-piece swimsuit. She looked good enough to eat. Her blond hair was pulled up in a ponytail, and her skin shone with coconut-scented sunscreen, so she also smelled good enough to eat.

He gave her a quick kiss. "Where should we put him?"

"How has he been doing?" She led the way upstairs. "Do you think he'll be okay in the cat room, or would he be better in a smaller space?"

"He's been doing really well. I let him out of the bathroom Friday morning, and he's had the run of the house ever since. He comes when I call him now."

"Okay. Good. Cat room it is, then." She opened the door and held it wide for him. "I'll set up the food station and fill a box with litter. Go ahead and let him out so he can explore."

While Heather set everything up, Adrian sat on the floor and opened the crate. "Come on out, Winky."

The cat hunched in the far corner of the crate and glared.

"Give him time." Heather sat cross-legged next to Adrian. "Has he had his medicine this morning?"

"Yep. He's been good about that too." Adrian had tied a small bag to the crate's handle. He untied it and gave it to Heather. "It's all in here. The antibiotic has to be refrigerated."

"I'll tell Abby to make sure he gets another dose tonight." After a second of silence, Heather looked at Adrian's watch. "I hope Winky decides to come out soon." As if in response, Winky slipped out of the carrier and started exploring. "We should head out soon. They'll be leaving the dock in an hour."

Adrian stuck his bottom lip out in an exaggerated pout. "And we'll be spending the whole day together, pretending we hardly know each other."

"I have good news that might make you feel better about that." She leaned over and kissed him. "My kids are all spending the night away from home tonight. The twins are going with Sara, and Erin's staying with a friend."

He felt a grin spread across his face. "Is that so?"

"I was thinking that maybe after your folks go to bed, you could slip away from the motel and spend a little time at my house."

"Oh, yeah?" He pulled her into his lap and kissed her thoroughly. "You want me to sneak over to your house and hide my car in the garage and everything, huh?" He slipped a hand under her beach sundress. "I think I might enjoy sneaking around with you."

"Meanwhile," she said primly, "while we're on the water today, you and the kids can get to know one another better, and you and I can pretend to be good friends."

He was already willing to spend the day with Heather's kids, but the imminent payoff for his sacrifice took him from willing to enthusiastic. He slipped his tongue between her lips and skimmed past her teeth to stroke the roof of her mouth. "I do have a slight problem though." He guided her hand down to underscore his predicament. "I'm not sure I'll be able to hide my reaction to you."

"I feel sorry for you," she said. She stroked his tongue with hers and slid her hand up and down his erection in the same rhythm. "But I'm not sure what I can do about it."

"I have an idea," he said, smiling against her mouth. "But we'll have to hurry."

Heather drove her car to the boat dock. It only made sense because she'd have to take Jasper back home after the party and drop the kids off for their spend-the-nights. But as she drove behind Adrian's fancy little convertible, she wished she could be sitting next to him, holding his hand.

Was she stupid to be so adamant about keeping their relationship a secret? Erin had taken the news better than Heather might have expected.

Caroline never complained about anything, so Heather knew she wouldn't make a fuss. But Caroline's quiet acceptance of everything was a problem in itself. The child's still waters ran so deep, Heather sometimes wondered if those depths were full of fears and insecurities she was unable to share.

Josh would be over-the-moon happy about it, but he was the main reason Heather wanted to take things slow. She didn't want him to get his hopes up unless she and Adrian were in a solid-feeling committed relationship.

She was right, Heather reassured herself, to keep quiet for now. No reason to spill anything until after Adrian had time to get to know the kids—and her—a lot better.

By the time they got to the Bayside Motel, the pontoon boat

was tied to the dock and loaded with water toys—boards and skis and kayaks and tubes. "Where have y'all been?" Abby called. "Why haven't you answered any of my texts? I sent about a dozen."

Adrian took a small duffel bag out of his trunk. "I've gotta go change."

Heather nodded. "I'll make our excuses." It was hard not to lean toward him and steal a kiss—especially when she was still feeling all tingly from their brief but passionate encounter in the shelter's small bathroom (the only room with a locking door).

"Sorry," Heather called out to Abby, then started walking toward the dock where everyone was gathered. "We had to get the cat settled at the shelter before we left."

Josh ran up to Heather, wrapped his arms around her hips, and squeezed. "Mommy!" He hardly ever called her Mommy. He was being dramatic, something he tended toward whenever he was in a crowd. He seemed to think that whenever he felt uncertain, the best remedy was to become the center of attention.

Heather clenched her teeth and hugged her son. "Hello, Joshua."

Caroline came running too, and plastered herself to Heather's side. Heather patted Caroline's back. "Hey, sweetie. Did you have fun riding over here with everyone?"

"Yes." Caroline nodded against Heather's hip. "But I missed you." Even though they'd been apart for little more than an hour.

"I missed you too, but I'm glad we can still have fun even when we're not together, aren't you?" Heather wished she could find a way to help Caroline become more independent, but it wasn't something she could just order up from the corner store. Having Adrian spend time with her kids while she was at work might help with that as well as allow them time to bond.

Adrian emerged from one of the motel rooms with his parents, whom Heather hadn't yet met. They had just crossed the motel's courtyard when Josh noticed them.

"Ade!" Josh catapulted into Adrian's arms and clung like a starfish on a rock.

"Hey, buddy." Adrian hugged Josh and smiled at Heather over her son's shoulder. "You ready to go waterskiing?"

"I don't know how to water-ski," Josh yelled in a shrill tone. "I'm only in first grade!"

"Really?" Adrian pulled back and stared at Josh with a fake-surprised look. "I thought you were in college already."

"Nope, but I can run really fast." Josh squirmed to get down. "You want to see?"

"From here to the picnic bench and back again. I'll time you." Adrian pressed a button on his watch. "Ready, set, go."

Josh took off running, and Adrian introduced Heather to his parents, Gordon and Eileen. Gordon was an older, rougher version of Adrian, a good-looking man in his early sixties with steel-gray hair and Adrian's blue eyes. Eileen, who stepped up and gave Heather a warm hug, had smiling brown eyes and honey-brown hair lightened to almost-blond by a liberal scattering of soft white strands. "We've already met your children," she said. "They are delightful."

"Mom," Erin yelled, waving from the dock. "Can I go with Abby and Quinn?"

Quinn brought over a couple of child-sized flotation vests. "These are for the twins."

"Thanks." Heather took the vests.

Quinn looked back at the teenagers, who stood next to the pontoon boat with Abby and the two dogs who'd been allowed to come, Jasper and Georgia. "Erin wants to come along and do beach patrol duty. We'll need to leave some people on the beach to watch all the stuff while I come back to get the rest of y'all."

"That's fine, as long as Abby will chaperone."

Quinn's fifteen-year-old son, Sean, looked like a young Keanu Reeves. Tall, broad-shouldered, with a soon-to-be-studly build enhanced by his tanned olive skin, tousled dark hair, and deep-indigo eyes, Sean was the sort to make a young girl's heart spin daydreams of happily ever after.

And even though Erin was younger than Sean, she showed a promise of beauty that could turn a young man's head. The clear retainers she wore at night had just about straightened her teeth, her long blond hair shone like spun gold in the sun, and she had developed a few curves that were emphasized by a string bikini Heather didn't remember buying for her barely teenage daughter. Erin had probably borrowed it from a friend.

The teens were both too beautiful, too young, and too inexperienced to be trusted alone with each other.

"I see what you're seeing." Quinn patted Heather's shoulder. "Don't worry. Abby will be with them. We won't have a problem."

"You've got a vest for Erin on the boat?"

"Yup." Quinn looked back at the dock, where Erin and Sean stood next to each other, talking and laughing. "We have more than enough flotation devices on both boats. Just need to make sure the littles keep theirs on all the time."

"They will."

"Abby's and my parents are already on the houseboat, and Mack has taken the speed boat with the propane grill and all the coolers to the floating dock. We'll be back to fetch y'all as soon as we unload all the toys."

Josh ran back, panting and out of breath. Adrian knelt and showed him the timer on his watch.

"Sorry we can't fit everyone on the pontoon," Quinn said with an apologetic glance all around, "but with all the toys…"

"It's fine," Heather assured him. "We'll use the time to apply sunscreen. Thanks, Quinn."

"Sure thing. I'll be back for y'all in a few." Quinn headed toward the boat, and minutes later, the pontoon took off, leaving Heather, Adrian, his parents, and Reva behind with the twins. By unspoken consent, everyone migrated to the tree-shaded picnic table at the water's edge.

"No fair," Josh pouted. "I wanted to go first."

"What?" Adrian's father pretended to have hurt feelings. "You don't want to hang out here with me? I bet I know where we can find some tadpoles."

Josh debated with himself for a second; then his expression brightened, and he grabbed Gordon's hand. "Show me."

"Mama." Caroline tugged at Heather's sundress, then whispered in a not-quite-quiet voice, "I need to potty."

"Here." Gordon reached into the pocket of his swim shorts and gave Heather the key to his motel room. "For anybody who wants to make a pit stop before we head out. Josh and I are on a mission to find tadpoles."

On the way back to the picnic table after taking Caroline to the bathroom, Heather let Caroline run ahead while she paused to savor the sight of Josh and Gordon wading at the water's edge. Her son was in hog heaven right now, doing little-boy things with a grandfatherly figure, something none of Heather's kids had experienced because she and Dale had both been estranged from their families.

With Gordon filling some of Josh's bottomless need for recognition, Adrian was free to give Caroline some attention. He sat next to her on the picnic table, bending toward her to hear something she was saying. As Heather watched her twins interacting with Adrian and his dad, she allowed herself to imagine how full their lives could be as part of a larger family.

Heather wasn't looking to replace Dale in her children's lives—or in hers, either. She had only just now come to terms with the idea of entering a new, independent phase of her life. Maybe she had no business even thinking of dating Adrian, much less of entertaining a dream of a deeper and more permanent relationship.

Adrian certainly wasn't at all the sort of guy she would have envisioned for herself or her children. He was polished, highly educated, a city sort of guy. The cozy little backwater of Magnolia Bay would hold no appeal for him. It couldn't hold a candle to his fancy loft in New Orleans, where he could order up gourmet meals or walk out his door and find live music and fine dining in a party-all-the-time atmosphere.

The snapshot images of Adrian talking to Caroline and of Josh wading with Adrian's father in the shallows were compelling. But could it ever be anything more than a dream?

She couldn't see how.

Chapter 15

ADRIAN SAT NEXT TO CAROLINE ON THE BENCH AND WATCHED his mom braid her long hair in a complicated plait that started as two braids and combined into one at the back of her neck. He bent down to meet the child's eyes. "Your fancy braid is very pretty, Caroline."

She tucked her chin and looked pleased but also painfully shy. "Thank you," she said so quietly he almost couldn't hear. He'd thought he'd made progress with Caroline when he brought her up in front of him to ride Charlie. But apparently, those two steps forward had been followed by one step back. If his relationship with Heather was going to go anywhere, he would have to make friends with all three of Heather's kids in a way that stuck.

He had his reservations, and no doubt Heather had hers. But his quest to win over Heather's kids had begun. Josh was so hungry for a daddy figure that befriending him was already a done deal. The girls, for different reasons, would be harder to get to know. He hoped that today, they could make a start. If he was lucky, by the end of the day, Heather would be able to see that he was trying.

Josh screamed, and everyone looked up to see him run back to the picnic table. After a quick glance, Reva and Heather went back to chatting. Josh leaped into Adrian's lap with high drama.

Adrian put a calming hand on the kid's back. "What happened?"

"Nothing happened," Gordon said, following more slowly. "Josh saw a little water snake."

"It was a water moccasin," Josh insisted. "I saw the inside of its mouth."

"Whatever kind of snake you saw from fifteen feet away, it's gone now." Gordon chuckled. "You probably scared the poor thing to death with all your screaming."

"I wasn't screaming," Josh was quick to say. "I was yelling." He sat still in Adrian's lap for a half second before jumping off again. "Let's go look for more tadpoles."

"We already found some," Gordon said to Josh. He sat on the end of the bench and patted the space beside him. "Let's sit here for a minute."

Though Adrian hadn't told either of his parents that there was anything brewing between him and Heather, they were both born grandparents, so they took Heather's twins under their wings. His dad seemed to glory in directing Josh's high energy. His mom seemed to know that Caroline needed to be finessed into moving out from under Heather's coattails, so she used her gentle wiles to charm the child.

The pontoon boat came chugging into view. "They're back," Josh yelled. He jumped down from the bench and ran to the dock.

"Josh, wait." Heather grabbed up her beach tote and the Ninja Turtle life vest and went after him. "You have to put your vest on."

Adrian's mom stood and jingled her room key. "Last chance for a pit stop before we leave. Any takers?" She and Reva headed toward the motel while Gordon ambled toward the dock.

Adrian picked up the other vest and turned toward Caroline. "Will you let me help you?"

Caroline looked at him with her mother's big green eyes and nodded slowly.

He pointed to the ground in front of him. "Come stand here."

She climbed down from the bench, as careful as her brother was bold. Standing in front of him, she held out her arms and let him slide the vest on. "It matches your bathing suit, doesn't it?" He adjusted the straps and buckled them. "Is pink your favorite color?"

"Yes," she whispered, her cheeks turning as pink as the Disney Princess flotation vest.

"I like pink too." He realized right away that he needed to ask her a question that couldn't be answered with a simple yes or no, but for the life of him, he couldn't think of one. He pointed out one of the princesses pictured on the vest. "This one's Aurora, I think."

She nodded. "Uh-huh."

He pointed to a different one. "Which one is this?"

"That's Jasmine." She pointed to another. "And that's Ariel."

Together, they identified all the princesses while the pontoon boat slowed past the NO WAKE sign and puttered up to the dock. Adrian held out a hand to Caroline. She hesitated, then took it.

She held his hand all the way to the pontoon boat.

Progress.

The large rectangular boat's flat platform rested on two long metal cylinders that floated on top of the water. At the back, where the outboard motor hung, a wide deck with a ladder on one side allowed people to enter and exit the water easily. The rest of the platform was enclosed on all sides by a low wall with a small entry gate.

This model—which Quinn had jokingly called Mack's happy divorce present to himself—featured padded leather seats all the way around, with a captain's chair and steering deck under a canopy in the center.

Gordon kept Josh from making a flying leap from the dock to the boat, taking him by the hand and guiding him over the gap instead. Once on the boat, Josh rushed over to pester Mack. Adrian held Heather's hand as she stepped in, then Caroline allowed him to lift her into Heather's outstretched arms. Once everyone had safely embarked, he untied the dock line, tossed it into the boat, and gave the boat a push away from the dock before he leaped in himself.

"Everybody settle in," Quinn said. "Here we go."

Reva and Adrian's parents sat at the back of the boat, laughing and chattering to one another as if they'd been friends for ages.

Heather took a corner seat at the front, with Caroline tucked close beside her. Josh was busy hopping from one seat to another.

Conscious of what it might look like to everyone if he and Heather sat too close, Adrian took the opposite corner. "Josh," he said. "Come here. You need to light somewhere so we can get going."

Josh sat next to Adrian, and Quinn guided the boat slowly past the NO WAKE sign, then pushed the throttle down. The pontoons kept the boat so stable that it felt like they were skimming over the water, while the tall, moss-draped trees on either side of the inlet zoomed past.

Heather closed her eyes and lifted her face to the stiff breeze that flirted with her bangs and made her ponytail flap out behind her. The older folks at the back of the boat were whooping and cackling with hilarity, but the wind caught their voices and tossed them out behind the boat, so there was no telling what they found so funny.

Clearly, though, they weren't paying any attention to anyone else, so Adrian felt safe enough to study Heather's blissful expression.

He hoped that maybe he had helped put that serene, joyful smile on her lips.

———————

Reva put a hand on Eileen's shoulder and leaned in close. "Do you see what I'm seeing?"

Eileen glanced at her son and leaned back to speak into Reva's ear—it was the only way to be heard over the wind and the sound of the boat's outboard motor, which was just a few feet behind them. "He's right smitten, isn't he?"

"I'd say so."

The inlet opened out onto the bay, and the water became

much choppier. Quinn pulled back on the throttle when the boat rounded a small marshy island between the boat launch and the bay. On the far side of the bay, a thin strip of barrier islands met the gulf. Beach condos on the peninsula looked like tiny sandcastles shrouded in mist.

Closer, but still some distance away, the sandy beach and the floating dock that anchored Mack's houseboat came into view. After being dumped by his wife (who, in Reva's opinion, had never deserved him anyway), Mack had traded the house he'd worked so hard to buy for a houseboat, a pontoon boat, and a speedboat. Now, he lived on the water, having traded his paid-off mortgage for a few rented boat slips.

Eileen pointed at the portable floating dock Quinn and Mack had built before Mack's divorce became final. "Is that where we're headed?"

"Yes. Mack towed the dock out there and dropped anchor this morning. He's been guarding it and the beach from interlopers ever since."

Labor Day weekend boaters would've been out early, snapping up the available strips of sandy beach. Not all of the bay's coastline was suitable for water sports and picnicking. Most, in fact, was marshy, full of water plants and lily pads and thick grassy reeds mixed with fallen logs and tree roots exposed by erosion from flooding.

Beautiful but wild. The land beyond was, in most places, impenetrable and unfit for human habitation, but it provided a lush Eden for wildlife.

"I'm sure Mack was glad to see Abby and the big kids show up to help," Eileen said.

As the pontoon boat advanced farther into the bay, other boats began to zip past, some towing skiers, others hauling huge inner tubes that bounced along while screeching kids struggled to hold on.

Quinn slowed the pontoon boat to a putter.

Gordon got up to stand next to the captain's chair and pointed out something on the marshy bank. Reva looked toward the front of the boat and noticed that Heather and Adrian had scooted closer to each other. The glances that passed between them were hot enough to light a match. "What do you think about all that?"

Eileen smiled. "I'd say it's about time. Heather seems like a nice girl."

"Oh, she is." Reva told Eileen about the loss Heather and her kids had endured. "She's due for a little happiness. It would be sweet to see something blossom between her and Adrian. But... would you mind the fact that she has three kids?"

"No, not at all... Oh, look at that." Eileen pointed out a bald eagle sitting at the top of a dead-looking cypress tree. "I think a ready-made family would be good for Adrian. Settle him down a bit. He... We..."

Eileen bit her lip and gave Reva a look that revealed the depth of what she was about to say. "Adrian lost a lot because of Hurricane Katrina. He spent his senior year in high school away from his friends and the rest of the family—we all had to relocate to Houston for nearly a year."

Reva nodded, encouraging Eileen to continue.

"I stayed with my sister and the younger kids, while Gordon went back to New Orleans and basically camped out to help with the cleanup and to rebuild the house. Adrian, being older, stayed with his cousin who was already in college. We didn't realize it at the time because we were all just doing the best we could in a bad situation, but Adrian felt very isolated, very...lost."

Reva put a hand on Eileen's arm. "I'm so sorry."

Eileen nodded. "I think that, in a way, everything that happened—and the way it happened—damaged Adrian's ability to connect with others. Not just people, but animals too. We lost the family cat, Buster, because he hid somewhere as a result of all the commotion, and we couldn't find him before we had to evacuate. We managed to get the horse on a rescue transport up north, but we didn't have a place to keep him after the storm went through, so we allowed him to be adopted by a family who wanted him."

Reva shook her head. "So many people and animals suffered in that storm."

"And afterward. Most of us are still scarred in some way. Adrian lost his ability to trust in the sweetness of life."

"I think Heather has lost some of that ability too," Reva said. "Her husband's death was so tragic, so sudden. And very upsetting, the way it happened. He died right in front of Heather and the kids."

Eileen made a tsking sound, then glanced toward the front of the boat. "But look…"

Adrian's arm was stretched across the back of the seat, just close enough to touch Heather's shoulder with his fingertips. Caroline and Josh sat between them with their heads down, both immersed in whatever game they were playing on someone's phone. Adrian and Heather weren't speaking, but they were looking at each other with small, secret smiles on their faces.

"Maybe they're beginning to heal each other," Eileen said.

Reva smiled. "I hope so."

———————————

Heather stretched out on a beach blanket next to Abby.

"Adrian sure is good with Caroline," Abby commented. He stood in waist-deep water, holding Caroline up while she dog-paddled toward Eileen. When they got within a couple feet of Eileen, he gave Caroline a little push through the water so she could paddle on her own the rest of the way. "I haven't seen her look so relaxed and happy since…well, since ever."

"He's pretty good all the way around," Heather agreed,

wondering every other minute whether she should 'fess up and tell everyone that she was falling in love—not just with Adrian, it turned out, but with his parents too. Eileen had taken Caroline under her wing. Gordon had kept Josh busy all day, hunting for minnows with a dip net in the shallow water—a surprisingly interesting activity given that they never caught a thing. "Adrian's parents are great too."

"They'd make wonderful grandparents for someone's kids," Abby said in a la-de-dah tone.

"I'm sure they would," Heather said, refusing to rise to the bait. "In fact, I think they already are. Don't Adrian's sisters have kids?"

Abby sat up and rooted through the cooler. "Yeah, but they live too far away. Gordon and Eileen need grandkids who live closer so they can do weekend sleepovers and such." She handed Heather a wine cooler. "Don't you think?"

Heather took the beverage but again refused to take the bait. "Maybe."

Quinn plopped down beside them, totally ruining the girlfriend vibe, so after a few minutes of polite conversation, Heather finished her watermelon cooler and waded out into the water toward the ongoing swimming lesson. She hoped her presence didn't ruin things—when Heather had tried to teach Caroline to swim, the child refused to budge off Heather's hip—but Adrian's laughter across the water pulled her like a magnet. "Look who's swimming," Heather praised. "Somebody's got the magic touch."

"It's me," Eileen said with a laugh. "I taught all my kids to swim, didn't I, Adrian?"

"Yes, ma'am," he agreed. "And now you've taught this one." He lifted Caroline out of the water and twirled her around. "Ain't that right, princess?"

Caroline laughed, her face lit like a candle. She even patted the side of Adrian's face with affection. "I can swim, Mama!" She squirmed for Adrian to put her back in the water. "Watch how far I can swim."

"Let's show her." Eileen backed up a few steps and held her arms out.

"Watch me, Mama," Caroline yelled, her voice as loud and enthusiastic as Heather had ever heard it.

"I'm watching, sweetheart." As Caroline paddled valiantly toward Eileen with her little chin barely above the water, Heather swallowed down the lump in her throat. Abby was right; Caroline hadn't really seemed happy at all since Dale died. But now, because of Adrian and his mother, Caroline was happy and unafraid. In Adrian's arms, Caroline felt safe.

At the thought, Heather realized for the first time that Caroline hadn't just been sad after Dale's death; she'd been fearful. A simple realization Heather should have snapped to long before now, but it rang in Heather's mind, an undisputed truth. For all her trying, Heather hadn't been able to make Caroline feel safe, but Adrian had.

Though Eileen had stepped away from Caroline before Adrian launched her into the water, she stepped forward to lift her up. Then, with a half twirl, she turned toward Heather. "Okay, Mama, ready to catch your girl?"

Heather held her arms out. "Swim to me, baby."

Eileen propelled Caroline through the water so she only had to paddle a few strokes to get to Heather, but the shared sense of accomplishment still made Heather's heart sing. "Whoo!" She hugged Caroline tight. "You can swim!"

Adrian waded forward and tucked a tendril of hair behind Caroline's ear. "But no swimming in the river behind your house—or anywhere besides the bathtub—without your mama or me right there with you, right?"

"I promise," Caroline said in an impatient tone that made it clear Adrian had already drilled the rule into her head. Then she leaned toward Adrian with her arms out.

He caught her up and held her close, smiling at Heather over Caroline's wet blond head. "Did you see Erin ski out of here a few minutes ago?"

"Yes, I did." Mack had been driving the speedboat, Reva had been spotting, and Sean had been sitting at the back of the boat, snapping pictures. "Thank you for that too." It felt like everyone in Heather's family had been existing in a state of suspended animation until Adrian came and woke them up.

Eileen waded past and patted Caroline's back. "You've worn me out, sweetie pie. I'm gonna go see if there's any lemonade left in one of those coolers on the beach."

"Lemonade!" Caroline jumped from Adrian's arms and went under for a second but popped back up undeterred. "I want lemonade," she sputtered, flailing her arms in the general direction of the shore.

Eileen grinned at Heather and boosted Caroline forward a bit. "Let's go then." She kept an unobtrusive hand beneath Caroline's belly to keep her from sinking. "Don't forget to kick."

As Eileen guided Caroline toward the beach, Heather and Adrian stood waist-deep in the water, close enough to touch but not daring to.

"Hey," he said, swiping a water slider away as it paddled just under the tea-brown surface.

"Hey," she answered, skimming her fingers through the gentle waves. She thought about saying that they could tell their secret now, get it over with. But something made her hold back. What if Adrian seduced them all into wanting him in their lives and then decided that country life in Magnolia Bay wasn't for him? Could they relocate to New Orleans, with its narrow streets and party atmosphere, with its close-together buildings and touristy culture?

Her kids were used to having space to roam and people around who knew who they were and where they lived. Erin couldn't make a wrong step without Heather knowing about it before nightfall. It wouldn't be like that in New Orleans.

Adrian stepped closer, still not touching but close enough for her to feel the warmth of the sun radiating off his tanned skin. "Your kids love me," he taunted, his voice soft, his gaze intense. He slipped a hand toward her, just under the surface of the water.

"I can tell." She reached for his hand and threaded her fingers through his. Anyone watching wouldn't know they were touching. She glanced toward the beach. No one seemed to be looking, but that didn't mean they weren't. "Thank you for making the effort."

"I honestly enjoyed spending time with your kids today." With the afternoon sun behind his head, his blue eyes looked dark, almost black. "I'm beginning to realize that this is about more than you and me."

"That's why it's so scary," she said. "I can fall in love with you and get over it if things don't work out. But what if they fall in love with you?"

He gave her that heartbreakingly beautiful smile of his. "Wouldn't that be a good thing?"

"It would, unless you decide you're not up for taking our package deal."

"I've already shown you that I'm willing to try, haven't I?"

"But trying might not be good enough. And you can't guarantee that you won't change your mind, can you?"

He made a move toward her, but she took a step back. "My kids have already lost their dad. I don't want to let them get used to having you in their lives only to lose you if you decide to leave."

"I won't do that. I wouldn't." His fingers squeezed hers under the water's surface. "Just like with Charlie, no matter what happens between you and me, if your kids need me, I'll show up."

"I'd like to think that's true," she said. "I hope it is."

Because this whole day had been like a fairy tale, complete with a handsome prince and fairy grandparents. But Heather couldn't help waiting for the other shoe to drop out of the sky. Ever since Dale died, she'd been just as fearful as Caroline, expecting that her whole world could come crashing down if she made one wrong move. The carefree day they'd just shared almost made the waiting worse because the higher she let her spirits rise, the farther and faster they would plummet down to earth.

———————

Hours later, Adrian paddled his two-person kayak up closer to Heather's. Even though each of them had one of the twins up front, he knew they weren't paying attention, so he reached out to take her hand. "It's been a great day, hasn't it?"

Heather linked her fingers through his for a brief squeeze before letting go. "Yes, it has."

Adrian felt elated by a sense of accomplishment. He'd taught Erin how to ski, Caroline could dog-paddle without help, and he'd broken through the barrier of her extreme shyness. In fact, when they'd set out on this last adventure of the day, she had easily agreed to sit in Adrian's kayak while Josh sat in Heather's.

Sunburned despite the liberal application of sunscreen, sore from the day's strenuous activity, he and Heather paddled back toward the beach in companionable silence. They beached the kayaks, and while the twins tossed the ball to Jasper and Georgia, the adults and the teenagers loaded the toys, the coolers, and the grill onto the pontoon boat.

Mack turned to Adrian with the slalom ski under one arm. "You didn't get to ski yet, did you?"

"Nah, but that's okay." He had actually enjoyed spending most of the day getting to know Heather's girls better. It seemed almost as if the universe had conspired to give him time with each of them. Sean had encouraged Erin to let Adrian teach her to ski, then spent the rest of the day helping her practice. Adrian's dad had taught Josh to dive off the floating dock while Adrian and his mother stood waist-deep in the water and taught Caroline to swim.

"You can ski back to the landing if you want," Mack said. "I'm taking the speedboat, and Reva's riding with me, but there's room for Heather and the twins, too, if they want to come along."

Adrian looked at Heather.

She shrugged. "Works for me."

"Okay, sure." Adrian reached out for the ski. "Let's do it."

The speedboat was beached on the shore. Heather and Reva climbed in, and Adrian lifted the twins into the boat. Reva pulled the anchor in while Mack pushed the boat away from the bank, then he jumped in and sat in the ski boat's captain chair and started the engine. Reva reached into one of the under-seat storage bins and tossed a life vest to Adrian.

"You want to do a beach start or a water start?" Mack yelled.

Adrian let the ski float beside him while he put the vest on. "Beach is fine." He couldn't help wanting to show off a bit for Heather.

"I'll spot," Reva offered.

"Thanks, Reva," Adrian said. Heather might be too distracted by the twins to be able to watch out for dangers like other boaters or submerged logs. It was always necessary from a safety stand-point to have a designated person to be a line of communication between the skier and the boat's driver. Reva would inform Mack if Adrian fell or if he decided to drop the rope and call it a day.

While the engine idled, Reva tossed the ski rope. Adrian caught it in midair, then waved to the twins as Mack backed the boat up and turned the bow toward the bay.

Adrian put the ski on and stood in knee-deep water with his right leg cocked to keep the ski's tip sticking out of the water. He held the ski rope and watched the length play out. When only a few feet of slack snaked out across the surface of the water, Mack idled the boat and turned back to look. "Hit it?"

Adrian gave a thumbs-up, and Mack pushed the throttle wide-open. A second later, Adrian was skimming across the water with the wind in his face and the turbulence stirred up from the boat's motor bumping under his ski. He pulled back on the double-handled rope and leaned right, jumping the wake onto smoother water. He rode that way for a while, waving to the twins who were both waving at him.

Then the real fun began. He zipped from left to right and back again, jumping the wake and using momentum to build speed on each end of the pendulum swing before crossing the wake again.

He did a few trick moves: a couple of turnarounds while jumping the wake, then skiing backward in the center of the wake. But when he turned back around after that one, he noticed that Heather was biting her pinkie nail and looking worried, so he decided from then on to enjoy a more sedate but still fun swing from one side to the other, over the wake and back again.

Reva stood and pointed out a good-sized stick bobbing in the water.

Adrian nodded and switched to the other side of the wake. Starting to get bored, he was thinking about dropping the rope and calling it a day when he noticed a twig sticking up in the water.

Then he hit the submerged log attached to the twig.

The rope ripped out of his hands, and the ski flew off his foot, wrenching his ankle and catapulting him up into the air. He cartwheeled down onto concrete-hard water, then somersaulted over the waves as a blinding spray of water went up his nose and down his throat.

He didn't even see the ski spinning through the air until it smacked him in the face.

―――――――――――

Heather screamed.

Reva pounded Mack on the back. "Stop! Stop. He's down."

Adrian floated, faceup at least but as limp and still as if he were dead. "Turn around, turn around," Heather yelled at Mack.

"I am," Mack yelled back. But he wasn't turning, not yet. The boat had to slow down first. "Is he okay?" Concentrating on driving the boat, Mack couldn't turn around to look.

"I don't think so," Reva answered. The fear in her voice ramped up Heather's fear. She'd seen the ski hit Adrian in the face. It had hit him *hard*. So hard that it had spun off to land in the choppy waves fifteen feet away.

"Hurry, hurry," Heather chanted. Adrian still hadn't moved. At least he wasn't facedown. If he had been, he would drown before they could get to him. And other boats were beginning to come in at the end of the day; someone not paying attention could run over him. "Oh my God, Mack. Hurry."

Mack finally got the boat turned around and headed back to where Adrian floated, his head tilted back in the water, his chest held up by the flotation vest.

"Can't you go any faster?"

"Mommy, Mommy," Heather heard Caroline saying as if from a long way away. "Is Adrian dead?"

Heather's mind flashed back to the scene of Dale's death, when the kids had been gathered around him, screaming and crying out for Heather to *do something*.

Then, as now, she had been powerless.

The boat pulled even with Adrian's lifeless body, and Mack cut the engine. "Reva. Drop the anchor."

Heather looked over the side of the boat and felt her face and hands go numb. Adrian's eyes were closed, his face a bloody mess.

Heather's head seemed to be floating high above her body. She couldn't go through this. Not again.

"Mommy," Caroline screamed. Heather knew her daughter's arms were wrapped around her, but she couldn't feel them. "Help him, Mommy. Help him," Caroline chanted, stringing more words together than she'd done in the last year. "Adrian's not dying, is he? He's not dying…?"

Joshua was uncharacteristically silent.

"Come here, baby." Heather heard Reva's soothing voice, felt her gentle hands breaking Caroline's death grip on Heather's legs. "You too, Joshua. We need to stay out of the way. Y'all come sit over here with me."

Mack jumped over the side of the boat with a splash, then towed Adrian toward the ladder at the back of the boat.

"He's breathing." Mack swam with one arm supporting Adrian's shoulders while he smacked Adrian's blood-smeared cheek with his other hand. "Adrian. Wake up. I need you to help me."

Adrian's head lolled, but his eyelids fluttered, and his lips moved. Mack clung to the boat's ladder with one hand and tried to lift Adrian's shoulders up.

"Reva. Heather. Help me lift him into the boat. I can't touch bottom here. I don't have any leverage."

"Yes," Reva said immediately.

Heather wasn't sure she could stand up without keeling over. She pulled herself together and leaned over the back of the boat and helped Reva grab Adrian by his upper arms.

Adrian's skin was slippery wet and chilled from being in the water, but beneath the chill, she felt the warmth of his muscled flesh.

Heather's rational mind tried to come online. *This is Adrian. He's hurt, but he'll be okay.* Ski accidents were rarely fatal.

The two women managed to lift Adrian up enough for Mack to get a foot onto the ladder.

Mack grabbed Adrian around the hips and powered up the ladder while Heather and Reva supported Adrian's shoulders and walked backward until they had him in the boat.

Heather collapsed on the floor of the boat and dropped her head to her knees. Reva put a hand on her shoulder. "Are you okay?"

Heather shook her head no. "Trying not to faint."

"Just breathe." Reva's voice sounded as if it was coming from a long way away. "I'm sure it's not as bad as it looks. He's got a gash on his forehead and maybe a broken nose, so he won't be so pretty for a while, but he'll be okay."

Heather could hear Caroline wailing in distress. Josh, always the loudest voice in the crowd, remained chillingly silent. She reached up to take Reva's hand. "I'll be okay. Please see to my kids."

Heather pressed her forehead to the boat's scratchy carpeting and gulped for air like a fish tossed up onto a bank. Reva's calm voice soothed her children, and Mack's strong, take-charge tones talked to Adrian. "How many fingers am I holding up? Okay... What year is it?"

Mack's tone changed when he talked to Reva. "I'm pretty sure he's got a concussion, and he's definitely gonna need stitches. Here. Put this..." His voice faded out, and Heather concentrated on breathing again. "...stop the bleeding, and..."

It wasn't the sight of blood that was getting to Heather; it was the thought that she could so easily lose Adrian. Maybe not from this accident, but what would stop him from dying some other way? He could have a car accident driving from Magnolia Bay to New Orleans. He could get bitten by a snake while hiking or fall off a mountain while climbing or plunge off a precipice while snow skiing or fall out of the sky while riding in an airplane on a business trip. He could die a thousand different ways, and if he did, she would be unable to do anything to stop it from happening.

"Call 911," she heard Mack say to Reva, "and get an ambulance to meet us..."

"Sit with him," Mack told Reva. "I'm gonna get us to the dock."

The boat started moving, and Heather eased upright slowly. Looking over the stern of the boat, she could see the slalom ski that had ruined Adrian's face getting smaller in the distance, innocently bobbing in the reeds at the water's edge.

"Heather." She heard Adrian's voice behind her.

"Don't try to sit up," Reva said.

"Heather," Adrian said again. His voice sounded wrong—weak, nasal, and slurred, even though she knew he hadn't been drinking at all today because he'd been so busy playing with her kids. And they had loved every minute of it. They were all falling in love with him, just as she was.

Just as she already had, God help her.

Damn him for doing this to them. Damn him for making them all fall in love with him and then doing this. "I'm okay, honey," he said in that stupid-sounding slurred voice. "It doesn't even hurt; it just feels numb."

Stupid idiot. Didn't he know that really bad injuries might not hurt at first because adrenaline kept the pain from kicking in? "I'd feel better if it did hurt," she said over her shoulder without looking at him. "Your fucking face has been laid open. It's supposed to hurt."

"Come here, baby."

"Don't try to sit up," Reva said again, her voice stern.

An indelible snapshot of Adrian's beautiful face covered in blood would be stuck in Heather's mind forever. Worse, the twins had seen it.

Heather realized in that moment how badly she had failed her poor kids by letting Adrian into their lives and allowing them to go through this kind of trauma all over again.

Chapter 16

THE AMBULANCE WAS PARKED NEXT TO THE BOAT RAMP. TWO medics stood on the dock holding a backboard. All business, Mack jumped out of the boat and tied it off at the dock.

Adrian sat up and batted Reva's hand away. "I can get out by myself."

"Fine." Reva held her hands up. "Do what you want." She got up and went over to comfort the twins, who huddled together on the bench seat at the bow.

Adrian got to his knees, feeling woozy, seeing double. The whole top of his head—including his face—was on fire.

Heather, still at the back of the boat, got to her knees too. Her face would have been pasty white if not for the beginnings of a mild sunburn. Even her lips were white.

"Heather," he said, but she looked away, her mouth tight.

Mack and the medics lifted Adrian out of the boat. Then without exactly knowing how it happened, he was inside the ambulance and strapped down to the gurney.

"Who's riding with?" one of the medics yelled. "Anybody?"

Reva held up a hand to signal them to wait, and she and Heather had a heated-looking discussion. Then Reva gathered the twins to her like a mother hen tucking two baby chicks under her wings, and Heather stomped toward the ambulance with her head down before climbing inside. One of the medics directed her to a small, out-of-the-way seat, and she buckled her seat belt, then clenched her fingers in her lap.

Heather watched with an unhappy look on her face while the medics checked him out. The whole time, they went on and on talking about Adrian's good luck. They chatted about how lucky he was that the leading edge of the ski had hit his forehead instead of his nose—which probably wasn't broken. His head was sliced open, he most likely had a concussion, and he ought to consider going as Frankenstein this Halloween. But the scar would fade over time because the ER surgeon on call this weekend was really good. (He could be a princess next Halloween.) The luckiest thing of all was that he hadn't ended up facedown in the water, because if he had, he'd be dead.

Yeah, Adrian was lucky. He didn't need the paramedics to tell him that.

He just didn't feel all that lucky right this minute.

He had told Heather it didn't hurt, hoping to make her feel a little better about the situation, but that tactic had backfired big-time.

Truth was, it *hadn't* hurt much at first. It had been numb but pulsating with every heartbeat, promising greater pain to come. The promised pain had arrived. His head pounded worse than the worst hangover of all time.

He reached out for Heather's hand, and she took it, but her hand felt limp in his. "I'm gonna be okay," he said. "You don't need to worry."

"I'm not worried," she answered, her voice dull. "But I thought you were dead." Her chin trembled, and she looked away, pressing her lips together and visibly composing herself.

Then she speared him with her tear-filled eyes, and the tears spilled over. "I thought you were dead," she whispered, her voice breaking. "And I can't go through that again." She swallowed and looked away. "Not ever again."

She was upset, understandably so. By the time they saw each other tomorrow at the shelter's grand opening, when she saw that he was fine—a little uglier than before, maybe, but fine—she would be over the shock of the accident, and they'd go back to where they'd been before this happened.

One of the medics reached over and patted Heather's shoulder; it was pretty close quarters in the ambulance, so they'd heard every word that was said. "Head wounds bleed a lot, ma'am, and they often look way worse than they are. This one was pretty bad, all right, and they'll make him stay overnight, for sure, because of the concussion. But he'll be okay."

The other medic chuckled. "I bet he won't go skiing again anytime soon. Not for the rest of this season, at least."

Adrian closed his eyes and let the medics' chatter wash over him. He was trying very hard not to vomit, but he wasn't holding out much hope of success.

And that was before the ambulance hit the highway with lights flashing and sirens blaring. The rocking motion of the ambulance didn't help to quell his nausea. But they got to the hospital without him tossing his cookies, and when the medics wheeled him into the ER, he was grateful that nobody expected him to walk.

Though the place bustled with hospital staff and the families of people who'd suffered Labor Day mishaps, it wasn't long before Adrian was installed in one of the curtained cubicles. A nurse inserted an IV and hung a bag of saline while Heather sent text updates from Adrian's phone.

"Your parents are on their way here now," Heather said without looking up. "Your dad's bringing my car; it's a good thing I left the keys in my beach bag on the pontoon."

"How are your kids?"

"Reva says they're fine. I told her to cancel their spend-the-night plans. She took them to her house, and she'll bring them here in a little while so I can take them home when I leave."

"That's good. Y'all need to rest." The saline drip seemed to be settling his stomach somehow. Thank God. He held out a hand to Heather. "Come here."

She looked reluctant, and though she put his phone down in her lap, she didn't budge from the chair.

He crooked his fingers. "Please."

She got up and came over to the hospital bed. He patted the thin mattress. She sat next to him, and he kept urging until she stretched out and put her head on his shoulder.

He stroked her hair. "You know I'm gonna be okay, right?"

"I know." Her voice sounded tired, resigned.

"So what's the matter?"

Before she could answer, Adrian's mother rushed into the cubicle. She gasped and cried out when she saw him. "Oh, Adrian, you could have been *killed*," she said so loudly that he cringed. That was not what Heather needed to hear right now. Heather sat up and tried to stand, but he wrapped an arm around her waist, so she perched on the side of the bed instead. "I'm fine, Mom. It looks worse than it is."

Gordon came in. "Whoa, son," he boomed in a too-loud voice. "You got yourself a good little whack on the head there."

A nurse wheeled in a tray with syringes and needles and a bunch of shiny silver implements. "Too many people in here," she said in a businesslike tone. "Somebody's gotta leave."

Heather stood, and this time, he let her. She leaned toward him as if she might give him a kiss, but instead, she took his hand and gave it a gentle squeeze. "I'll see you tomorrow."

———————————

Heather walked out of the ER. Gordon caught up with her after she'd walked through the automatic doors that led to the parking lot.

"Heather." He put a hand on her arm. "You won't get far without these." He pressed her car keys into her palm. "Your car's in the first row. Can't miss it. Your beach tote is on the front seat." He studied her face. "Are you okay?" His voice sounded gruff. Worried.

She pressed her lips together and blinked back tears. Unable to speak, she shook her head. He opened his arms, and the next thing she knew, she was enveloped in Adrian's father's comforting embrace. He patted her back. "He's going to be all right," he soothed. "That boy's hardheaded."

She choked on a laugh. "Not hardheaded enough, apparently."

"So he'll have a new dent in his noggin." He drew her away from the doors as a couple walked in carrying a crying child. "It'll make him look more manly."

"I know." Heather stepped back and wiped her tears. "It's just… It was hard seeing him unconscious and bleeding. I felt so…helpless." The worst of it was knowing that anything could happen to him, at any time, and she'd be just that helpless all over again. "And he's such a daredevil. Skiing backward…"

"Awww." Gordon chuckled and patted her shoulder awkwardly. "Skiing backward isn't that big a deal. He's no more a daredevil than any man I know."

"Well, then, you're *all* crazy." She sniffed and tried to smile. "But that doesn't much help my feelings." Today, she'd begun to imagine her life with Adrian in it, not just as a temporary bridge from widowhood back to womanhood but as something more— something she wasn't yet ready to put a name to, especially now that it had almost been snatched away. "Anyhow." She patted Gordon's shoulder. "Thanks for bringing my car."

"Happy to do it." Gordon smiled before he turned to go, the ghost of Adrian's smile on an older man's face. A glimpse into a future with Adrian that she wondered if she'd ever see. She'd thought there wouldn't be any harm in having a quiet fling with Adrian and being open to the possibility of something more developing between them. But seeing him with her kids today, she'd started falling in love with him. Worse, so had they.

Was today's accident the wake-up call she needed to put on the brakes before they all got their hearts broken again? Life without Adrian would be smaller, maybe, but more predictable. Safer.

Reva pulled into the parking lot and parked next to Heather's car. Her window came down, and she waved. "How's Adrian?"

"Concussion and stitches, just like Mack said. He'll be staying overnight for observation."

The twins bolted out of the back seat of Reva's sedan and clung to her legs, effectively hobbling her. "Can we go see him?" Josh asked in a whiny tone. "I want to see him." Apparently, Josh had found his voice again. "Does he have stitches?"

Erin got out of the car holding Jasper's leash, then made the dog sit long enough for her to peel Josh off Heather's leg. "Come on, dude." She reached for Heather's keys. "Let's go get in the car."

"Is Adrian gonna be okay, Mommy?" Caroline asked. "He's not gonna be dead like Daddy, is he?"

"No, baby. Adrian is not going to die." Not this time, anyway. Who knew what would happen the next time he decided to be a stupid daredevil cowboy. "It's been a long, tiring day. Let's go home."

Heather thanked Reva and drove home with Joshua keeping up a steady stream of chatter from the back seat. In the house, Erin helped out without being asked, directing the twins upstairs to take their baths while Heather went to the downstairs master suite to take off her bloodstained clothes and have a hot shower.

Dressed in her pajamas, she rolled up the bloody swimsuit and beach cover-up and stuffed them in the kitchen trash bin. They'd wash, but she didn't think she'd ever want to wear them again. The television blared from the den, and Erin stood at the stove, making grilled cheese sandwiches. "Dinner's almost ready," Erin said over her shoulder. "I told the twins they could eat in the den tonight. I hope that's okay."

Heather sat at the bar. "That's fine. Thank you for taking over."

"I could tell you're upset about what happened to Adrian." Erin set a plate in front of Heather. "Was it really as bad as the twins said?"

Heather pushed the plate away. "I don't think I can eat anything tonight." Her stomach was still in knots. "It was as bad as they said. Or worse."

"I'm sorry." Erin pushed the plate in front of Heather again. "Once you start eating, it'll get easier."

Yes. Heather remembered that from last time. Erin took plates for her siblings into the den. Heather took a small bite of the warm, buttery bread and melted cheese, and made herself chew until she could swallow. The second bite went down more easily.

After dinner, Heather cleaned the kitchen and sent the kids up to bed with a promise to tuck them in later. She checked on Erin first. "Hey," she said quietly after tapping on the door.

"Come in," Erin said, her voice sleepy.

"Just seeing if you want to talk about the day."

"Sure." Erin sat up in bed. "I had a really good time. I'm sorry about how it ended for y'all, though."

Heather sat on the edge of Erin's bed. "You learned how to ski."

"Adrian was a good teacher." Erin fiddled with the end of her braid. "He's really nice, Mom."

Heather nodded. "Yes, he is."

"I'm sorry I pitched a fit about y'all kissing before."

"That's okay." Heather patted Erin's leg through the comforter. "I know it was a bit of a shock."

Erin chuckled. "It was. But you know, now that I've had time to get used to the idea, I think Adrian will be good for you. And for us too." A mischievous grin spread across her face. "If y'all get married, all the girls will be jealous that I have such a hot stepfather."

"Well, about that…" Heather looked down and picked at a tiny pinhole in her pajamas. "I don't think Adrian and I are going to be a thing after all."

"Why not?" Erin sounded disappointed. "What happened?"

Heather shrugged. "I'm not ready for a relationship."

"But Mom," Erin argued, "Adrian's kind of a catch, and he's probably not the waiting-around type."

Heather patted Erin's leg again. "We don't have to think about that right now. Tomorrow is a new day, and we have to get up early for the shelter's grand opening."

Heather stood and turned to go, but Erin called her back. "Mom."

"Yes?"

"What did you think of Sean?"

"Besides the fact that he's way cute?"

"He's really nice too," Erin said. "I think I might have a little crush on him. Do you think he'd go out with me?"

Heather sat back down on the bed. "I don't know, sweetie. I mean, he'd be a fool not to want to go out with you, but who knows what's in the minds of young men? You are a couple years behind him in school."

"He held my hand today."

"He did?" Heather tried not to look shocked. She and Abby had thought that all the adults were watching those kids with hawklike precision. "When?"

"When he helped me get in the boat—and out of it too."

"Oh." Heather's relief must have showed in her tone, but Erin shot it down.

"He held my hand longer than he needed to, I mean."

"Oh. That's...um... That's good, I guess." They'd have to watch the kids even closer than they had been.

Erin laughed. "Sorry, Mom. I didn't mean to scare you."

"No, it's okay." Heather smiled. "You didn't scare me." Much. "But if you want to impress Sean with your wit and beauty tomorrow, you should try to get enough sleep tonight."

"Night, Mom."

"Night, sweetie." Heather turned out Erin's light and pulled the door closed, then went across the hall to Josh's room. He was already asleep, with his face buried in the pillow and his covers halfway off the bed. Jasper looked up from the foot of the bed and wagged his bob tail.

Heather crossed the hall to check on Caroline. It seemed that she was asleep too, with the covers pulled up over her head. But when Heather opened the door wider, Caroline flung the covers off and sat up. "Mama…" Caroline leaped off the bed and ran to hug Heather. "Can I sleep in your bed tonight?"

Heather squatted down to meet Caroline's eyes. "Why, baby?"

"I had that nightmare about Daddy again, that he was coming after me with his face all puffy and blue and his tongue sticking out."

"Aww." Heather brushed Caroline's hair away from her forehead. She was hot and sweaty from hiding under the covers. "I'm sorry." Hopefully, the trauma would be short-lived this time because Adrian was going to be okay, and because Caroline hadn't had time to learn to love him and to think of him as a daddy. "Sure, you can sleep with me tonight."

"I tried to go back to sleep," Caroline said, "but every time I close my eyes, I see Adrian with blood all over his face… Or sometimes I see Daddy instead."

"Come on." Heather held out a hand. "Let's go downstairs. I'll tuck you into my bed and tell you a story."

Caroline slept fitfully that night, and Heather hardly slept at all, so she was able to notice when Caroline's dreams turned dark and soothe her with a gentle touch. Heather spent most of the night staring at the ceiling because whenever she closed her eyes, she saw Adrian's beautiful, ruined face. There were times when she drifted off, but either Caroline's nightmares or her own kept her from getting truly restful sleep.

The drastic measure of breaking up with him had crossed her mind when she was still reeling with shock, but now that she'd had time to think it over, she knew she didn't want to break things off with him completely. He was the best thing that had happened to her and her kids in a long time.

The accident wasn't his fault. He'd been a daredevil cowboy when he was skiing backward, but the ski hitting a log could have happened to anyone. Erin had been skiing that day too. It could have happened to her. Accidents happened.

Heather knew, intellectually, that pulling the plug on her new relationship with Adrian wouldn't stop anyone she loved from experiencing harm or loss. But the whole thing had spooked her and made her realize that their relationship was developing too quickly.

If it had only been about her, she'd dive in and never look back. But as a mother, she had to protect her kids from the emotional backlash that might happen if they fell in love with Adrian as a father figure and things didn't work out.

Adrian had said that he'd be there for her kids—and for Charlie—no matter what she decided about their relationship. They'd made a pinkie swear that they would always be friends. If all that was true, then Adrian would understand when she told him tomorrow that they needed to go back to being friends and let any relationship that might grow out of that friendship evolve more slowly.

With that decision made just as the sky began to lighten outside her bedroom window, Heather finally let herself sleep.

———

Winky sat in the towel-lined crate that smelled like Adrian's house. All alone in the dark room that didn't smell like anywhere he'd ever been before, Winky wondered why he'd been abandoned.

He had tried to connect his mind to Adrian's several times, but it wasn't working. Adrian's mind was encased in a dark fog that Winky couldn't penetrate. The only explanation that made sense was that Winky's trusted human friend had closed the door of communication, and Winky didn't know why.

Had he not been good? He'd done his best.

He'd been tricked into surrendering his freedom and opening his heart, only to be left behind.

He vowed to himself that he would never trust humans again. He vowed that if someone opened the door to the outside, he would take the chance and run. He knew the way back to freedom because he'd paid attention when Adrian carried him up the stairs in the crate. When Winky got free, he would go back to being untethered to anyone. He would go back to being independent. He would go back to fighting for survival. He would challenge Old Gray, and this time, he would finally beat the old warrior.

Because Winky's time with humans had changed him.

He had learned how to love, and now that his love had been rejected, he was learning how to hate.

———————

Leaving Jasper at home, Heather and the kids arrived at the shelter about an hour before the grand opening of Magnolia Bay's Furever Love Animal Shelter. The fund-raiser and celebration aspect of the grand opening would take place entirely at Bayside Barn under the direction of Reva and the barn volunteers. Abby and Heather would take turns giving guided tours of the shelter every half hour.

The kids scattered immediately. Erin had been exchanging texts all morning with Quinn's son, Sean, and the teenagers had arranged to meet up in the pavilion next door at Bayside Barn. The twins made a beeline for the bouncy house, under strict instructions not to go inside unless and until an adult was there to supervise. One cracked-open head a week, Heather had told them, was more than enough for her.

Heather walked over to where Quinn had set up a row of tents along the tree-shaded fence in the shelter's parking lot. He had also erected a rope barrier marked with flapping flags to keep idiots from attempting to drive or park too close to the adoption tents. Heather waved to her friend Sara Prather. The editor and photographer of the Magnolia Bay news flyer and VP of the Magnolia Bay

Elementary School's PTA, Sara was directing several people who were unloading dog crates from vans and walking dogs around the parking lot.

Sara had organized and advertised an adoption event for rescue organizations and shelters from neighboring towns. Arrangements had been made for the animals who didn't find forever homes today to become the first shelter residents. The hope was to foster long-term relationships between this shelter and others in order to pool resources to find homes for animals in need.

Sara's long copper hair glowed like a new penny in the sun as she waved to Heather and motioned her over. Sara pulled Heather aside and spoke quietly. "I heard about Adrian's accident yesterday. Is he going to be okay?"

"I got a text from his mother this morning. She says he'll be fine. They kept him in the hospital overnight, but they're going to release him later today."

"Wow." Sara gave Heather a penetrating look. "Was it very bad?"

Heather nodded. "The ski sliced his forehead open. There was so much blood." She closed her eyes and shook her head, dispelling the memory. "I almost fainted." She didn't add that the reason she'd almost fainted wasn't simply because there was blood. She'd almost fainted because it was Adrian's blood.

"Quinn said your kids were in the boat when it happened and that y'all were all very upset and worried for Adrian."

"We were hysterical." She didn't bother to split hairs about which of her kids were there and which weren't. "He was knocked out at first. It looked like he was dead. It was…horrible."

Sara made a soft sound of commiseration. "That's awful. Quinn said that you and your kids are really close with Adrian." Sara cocked her head and put her hands on her hips, assuming the stance of a good friend who's been unfairly left out of the loop. "I didn't know that."

Heather shrugged. "He comes over sometimes to ride Charlie, that's all." But her blush gave her away. She could feel it creeping up her neck and into her cheeks, making the heat of her slight sunburn glow even hotter.

"Um-hmm," Sara said in a skeptical voice. "I see how it is."

"No," Heather hit back. "No. You don't see how it is. There is nothing between Adrian and me but friendship." At least, Heather hoped they could still have a friendship once she asked him to cool their relationship for a while, but that remained to be seen. Since Adrian lived in New Orleans and she lived in Magnolia Bay, was it even practical to expect anything to come of their mutual attraction? Would any of it even matter in a few months' time?

"Just friendship." Sara scoffed. "I've known you since third grade. And I didn't fall off the turnip truck yesterday."

"Just friendship," Heather repeated. "If that."

A rescue volunteer came up to them, leading a charmingly scruffy midsize dog on a leash. "I'm sorry," she said to Sara, "but we totally forgot to bring poop bags. Do y'all have any to spare?"

Sara turned toward Heather.

"Yes, of course," Heather answered. "Come with me."

"It's turned out to be a beautiful day," the woman commented on their way across the parking lot. "Hasn't it?"

Heather looked up at the endless blue sky for the first time that day. She'd been so preoccupied with her worry over Adrian and their relationship that she'd completely forgotten to ground herself in the here and now. The weather had indeed cooperated to ensure a perfect day. A tropical storm brewing in the gulf, the first storm of this hurricane season, was still several days from landfall. It hadn't yet sent a cloud into the sky, but already it created a lovely warm breeze that flirted with the skirt of Heather's sundress. "It's perfect," Heather agreed. "I'm so glad y'all could come and be a part of our celebration."

Heather took the woman into the shelter and provided her with poop bags. "Best of luck finding homes for the dogs you brought to the adoption event today." They chatted all the way back to the adoption event, then Heather waved to Sara and walked through the large drive-through gate that had been left open between the shelter and Bayside Barn.

The pre-storm breeze flirted playfully with the flags that decorated the food booths, and fluttered the edges of the disposable tablecloths on the tables in the pavilion. In early September down here, the weather was still hot as blazes, so these breezy days before a storm brought welcome relief from the oppressive, muggy heat that often persisted into October.

Most of the tropical storms in the gulf either fizzled out or went somewhere else. Gulf Coast residents took the threat of storms with a grain of salt until they knew they had a real and imminent danger to guard against or flee from. There was no use fretting; people did what they could to prevent damage, then prepared to hunker down or flee as the situation evolved.

As with Bayside Barn, the shelter was prepared to ride out all but the most severe hurricanes. The new buildings at the shelter had all been built to withstand a Category 5 storm. Part of the shelter's planning phase had included coming up with a hurricane preparedness plan, and the team had decided that animals housed in the older buildings would be evacuated for a storm rated Category 3 or higher, just to be safe.

Worried about the conversation she planned to have with Adrian, Heather sought out Reva, who always made her feel better, no matter what was going on. She found her standing near the portable corral where the two ponies, Sunshine and Midnight, were decked out with flowers and ribbons braided into their manes and tails. "Ready for the pony rides, I see."

"Yep." Reva nodded toward the big red barn. "And Sean and Erin are bringing out the donkeys now." The donkeys, Elijah and Miriam, looked comical and cute in flower-bedecked straw hats with holes cut out for their ears. "I've tasked them with making sure that the equines and their handlers have plenty of water and time to rest in between rides."

"Erin will love that." Heather noticed the happy glow on her daughter's face as Erin chatted with the handsome teen. "Sean seems not to mind either."

"They're both pretty taken with each other." Reva glanced at her watch. "People will be arriving soon. Are you and Abby set to give shelter tours?"

"I'll walk over in a minute." Someone had set up a canopy by the big gate between the properties with a sign advertising shelter tours every half hour. "I noticed the tour station when I walked past."

Reva opened the corral gate so Erin and Sean could lead the donkeys through. "Y'all all set?" she asked the kids.

At their thumbs-up, Reva and Heather walked toward the dividing wall between the two properties. Food tents with festive banners lined the Bayside Barn parking lot, which would remain closed to vehicles today. A critter-petting enclosure had been erected outside the barn, and volunteers wearing colorful Bayside Barn T-shirts were beginning to take their stations. Tickets for food and fun would be sold at the gate by the road and at the pavilion, which had been set up as a food court with tables and chairs. "How's Adrian doing today?" Reva asked. "Have you heard?"

Heather filled Reva in on the text Eileen had sent earlier. "I'm worried about seeing him though."

Reva ran a hand down Heather's arm. "Why?"

Heather shrugged. "I'm going to tell him that we need to go back to being friends. I had no business thinking..." She shrugged again, then left it at that.

"Thinking what?" Reva pressed. "Thinking you deserve to be happy?"

"Starting something this intense with Adrian was stupid. I'm not ready for a romantic relationship."

Reva made a tsking sound. "I wouldn't have pegged you as a coward."

Heather lifted her chin. "The kids and I were just beginning to move on with our lives after Dale's death. Starting to gain some equilibrium. But I let Adrian get too close too fast, and when he got hurt, it put us right back where we started. I just need to back up a bit and reassess."

"I can see how bringing a new man into your life might stir old ghosts, and his accident was upsetting, but—"

"Caroline had that old nightmare about Dale dying last night," Heather interrupted. "She hasn't had that nightmare in months, but seeing Adrian so hurt brought it all back."

"Sure it did." Reva's voice was soft, and she put a gentle hand on Heather's back. "But that doesn't mean you should give up trying to be happy, does it?"

"I'm not giving up. I'm just…postponing." Heather's eyes stung with tears, but she blinked them away. "I think that Adrian and I need to learn how to be friends before we think about being lovers." She swallowed. "If the kids and I fall in love with Adrian and anything happens to him, we won't survive it."

Reva rubbed Heather's back softly. "And what if you've already fallen in love with him?"

Heather straightened her spine. "I can't afford to think about that."

Chapter 17

ADRIAN FELT LIKE GROWLING AT EVERYONE WHO GAVE HIM shocked glances as he walked past the people leaving Bayside Barn and heading toward their cars. His forehead and nose were both bandaged, and even though he wore his sunglasses, the entire top half of his face was bruised and swollen.

As the medics had predicted, he did indeed look like Frankenstein.

At the gate, he paid the entry fee for himself and his parents and bought a bunch of tickets for them plus more for Heather's kids. "Y'all have fun," he said to his parents. "I'm gonna go find Heather."

Even this late in the afternoon, the place was packed. The hot breeze carried the sound of a live band playing Zydeco music along with the mingled scents of barbecue, funnel cake, and grilled corn on the cob.

Adrian found Erin and Sean taking tickets for the pony and donkey rides. Erin's eyes went wide, and her mouth dropped open.

Seeing the expression on her face, Sean followed her gaze. "Whoa," Sean said. "Holy shit, Batman."

Surprising Adrian, Erin gave him a hug. "I'm so glad you're okay." She pulled away and studied his face. "I mean, I hope you're okay. At least you're walking, right? I mean, at least you're not—"

"Right." He was glad he wasn't dead too. "I might not win any beauty contests for a while, but I'm gonna be okay."

"Can I see?" She made a motion asking him to remove his sunglasses.

He lifted them up for a second, revealing two spectacularly black eyes.

Erin winced, and Sean turned away to take someone's tickets and tell them where to stand to wait for the next group's ride. But not before Adrian saw the pained look on Sean's face. "It's not as bad as it looks," he said to both teens. Then, to Erin, "Do you know where your mom is?"

Erin pointed in the direction of the gate between the shelter and the barn. "She and Abby are taking turns giving shelter tours."

He had walked right past there, so Heather must have been giving a tour. "Okay, thanks. What about the twins?"

Erin shrugged. "Around here somewhere. They ran out of tickets a while back, so…" She shrugged again.

"Okay. If you see them, tell them to come find me at the shelter. I've got more tickets for them."

"Will do." Erin hugged him again. "I'm glad you're okay."

"Thanks." Adrian hadn't walked ten feet before he was tackled from behind, and two spindly little arms wrapped around his legs. He'd know that tackle and those spindly little arms anywhere. "Josh, hey."

"Ade! You came!" Josh released him, and Adrian turned to see Josh, Caroline, and another kid about their same size staring at him. "Whoa!" Josh yelled, apparently delighted at Adrian's gruesome appearance. "You're all bruised up. Can I see your scars?"

"Maybe later."

Caroline stood behind the boys, looking uncomfortable. Adrian knelt. "Come here, Caroline."

She eased forward, and he gently guided her to sit on his knee. "I'm sorry you had to see what happened yesterday. I know that was very upsetting for you."

She nodded, her green eyes solemn.

"But I'm okay now."

She didn't say anything. She just stared.

"Are you okay?"

She stuck her thumb in her mouth and shrugged.

"She had nightmares," Josh offered. "Didn't you, Caroline?"

She nodded.

He smoothed her long blond hair. "I'm really sorry about that."

"Did you get stitches?" Josh asked, clearly enthralled with the idea.

"Yep." When Adrian looked at Josh, he noticed Caroline studying his face. When he turned his head, she would've been able to see the bruised skin beneath his sunglasses. Not black, exactly, but certainly a nice deep purple.

"How many?" the other kid, a boy with curly red hair and freckles, spoke up.

"Forty-six," Adrian answered.

"Wow," both boys said at once.

"Did it hurt?" Caroline asked in a soft, hesitant voice.

Adrian thought about sugarcoating it, but he knew Caroline would know better, and he wanted her to trust him. "Yes, it did. It hurt pretty bad. But not the getting-stitches part. They gave me shots so that part didn't hurt."

"Shots hurt," Caroline said. "Don't they?"

He smiled. "Yeah, but not much because after the first few shots, everything starts to go numb."

She reached up and touched the bruise that wasn't quite hidden by his sunglasses.

"Is your nose broke?" Josh asked with avid curiosity.

"No. My nose isn't broken." They'd done a CT scan to determine the severity of his concussion, so even though his nose looked broken, they knew for sure that it wasn't.

"Mama said you had a combustion, though."

Adrian laughed, then winced because any kind of movement still hurt like hell. "I had a concussion. But it's going to be okay too."

"Okay, well," Josh said, now that all the fun of examining Adrian's injuries was over. "Max and me are gonna go play. Caroline, are you coming?"

Caroline looked at the boys, then at Adrian, weighing her options.

"You can come with me if you like," he said to her. "I'm gonna go find your mother."

She smiled at him, a tiny upward tilt of her lips. "I'll come with you."

Adrian stood, and Caroline slipped her hand into his. He gave a handful of tickets to Josh, who yelled, "Thanks, Ade." After counting his ticket windfall, Josh grinned. "I'll split with ya," he promised his friend, and both boys took off in the direction of the bouncy house.

"I've got tickets for you too, Caroline, if you want to play any of the games."

"No, thank you. But after we find Mama, can we go see the puppies?"

"Sure thing." They went to the tent where the shelter tours started. Abby was sitting in one of the two chairs, reading a book. Her wavy brown hair was pulled back in a ponytail, a few wisps escaping to twirl down her neck. She wore a cute sundress and sandals but looked a little wilted in spite of the warm breeze.

"Hey, Abby," Adrian said.

She looked up from the book she was reading. "Holy sh…" Her wide hazel eyes flickered from him to Caroline. "Holy…um…sheep."

Abby set her book aside and walked over to study Adrian's face. Gingerly, she lifted his sunglasses, just enough to see his two black eyes, before easing them gently back down. "You're lucky to be alive, man," she whispered.

"So I've been told. About a million times."

"I didn't think…" Abby swallowed. "It's worse than I imagined."

He cut his eyes down toward Caroline. "I'm fine," he said with emphasis. "The bruises will fade in a few days." Or weeks, whatever. "Heather's giving a tour, I guess?"

"Yeah. She'll be done in a few minutes if you want to wait here."

"Then we're gonna go look at the puppies," Caroline announced. He could tell that his accident had set his relationship with Caroline back a bit, but once again, progress was being made.

"Yep, we are," he agreed, smiling down at her. "I just hope they're not too cute because I'm pretty sure your mama wouldn't want us bringing home a new puppy, huh?"

"Adrian," Heather said from behind him. "Can we talk in private for a few minutes?"

He turned, smiling, but felt the smile die when he saw her expression. Remote, resolute, regretful. The distance he'd sensed between them at the hospital hadn't decreased overnight, as he'd hoped. Instead, it seemed that though they stood next to each other, they were worlds apart.

Heather turned to Abby. "Don't you think we can stop doing tours at this point?" Her tone was light, but he knew she was faking a nonchalance she didn't feel.

"Yeah, sure." Abby sounded puzzled but agreeable. "Everyone who wanted a tour has probably already done it."

Heather knelt to talk to Caroline. "How about if Abby takes you to get a snack or something?"

"But Adrian was going to take me to see the puppies," Caroline said in a quiet, pleading tone. "I want to see the puppies."

"I'll take you to see the puppies." Abby held out a hand to Caroline. "Come on."

Instead of taking Abby's hand, Caroline stepped up to Adrian and raised her arms, a silent signal for him to pick her up. With an apologetic glance to Heather for making her wait, he lifted Caroline into his arms and turned slightly away from both Heather and Abby.

Caroline took his face in her small hands. "I'm sorry you got hurt," she whispered, "but I'm glad you're gonna be okay."

Touched by her sincerity, Adrian felt the unaccustomed sting of tears behind his eyes. How long had it been since he'd cried? He couldn't remember.

"Thank you, Caroline." He hugged the child close, and when she patted his back and put her head on his shoulder, he realized for the first time that he had already begun to love each of Heather's kids.

He loved Josh's wild exuberance, Caroline's quiet intelligence, and even Erin's passionate outspokenness. In the hospital last night, he'd had plenty of time to think about the life he'd been leading and the one he wanted to reach out for. He had begun to believe that maybe his life could be about more than his work and his self-indulgent pursuit of the next fun adventure. Maybe he could fit into Heather's life, and if he tried hard enough, he could be a good daddy to her kids.

But now, watching Heather's expressive face, he wondered if this would be the last time he saw any of them.

Heather spotted Reva walking toward them from the aviary with Freddy the macaw on her arm and Georgia trotting along beside her. Heather took Adrian's arm and headed in that direction. They met up with Reva near the fence that separated Reva's private residence from Bayside Barn's public venue. "Reva," Heather asked, "can we use your house for a minute? I want to talk to Adrian somewhere private."

"Sure," Reva said. "Just don't let any of the critters out. I've put Jack and Winky in there for the day to avoid getting them stressed with all the people around. Winky was in a hell of a mood, so I put him in a big dog crate in the laundry room. But his cat crate is right there, Adrian, so you can take him with you when you're ready to go back home. Just be careful with the transfer because if he manages to slip out of the house, he won't be coming back."

"We'll be careful," Heather promised.

Reva looked back and forth between them, her expression concerned. "Is everything okay?"

Heather hesitated, but Adrian answered. "Everything's fine, Reva."

"Thanks," Heather added. "We won't be long."

Inside Reva's old-fashioned farmhouse, a welling-up of love for Adrian threatened to swamp Heather's determination to pump the brakes on their relationship, but she couldn't allow that to happen. Gathering courage to say what had to be said, she perched on the edge of an overstuffed chair. Jack, the new three-legged dog, came into the room quietly. He leaned against Heather's leg.

Adrian pulled an ottoman up close to Heather's chair, sat in front of her, and slipped his sunglasses up onto his head.

She stifled a gasp at the bruising around his eyes that made the irises seem all the more blue. Without her consent, her arm reached out and her fingertips touched the swollen skin. Then her brain kicked in, and she pulled her hand back as if she'd touched a hot stove.

Adrian leaned forward and grabbed Heather's hands in his. "I can tell you're gearing up to kick me to the curb, but before you say anything, please hear me out. This thing between us is happening so fast that it scares you—hell, it scares me too. I know you're thinking that the accident was a wake-up call, a chance to back out."

"Not back out. I do think we need to back up to being friends though."

"Of course we can be friends, sure. But I had a lot of time with nothing to do but think last night, and I've realized that I want more than that."

"I've had time to think too. And I'm not capable of more than friendship right now."

"I know that the accident was traumatic. I get that. But it doesn't have to change anything between us."

"Doesn't it?" Heather pulled her hands out of his and crossed her arms. "From my perspective," Heather said with emphasis, "it changes everything."

"No, it doesn't." He bolted to his feet and paced the braided rug between the couch and Heather's chair. "It shouldn't."

"It changes everything because it made me realize that I've been selfish in thinking that I could have a relationship with you or with anyone. I'm a mother, first and foremost. My first...no, my *only* responsibility is to protect my kids."

"I'm a threat to your kids?" Adrian flung his hands up. "How, exactly? You know I would never hurt your children. I wouldn't harm them in any way. In fact, I would do anything to protect them. Even if you kicked me to the curb, I would still give my life to protect any one of them or you."

"I know that, Adrian." Heather kept her voice level. "But first of all, I'm not kicking you to the curb. I'm resetting our relationship before we're in too deep to back out."

"Ha!" He pointed an accusing finger at her face. "So. Now you admit it. You do want to back out. You *are* kicking me to the curb."

"No, I'm not. You're twisting my words. I just want to go back to being friends while we still can."

"You haven't dated enough to know this, but the friend zone is the death knell for a romantic relationship."

"We haven't known each other long enough to call this a relationship though, have we?"

"Not a... Are you kidding me? What you're saying makes zero sense." He crossed his arms and studied her, his mouth tight. With exaggerated patience, he walked over to the couch and threw himself into it. "But I'm willing to listen. Go ahead. Shoot."

In the silence marred only by the ticking grandfather clock, she gathered her thoughts. Honesty, she decided, would be her only recourse because he could read her too well to accept a lie. "I'm falling in love you, Adrian. And you're right. It scares the hell out of me."

He nodded, accepting her first declaration of love with little outward emotion beyond the movement of his throat when he swallowed.

The ticking clock marked time.

"I lost more than a year of my life when Dale died. So did my kids. We're only just now getting over it, and in some ways, we'll never be over it. Seeing...watching Dale die, right in front of us, and not being able to do anything about it... We were all scarred by it in different ways."

Adrian nodded. "I understand that." To his credit, he didn't follow up with a *But...*, though she knew he wanted to.

"The bottom line is, I may have already made the mistake of falling in love with you. But the kids aren't there yet. I need to protect them from making that same mistake. Because if we allow you to take Dale's place—"

"I don't want to take Dale's place," Adrian butted in, his voice earnest. "He will always be your kids' father. I wouldn't try to diminish his memory."

"I know, Adrian, but it's not even about that."

"Then what's it about?"

"I can't..." Sudden tears swamped the back of her throat, and she tilted her head back to keep them from flooding her eyes too. She felt him touch her knee and tilted her legs gently away from him to the other side of the chair. "I can't let you into our lives as anything more than a friend because none of us would survive it if anything happened to you. Maybe one day..."

He moved back to the ottoman and grabbed her arms, forcing her to look into his poor, bruised eyes. "Nothing is going to happen to me. I promise."

She touched his cheek. "But it already has, and it could again. It's a miracle you're not dead, Adrian. And if you had been..." This time, she couldn't stop the tears from filling her eyes and spilling over. "I barely managed to keep it together when Dale died. There were days…weeks…" She gave a huff of sad laughter. "Hell, there were whole months when I thought I'd go crazy."

"But you didn't."

Confessing it all, she realized, was the only way to get through this. "I actually did go crazy sometimes." She looked into his eyes and allowed herself to show him everything she felt. Maybe letting him know how toxic too much love could be would convince him when nothing else could. "I love my children, of course. You know that."

"Everyone knows that, Heather. It's evident in everything you do."

"But Dale was my soul mate. We were everything to each other. When he died, I did go a little bit crazy. I screamed at Josh to go get the EpiPen, not thinking that he was too little to reach it. I screamed at Caroline to go find my phone so we could call for an ambulance. I screamed at Erin to get the damn horse out of the way because I was too scared to do it and I didn't want to leave Dale's side. My poor kids…"

Heather took a shuddering breath and wiped her eyes with the tissue Adrian pressed into her hand. "My poor kids were rushing all over the place, trying to save their daddy, while all I did was sit there and hold his hand and scream at them."

"It was an emergency situation," he said, too quick to make excuses for her. "Of course you would be frantic."

"But it wasn't just then that I was a bad mother. There were days afterward when I couldn't get out of bed. I just…checked out. Erin had to step up and be the twins' mother because I…I just couldn't. She took care of me when I should have been taking care of her. She taught herself to cook, brought me food, encouraged me to eat…. I didn't even care that my children needed me. Sometimes, I'd send them outside to play so I could lock myself in my bathroom and scream until my throat was sore.

"If anyone had known how badly I was coping… If the kids had said anything to their teachers, the authorities would have taken my kids away from me. And they'd have been right to do it."

She paused to let that sink in before hitting him with the worst of it. "There were times when I let my children take care of themselves while I locked myself in my bedroom because I was afraid of what I might do to them."

"You would never hurt your children."

"Wouldn't I?" She twisted the tissue he'd given her. "How would you know?"

"I know you better than to think you could harm your kids." He put a hand over hers. "You should know yourself better than to think that."

"Pushed to the brink, anyone is capable of anything. My mother taught me that, when my father left us and she took it out on me. For years, she took it out on me. And that's a lesson I'll never forget. My kids and I have finally made it out of the woods, and now you're trying to lure us right back in."

"But, Heather, you're not your mother. And I'm not Dale. I don't have any allergies. If a bee stung me—"

"It was hornets."

"Fine. Hornets, bees, whatever. If anything stings me, I'm not going to die."

"And Dale wouldn't have died if he'd carried his EpiPen with him like any normal person would have. But he didn't because he was too much of a *fucking cowboy* to take simple precautions." One of Reva's cats hopped into her lap, and she petted its soft fur. "You're just like him in that respect. You were a fucking cowboy on that ski yesterday. Skiing backward, doing 360s—"

He scoffed. "I go skiing like three times a year. I'll never ski again if that's what it takes—"

"Yeah, but what about all the other stuff you like to do? Hiking, you could get bit by a snake. Riding Charlie, you could fall off. My point is, I'm not capable of a romantic relationship with you right now."

"And if that's not enough for me?" His eyes had gone dark, his voice deadly soft.

"Maybe our friendship will evolve into something more—and I hope it does—but I can't promise that it will. I'm not ready—"

He stood and looked down at her, his expression grim. A slow-simmering anger had begun to build behind his eyes. "So you're saying you don't want any claim on me besides friendship. I can date who I want, fuck who I want, do whatever I want, and it won't bother you. I'm no different to you than Quinn or Mack."

"Of course you're different." She'd said she was falling in love with him, but he seemed not to remember that now. How had this conversation devolved so suddenly? She wanted to apologize, to take it back, to jump up and wrap her arms around him. But instead she forced herself to sit still. With her hands buried in the cat's fur, she closed her eyes and tried to gather her thoughts, to figure out what she could say to make him understand. "I'm not breaking up with you, Adrian. I just want to put the brakes on us for a while. That's all."

"Yeah?" His voice sounded cold and distant. "And how long is a while?"

"I don't know."

"A day? A month? A year?"

The anger in his voice brought tears to her eyes, but she blinked them back. "I don't know. Maybe a year? Or a few months?"

"Sorry, honey." The endearment sounded like a curse. "That ain't gonna work for me."

"But…" She wanted to remind him of their pinkie swear to always be friends no matter what. But when she looked up at him, his expression took her breath away, and the words she wanted to say shriveled in her throat.

"I guess I'll see you at the shelter sometime. Friend." Then he turned and walked out, closing the door with a soft and final click.

Reva stood with Abby at the adoption event, watching Caroline commune with one of the adoptable dogs through the bars of his crate. Heather walked toward them, holding Josh by the hand and looking straight ahead with a miserable expression on her face. "Uh-oh," Reva said to Abby under her breath. "This doesn't bode well."

"What is going on?" Abby asked, also talking quietly. "I noticed a high degree of tension between Heather and Adrian earlier."

"It appears that she just broke up with him," Reva said, not particularly caring that she was betraying a confidence. Heather needed to have her butt spanked, and Reva had been hoping that Adrian would do it—sweetly, of course.

"What?" Abby squeaked. Then she lowered her voice. "I didn't even know they were a *thing*."

"For about two minutes, maybe," Reva said. "But it looks like Heather's gone and trashed it." She shook her head and made a tsking sound. When Heather reached them, Reva narrowed her eyes and speared Heather with a *look*.

"Don't judge me," Heather said, her voice wobbly.

"None of my business." But her heart ached for all of them. Not just Heather and Adrian, who Reva hoped would go to his friend Quinn for solace and advice, but for Heather's kids and that poor horse. Charlie had allowed himself to trust, only to be abandoned by someone he loved yet again. "I guess you're grown-up enough to do what you think is best."

Reva knew her tone suggested otherwise. She could abide foolishness in strangers, but when she saw someone she loved making a mess of their lives—and therefore also the lives of their animals, who had no say in the matter—Reva had to admit that she sometimes took it a bit personally. "Is Adrian taking Winky with him?"

"He didn't take him when he walked out."

"Great," Reva said. "I guess I'll find out what kind of mess that cat has become when I get back to my house."

"I guess you will," Heather agreed. She shifted her focus to Abby. "I'm going to take Josh and Caroline home now. Do you think you could get Quinn to give Erin a ride home later? She wants to stay and help with the cleanup."

Abby nodded. "Sure. Or I'll take her myself. No problem."

"Thank you. Come on, Caroline. It's time to go."

Caroline popped up like one of those suction-cup frogs. "Okay, Mama."

As Heather walked away with the twins, Reva noticed how brittle she looked, as if she was barely holding herself together. Did Heather think this self-inflicted trauma was better than reaching out for the chance at happiness the universe held out to her? Reva shook her head. "I hope I'm never guilty of whacking a gift horse on the rump and telling it to get the hell away from me."

Sara sidled up to Reva and Abby. "What is going on?"

"I've said too much already," Reva said, "but you should give Heather a call later on. She'll need a friend to talk to, and I've already tried. It's someone else's turn, I think."

"Okay, I will." Sara turned to Abby. "Now that y'all have the grand opening out of the way, I guess you'll be shifting to wedding planning?"

"It's mostly done," Abby said. "All but the actual decorating and last-minute stuff. Thanks for offering your photography skills on the day."

"It was the best wedding gift I could think of," Sara answered. "I'm honored that you're taking me up on it."

"Do you know that in all the years Bayside Barn has been in operation," Reva said, "it's never been a wedding venue before? This'll be a first. I wish we had time to grow some jasmine or climbing roses on the arbor Quinn is building for the ceremony."

"Ribbons and plastic flowers will be fine for us," Abby said. "And

I'll plant something pretty afterward to commemorate the occasion. Maybe whoever gets married there next will reap the benefit."

"Yeah, and I was hoping it would be…" Reva sighed. "Never mind."

A really tall guy—had to be six foot six—came up to them.

"Hello, ladies," he said in a deep, silky voice.

They all looked way, way up to meet his serious—and seriously attractive—chocolate-brown eyes.

Abby and Reva both answered, "Yes?"

Sara said "Hello" in a tone that suggested she'd just had the wind knocked out of her sails. And rightly so, Reva thought. This guy was serious eye candy. Not as pretty as Heather's Adrian, but then again, there was no comparing Superman to Kylo Ren, was there?

This guy, whose long black hair fell in loose waves to his wide shoulders, didn't have the sort of face you'd call gorgeous or even traditionally handsome. A better description would be…arresting. Compelling.

"Hey, um…" He seemed adorably abashed being the object of such close regard. "I'm here to help my friends"—he glanced over at a polished-looking couple who were bending down to look at some dogs in a nearby kennel—"choose the right dog for them."

Reva took charge, hoping that Sara would remember to close her mouth sometime soon. "Sure. I'll help you find the right people to talk with." Reva looped her arm through his and walked toward his friends. "Were you interested in a certain dog?"

He pointed out a black mastiff-Rottweiler dog inside a huge kennel that was still only big enough for the dog to stand up and turn around. "This one, I think."

Reva looked around and couldn't find any of the folks wearing the T-shirts that would identify them as volunteers for the organization manning this tent. "I'm sorry. I don't see any of the right people here at the moment."

Reva glanced over at Sara, who had composed herself and was now smiling instead of looking as if she'd been smacked upside the head. "Sara, could you come over here? Maybe you can help... um..." She looked way up at the guy's...smoldering sex appeal. That was another good description that had eluded her before. "I'm sorry. I didn't get your name?"

"Justin." He stuck out a hand, and when she shook hands with him, his hand completely engulfed hers. "Justin Reed. I'm a dog trainer. I'm helping my friends choose the right dog. We'd like to take him on-leash, maybe to one of those fenced areas, if that's okay, and work with him a little."

Sara came over with her phone in her hand. "I just sent a text. They're next door grabbing something to eat. Said they'd left a note that they'd be right back, but it must have blown away." She smiled at Justin, and a gust of wind caught her long copper curls and sent them flying, proving her point. "I don't doubt it, either. This wind!"

"Sara, this is Justin," Reva said. "Can you help him and his friends take this dog to one of the play yards?"

"Yes, of course." Sara bent down to unhook the leash that had been fastened to the door of the crate, then asked the big black dog to sit. He sat, and Reva sent a silent "Good job" to the dog, who cocked his ears and glanced toward her but went back to staring straight ahead while Sara unlatched the crate door and hooked the leash to his collar.

Reva's phone in her pocket beeped with a loud emergency alert alarm. She let out a surprised yelp and just about jumped out of her skin. Several other phones nearby went off as well, and a ripple of "Whoos!" and "Ohs!" and "Ooohs!" went through the crowd. Reva silenced her phone and was still reading the message when the alarm went off again. "I get it," she fussed at her phone, hitting the mute button for the second time.

Sara gave the leash to Justin. Without speaking a word, Justin looked down at the dog, who responded immediately by sitting at Justin's side and training his gaze on Justin, awaiting further instruction. The couple who'd come with Justin so he could help them choose a dog sidled up to join the conversation. "What's going on?" the pretty blond woman asked. "Was that an Amber Alert?"

"Incoming storm alert," Reva answered absently. They had thirty-six hours' notice to prepare for the arrival of a tropical storm with the potential to become a hurricane. But she was more interested in the arrival of *this* guy, a kindred spirit, whether he knew it or not.

Reva had never met another animal communicator before, aside from her niece, Abby, whom Reva had trained herself. But this big guy standing in front of her definitely was one.

Did he know it? Or was he like Cesar Milan, who seemed to think that his training ability was all due to the accurate observation of body language and the astute application of behavior modification techniques?

"Yeah?" Justin looked up at the still-clear-blue skies. "When?"

She flapped a hand. "Couple days. It's just a tropical storm. I doubt it'll turn into more than a Category 1, if that. We'll be fine."

The woman's eyes opened wide. "You mean a *hurricane*?"

"Just a little one. More likely, just a tropical storm."

"We're from California," she said. "We're used to earthquakes and fires. Aren't you worried?"

"If it was expected to be bigger, yes, we'd be worried. But with these smaller storms, we're more concerned with flooding than wind. And we're on high ground here. This bluff has been built up over centuries."

"Sounds like you've got everything under control, but..." Justin took his wallet out of his back pocket and flipped it open one-handed while the dog at his side looked on with interest. "If you do need help with evacuating the animals, we can provide transportation." He gave Reva his business card.

"Oh, yes," the pretty lady said. "We'll be filming in New Orleans for the next few months. We have access to any sort of vehicle you'd want. Buses, ambulances, whatever. The props department can get anything. If y'all need help, let Justin know."

"Thank you." Reva looked down at Justin's business card. "We will."

Now, she was the one who probably looked like she'd been smacked upside the head, and she reminded herself to close her mouth. Justin wasn't just a dog trainer; he was an animal trainer for the film industry. His picture showed him cozying up to a full-grown tiger, something that made Reva feel immediately and intensely jealous.

"Sara," Reva said weakly, "would you please show Justin and his friends to the play yard? I need to see how things are going next door."

Maybe Justin and Sara would hit it off and exchange numbers. They clearly had some chemical thing going between them. But since Reva had struck out matchmaking between Heather and Adrian—who had seemed so *right* for each other—she might as well put any ideas about those other two out of her head.

Reva went back to her house, wondering what sort of state she'd find Winky in. Poor cat had been bounced around so much in such a short amount of time that she feared he would never trust humans again. "Winky?" Reva walked toward his crate in the laundry room. "How you doing, kitty?"

The poor cat sat in his litter box, his face tucked into the far back corner of the crate. His head was down; his eyes were closed. Reva cautiously opened the crate door in case he thought about running, but he sat still and unresponsive. She reached into the crate to touch his hunched back. He didn't flinch or hiss or try to run. He didn't move at all. "Hey, buddy. What's wrong, huh?"

She knew what was wrong, but she was hoping to start a dialogue, to get him to express his feelings about being abandoned. "Do you feel like talking about it?"

She didn't get a sense of yes or no. She didn't get anything at all. Winky had shut down emotionally to such a degree that Reva couldn't reach him.

───────────

Adrian sat on his balcony early the next morning and watched the river drift past. He still had trouble believing that Heather had kicked him into the friend zone, which honestly wasn't that far from the curb. He knew exactly what the *let's be friends* line meant because he'd used it himself more times than he could count.

He'd used it on Jamie, who'd been just as ready to move on as he had, so they'd actually been able to *be* friends after the breakup. But no mistake; it had been a breakup. That's exactly what *let's be friends* meant. He learned that when his high school girlfriend found somebody new the month after he moved to Houston. *Let's be friends.* Yeah, right.

He missed Heather already.

He missed her kids.

He even missed the damn cat and regretted not taking Winky with him when he left. Winky would have given him some comfort. But at the time, Adrian hadn't wanted to take even a minute to do what needed to be done to make that happen. He'd been so angry and upset that he hadn't wanted to do anything other than get the hell out of there.

He was halfway home before he realized that his parents would be worried that he'd just disappeared. He pulled over and sent a text claiming that something work-related had come up and he had to return to New Orleans right away. Then he sent step-by-step instructions they could follow to get to the highway when they were ready to head home.

He couldn't believe he'd run away like an embarrassed kid.

Stupid. He had been too shell-shocked to think straight, as numb as he'd been when that ski first hit him in the face.

The pain was coming on stronger now, along with a hefty dose of anger at Heather for not even giving them a chance. He felt as isolated and uprooted now as he had when Hurricane Katrina had torn through New Orleans and ripped through his life.

Adrian realized that because of what he'd been through, he could empathize with animals whose lives were impacted by events over which they had no control. Adrian had promised to ride Charlie no matter what happened with Heather. The poor horse had done nothing wrong. But now, through no fault of his own, Charlie would be stuck in his stall again with no one to ride him.

Okay, not strictly true because Adrian felt sure Quinn would spend time with the horse. But for Quinn, it would be a perfunctory obligation. For Adrian, it had been a pleasure and a joy. For him and for Charlie, it had been the beginning of a relationship.

And hell, he had relationships with Heather's kids too, no matter what she thought. What right did she have to yank the foundations out from under all those relationships?

Tired of sitting on the balcony and fuming all by himself, he thought about calling Jamie but decided against it. Fuck-buddy sex wasn't going to help his situation, and he liked Jamie too much to damage the friendship they'd managed to salvage from the ashes of a few too many meaningless hookups.

Besides, Jamie wasn't Heather. The only reason he and Jamie had managed to be friends after being lovers was that neither of them really *wanted* the other. And he did want Heather. Still.

Aimless, he went back inside and turned on his laptop. Took care of some business, billed some clients, took on that new job he'd been angling for. They wanted him to come to Dallas to meet everyone and observe the company setup in person, so fine, he'd go to Dallas. He e-signed the contract, made the bookings, then emailed his itinerary to the company president. He would fly out first thing in the morning, then stay for a couple of weeks. That should get him over the worst of this.

By the time he got home from Dallas, he would be over his failed-before-it-even-got-started relationship with Heather.

And, he realized, it was just as well that he hadn't brought the cat.

But dammit, he deserved a chance to say goodbye to Charlie. He sent a text to Heather:

> I'll be going out of town for a few days. I'm going to your place today to ride Charlie one more time before I leave. I'll come when you're at work and the kids are at school.

He didn't ask Heather for permission. Fuck getting her permission. Adrian had made a promise to that horse, and he intended to keep it. He'd go today and spend some quality time with Charlie. He'd double-check with Quinn that he would be around to ride Charlie while he was away.

And when Adrian got back from Dallas, he would insist on the right to continue riding Charlie on a regular basis. Hell, maybe he'd even insist on buying the horse from her. There were plenty of high-dollar full-board horse barns around here where he could rent a stall.

It wasn't like Heather spent any time with Charlie anyway beyond the bare minimum required for the horse's upkeep. Maybe she would let him buy Charlie. Then at least he'd get a horse out of the deal instead of walking away with nothing but a broken heart.

With a plan in mind and a tiny ember of resentment burning in his heart, he dressed in jeans and boots and a thin old T-shirt for riding, then stuffed a change of clothes and a pair of tennis shoes into his gym bag.

A message came through from Heather:

That's fine! Charlie will be glad to see you.

It seemed from the breezy tone of her text that she was already comfortable with her decision to put him in the friend zone. But then, a second later, another message came through.

Please be careful.

Adrian flipped a bird at his phone and headed out the door.

Chapter 18

WINKY HAD TO HAVE HIS MEDICINE, SO NEITHER HE NOR REVA had any choice but to engage in armed combat over it, Winky armed with claws and teeth, Reva armed with a thick beach towel and determination. She wrapped him in the towel and tried to stick the medicine-dosing syringe in his mouth, but he managed to break free and skedaddle between the washer and the dryer.

Given Winky's current attitude, dosing him had become a two-person job, but Abby and Heather were outside taking down the last vestiges of yesterday's celebration and preparing for the incoming storm: bringing the pool patio furniture into the barn, bungee-cording the heavy polyethylene rocking chairs to the porch railings, taking down hanging ferns, wind chimes, and bird feeders.

Quinn was taking each of the vehicles to fill with gasoline and topping up jerricans for the portable generators because Reva's house didn't have a fancy propane-powered generator like the shelter did. Quinn was also exchanging propane tanks for the grill. Even though this storm was only a tropical storm, it probably wouldn't be the last one this hurricane season.

Quinn's attitude was that they might as well be prepared for anything, and whatever supplies they didn't use this time, they'd have on hand for the next storm. Reva appreciated his foresight.

Reva found Winky hiding behind the dryer. "Thanks a bunch, Winky." The damn cat had managed to disconnect the dryer hose in the process of hunkering down between the dryer and the laundry room wall. "Come out," she threatened, "or I will move the dryer and drag you out."

He hissed and growled in defiance.

Reva closed the laundry room door and put her back into the effort of moving the dryer. When she'd moved the dryer out far enough to squeeze through the gap, she tossed the towel over the cowering cat and scooped him up.

She got a few scratches for her efforts but finally managed to dose him with both medicines, then threw him none too gently into the big dog crate she had outfitted for him.

Hissing, Winky leaped into the litter box at the back of the crate. His one good eye was narrowed, but the other one was nearly shut. Despite the faithful and liberal application of the antibiotic ointment, that eye wasn't getting better.

It looked worse.

Reva closed her eyes and tried to connect with the cat. "How bad does your eye hurt? The same as before? Better? Worse?"

Nothing. She got nothing. She opened her eyes to see that Winky had turned his back on her. "Fine, then," she said in a huff.

But it wasn't fine. Winky was being a turd, yes, but he had good reason. He'd made a giant leap of faith in trusting Adrian, and Adrian had betrayed that trust by abandoning him. No wonder Winky was mad. He had every right to be acting out, and his crappy attitude wasn't a good-enough reason for Reva to deny him the veterinary care she was pretty sure he needed, even though he refused to tell her how he felt.

Reva called Mack on his cell, and though he was at the office, he answered.

"Hey." Mack always had been a man of few words.

"That cat's eye isn't getting any better. I'm worried. Either that ointment isn't working, or—"

"Bring him in."

Reva threw the towel over the cat for the second time that day, dragged him out of the big crate, and deposited him in a smaller one she could carry by herself. She sent Abby a text to let her know she was heading to the vet and offered to swing by the grocery store on the way home if Abby wanted to text a list. She left Georgia and Jack piled up on the couch watching Dog TV, then drove into town to Mack's vet clinic with the cat carrier on the passenger seat.

Bypassing the waiting room for the people who hadn't spent enough money at the vet to pay for Mack's truck, Reva went through the back door, Mack's private entrance. "Hey, Mack," she called. "I'm here."

Mack's latest vet tech, the pretty girl with a purple braid, came around the corner, drying her hands on a paper towel. "Hey, Reva. Mack said for you to wait for him in exam room two. He's with another client right now, but he'll be with you soon."

"Thanks." Reva took Winky to the exam room, then sat in a chair and checked her messages. One from Abby with a grocery list and another from Quinn, though she didn't have time to open it because Mack walked in.

"Hey," he said, the lines beside his whiskey-brown eyes crinkling with his smile. "How's Adrian?" Mack stuck his hands in the back pockets of his jeans. "Have you heard anything?"

"He'll live."

Mack turned and peered out into the hallway, then turned back to Reva. "I'm sorry. I thought my friend Reva was in here. You might have seen her? Earth-mother type, all sweet and understanding and 'Kumbaya'?"

Reva pursed her lips and gave him the stink eye.

"She's probably somewhere around here," he kept on, hanging on to the doorframe with a big grin pasted on his face, "talking about how we're all interconnected fragments of divine source energy expressing itself in physical form and all that shit."

"It's too bad you're not as funny as you think you are. I really hate it for you."

He stepped fully into the room and closed the door behind him. "What's wrong, darlin'?"

"I'm just mad," Reva confessed. "I'm mad at Heather for dumping Adrian, and I'm mad at Adrian for dumping this cat. Winky was just learning to trust people, and now we'll have to start all over again trying to tame him."

"Awww, come here." Mack wrapped his brawny arms around Reva and gave her a big, friendly, bearlike hug. She laid her head on his wide, hard chest, wrapped her arms around his thick, muscular waist, and allowed herself to absorb the comfort he offered. He patted her back. "I'm sorry we lowly humans are often such a disappointment to you."

She swatted his butt and stepped away. "Thanks, Mack." He was such an adorable jerk. "You always know just what to say to make me feel better."

He grinned and ran a hand over his short dark hair that he'd probably cut with dog grooming clippers. The man was unashamed—and maybe even proud—of his rough edges. "Let's take a look at that cat."

Together, they managed to get the resistant feline out of the crate and wrapped in the towel, kitty taco–style.

While Reva held Winky securely, Mack's long, blunt fingers gently pried open the cat's irritated eyelid. "Yeah, I'm sorry to say, it looks like he's gonna lose this eye. You see how the eyeball looks like it's getting smaller? It's gonna keep bothering him unless we do something about it."

"By do something, I assume you mean remove the eyeball and sew the eyelid shut?"

"Yep, sorry. I think it's the best thing. Especially since he's still half-wild and giving him that medicine is such an ordeal. You need to be working to build trust, not holding him down and torturing him twice a day. He prob'ly can't see much out of that eye anyway. And it's bound to get worse, not better."

"Okay." Mack wasn't the sort to suggest a pricey procedure if it wasn't necessary. "Can you do it today?"

Mack reached out with one finger to stroke the cat's head. "Have you fed him anything today?"

"I gave him food, but he hasn't touched it." Reva rocked the cat gently, soothing it the same way she would a swaddled infant.

Mack nodded. "I'll do it today. You can pick him up around 4:30."

He touched her shoulder and gave her a small, compassionate smile. "I know that's not what you wanted to hear, but it's the best thing."

"I know. Can I sit with him for a few minutes before you take him?"

"Sure." Mack put a hand on the doorknob. "I'll send Sandy back here to get him in a bit."

After Mack left, Reva sat in a chair by the window, closed her eyes, and took a couple of breaths to clear her mind. Even though she held Winky in her arms, she tried to connect in by imagining that he was sitting in front of her and giving her his attention. After forty forevers, she still couldn't imagine him doing anything other than ignoring her.

But finally, she looked down to see him twitch one ear in her direction. Listening, at least. She explained the medical situation at hand, but when she asked whether Winky understood, all she got was "Don't care." Then, after another long moment, "Why did Adrian abandon me?"

"Adrian was planning to take you home with him, but a lot of things happened that kept him from doing it."

Winky opened up to Reva about his effort to connect with Adrian when he didn't come back to get him from the shelter. "I kept asking where he was, and all I could see was a dark fog. He was hiding from me."

"No, he wasn't hiding. He was at the hospital, zonked out on painkillers." Reva reminded Winky of how he'd felt when he'd been given anesthesia for the neuter surgery.

Determined to feel sorry for himself, Winky hid his head in the crook of Reva's elbow. "He threw me away. He doesn't care about me."

Reva explained that because Adrian's feelings were hurt over being discarded by Heather, he had, unfortunately, discarded Winky. A delicate thing to explain to someone who'd just been ditched by their beloved. But being a multispecies family therapist had its challenges. "Humans and their messed-up love lives can be hard on the animals who love them."

Reva had expected Winky to react badly to the news, but instead, Winky lifted his head and stared out the exam-room window with an intense expression on his face. It was clear that he was percolating on a solution.

"What do you think we should do?" she asked.

"I need to be with Heather," Winky replied. "If she will take me home with her, I can convince her to take Adrian back. Then he will take *me* back."

"But how will you do that?"

"I don't know," Winky answered. "But I'll figure that out when I get there."

———————

A call came through from Quinn when Adrian had just finished saddling Charlie. "Hey, Ade," Quinn said. "Just checking up on you. Abby told me what happened yesterday. That's raw, man."

Raw described it pretty well, Adrian thought. "Yeah, well." There wasn't much to be said about the fact that Heather was done with him. "That which doesn't kill us and all that bullshit." Adrian left Charlie tied to the stall's window bars, then sat on a hay bale to talk to Quinn. "How'd the event go yesterday?"

"All good," Quinn said. "Made a bunch of money, enough to pay for those generators y'all picked up for the shelter plus a little left over."

The reminder of Adrian's night with Heather stung. He'd thought it had meant something to her, but he guessed he was wrong. "Well, I'd better go. I've got this horse saddled up, and—"

"Oh, you're at Heather's house now?"

"Out in the barn, yeah."

"I'll swing by and visit for a sec. I've got a trailer load of hay; stocking up in case we're not able to go out for a while after the storm."

"What storm?"

Quinn laughed. "The tropical storm that's supposed to make landfall in the next few hours. You haven't heard about it?"

"I haven't been paying that much attention, what with having my face bashed in and getting dumped and all." Adrian looked down at the bales he was sitting on, then glanced around the barn. These two bales appeared to be all Charlie had. "Did Heather tell you to pick up any extra for Charlie?"

"No. I should have asked, but the girls have been busy, cleaning up and nailing down anything that might fly off in the wind. I can give Charlie some of this hay, no problem. I'll see you in a bit."

Adrian put his phone on a nearby shelf and tightened Charlie's cinch strap, then led him out of the barn and into the field. A gusty wind blew leaves off the trees and carried them tumbling sideways along invisible currents of turbulent air. The sky was filled with fast-moving clouds that were more white than gray. They weren't likely to drop any rain yet, but the cool mist in the air promised rain later in the day, well in advance of the expected storm.

Adrian accepted the fact that he might be driving home in a downpour.

He and Charlie had a good ride, walking to warm up and build rapport, then racing to blow off steam and get a good workout. Charlie kept veering toward the woodland trail behind Heather's house, and though Adrian had promised Heather that he wouldn't ride off the property without her consent, he was dealing with a hefty dose of fuck-it energy right now, so with a muttered "What the hell," he rode up to the gate that led to the woods then leaned down and opened it to let Charlie walk through.

Heather had elicited that promise from Adrian because she'd been worried about him. It wasn't as if she cared all that much what happened to him now. And anyway, nothing bad was likely to happen if he and Charlie took a nice quiet ride through the woods.

Then Adrian remembered that Quinn was planning to stop by.

If Adrian was off riding Charlie in the woods—especially given that Adrian had left his phone in the barn—he and Quinn might miss each other. And even though Heather had said she'd make arrangements for Quinn to ride Charlie, Adrian didn't want to leave it completely up to her. No reason he shouldn't at least give Quinn a heads-up.

Rather than going back through the gate he'd just closed, Adrian rode Charlie around the perimeter of the field and along the road to Heather's house. Quinn came into the barn, just as Adrian had unsaddled Charlie and was about to brush him down.

"Hey." Adrian looked out the open barn door at Quinn's truck and the trailer it pulled. "What's with the horse trailer? When you said you had a trailer load of hay, I was imagining the flatbed."

"Didn't want to take the chance of the hay getting rained on."

Quinn came closer to inspect Adrian's injuries and whistled. "Jeez-o-Pete." Adrian had dispensed with the bandages this morning, so his bruises and the long line of stitches across his forehead plus the glued-together cut across the bridge of his nose were on full display. "I didn't know it was that bad."

"Bad enough," Adrian agreed. "So give me the scoop on the storm."

"The wind isn't supposed to be too bad, but it's moving slow, so it'll be dumping a lot of rain."

Adrian looked out the window of Charlie's stall toward the river that flowed not far behind Heather's house. Her house was built up several feet above the ground. The barn, which was closer to the river, was not. "Has this place ever flooded?"

"No idea," Quinn said. "But the slope from the barn to the river is pretty flat. I'd say it's an extreme possibility. Especially if the storm parks on top of us for any length of time. It's predicted to go right over Magnolia Bay."

What would Heather do if this place flooded? Had she ever gotten new tires for Charlie's old dilapidated trailer so she could evacuate him? Could she even load him in the trailer if that became necessary? And what if the storm winds were worse than predicted?

Adrian observed the construction of Charlie's barn with a critical eye and decided that even a small wind could tear this simply built structure apart. The eight-inch-thick poles that held up the metal roof could snap off in a high wind. And though they were probably sunk in concrete, if the ground around them became saturated, the posts could shift, causing the roof to collapse.

Bayside Barn's thick steel support beams were bolted into a two-foot-thick concrete slab.

The roof of this barn consisted of corrugated roofing metal screwed into flimsy, hollow metal supports that could twist or be ripped off in a bad thunderstorm, let alone a hurricane.

Bayside Barn's roof was constructed with corrugated roofing metal over tar-paper-covered OSB over two-by-eight wood beams spanning solid steel I-beams.

In any sort of imminent weather event, Charlie should be

somewhere safer than this. "Do you think Reva could make room for Charlie at Bayside Barn?"

"Yeah, sure. We built all new enclosures for the smaller grazing critters at the farm so the barn would have a few extra stalls for the shelter's use."

Adrian rested a hand on Charlie's broad back. "You got room in that trailer to load him up?"

"We'll have to shift the hay to one side, but yeah." Quinn narrowed his gaze at Adrian. "You gonna run this past Heather first?"

"She'd probably take it better coming from you," he suggested.

"I'm not walking into that buzz saw." Quinn looked up at the barn's roof, and his gaze traveled from point to point, clearly assessing the building's structural integrity. "She's likely to resist either of us interfering in what she sees as her business."

Adrian knew what Quinn was thinking, but he asked the question anyway. "Do you think this place is safe for Charlie to be in right now, given the current weather predictions?"

"Nope." Quinn put his hands in his pockets. "I wouldn't keep my horse here. If I had one, that is."

Adrian walked over to the shelf where he'd left his phone. "I'm gonna call Heather." He tried, but she didn't answer. Nobody answered the shelter's landline either. They were probably all outside preparing for the storm. "Either she's ignoring my call, or she's too busy to answer."

"They're busy, for sure. But if we are gonna move Charlie, we should do it now," Quinn suggested, "since I'm already here with the trailer and it's not yet pouring rain."

Adrian felt a grin tugging at the corners of his mouth. "You thinking what I'm thinking?"

Quinn looked resigned. "Better to apologize later than to ask permission now?"

"You'll still have to work with her," Adrian felt obliged to point out. "Whereas my walking papers have already been issued."

"*Au contraire, mon frère.* I have fulfilled my obligations to the animal shelter as of yesterday's grand opening."

"So…" Adrian felt a spark of excitement, which he had to admit felt a whole lot better than the sadness and anger he'd been carrying since yesterday at about this time. "You up for adding horse thievery to your rap sheet? I am if you are."

"Well, technically, it's not thievery if we're just temporarily relocating the horse for a good reason, is it?"

Adrian shrugged. "I don't know. I think we'd have to consult a lawyer to determine that for sure."

"And anyway, those drunk and disorderly charges were dismissed, if you'll remember."

"Noted." Adrian looked at his watch. "If we're gonna do this, we'd better get busy."

"You need to at least inform her of what we've done and why so she doesn't come out here to feed Charlie and have a cow when she finds him gone."

"Agreed." Adrian tried to call Heather once more, but again the call went to voicemail. He left a message, knowing she might not listen to it. She was ignoring him, and he wasn't surprised. "I'll send her a text as soon as we hit the road."

Heather waved to Quinn when she met his truck on the road, pulling the horse trailer he had taken to fill with hay in advance of the storm. Adrian's car was following right behind. On their way to the shelter, she guessed.

She hoped Adrian wasn't going there to get Winky (whose name would be an even better fit for him now that he only had one eye) because Heather had just signed the adoption papers and was on her way to the vet's office to get him.

She truly hoped Adrian hadn't decided that he wanted to keep

Winky because she didn't want him to think she was taking the cat away from him out of spite. Unfortunately, right now, anything she said or did was likely to be taken the wrong way. Adrian was angry, and she understood now that he had taken her request for friendship the wrong way. She'd talked to Sara, who'd commiserated with Heather but also helped her see his point of view. His ego was bruised, and Heather hoped that once he'd had some time to think it over, he'd realize that backing up wasn't the same as backing out.

But for now, he thought he'd been dumped. That was his reality. Thinking she'd dumped him was bad enough. Thinking she'd dumped him and taken his cat would be worse.

But Winky was going home with her now, not Adrian, no matter what either of them preferred. She had already told her kids, and they were all excited, so that was that.

Reva had laid it on pretty thick about how Heather's dumping of Adrian had led to his dumping of Winky and why Heather owed it to Winky to give the cat a loving forever home. Heather had tried to explain that from her point of view, Adrian had been the one to walk away, but Reva had flapped her hands and said, "Not my circus, not my monkeys. Are you gonna take the cat or not?"

Heather had been leery of the idea of having Jasper and Winky together in the same house, but Reva claimed to have communicated with both parties and negotiated a mutual peacekeeping agreement.

So, here Heather was, leaving work early to do some pre-storm grocery shopping and then make it to the vet by 4:30 to pick up the cat. Heather wished she had time to run by the house and change clothes—even take a shower—before going to Mack's vet clinic. She was way past the point in her life when she needed to impress anyone, but she didn't want to offend anyone, either. And the sad fact was, she had worked so hard today to batten down the hatches at the shelter and the barn that she knew for a fact that she… Well, she wouldn't say she stank exactly, but she wasn't as *fresh* as she'd prefer.

She had, in fact, at one point in the day been so hot and drenched in sweat that when she took her phone out of her back pocket, the screen displayed a *device overheating* message shortly before going black. And on top of that, the thing was so wet that she feared for its battery. Reva had given her a bag of rice and a couple of cool packs, and Heather's hopefully not-dead phone was turned off and (please God) recovering in the side pocket of her laptop case.

But the pre-storm preparations at the shelter and the barn were necessary, and when Heather got home, she would have to do them all over again at her house. Fortunately, there wasn't much to do at her place that she hadn't done already, except shop for enough groceries to get the family through a week and then tend to Charlie.

Heather had Charlie's safety concerns covered. She had spoken to her neighbor up the hill earlier in the day—before her phone died—and the woman had said that yes, of course, Charlie could bunk with her horse in their much nicer barn that wasn't in danger of flooding or blowing away.

The neighbor and her husband had given shelter to Charlie in past storms, and the lady reiterated that they were happy to have Charlie hang out at their place anytime.

Heather and Erin just needed to pack up a few gallon Ziploc bags with horse food, then lead Charlie up the hill. The neighbors had more than enough hay, and the lady had joked that if Heather tried to bring more hay, she would stuff it down Heather's shirt.

Heather did the grocery shopping and also bought a gift bag and filled it with some weather-the-storm essentials for her nice neighbors: flashlights, batteries, candles, a bottle of wine, and some edible goodies that wouldn't require refrigeration.

It was good to have good neighbors, and Heather wanted hers

to know how much they were appreciated. She also bought all the supplies Winky would need, then picked him up at the vet. When she got home, she got Winky settled in the mudroom. Then she carried an armload of grocery bags into the kitchen, set the bags on the counter, and walked to the bottom of the stairs. "Kids," she yelled, "please come help with the groceries."

"Okay," Josh answered. She heard his bedroom door open. "I'm putting my shoes on."

"Thank you, Josh. Please make sure your sisters heard me." Jasper came running down the stairs, bypassing Heather in a bee-line for the mudroom. "Do not bother that cat," she said to the dog, who ignored her.

While the kids brought in the groceries and put everything away, Heather started a big pot of soup, using up as much of the food in her freezer as possible so it wouldn't go bad if the power went out. Also, if the power stayed out for a while, they'd have something quick and easy to warm up on the gas stove. She made plenty, enough to take some to the neighbors when they brought Charlie over there.

When everything was done and the soup had cooled enough to transfer the neighbors' portion to a big Pyrex bowl with a lid, Heather and Erin gathered all the gifts for the neighbors and took a handful of Ziplocs out to the barn to fill with Charlie's food. "Would you bring Charlie in from the field while I scoop his food?"

"Sure." Erin took the halter and lead rope off the hook next to Charlie's empty stall and walked to the open barn door that led to the field. "Mom?" she said a second later, her voice tentative. "Charlie's not out here."

"What?" Heather zipped the last bag shut and put it in the feed bucket with the others. She dusted her hands off and walked to where Erin was standing in puzzlement. "He's got to be…"

But he wasn't. The big open field didn't have any nooks or

crannies where a thousand-pound horse might hide. And Charlie wasn't there. "What on earth...?" Then Heather remembered seeing Quinn's truck pulling a horse trailer that Heather had assumed was full of hay.

And Adrian's car was right behind it.

"Those fuckers," she muttered under her breath. What in the world were they up to? Why would Quinn and Adrian take Charlie without... Then she remembered that her phone was sitting in a bag of rice in the side pocket of her laptop case. "Help me bring all this stuff back inside," she said to Erin. "I've got to make a call."

"Are you going to call the police?"

"No. I think I know where Charlie is. I bet Quinn and Adrian decided to take him to Bayside Barn." And she couldn't even be mad about it, since she hadn't been available for them to call. They'd probably decided between the two of them that she didn't have the good sense to make provisions for Charlie's safety during the coming storm.

Their mutual vote of nonconfidence got up her nose, but again, given her previous track record, she couldn't much blame them for that either.

She dug her phone out of the rice, and it turned on without a hitch. She could see that Adrian had tried to call several times. She didn't want to risk hearing the residual anger in his voice, so she sent a text:

Hey, did you and Quinn steal my horse?

His reply came in under a minute:

We did. Friends helping friends.

"Passive-aggressive much?" She refrained from chastising him about the fact that she had the situation handled and didn't need him and Quinn butting in, because what would be the point? Heather knew Charlie was fine, probably munching hay at Bayside Barn by now. No harm, no foul, and she had bigger fish to fry.

I had it covered, but thanks for helping, friend.

"Come on," she said to Erin. "We've got a lot of work to do before it gets dark."

———————————

The next day, Adrian leaned back in the first-class seat to Dallas and signaled the flight attendant for another Bloody Mary. He'd driven home late yesterday evening after dropping Charlie off at Bayside Barn. It had rained all the way home, but he'd driven in worse weather. After all the pre-storm hoopla, it had ended up being a nonevent, a blustery wind and a whole bunch of rain but nothing extreme enough to warrant all that preparation.

He sipped his drink and glanced idly around the cabin. The woman across the aisle was exactly his type. He studied her when she wasn't looking.

Her makeup was a work of art. Her expertly crafted hair was blond, but not Heather's sort of blond—more like an artist's palette of highlights and lowlights and everything in between, shown to best advantage by a perfectly shaped cut and ten minutes with a blow dryer, flat iron, and curling iron. Her fingernails were too perfect to be real, her silk blouse and linen pencil skirt were smooth and unwrinkled, and the shoes she had tucked neatly under the seat in front of her were pointy-toed high heels. Her bright-red pedicured toenails peeked through the shiny hose that covered her ballet-barre-class legs.

The mimosa she sipped from a champagne flute had a neat

circle of red lipstick on the rim, and whenever she sipped, she always placed her lips in that exact spot.

This dry-clean-only woman was Heather's exact opposite. Exactly his type.

He looked away before she noticed him looking. Before Heather, he'd have flirted. But he knew that if he caught this bright little fish, he wouldn't have the heart to do anything other than throw her back into the water.

Opening his laptop, he got to work tweaking his presentation for the Dallas client. When the plane started its descent, he slipped his laptop into his briefcase. At the end of the flight, he was the first to stand and grab his bags from the overhead bin. He hustled out of there in a hurry, though he had more than enough time to check in to the hotel, prepare for the presentation, and get to the meeting on time.

The week in Dallas evolved into two weeks, then three. He wowed his new client with his dedication and attention to detail. He started work early and kept at it till long after dark. Fueled by coffee and alcohol, he made a truly disgusting amount of money and secured a long-term client in the process.

But none of it made him happy.

Working at the shelter more than full-time in these first few weeks was eating Heather's lunch, but she and the kids were working it out. They had begun to fall into a routine, with the kids coming on the bus to the shelter half the time and home half the time. On the kids' home days, Heather pushed the two employees she'd hired to finish by 5:00 so the kids would only have to be alone for an hour or so. On their shelter afternoons, she stayed late and caught up on shelter laundry and paperwork.

She almost didn't have time to miss Adrian.

She had decided to keep Charlie at Bayside Barn—temporarily at least—and made a point of coming early each morning to feed him sliced apples before turning him out into the field for a day of grazing. Charlie enjoyed the company of the other animals, so paying a smaller-than-fair boarding fee—which was all Reva would accept—was well worth the money. (Especially now that she actually *had* money.) Quinn or his son, Sean, rode Charlie once or twice a week, and Sean kept Charlie well groomed.

Charlie didn't have time to miss Adrian either.

Winky was still a standoffish little pisser; he had managed to escape the mudroom in less than twenty-four hours and disappeared to nobody-knew-where for almost a week. They'd only known he was still in the house because the food in his kibble bowl was steadily disappearing and the litter box was being used.

He also peed in other places—Heather's shoes, the bathroom rug, even the kitchen counter—just to make a point. He'd begun to be more visible lately; sitting on some piece of furniture or other, high up enough to glare down at the family in general and Jasper in particular. Heather hadn't been able to find any more of Winky's hygiene indiscretions recently, but her closet was beginning to smell vaguely of cat piss.

According to Reva, Winky *did* have time to miss Adrian.

But Heather couldn't do anything about that other than keeping her closet door closed.

Some of the grants Adrian had applied for needed his attention, and Abby lived in fear of messing up on OSHA-compliance rules or nonprofit paperwork requirements. Desperate to get a handle on the things for which they had depended on Adrian, Abby had sent texts and emails, only to receive immediate out-of-office responses but no follow-ups. Abby and Heather did their best to take up Adrian's slack, but it wasn't easy, and the uncertainty of it all ignited Abby's anxiety.

But all in all, the new shelter was running smoothly, and people from the community were beginning to bring in—and adopt out—animals. Heather stayed busy, and she loved her new job because it gave her a sense of purpose and worth. But Adrian kept invading her dreams—and often her nightmares—so she wasn't sleeping well, and none of the things she spent her days doing made her happy.

Winky roamed the house alone, looking for a new way to show his displeasure. *That dog*, as he had taken to calling Jasper, had gone with Heather to the shelter as usual, so Winky had the place to himself, but it didn't give him any joy.

He had hoped that coming here to live with Heather would allow him to encourage her to take Adrian back so they could all be together. But Heather had begun keeping many of the doors closed, and he was running out of new and interesting places to pee. He settled for scratching at the doorframe to Heather's closet until the soft wood hung in curling shreds and tiny paint chips littered the carpet, which he had also peed on for good measure.

Then, all out of pee, Winky sat on the back of the couch and looked out the window at all the tasty little birds who clustered around the bird feeder with complete impunity.

Reva popped into his head, asking him once again to please stop peeing outside the litter box.

He replied, once again, that he would stop peeing when Adrian showed up.

Reva tried to explain that this rift in Winky's intended family was as much Adrian's fault as Heather's because while she had started the problem by being too afraid to love him with her whole heart, he had finished it by stomping off in a huff instead of attempting to understand.

Fine, whatever. When Adrian showed up, Winky would pee on his shoes. But Adrian wasn't here, and neither were his shoes, so all Winky could do was torture Heather and hope it would force her to bring Adrian home where he belonged.

They were at a temporary impasse, but Winky was determined to win the war. However, even a cat of means such as himself had few weapons at his disposal. Winky leaped onto the bookshelf and knocked off a few framed photos, then headed back to the kitchen to drink as much water as he could hold.

Chapter 19

HUNGOVER FROM THE SEE-YA-LATER BAR PARTY THE NIGHT before, Adrian boarded the plane back to NOLA feeling like a piping-hot stack of ass. His head pounded, his mouth was dry and sour-tasting, and his gut felt rough and jumpy. The cold shower had done nothing to loosen the vise squeezing his temples, and the supplements and painkillers he'd taken this morning only sat in his stomach and disagreed with one another while he suffered.

"Bloody Mary," he said to the flight attendant when she walked past. Hair of the dog might help; it was all he had left to fall back on since the bacon, grilled cheese, and fizzy fountain Coke he'd had for breakfast hadn't yet managed to soak up the alcohol permeating the tissues of his digestive tract. He'd made an appointment at the Remedy Room for an IV hangover cure, but he had to get through the flight first. He closed his eyes, clutched the armrest of his first-class seat, and tried to hold on until then.

The flight attendant brought his drink, and he cracked one eye open just enough to grab the cool glass and bring it to his mouth with trembling fingers.

As he sipped his drink, he vowed never to drink alcohol again.

Never again, after he finished this Bloody Mary.

"Well, hello, you," a smooth, feminine voice said from across the aisle. "Don't I recognize you from our flight to Dallas a few weeks ago?"

He turned his head as slowly as he could manage and opened his eyes just enough to spy the woman through slitted eyelids. It was the perfect-for-him woman from the flight out, sitting in the very same seat as before.

"I was planning to give you my card so we could get together sometime, but you hyper-spaced out of that plane like you had somewhere to go." She extended a manicured hand across the aisle. "Hi. I'm Tina Tanner. I'm a headhunter for the Benson Group."

"Really?" He'd used that group before to staff new and merging companies. He shook her hand without moving any more than necessary. "I'm glad you reached out…so to speak. I just recommended your company to a new client."

He introduced himself, and they exchanged cards. He glanced at hers to remind him of the name she'd just said but he hadn't paid attention to: Tina Tanner. He repeated the name silently to himself so he wouldn't forget. Tinatanner Tinatanner.

They talked for a bit about mutual clients and businesses they'd worked for in the past, but when the conversation lagged, she gave him a sympathetic look. "Rough night?"

"Nothing wrong with the night besides the fact that I heartily regret it this morning."

She laughed, a light trill that made his teeth ache. "Poor you."

He lifted his glass, took a sip, and winced as the acidic drink coated his esophagus. "Hair of the dog isn't working today."

They talked hangover cures for a minute, but when the plane hit some turbulence and he had to close his eyes to weather the bumps without hurling, she took pity on him and minded her own business for the rest of the flight.

As they headed down the Jetway toward the terminal, she walked faster to keep up with him. "I apologize in advance for being so bold," she said, "but I've learned to go after what interests me in life, and you interest me."

His bloodshot eyes felt grainy when he glanced over at her.

"If you're not married or otherwise taken—"

"Not married, not taken," he growled. Thanks to Heather, Tinatanner might just get what she was after.

———————

Feeling marginally better after the IV hangover cure, Adrian went back to his loft determined to take a restorative nap. Jamie, possessing her usual radar, opened her door just as he passed by. "Hey, neighbor," she sang. "I can't see the surface of my dining table any longer because it's covered with your packages. You want to come get them so I can eat at my table one of these days?"

He turned and focused a bleary eye on her. "Can it wait until after I take a nap?"

"Oh, man," she said. "You look rough."

"You should have seen me earlier," he replied. "If I promise to take you to dinner or something, can my packages hold down your dining table for another hour or two?"

"Sure." She cocked her head to one side. "Is there anything I can get you?"

"Thanks, but I think what I need more than anything is sleep."

"Okay, friend." Jamie smiled, a sunny smile that lit up her face. "Have a nice nap."

He nodded and made a sound that was supposed to be an acknowledgment, but it came out sounding more like a growl.

Inside his loft, he dumped everything by the door, filled a glass with water he didn't drink, stripped down to his underwear, and climbed into bed. But sleep proved elusive. Shreds of thoughts teased his consciousness, preventing him from letting go. He thought of the emails and texts from Abby that he'd ignored, letting his auto-responder settings do the talking.

Quinn had sent a few texts, *just checking in.*

Adrian had responded to those using the phone's auto-fill options. He hadn't heard anything from Heather.

The nap didn't take, but at least he managed to lie there long enough to give his aching muscles and joints a rest. Yesterday's bender had him tied up in knots, and he resolved to book a massage as soon as he got up. But would that even help? Maybe his problem wasn't the lingering hangover. Maybe it was the realization that all the small self-indulgences he had once reveled in now felt shallow and meaningless compared to the life he had begun to imagine with Heather and her kids.

He sat on the balcony, but the mighty Mississippi rushing past didn't magically carry his woes away.

He played the piano, but the music didn't soothe him either.

Admitting defeat, he dressed in jeans and a plain white T-shirt, pocketed his keys, and walked barefoot across the hall to knock on Jamie's door.

She opened the door with a smile, her newly whitened teeth blinding him. Her hair was pink today, he noticed. It matched her strappy pink dress and mani-pedi.

"You're all matchy-matchy today," he commented.

"Thank you… I guess." She stood back to let him walk past. "Did you have a nice nap?"

He lowered his eyebrows with a *don't even start* look.

"Okay," she said. "Have a seat on the therapist's couch and tell Auntie Jamie all about it."

He collapsed on the couch. "I don't know. I guess I'm… depressed or something."

She sat on the chair across from him. "What happened?"

He leaned forward, put his head in his hands, and told her the whole story. "I honestly don't know what to do to get back on track. I've tried to go back to my old life, but it doesn't seem to fit anymore. It's like I'm trying to wear a pair of jeans that used to fit in high school, but now they're too tight in all the wrong places. Maybe I need a prescription for Xanax."

She came over to the couch and put an arm around his shoulder.

Then she took one of his hands and held it tight. "If all she can offer you is her friendship, then you need to take it."

He scoffed. "Bullshit."

Jamie put her head on his shoulder. "Hon, how do you think I felt when you booted me from your bed to the friend zone, hmmm?"

He looked at her in surprise. "I thought you felt the same way. You never—"

"I never let you see that you'd broken my heart, but believe me, you did."

"But—"

"Ade, we can't make people love us the way we want to be loved. But we can allow them to love us in whatever way they're capable of loving."

"Well, shit." He leaned back against the couch cushions, and Jamie leaned back, too, looking over at him with a soft expression. She didn't say anything, just gave him the space he needed to mull over what she'd said. "So what do I do now?" he asked.

"Go back to Magnolia Bay and be her friend. Give her your whole heart, and see if she can find a way to fit it into her life."

———

Heather wished she'd taken the time to bring the real ladder into the shelter's laundry room instead of trying to reach the top shelf by standing on tiptoe on the stepladder. They'd just received a fabulous donation of a dozen fleece blankets, and she was unsuccessfully trying to store them on the shelf above the dryer. She planned to take them home to cut them into dog-blanket-sized squares and hem the edges, but not anytime soon.

"This. Is. Not. Working." Violating all sorts of safety regulations, she climbed onto the dryer, got to her knees with a stack of folded blankets in her arms, and slowly got her feet under her to stand.

"I know you miss me, Heather, but it's not worth killing yourself over."

She turned in surprise at the sound of Adrian's deep, teasing voice and nearly lost her balance. He knocked the stepladder out of the way and grabbed her hips to steady her. "Anyway," he said, "taking a header off the washing machine isn't likely to kill you. Maybe just put you on crutches for a while."

She set the blankets on the highest shelf, then turned around and eased down to sit on the dryer. "It's a dryer, not a washing machine," she corrected him. "And I'm not trying to kill myself over you. If you must know, I've been so busy, I've hardly had time to think of you."

He took her hand in his. "I see you're still wearing your... friendship ring."

She shrugged. "Why not? You gave it to me no strings attached, so it's mine to wear, is it not?"

"Absolutely."

Without being asked, he put his hands around her waist and plucked her off the dryer, setting her firmly on her feet. "Abby's been blowing up my phone about some paperwork, but she's not in the front office."

"She's gone to the pet store to pick up some soon-to-be expired dog food they're donating." She brushed her hands on her jeans and glanced at Adrian from under her lashes. He looked tired. Still gorgeous as ever, even with those dark smudges under his eyes. The scar across his forehead was still red but not raised. The medics had been right; he'd lucked into a good surgeon who knew how to sew a fine stitch. In time, the scar would fade away. "Kind of you to grace us with your presence finally."

"I've been out of town on business until yesterday."

"Abby will be happy to see you. She needs the help, and legalese is not my first language." She turned her back on him. "I'll show you where everything is. You can use my desk."

"I was thinking that after I finish here," he said as he followed her down the hall, "I'd go to your place and ride Charlie, if that's okay."

"Charlie would love a nice ride, I'm sure," she said over her shoulder. "But he's not at my house anymore."

"He's not?"

"He's still at Bayside Barn. He likes it there, and I can afford to board him now, so…" She opened the file cabinet behind the two catty-corner office desks and set a thick manila folder on her desk. "It's filed under A, for Adrian's to-do list. Do you need anything else before I get back to work?"

———————

Charlie was hanging out in the field with the horses and donkeys, munching sweet grass while the sun warmed his back, when he heard a familiar whistle. His head popped up, eyes wide, a tangle of grass hanging from his lips.

The whistle came again. Charlie ran for the fence to meet Adrian, who stood at the gate with a saddle on his hip and a bridle hanging from his fingers. Adrian set the saddle on the fence rail and leaned over the fence to slip the bit into Charlie's mouth and fasten the bridle. Then he opened the gate and led Charlie through to finish saddling him up.

Charlie was so excited to see Adrian that he snorted and pranced. Adrian laughed but didn't allow Charlie to run the way he wanted to. Instead, they took a slow walk through the gates of Bayside Barn and then ambled along the mowed edges of the blacktop, communing without words and getting reacquainted.

Charlie tossed his head and did a little dance. His person was back.

———————

Adrian pulled into Heather's driveway and got out of his car with the key to her house in his hand. Reva and Heather had cornered him at the animal shelter on his first day back and insisted that he spend some time with Winky before the cat destroyed Heather's house.

Adrian didn't give either of them the satisfaction of knowing he'd been hoping for the invite to Heather's house. Instead, he made some noise about not having all the time in the world to jaunt all over Magnolia Bay, and then he finessed the situation so he'd still be there when Heather's kids got home from school.

He was taking Jamie's advice about letting Heather decide how much of him she wanted in her life, but that didn't mean he couldn't grease the skids a little by doing exactly what she'd asked him to do when she still wanted him: getting to know her kids.

The house was quiet when he walked in. Jasper was at the shelter with Heather, and the kids weren't home yet. "Winky? Here, kitty, kitty." Heather had told him to make himself at home, so he took off his shoes and left them by the back door, then tossed the keys on the kitchen counter and checked the fridge. No beer, but he grabbed a soda, popped the top, and ambled into the den. "Winky?"

The cat leaped down from the bookshelf and sauntered over, meowing and purring like Quinn's Harley. Adrian sat in the recliner and turned on the TV. Winky jumped into his lap and paraded in circles, rubbing his head all over Adrian's shirt and drooling with ecstasy.

He petted the cat's head and flipped to the sports channel. "I'm glad to see you too, buddy."

Adrian and Winky watched tennis together until the kids got home. Josh slammed through the back door first. "Ade!" Apparently realizing the imminent pouncing that was about to occur, Winky took off and ran out of the room a half second before Josh leaped into Adrian's lap. "You're here!"

Caroline came in more slowly, a shy smile on her face. She leaned against the recliner and patted his shoulder but didn't say anything. They'd taken two steps back while he'd been gone, but Adrian knew that with patience, he'd be able to make up for lost time.

―――――

Disturbed by the disruptive young human, Winky ran into the kitchen and hunched in front of the communal water bowl he shared with the dog. Winky lapped up some water, wrinkling his nose at the knowledge that even though the water in the bowl was fresh from this morning, he was still sharing saliva with a canine.

Why couldn't it go back to being just him and Adrian, like before?

Winky had manipulated the humans successfully so far, but he knew that the subtlety of subterfuge was an art that took time and strategic planning to implement. He cocked his head at the sound of high-pitched human voices melding with Adrian's more soothing tones.

Winky drank his fill, then sauntered over to where Adrian's shoes had been left by the door. He sniffed the new-smelling shoes and considered his options. He knew that he had the ability to make his displeasure known and push these humans to the next level of compliance, but he struggled with the decision.

He had used his powers of persuasion to encourage Heather to bring Adrian back to the family—and therefore back to Winky— where he belonged. The undisciplined dog and the small, squeaky humans were less-than-ideal aspects of Winky's life now, but he had only just now convinced Heather to do the next right thing in bringing Adrian home.

Maybe he should save his super-powers of pee for another day. Humans, after all, were slow creatures who needed time to adapt to new circumstances. Winky settled for rubbing his face against the shoes to put his scent on top of the new leather smell.

Humans were a simple species who seemed not to understand anything about scent-marking. But Jasper, at least, would understand that he came in second-place when it came to Adrian.

It had been a good day, Winky decided as he headed to his domain in the laundry room.

Tomorrow, he would decide how to wield his powers of persuasion. For now, he'd content himself with checking whether the kibble in his bowl was still fresh enough to eat, or whether it needed to be knocked down from the shelf onto the laundry room floor.

Adrian's Wednesday afternoon visits to Heather's house while she was at work became a regular thing, and since he'd offered, Heather had even taken to leaving him little honey-do notes on the counter along with money for a pizza dinner. (He didn't need the money, obviously, but she insisted.) He figured that his ability to change the menu one day a week meant he was making progress.

The routine he had feared would be boring became comforting instead. Every Wednesday, he let himself into the house and took off his shoes, grabbed a cold beer from the fridge, and turned on the TV. Winky sat in his lap while he watched the sports channel, and to hear Heather tell it, Winky's failure to use the litter box was a thing of the past. He still scratched the doorframes, but as Adrian told Reva, everybody's gotta be thankful for what they've got now and hold out hope for more of what they want in the future.

The Wednesday after Halloween, a chilly breeze promised rain along with the first hint of almost-fall weather in the sunny South. Instead of watching TV with Winky, Adrian took the ladder out of the pole barn and propped it against the side of the house. He'd just finished cleaning the gutters when the school bus stopped and the twins scrambled out and ran toward the house. Adrian climbed down from the ladder and took off his work gloves in time to catch Josh's tackle. "Hey, buddy. How was school?"

"Good. I didn't get in trouble at all this week."

Adrian patted the kid's back. "That's okay. The week's not over yet."

Caroline held up a gold-edged certificate. "I won the best book contest," she announced. "You want me to read it to you?" The kids had been making their own stapled-together books in class during the month of October in anticipation of the upcoming book fair in November. He'd been hearing all about it.

"Sure. Let's go inside." Caroline grabbed his hand and swung it while she skipped along. Somehow, he'd ended up carrying her backpack. Cunning little critter. He hadn't even noticed. He set her backpack on the bench by the back door. "Y'all wash up first, and I'll set out some snacks, okay?"

After snacks, Caroline brought out the dog-eared, stapled-together book. "Sit," she demanded, "so I can read my book to you."

He sat in the recliner, and she climbed onto his lap.

"My family." The carefully crafted title on the front cover was written in crayon.

The first page was a cartoonish picture she had drawn of Jasper. "Jasper is my dog," she read. "He likes treats."

Next, a picture of a one-eyed cat. "Winky is my cat. He likes to pee."

Adrian stifled a laugh at the next picture: a wild-eyed woman with an hourglass shape and yellow hair. "Heather is my mama. She likes to cook."

She turned another page. "Erin is my sister. She likes to read."

"Josh is my brother. He likes to make messes."

The next page had a picture of a man with wings. "Dale is my daddy. He likes to fly in heaven."

Then she turned to the last page. "Adrian is my mama's special friend. He likes to drive her crazy."

She closed the book and hopped down. "The end!"

———————

Adrian closed the sliding door of Charlie's stall at the far end of the barn, then turned off the barn lights. Abby and Reva had already put the rest of the barn critters up in their stalls a little early because of another incoming storm. This one was expected to roll in just after dark as a strong Category 2.

"You want a beer?" Quinn asked as they headed down the flagstone walkway toward Reva's house.

Adrian glanced at his watch. "Just one. I've gotta catch a flight to Dallas early tomorrow morning, and I want to be back in NOLA before the storm hits. Anything else need doing before I head out?"

"Let's ask." Quinn opened the door to Reva's house. "Welcome to Dog Heaven."

"Shit," Adrian said with a laugh as he was mobbed by dogs, each of them leaping up and vying for attention while Georgia and Wolf and Jack looked on with disdain from their perches on the couch. "Now, I definitely need a beer. Why are all these dogs here instead of the shelter?"

"This is insane," Quinn muttered as he squeezed through the door without allowing any dogs to escape. Abby and Reva were nowhere to be seen, but the kitchen smelled divine, the air scented by whatever was cooking on the gas stove. Quinn took several dog biscuits from the antique cookie jar on the counter. "These are the dogs Reva says are too afraid of bad weather to stay over there during a storm. Even though those kennels are better built and safer in a hurricane than this old farmhouse. Come here, dogs."

Quinn lured all the new dogs (which turned out to be only

four, not the fifty-four it had seemed like when they were leaping against Adrian's legs) into the metal crates that had been lined up along the kitchen's island. Then he took three treats to the resident dogs, who had waited patiently on the couch.

Reva had them trained that treats came to them, so they didn't have to enter the fray of undisciplined dogs who thought they had to clamor to get what they wanted. If Adrian ever got a dog, he decided, he would take it to live with Reva for a couple of weeks before bringing it home.

After dealing with the new four-legged ruffians, Quinn took a couple of beers out of the fridge and handed one over before taking a seat at the oak dining table. "Wonder where the girls are?"

"Here," Reva answered, coming into the kitchen from the laundry room. "We brought all the parrots in for the storm." Loud squawks from the laundry room confirmed Reva's statement. "They're not happy about my decision to make them stay in travel cages overnight, but I didn't want them to be out there in the aviary where I can't check on them if it gets bad."

Abby closed the laundry room door, muting the sound of squawking, but not by much. "If we're gonna blow away," she said, "we're gonna blow away together." She walked into the kitchen. "Who wants wine?"

Adrian held up his beer. "Quinn and I have beer already, thanks."

A text pinged in Adrian's pocket. He felt a zip of anticipation when he checked his phone, but the text wasn't from Heather. "My flight's been delayed because of the storm," he read out loud. "I can reschedule without penalty if I want."

"You know it'll be canceled." Abby uncorked a bottle of red and brought it to the table with empty wineglasses for her and Reva. She sat next to Quinn at the table and pulled up the weather app on her phone, then showed it to Adrian. "See? You'll be driving back to NOLA for nothing. You might as well cancel the flight and tell those folks in Dallas not to expect you until next week."

"You could hunker down here," Reva offered. "We'll be doing the storm watch together from here. We have the shelter's security camera feed on Abby's computer, so we'll know how the animals there are doing. Abby and Quinn have dibs on the guest room, but the couch's pullout bed is surprisingly comfy."

Adrian looked at Quinn. "Y'all aren't staying at the cabin?" They'd finally finished the cabin they'd been building on Reva's property.

"The power's bound to go out, and our new cabin doesn't have a generator," Quinn answered.

"This storm's expected to spawn tornadoes," Abby said. "Even the outer bands could be dangerous. You should stay here. Quinn and I can always stay at the shelter's pool house."

"I wish you'd stay," Reva added, "so we don't have to worry about you driving back to New Orleans."

"Thanks, Reva. I'll take you up on that offer." The sense of camaraderie Adrian felt here was completely different from his experience of Katrina. "I'd rather blow away with y'all than be sucked up in a tornado all by myself on the road between here and New Orleans."

After Heather fed the kids a quick dinner of soup and saltines, they worked together to bring in the potted plants and the hummingbird feeders from the back porch. Anything that might blow away from the barn aisle or the shelves got put in Charlie's empty stall, along with the chairs that normally lived on the boat dock out back.

It was the third storm this season, and their storm preparations had become routine. Adrian had offered to help, but she'd turned him down because he had plans to go to Dallas the next day and she didn't want to impose. He already did so much around here that he was in danger of earning his way out of the friend zone. She was tempted, but she knew that once she made that decision, there would be no going back.

When all the work was done, Heather sent the kids inside with instructions to take baths and get dressed in their pajamas. Afterward, she and the kids and Jasper gathered in the den. Winky was who-knew-where, as usual. Adrian was his favorite person; the rest of them he could take or leave, and he usually chose to leave them.

The first two storms of the season had been little more than heavy rainstorms, not worth staying up over. But this one promised to be a doozy, so Heather knew they'd probably be up late, paying attention.

She did wish that Adrian was here with them—and well aware that he would have been if she'd invited him. She could imagine that he would sit next to her in the middle of the couch and Josh would sit in Adrian's lap. Caroline would sit next to Heather on the other side, and Erin would take the recliner and only halfway pay attention to the weather updates while she and her friends sent messages to one another. Jasper would curl up on the recliner's footrest, and Erin would wage a constant battle to keep it from folding up under Jasper's weight.

The reality differed from the dream.

Heather made popcorn, and the kids chose to watch *Cinderella* while the weather channel occupied a corner of the TV screen. All the humans sat on the couch, with Heather and Erin on the outside and the twins in the middle. Jasper took the recliner.

The kids focused on the movie while Heather watched the storm track closer to them without worrying too much. They'd slept right through worse storms than this one was predicted to be. It was only a Category 2, and though it was moving slowly, Heather knew that the house should stay high and dry and Charlie was safe at Bayside Barn.

Caroline sat next to Heather and held her hand, playing with her fingers. "I like your ring, Mommy."

"I know you do." Caroline not-so-secretly wanted Heather's poison ring for herself. The telling part of that statement was the word *Mommy*. The kids only called her that when they were feeling unsure. The kids knew something was up because of the hype they'd heard at school and the fact that school was scheduled to be closed for the rest of the week.

That was why they'd started the hurricane party tradition when Erin was little. When tucking her into bed and instructing her not to worry hadn't helped at all, Heather and Dale had made a fun evening of storm-watching instead. It had become a family tradition.

Caroline fiddled with the latch mechanism of Heather's ring, and for the first time, she managed to pop it open. "There's a secret compartment." Caroline's eyes shone bright. "What's it for?"

"It's a poison ring," Erin said. "Back in the old days, women wore rings filled with poison in case they needed to protect themselves."

"From what?" Caroline asked.

Heather gave Erin a *shut up, please* look.

Erin went back to watching the movie, but the damage was done. Heather patted Caroline's hand. "Nobody needs poison to protect themselves nowadays. I just liked the ring because it's pretty."

"So you bought it?" Josh asked. Nobody had asked the question when she'd first shown off her ring the night she gave the kids the presents she'd bought for them in New Orleans. She had given the impression she'd bought it for herself instead of saying it explicitly. She could have avoided the question by taking the ring off, but she hadn't been able to make herself do it. Now, she couldn't bring herself to lie. And besides, it didn't matter anymore. "Adrian bought it for me when we went to New Orleans."

"It's a magic ring," Caroline breathed, probably inspired by the kiddie movie they were watching. "We should put a magic potion in it."

"That's a great idea, sweetie." Heather brushed Caroline's drying hair away from her face.

"I know what!" Caroline jumped up. "I'll be right back." She came back a minute later holding the glitter-filled fairy dust pendant that had come with her ballerina fairy doll. "You can put magic fairy dust in it." Caroline pulled the cork out of the tiny vial. "But first, you have to make a wish."

"Okay," Heather promised, holding her hand out. "I will." Heather closed her eyes and pretended to make a wish.

"You have to say it out loud," Caroline insisted.

Heather closed her eyes again and thought of the wish she wanted more than anything. "I wish that our family will always be happy and safe."

"Have you not been watching the movie?" Erin tossed a kernel of popcorn at Heather, but it landed in Caroline's lap. "You have to be more specific than that."

"I wish—"

"It has to be about true love," Caroline said. "You have to wish for a true love that will make you happy ever after."

"Wish for true love with Ade," Josh yelled.

"You have to say it out loud." Caroline held the vial of glitter over the poison ring's empty chamber. "I wish for..."

Heather chuckled. "Okay, fine. I wish for a happy-ever-after love with...someone at some point. How's that?"

Erin tossed more popcorn at Heather. "Be specific."

"Well, what if I don't know who my handsome prince should be?"

"He has to have a task," Erin said, "and a deadline. Like how Sleeping Beauty's prince had to hack through the thorny forest or—"

"Or how Cinderella's coach would turn to a pumpkin at midnight," Caroline added.

"I still think you should choose Ade," Josh said. "He's the best."

"I wish for my handsome prince—who shall remain nameless until he reveals himself—to come to me before midnight tonight, even though he'll have to hack through a forest to get here."

Caroline sprinkled some glitter into the ring, then closed the compartment. "Now," she proclaimed, "you'll live happy ever after."

Heather kissed the top of Caroline's head. "I'm already happy ever after."

When the movie ended, Heather sent the twins upstairs to brush their teeth, then tucked them into bed. She set a small flashlight on each of their bedside tables in case the power went out. Jasper, as usual, slept on Josh's bed. He always curled up at the foot of the bed at first, then moved up to the pillows after Heather had closed Josh's bedroom door. In the morning, Josh and Jasper would be curled up together under the covers like two peas in a pod.

When Heather came back downstairs, Erin had moved to the recliner, and Winky was doing a good loaf-of-bread imitation in Erin's lap. Erin stroked Winky's fur. "He said he was ready to come out now that the heathens are all upstairs."

Heather almost laughed. Reva must have given Heather's kids a good dose of animal communication propaganda. Even before Reva confessed to Heather about the extent of her abilities, she had always made offhand comments about animals' thoughts and feelings. Planting seeds.

Erin petted Winky's head. "Can we watch another movie, since there's no school tomorrow?"

"Sure." Heather stood and gathered the popcorn bowl and the twins' glasses. "You pick one while I clean the kitchen real quick and start a load of laundry."

While Heather cleaned the kitchen and tossed the last of the

dirty clothes into the washer, she reflected how storm preparation was a lot like nesting before the birth of a baby. Knowing
that she—or the power—might be out of commission for a few
days, Heather felt compelled to make sure that she caught up on
all the chores beforehand. She put the clothes from the dryer into
a laundry basket and brought them into the den for folding.

"I wish I could help," Erin said with a smirk, "but I can't because
there's a cat in my lap."

"Awww," Heather said with an indulgent smile, "that's too bad
for me, I guess."

"Yep. Too bad for you." Erin pointed the remote at the TV.
"We're watching *13 Going on 30.*"

"Perfect."

When the laundry was all folded and in baskets in front of
the coffee table, Heather stretched out on the couch to finish
watching the movie. She woke with a start at the jarring sound
of the emergency alert on both cell phones going off at the same
time.

"Dammit, cat," Erin cursed when Winky leaped out of her lap.

"Watch your language, young lady," Heather scolded. She
picked up her phone to read the alert message: Tornado warning
in your area. Take cover immediately.

"Winky scratched my legs." Erin sat up, rubbing her thighs.

"He was scared. He couldn't help it." Heather took one of the
flashlights off the table and pointed it out the den windows into
the darkness. The electricity had gone out after she fell asleep, so
the back porch lights were off. The flashlight against the window
showed her own reflection and the room behind her more than
it revealed what was going on outside. All she could see through
the rain-slashed windows was the movement of the tall water
oaks and willows between the house and the river, swaying in
the stiff wind.

"I don't know where Winky went," Erin said. "Kitty, kitty?"

She turned on the other flashlight and started searching for the errant cat.

"He's hiding under something," Heather said absently. "As usual."

Heather wondered if she should do something, like maybe wake up the twins and have them come downstairs. "He'll come out when he's ready."

"Okay, fine. I'm going up to—" A huge crash rattled the windows. "Shit, Mom!" Erin's eyes went wide with panic. The crash had sounded like a bomb going off. The muted roar of rain pounding on the roof and windows stopped, replaced by the even louder roar of a high wind.

"Go get in my bathroom. Now." Heather ran to the stairs, yelling for the twins. "Josh! Caroline! Get down here!"

Jasper barked, but neither of the kids' bedroom doors opened. Heather ran up the stairs, opening Josh's door, then rushing to open Caroline's. She hauled Caroline out of her bed, dragging her by the arm to Josh's room. Jasper had woken Josh up; he was sitting up in bed, rubbing his eyes. "What?"

"Go downstairs. Take Jasper with you." She dragged Josh out of bed and put his hand in Caroline's, then pushed them both to the bedroom doorway. "Wait for me in my bathroom." A windowless room in the center of the house, the master bathroom would be the safest place should a tornado hit the house. "Hurry."

"Mommy," Caroline whined. "What's happening?"

"Go," she yelled. "I'm right behind you." She whipped the covers off Josh's bed, then manhandled the twin-sized mattress to the door. Holding on to Jasper's collar, Josh hesitated on the landing. Thunder boomed, followed closely by a burst of lightning. "Run," Heather commanded. "Both of you. Do what I said."

This time, they obeyed, and Heather struggled to pull the heavy mattress down the stairs and around the corner of the newel post toward the master bathroom. She would make the kids sit in the bathtub with the mattress on top of them so if the house came crashing down, they would be protected from falling debris.

Another crash sounded—something big hitting the house. "Mom," Erin wailed, "I'm worried about Winky."

"He'll be fine. He's a smart cat, and he's hiding under something, I'm sure. And that's exactly what I need y'all to do." With Erin's help, Heather wedged the mattress over the bathtub enclosure to make a padded roof several feet above the tub. "Get in the bathtub," she ordered the kids.

They climbed in and sat, with Erin in the middle, her arms around each of the twins. Jasper hopped in and laid across their legs, panting with anxiety. Heather closed the toilet lid and sat beside them to check the weather app on her phone. The storm had made landfall, and they were just now experiencing the outer bands of it. Things would get much worse before they got better. She set her phone on the rim of the tub, dropped her face into her hands, and prayed.

The wind outside howled like a mad thing trying to break in.

Chapter 20

"MOM?" ERIN'S VOICE SOUNDED SMALL AND FRIGHTENED. "DO you smell smoke?"

Heather sat up. She'd been so focused on the howling of the wind and the sounds of things battering the house that she hadn't thought of much else. But she did smell a faint whiff of smoke. "Stay here," she said to the kids. "I'll be right back."

Taking the flashlight, she went to the bathroom door and opened it a tiny crack. The smell of smoke was stronger but still not terrible. The sound of the howling wind was worse, and she could hear rain again.

"Stay here," she repeated. If lightning had struck the house and caused a fire, the rain may have already put it out. The kids were safer from fire at the moment than they would be from the storm's continuing fury. She crept out into the hallway, closing the bathroom door behind her.

A hard, driving rain slashed down on her, even though she stood in the middle of her house. Lightning flashed, illuminating the sky above her.

A huge chunk of the roof had been smashed in by a fallen tree.

Heather panned her flashlight over a hellish scene of destruction.

Whatever had been burning was burning no longer. Rain hissed and sizzled in the cracked-open center of a huge oak tree that rested against the stairs after smashing through Josh and Caroline's upstairs rooms. Weak tendrils of smoke rose from a pile of rubble buried under the branches of the massive tree that had once dominated the front yard and had survived many storms worse than this one.

Heather took a breath to calm herself. She would assess the

damage as best she could, then decide whether they were safer hunkering down or whether they should try to flee before the second half of the storm hit.

She took a few steps and shone the flashlight's beam into the kitchen. That end of the house was still intact. She went back to the bathroom and opened the door just a crack. "There was a fire," she said, surprised at how calm her voice sounded, "but it's out now. I'm gonna go look for Winky, and I want y'all to stay in this bathroom with the door closed until I get back."

Heather went back out into the hallway, where leaves skittered along the wet, slippery floor tiles. She said a prayer of thanks that she hadn't removed her tennis shoes before falling asleep in front of the television. Neither had Erin; if they had to, each of them could carry one the twins if they needed to get out of here.

For now, though, it seemed best to stay put. The biggest tree had already fallen, and it was probably the only one close enough to fall on the house.

"Winky," she called, "Here, kitty, kitty."

Winky meowed, a plaintive sound coming from the depths of the den. Heather stepped over broken glass and a scattering of small branches that had blown into the house, heading toward Winky's meow, which seemed to be coming from under a bookcase that had come loose from the wall and fallen forward until it hit the back of the couch. Heather squatted down and shone the light into the cavelike hole where Winky's one eye shone from the very back corner.

"Come here, kitty, kitty," she called. Winky stared, unblinking, but refused to budge. He seemed unharmed, but he clearly didn't trust Heather enough to come out.

The bookcase had fallen as far as it was going to fall. It was almost as good a shelter as the bathroom where Heather's kids huddled under a mattress. And Heather wasn't going to crawl on her knees through the broken picture frames and glass shards that littered the floor beneath the fallen shelves.

"Okay, buddy. You can stay there if that's what you want."

Heather went back through the kitchen. On impulse, she opened the refrigerator and took out a few sodas, then reached into the scattered contents of the pantry and found a full package of Oreos to take back to the kids. She even managed to find a box of dog biscuits for Jasper.

In the bathroom, she gave the kids and Jasper their treats, then sat back down and reached for her phone. It seemed that maybe they were in the eye of the storm, but she wanted to check the weather app.

Josh greeted her with "Where's Winky? Is the storm over?"

"I'm tired of sitting in the bathtub," Caroline whined. "Can we go sit in the den?"

"Shush, y'all," Erin said. "Mama will tell us when we can move."

"I wish we'd brought pillows to sit on," Josh said. "My butt's gone to sleep."

"Where's Winky?" Erin asked. "Did you find him?"

"I found him. He's okay, but he won't come to me. Now, y'all hush for a minute while I check the weather."

Though the circulating winds were fast and fierce, the storm system itself was moving slowly, only a couple of miles per hour. The calmer weather inside the eye of the storm might only last a couple of hours, so if they were going to get out, they should do it now. "Y'all stay here. I'll be back in a minute. I'm gonna go check to see if the car is okay."

The door from the house into the garage stuck when she tried to open it, but she wrestled with it until it popped open. The garage and the car appeared to be untouched, though the metal garage door was blown outward and flapped like a sail in the wind.

It would bash against the hood of the car if Heather tried to back the car out past it. Would it be worth the risk? She stepped toward the opening and scanned the area with the flashlight's beam. The barn was gone, swept away as if it had never existed. Only a raw patch of red dirt remained. And the driveway...

"Well, shit."

The driveway was blocked by an enormous fallen tree.

The power had gone out hours ago, but the gas-powered generator hummed on the patio at Reva's, keeping the lights, the fridge, and the television going. They'd lost satellite reception even before the power went out, but they had a good-sized stack of DVDs to watch—more than enough to get them through the storm. They followed the storm on their phones' weather apps. The eye wall had just passed, so they were almost halfway through.

Adrian's phone buzzed. When he saw it was Heather calling, he jumped up from the couch, dumping the dog in his lap onto the floor. "Sorry, bud." Everybody, humans and animals, stared at him. "It's Heather." He looked at Reva. "Where can I...?"

She pointed to a closed door at the end of a short hallway. "My bedroom's quiet."

Adrian answered the call as soon as he stepped into the hallway, expecting to hear Heather's voice. Instead, it was Josh. "Ade?" His voice trembled with fear. "Can you come help us?"

Adrenaline flooded Adrian's body. He leaned against the wall. "What's happened? Is your mom okay?"

"She's gone out to see if the car is okay. But Winky won't come to her."

That made no sense. What could the car and the cat possibly have to do with each other? "Josh, let me talk to Erin, please."

When Erin answered, Adrian asked her to tell him what was going on.

"I peeked out the bathroom door when Mom left to check on

the car," Erin confessed. "Part of the roof is gone, and there's a big tree in the hallway. It was on fire at first, but the rain put the fire out. But Winky wouldn't—"

"Where are y'all?" Adrian cut her off. "Where in the house, I mean."

"We're downstairs, in Mom's bathroom. She made us sit in the bathtub with a mattress over our heads."

"Good." Thank God. If he was lucky, he'd have two hours to get them out of there before they were hit with the back side of the storm. "When she gets back from checking the car, tell her that I am on my way and that she is to get in that bathtub with the rest of you and wait for me to get there. I don't want any of you to leave that bathroom under any circumstances. Do you hear me?"

"Yes, sir."

"I will be there as soon as I can."

"But what about Winky?"

"I will deal with the cat. Y'all stay put, and make your mama stay put too."

"Yes, sir."

"Promise me."

"I promise."

"I'm on my way."

When Adrian got back to the living room, none of the humans were there. Reva hurried in from the kitchen and handed him a plastic grocery bag. "Flashlights, first aid kit, bottled water."

Abby came from the laundry room with another bag. "It's full of towels in case y'all get wet." She shrugged. "I didn't know what else you might need."

"Cat crate," Reva reminded her. "They'll need one for Winky."

Abby went back for the crate, and Quinn opened the sliding glass door by the patio. "I've got the chainsaw and an ax in the back of the truck. Let's go."

"Be careful." Abby came back with the crate. She kissed Quinn and hugged Adrian. "Come back safe."

"Watch for downed power lines," Reva yelled at them as they ran to the truck. "And don't drive through standing water."

"Hurry back," Abby yelled.

"Keep us posted," Reva added. "We'll be worried until y'all get back safe."

"Thanks for driving," Adrian told Quinn as the truck peeled out of the driveway. He knew if he'd been driving, he might have taken risks that Quinn wouldn't. "But we only have a couple of hours before the back side of the storm hits us. Can't you go any faster?"

"I'm going fast enough." The windshield wipers cut through the slashing rain; the headlights illuminated vegetation bowing and swaying along the sides of the road. "My speed isn't as much as factor as…" Quinn tapped the brakes, then eased to a stop in front of an uprooted pine tree. "Fallen trees blocking the road."

"Dammit to hell." Adrian jumped out of the truck and grabbed the chainsaw. He cut the tree's trunk into manageable-sized pieces, then he and Quinn moved the logs off the pavement, clearing a space just wide enough for the truck to pass.

They made it another mile before another tree blocked the road and a mile after that before they had to turn around and find a new route to avoid a downed power line.

"Fuck me," Adrian cursed when they had to stop for the ump-teenth time. "This had better be the last tree we have to move off the road. I feel like we've cut through a forest of trees already."

"We'll get there," Quinn said. "And getting back will be easier unless more trees fall across the roads we've already cleared."

When Quinn's truck finally pulled into Heather's driveway—which was blocked by another huge tree—Adrian jumped out of the truck and climbed over the tree before the truck had fully stopped.

The big showcase oak in Heather's front yard had uprooted and crashed through the roof, crushing the front wall of the house.

Thank God the kids hadn't been in their bedrooms at the time. The garage door hung like a limp sheet on a clothesline, flapping weakly in the slightly calmer wind of the storm's wide eye. Adrian went around back and entered the house through the back-porch door into the den. "Jesus." The whole place was a disaster. The house Heather was so proud of was a total write-off.

He went through the master bedroom and yanked open the bathroom door. Jasper barked, and Heather leaped up and ran into his arms, hugging him fiercely. "What are you doing here?"

"Josh called me."

"I know. The kids told me. But still… Are you crazy? Don't you know it's dangerous for you to be out driving in the middle of a hurricane?"

"I would drive anywhere, anytime, to get to y'all." He tucked a curl behind her ear. "You should know that."

"I do know that." She touched the side of his face. "I've never doubted it." But she didn't say that it made any difference. She didn't say that she'd made a mistake and wanted him back. But…she also didn't stop hugging him. He decided to take that as a good sign.

Caroline and Josh scrambled over the edge of the bathtub and rushed across the small room to hug Adrian's legs. "We were so scared," Caroline said, her thin arms squeezing tight.

Adrian put a hand on Caroline's soft hair. "Everything is gonna be okay now."

"Thank you for coming to get us," Heather whispered. She cupped his face in her palms and stared into his eyes for a long second, then gently kissed his cheek.

"Didn't Erin tell you to get in the bathtub with the kids?" he whispered so the kids wouldn't hear the fear in his voice. "What if the ceiling fell?"

"I would have gotten in that bathtub if my butt wasn't so wide." She smiled with just the hint of a tease. "I guess I'll have to lose weight before the next storm."

He took a chance and slid a hand down to lightly cup her very fine ass. "Maybe we'll have to make sure your next house has a bigger bathtub in the master suite."

"Ew," Erin said in disgust from behind them. "Get a room."

"We're about to," he promised. "Come here." He gathered Erin into his embrace, too, and with his arms around all four members of the family he had come to love, he closed his eyes and said a quick prayer of thanks for their safety. He knew that there was still a lot to be worked out between him and Heather, but that kiss gave him a little bit of hope that it could be done.

"Guess what time it is?" Josh said randomly.

"I don't know," Adrian answered. "What time is it?"

"Eleven fifty-five." Josh held up Heather's phone to show the time on the screen. "You got here just in time."

"Did you have to hack through a forest to get here?" Caroline asked with a hint of awe in her voice.

"Matter of fact, I did," he answered. Then he whispered in Heather's ear, "What are they going on about?"

Quinn stepped around the corner with a flashlight. "Dude. Why do you have glitter all over your face?"

"It's because he's Mommy's handsome prince," Caroline answered.

———

Heather tucked all three of her kids into the queen-sized bed in Reva's guest room. Jasper was curled up at the foot of the bed, and miraculously, for once, Winky didn't seem to mind sleeping on the same bed as the dog. Winky was relaxing on top of Erin. "I'm sorry y'all will be sleeping a little closer than you're used to."

"That's okay," Erin said, petting Winky, whose loud purr competed with the roar of the torrential rain pelting the metal roof. "We're gonna want to sleep close for a while, I think."

"That was a scary storm," Caroline said. "I hope nothing like that happens ever again."

"I hope so too," Heather answered, but she realized that she couldn't promise safety, not to her kids, and not to herself either. Especially when the second half of the storm was still roaring outside Reva's house. "But I will be close by, in the living room, watching the weather. And I'll take care of you if anything happens."

"Adrian too, right?" Caroline asked. "He'll take care of us."

Josh pulled at the sleeve of Heather's T-shirt. "I saw you kissing Ade. Are y'all gonna get married?"

"Now that he's your handsome prince," Erin added with a happy smirk.

"I don't know." Heather regretted how badly she'd blown it with Adrian, and she could only hope he'd give her another chance. "Maybe one of these days, a long time from now." She smoothed down her son's hair, where a cowlick kicked up a rooster tail along his hairline. "If we did, would that be okay with you?"

"Yeah!" Josh yelled. Then he moderated his volume a bit. "Yeah."

"What about you, Caroline? What would you think about that?"

Caroline nodded, a solemn expression on her face. "He *is* your handsome prince, so I think you have to." She turned her head on the pillow to look at Erin. "Isn't that the rule? I mean, he did pass the test on time."

Erin grinned. "Maybe we have to let Adrian and Mama figure it out for themselves."

Heather gave kisses to each of the kids. "That's a good idea." She petted Winky and Jasper, then turned out the bedroom light. "We'll be right outside the door if you need us."

Leaving the bedroom door open a crack, Heather went back to Reva's cozy living room, where Reva was dozing in the recliner with Georgia while Abby and Quinn cuddled on the couch with Wolf. Adrian moved Jack, the three-legged puppy, fully into his lap, then patted the empty place beside him on the love seat. Heather sat with a sigh, finally allowing herself to relax fully. Adrian reached out casually and pulled her close, snuggled against his side. She put her head on his chest, and he maneuvered her feet with his until they were entwined on the same ottoman.

"Adrian—" she started to say something to clear the air between them.

"Shhh," he said. "We'll talk later."

She let him shush her. They weren't the only ones in the room, and she hadn't known what to say anyway. Maybe all this closeness was premature. Maybe they were both too emotionally worn out to be thinking clearly, but for now, at least, this felt right. Jack must have thought so too, because he stretched out across both their laps with a groan of contentment.

Adrian kissed the top of Heather's head. "Is your crew all tucked in?"

She petted the dog's softly folded ears. "All safe and sound, thanks to you."

"Thanks to you," he corrected. "You were very brave, and very smart to put that mattress over them. You did everything right."

"I guess maybe I did. But I'm so glad you rescued us before the back half of the storm went through. I don't think that bathroom ceiling will hold up for long in all this wind and rain."

"Is the house as bad as Quinn said?" Abby asked quietly. "I mean, is it…gone?"

"Pretty much," Heather answered. "At least too damaged to repair. The stuff we brought with us—the two laundry baskets full of clothes and the shoes that were in the mudroom—may be all we can salvage."

"We'll know more in the morning," Adrian said. "As soon as the rain stops, we'll go see what's what."

"It's all just stuff," Heather said, though the loss of all the family photographs stung. "None of it really matters, though, because we're all safe. Thanks to Adrian and Quinn."

"It was nothing," Quinn said in a joking tone. "We save the world all the time, don't we, Ade?"

"Yeah," Adrian agreed quietly. "But we save the ones we love first, if we can."

Heather felt a tight knot inside her heart unravel at his words. *We save the ones we love…if we can.*

But what if we can't save the ones we love?

Does that mean we don't ever deserve to love again?

Heather wondered for the first time whether her reluctance to allow Adrian into her life was about more than the fear of her and the kids losing him and of having to go through that pain all over again. Was she also denying herself another chance at love because she thought she didn't deserve it?

Maybe she wasn't as weak and helpless as she'd thought. Maybe she did have the strength to save the ones she loved, at least some of the time.

And maybe she did deserve to love again.

The wind buffeted the house, making the siding clack. "Listen to that," Abby said.

The two couples sat through the rest of the storm, quietly talking while Reva snoozed. When the rain stopped and the wind died down, Quinn walked over to the wall of windows that faced the pool and peered out. "We're through the worst of it." He held a hand out to Abby. "You ready to go to bed?"

"Yeah, sure." Abby stretched and yawned, and Wolf hopped down off the couch, his fluffy tail swaying. "Let's go."

Quinn touched Reva's shoulder. "Storm's passed. We're going to bed."

Georgia hopped down from the recliner and waited with tail-wagging anticipation for Reva to go to bed. Jack did the same. "Doggies have spoken." She collapsed the footrest and stood. "Clean bedding for that pullout bed is stored in the ottoman y'all have your feet on. Sleep well, everyone." She moved off toward her bedroom with the two dogs behind her. "See y'all in the morning."

When everyone had left, Adrian tipped Heather's chin up and gave her a searching look. "I'll sleep in the recliner if that's what you want. But I would much prefer to sleep with my arms around you."

She took his face in her hands and kissed him. "I love you." She pulled back just enough to stare into his eyes. "And I'm sorry for pushing you away when I got scared." And the minute she admitted to being scared, she got even more scared, too scared to look into his eyes any longer.

She snuggled down into his embrace, put her head on his chest, and lowered her voice to a whisper. "I know it doesn't make much sense, but in some convoluted dark alley of my mind, I thought that pushing you back to the friend zone you would keep you safe. I know it sounds crazy. Probably because it is." She let out a little huff of laughter. "I might have to admit that I'm crazy."

He hugged her so hard that she could feel his arms tremble. "I'm not going to let you get away from me after this," he said in a whisper. "You scared me so bad, I'm not gonna let you out of my sight for a long time."

———

The next day, the two couples piled into Quinn's truck, prepared to work most of the day at Heather's place and salvage what they could. The truck bed was loaded with the chainsaw and a few other implements of destruction, and the flatbed trailer was hooked up to the bumper hitch. "Y'all be careful," Reva said. "Make sure the power's off before you start sawing stuff."

"We will," Quinn promised with a smile and a wave. "Not stupid," he added more quietly when Reva turned away to pick up a stack of plastic bins she'd gathered in case they found anything in the rubble of Heather's house that was worth saving.

"I heard that," Reva said to Quinn through the truck's open back door. She set the bins on the seat next to Heather. "The kids and I will hold down the fort here. Y'all stay safe."

Quinn drove along the same route they'd cleared the night before.

Adrian only had to get out once to drag a small tree over to the side of the road. As he did, he noticed a HOUSE FOR SALE sign lying in the ditch near a gently winding drive that led down a hill and over a picturesque bridge spanning a sweet little creek.

It was that cute farmhouse Heather had pointed out when they'd gone for their joyride that eventually wound up at Big Daddy's Bar & Grill. The white house at the top of the hill sat stately and serene behind a rustic wood farm fence. Beyond the house, a cute red barn. Adrian took his phone out of his pocket and took a picture of the sign, then another of the address on the sideways-leaning mailbox.

Abby rolled down the truck's window and leaned out. "What are you doing?"

"Nothing." He put his phone back in his pocket and walked back to the truck. "Just enjoying the view." He was so going to call that real estate agent the second he found a few minutes of privacy. It was too early for him and Heather to talk about commitment, and that was okay. But if she liked that sweet little house, he could help her and the kids get settled there, and he'd stay in his loft in New Orleans for as long as it took for them to figure things out. She could take all the time she needed to get used to the idea of them as a couple and a family.

She was worth the wait.

Friday afternoon, Heather finished her shelter work for the day and walked over to Reva's, where she and the kids were staying until they found another place. Heather had been apartment hunting because she had neither the money nor the heart to start looking for a house to buy. She was still dithering with the two insurance companies—hazard and flood—who were arguing over which insurance agency was responsible for which portion of the disaster her house had become.

Meanwhile, it was becoming more and more apparent that most apartments had pet restrictions that cut out one or both of their animal family members, and no way was Heather considering anyplace that didn't welcome every member of her multispecies family.

Reva was stuck with them for now, but Heather was doing her best to help out and simultaneously stay out of the way. Tonight, the twins were going home from school with Sara and her son, Max, to spend the night. Erin was at one of her yearbook club meetings at Sierra's house and would be dropped off later by one of Sierra's parents.

Heather's heart did a happy twirl when she walked through the swing gate to Bayside Barn and saw Adrian's car parked by the barn. He was probably still out riding Charlie, so she went to Reva's guest bathroom, showered, and changed into clean clothes. She dressed more carefully than usual, in a pretty A-line sundress topped with a bolero-style cardigan.

She hoped to lure him into going on an almost-date so they could have a private conversation in a relaxed location where they weren't likely to be disturbed by kids or dogs or people. She hadn't decided where that might be, but honestly, she'd be happy enough if they could just drive somewhere together and pull over to side of the road.

Maybe on a lonely country road.

Where nobody else ever went.

She walked into the kitchen as Reva came through the back door. "Well," Reva purred, "don't you look pretty."

"I'm…" Heather could feel her cheeks turning pink. "I'm just…"

Reva chuckled. "I know what you're just, and I totally approve." She uncorked a bottle of white wine from the fridge and poured a thin sliver of wine into two wineglasses. "Not that it's any of my business." She held a glass out to Heather, then clinked them in a toast. "To new beginnings."

They both took a sip, then Reva tilted her head toward the barn. "Adrian is in the barn, putting Charlie up after their ride. In case you're interested."

"Oh, thanks." Heather knocked back the rest of her wine—just a sip, but still—then pressed her hand to her chest and coughed. Light-headed, she set the glass on the counter and wobbled to the door.

"Lightweight," Reva teased. "Y'all have fun. I'll feed Jasper when I feed Georgia, and I'll be watching for Erin to come home. Feel free to take your time."

Heather stepped into the barn just as Adrian was closing Charlie's stall door. "Hey. I was hoping I could convince you to go on a…on a date, I guess…before you head back to New Orleans."

He slid the latch home with a quiet click. "I'm kind of horsey and sweaty…"

She stepped closer. "I don't care."

"Okay. There's something I'd like to show you anyway. Maybe we could do that too, while we're out."

"Whatever you want."

"Um…" He ran a hand down his sweat-soaked T-shirt, smearing a bright-green slime mark that slashed across it. "I have a change of clothes in my car, if you wouldn't mind giving me time for a quick shower first. Quinn said I could use the shower in the pool house whenever I want, now that they've moved into the cabin."

"I'll visit with Charlie while I wait. See you in…" She looked at an imaginary wristwatch. "Fifteen minutes?"

He grinned. "Five, tops."

True to his word, he came back soon, though her imaginary

wristwatch wasn't accurate enough for her to be sure. Dressed in a pair of clean jeans and a black T-shirt, with comb marks furrowing his dark hair, he looked like a movie poster of a sexy cowboy. "I'm ready."

She walked toward him slowly, then leaned into him and tilted her face up to invite a kiss. "You sure?"

He used his thumb and forefinger to tip her chin up just a bit more. His mouth hovered a breath above hers. "I think we need to collect more data before I can make a...firm...decision."

She closed her eyes, but instead of kissing her, he put an arm around her waist and guided her through the barn to his convertible. He helped her into the passenger seat, then came around the hood to get into the driver's seat and start the engine. "Was there anywhere you were dead set on going?"

"Somewhere private?"

"Your wish is my command." He put the car in reverse and backed down the drive so fast she had to close her eyes. "Buckle your seat belt. We're going on another joyride."

"Where are we going?"

"I want to show you my new business venture." He reached over and took her hand. "What did you want to talk to me about?"

"Well..." She brought her right hand up to chew on her pinkie fingernail. "I know that Charlie is happy at Bayside Barn, but I also know that you're his favorite person, and maybe it's selfish of me to keep him so close to me when I could let you keep him instead."

"Keep him?" Adrian glanced at her briefly before returning his attention to the road. "What do you mean?"

"There are some nice full-board horse barns in New Orleans. You could ride him every day if he were yours. If he lived closer to you instead of closer to me."

Adrian nodded. "I see what you're saying."

"And?"

"Let me show you my new business venture."

She hadn't been paying attention to where they were going, but he turned down the driveway of the cute farmhouse she'd noticed on their first joyride, where he'd pretended to claim the John Deere tractor some guy was driving. "I've been thinking of becoming a real estate baron. Buying up properties and renting them out—or renovating and selling, whatever." The car's tires bumped over the slats in the wooden bridge. "What do you think of this place for you and the kids? House, barn, and pool, on ten acres with fencing and cross-fencing."

"It's lovely, but I can't afford this." The modern farmhouse on the hill was beautiful. With its wide wraparound porch, white-plank exterior, and dark-charcoal roof and trim, it was exactly the sort of house Heather would choose for herself if money were no object. Her house—the one she'd just lost—had been nice, but this one was extravagant.

"But *I* can afford it." Adrian drove through the open gate of the weathered-wood farm fence and parked on the T-shaped concrete drive. "It's an investment. I wouldn't expect my renter to pay anything near what it costs to own." He brought her hand to his lips and kissed her knuckles. "I'd expect to lose money. It's a tax write-off."

She smiled at him. "You are so full of shit."

"Come see." They got out of the car and walked along the concrete path that wound through the beautifully landscaped area surrounding the house. He slipped an arm through hers and gestured grandly with his other arm at the property, from the polished-concrete back porch overlooking the pool to the fancy red barn situated a hundred feet away at the back side of the hill. "Wouldn't Charlie love this?"

"Charlie doesn't care where he is as long as someone there loves him."

"Truer words..." Adrian smiled down at her.

"Wait." She put a hand on his arm. "We need to talk."

"Okay." He stood next to her, looking uncharacteristically apprehensive. "Let's talk."

"Adrian, this is such a sweet gesture, but..." She took his hands in hers. "I can only accept it under one condition."

His lips tightened, but he didn't say anything. He nodded for her to continue. "Go on."

"I need to know that the kids and I won't be staying by ourselves here for long." She threaded her fingers through his and squeezed. "I need to know that one of these days, maybe sooner than later, you'll be living here with us. If you'll have us, I want us to be a family."

"Well, Heather." His apprehensive expression morphed into a huge smile. "Are you proposing to me?"

She smiled back, all her fears washed away by a flood of joy. "I guess I am."

He laughed, then threw his arms around her and held her tight. "Heather, I love you so much."

She hugged him back with all her strength. "Is that a yes?"

"Hell yes, that's a yes."

Epilogue

WHEN CHARLIE HEARD ADRIAN SAY, "LOAD UP!" IN THAT HAPPY tone, he bolted toward the new, fancy horse trailer, moving so quickly that he almost stepped on Jasper, who had some silly thought in his head that he was helping by getting underfoot.

Jasper didn't seem to care when he almost got stepped on, though, because honestly, the dog didn't have more than two thoughts in his head to rub together at a time, and he had already moved on from "How long has it been since breakfast?" to "How close is it to dinnertime?"

Charlie leaped into the trailer and stepped right up to the tie-down loop at the front, then stood still so Adrian could fasten the lead rope. "You're okay, boy," Adrian whispered in Charlie's ear. "We're going home now, and when we get there, a special surprise will be waiting for you."

Charlie's skin quivered with anticipation. He didn't know where he was going, though Heather had tried to explain with words, and Adrian had sent the emotions of love and acceptance and anticipation.

Reva had shown him mind pictures of the place: a barn with a view of a huge green pasture bordered by tall trees. She'd also shown pictures of his family: Adrian and Heather, Erin, Josh and Caroline, Jasper and Winky—the one-eyed cat who Charlie hadn't yet met but who'd been communicating with him for quite some time.

Charlie knew already that Winky would be a friend. Winky had been sending mind pictures, too, along with messages informing Charlie that Winky would be in charge of the barn. Charlie would have to obey Winky in all barn matters because Winky had been there first and had marked out his territory by rubbing his scent on all the important pillars and posts.

Charlie was happy to bow to Winky's rule because Winky had also promised that no intruders would be allowed to eat Charlie's grain under the watch of Winky's one good eye. Charlie had seen firsthand how Reva's cats used scent marking and other magical means to keep intruders from venturing into Bayside Barn, and Charlie knew that he was lucky to have a magical cat in charge of his new barn.

But what nobody, not even Reva, would tell Charlie was the surprise that was waiting for him in the home he hadn't yet seen.

Charlie spread his legs to balance as Adrian drove the new truck and trailer down the gravel drive of Bayside Barn. He whinnied goodbye to his friends, Sunshine and Midnight and Miriam and Elijah. He snorted a good riddance to Gregory the goat, who possessed, in Charlie's opinion, an overinflated ego that deserved a good popping.

Adrian had tied the lead rope so tightly to the tie-down that Charlie couldn't see much outside the trailer, but he smelled the pine trees and the green grass and the clear spring water of his new home before the truck slowed, and the trailer under his hooves bumped to a near-stop before turning.

Home.

This was a new place that Charlie had never seen before, but already, it smelled like home.

But there was a new smell, a different smell, one he'd never encountered before, carried on the fresh wind that cut through the humid heat and sent leaves flying. A scent that made Charlie's ears prick forward and his tail arch up and his hooves dance against the newly milled boards beneath them.

Charlie strained against the lead rope to look out the trailer's slatted window openings, but he couldn't see.

He could only smell the scent that brought back his days of

youth and vigor, days when love was in the air and anything was possible.

The trailer rocked to a stop. The truck's diesel engine stilled. The trailer's door behind Charlie opened with a giant, screeching squeal.

Adrian walked up behind Charlie and stood on the other side of the trailer's central divide. Adrian cooed soft words and made soothing clicking sounds with his tongue while he untied Charlie's lead rope and backed him out of the trailer, step by step.

When Charlie's hooves hit the hard concrete driveway and Adrian grabbed the lead rope to circle him back around, Charlie lifted his head and breathed in, inflating his nostrils to catch the elusive scent that had him so enthralled.

He remembered the words his humans had said about what he would find at the end of this next journey: *present* and *surprise*.

No wonder animals didn't bother with human words because they couldn't begin to express a reality that went far beyond words.

Charlie tugged at the lead rope and rushed toward the pasture where his future waited for him, her chestnut coat gleaming, her beautiful neck arched and high, her tail raised, and her nostrils flaring as her eyes locked with his.

Charlie realized in that moment that he had been waiting all his life for her and that every worry, every hardship, every loss, and even every love he'd endured in his life had been leading him to her.

Heather opened the pasture gate, and Charlie jerked his head and ripped the lead rope from Adrian's hands, then ran through the open gate to meet his mate.

The lead rope flew out behind him, flapping against his back and tangling in his tail. He would apologize to Adrian later, but right now, he couldn't bring himself to wait for permission to begin living the rest of his life.

Acknowledgments

As always, I have many people to thank for their invaluable help and support during the writing of this book. I know that words will fail to express the depth of my heartfelt appreciation, but I want to try, so here goes:

I owe a BIG thank you to...

Brandon James, director of the Atmore/PCI animal shelter, for taking the time to answer my questions about creating and sustaining a small-town animal shelter. You've done so much good for your community. Your driveway in Heaven is paved in gold, studded with diamonds, and lined with dogs and cats waiting for you to unlock the door to the mansion so they can come inside.

Lisa Miller, for your friendship and encouragement, and for creating your amazing Story Structure Safari method that I always use to assemble the bones of every book I write.

Margie Lawson, for helping writers to hone their craft, share what they've learned, and meet up with kindred spirits. I've learned so much and met so many friends through Lawson Writer's Academy.

Deb Werksman, the world's best editor, for bringing out the best in my writing. Your sharp eye and delicately wielded scalpel make all the difference. If you ever get tired of being an editor, you'd make a fine plastic surgeon.

Everyone at Sourcebooks! Your dedication makes every book an enjoyable experience for readers, but also for authors. Special thanks to Susie Benton and Christa Désir for your sensitive and insightful edits, to Jessica Smith for your diligence, determination, and guidance in the copy editing phase, to Stefani Sloma for taking the terror out of marketing, to Beth Sochacki for including me in fun author events, to Rachel Gilmer for organizing the launches, and to everyone else on the team, many whose names I don't even know, for everything they did to make this book a reality.

Lesley Sabga at the Seymour Agency for your first-read notes, brainstorming, and regular check-ins to make sure all is well, and Nicole Resciniti for always being just an email away.

JoAnn Sky and the Plotting Wenches (That sounds like a great name for a band, doesn't it?) for brainstorming and first reads.

Katrina Martin, my virtual executive assistant, for fulfilling my lifelong dream of having a trusted friend who possesses the wits and the will to wrangle my inbox, plan my days, and make sure I do yoga most mornings.

Jennifer Newell of SB Creative Content for taking the text and photos I toss at you and somehow turning them into a beautiful website, and a newsletter that actually goes out to subscribers almost every month! (When it doesn't, it's my fault, not Jennifer's.)

Shelley Glass, my neighbor and friend, for making sure we didn't starve when I was too busy writing to cook.

My critters, for always giving me plenty of animal stories to write about.

My kids, Christopher, Tessa, and Natalie, for each doing their part to help out. Natalie for helping me to wrangle the social media octopus into a jar. Tessa for holding down the fort and spreading the word. Christopher for offering his lake cabin when I need some quiet writing time—look out, I'm headed there now.

My husband, Hans, for always believing and understanding, and for shining a flashlight on the path so I can follow my dream.

WARM NIGHTS IN MAGNOLIA BAY

Welcome to Magnolia Bay, a heartwarming new series
with Southern flair from author Babette de Jongh.

Abby Curtis lands on Aunt Reva's doorstep at Bayside Barn with nowhere
to go but up. Learning animal communication from her aunt while taking
care of the motley assortment of rescue animals on the farm is an important part of Abby's healing process. She is eager to begin a new life on her
own, but she isn't prepared for the magnetism between her and her wildly
handsome and distracting new neighbor…

For more info about Sourcebooks's
books and authors, visit:
sourcebooks.com

RESCUE ME

In this fresh, poignant series by award-winning author
Debbie Burns, every heart has a forever home.

A New Leash on Love

When Craig Williams arrived at the local no-kill animal shelter for help, he didn't expect a fiery young woman to blaze into his life. But the more time he spends with Megan, the more he realizes it's not just animals she's adept at saving...

Sit, Stay, Love

For devoted no-kill shelter worker Kelsey Sutton, rehabbing a group of rescue dogs is a welcome challenge. Working with a sexy ex-military dog handler who needs some TLC himself? That's a whole different story...

My Forever Home

There's no denying Tess Grasso has a way with animals, but when she helps Mason Redding give a free-spirited stray a second chance, this husky might teach them a few things about faith, love, and forgiveness.

Love at First Bark

Animal portrait painter Mia Chambers and architect Ben Thomas share a complicated history. When they help with a large-scale animal rescue, they suddenly find that opening their hearts and homes can lead to so many upheavals…and new beginnings…

Head Over Paws

Veterinarian Gabe Wentworth has sworn off women, but when he meets volunteer rescue driver Olivia Graham, he can't deny the attraction. The more Gabe learns about a woman who risks everything to save animals, the more he might be willing risk…

To Be Loved By You

Therapist Jeremy Washington and yoga teacher Ava Graham are as different as two people can be, but when they work together to match up puppies and kids in need, Jeremy starts to see there's something very true to the theory that opposites attract.

THAT DEEP RIVER FEELING

Romance has an Alaska homecoming in this
bold, sexy series from Jackie Ashenden.

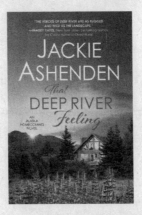

Zeke Calhoun doesn't care much about Deep River, but he'll do just
about anything to keep the last promise he made—to look out for his
best friend's sister.

As the sole police officer in Deep River, Morgan West won't be
bossed around, but Zeke is irresistible. He's tough, challenging, and all
kinds of sexy, but getting involved is the last thing on Morgan's mind...

**"The heroes of Deep River are as rugged
and wild as the landscape."**
—Maisey Yates, *New York Times* bestselling author

WELCOME BACK TO RAMBLING, TEXAS

From acclaimed author June Faver: the women of Rambling tackle small-town living in the heart of Texas Hill Country.

Reggie Lee Stafford is a hometown girl living in Rambling, the small Texas town where she was born. As a single mother, her world revolves around her young daughter and her beloved job at the local newspaper. But her peaceful life is turned upside down when Frank Bell—the bane of Reggie's teenage existence—returns to town to claim his vast inheritance.

"June Faver is a must-read author."
—*Harlequin Junkie*

For more info about Sourcebooks's
books and authors, visit:
sourcebooks.com

COLD NOSE, WARM HEART

First in a fun, funny contemporary romance series about the passions and perils of a local dog park in trendy Miami Beach.

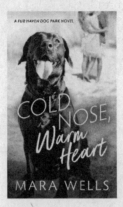

All Caleb Donovan has to do to redeem his family name is take a rundown Miami Beach apartment building and turn it into luxury condos. Easy, right? Unfortunately, that would also turn the local dog park into a parking lot and the neighbors aren't having it. Caleb is faced with outright revolt, led by smart, beautiful building manager Riley Carson and her poodle, LouLou.

For Caleb, this project should have been a slam dunk. But even more challenging than the neighborhood resistance is the mutual attraction between him and Riley. It would be so much easier just to stay enemies. Can Riley and her canine sidekick convince Caleb that what's best for business isn't always best for the heart?

"Full of humor and heart."
—*Publishers Weekly*

For more info about Sourcebooks's books and authors, visit:
sourcebooks.com